Spirit

Elizabeth slowly continued her walk towards Main
Street, frowning in perplexity. Why had the girl seemed
so familiar? It was almost as if Elizabeth had known her
all her life; and yet she knew for sure she hadn't.

It was only when she reached Main Street and saw
the sign across the street saying Walter K. Ede & Son,
Mortician, that she was seized with the most horrific of
thoughts. She turned, and stared back down the street,
and she was so frightened that she felt as if centipedes
were crawling in her hair.

'Peggy,' she whispered. Then she screamed out,
'*Peggy?*'

Graham Masterton is one of the world's bestselling
horror writers. His novels include *Manitou, Black Angel,
Prey, Burial, The Sleepless* and *Flesh and Blood*. He lives in
Surrey with his wife and three sons.

Spirit

GRAHAM MASTERTON

Mandarin

A Mandarin Paperback
SPIRIT

First published in Great Britain 1995
by William Heinemann Ltd
This edition published 1995
by Mandarin Paperbacks
an imprint of Reed International Books Ltd
Michelin House, 81 Fulham Road, London SW3 6RB
and Auckland, Melbourne, Singapore and Toronto

Reprinted 1995, 1996 (twice)

Copyright © Graham Masterton 1995
The author has asserted his moral rights

A CIP catalogue record for this title
is available from the British Library
ISBN 0 7493 1668 3

Printed and bound in Great Britain
by Cox & Wyman Ltd, Reading, Berkshire

To my mother, Mary, with love.

The Chilling

'She was exquisitely fair and delicate,
but entirely of ice – glittering, dazzling ice'

The Chilling

One

Elizabeth glimpsed Peggy running around the side of the house, a little mouse-grey furry figure barely visible through the duck's-down snowflakes, and for one moment she felt as if something terrible were about to happen.

In the distance, she heard the school clock striking, its tone flattened by the cold. *Dongg.*

Elizabeth stopped, crimson-cheeked, runny-nosed, panting. She stared at the empty garden, and at the white weather-boarded corner around which Peggy had vanished so completely, as if running from one life into the next.

The garden seemed to be holding its breath, hushed, with its dark snow-blanketed fir trees, and its curved, wind-razored drifts. All Elizabeth could hear was the occasional shuddering of overladen branches as they dropped their little offerings of snow. But there was nothing else. The huge, empty sound of nothing else. Sky, garden, house, and that was all.

She turned around, uncertain, nine years old. She wiped her nose on the back of a red woollen glove. She wondered if she ought to run after Peggy, but she guessed that Peggy would have scrambled through the hedge at the back of the conservatory, and along the patio, and around the kitchen garden; and that by now she would probably be crouching in the shed, giggling and sniffing and sure that nobody could find her.

But Elizabeth was still disturbed by that *feeling*. That deep, inexplicable feeling, which had glided through her mind like a huge black shark gliding through cold black water without disturbing the surface.

She knew for sure that Peggy was hiding in the shed. Where

3

else would she go? But she felt more strongly that Peggy had gone; that Peggy had disappeared; and that she would never see Peggy again, ever.

She called, 'Peggy! Peggy, where are you?' But the garden remained snow-muffled and silent; and she hesitated; and stopped.

'*Peggy, where are you?*' But there was no reply. Elizabeth hated the sound of her own voice.

'Peggy!' she called. Then she called, 'Laura!'

Eventually, Laura came struggling across the garden in her poppy-red corduroy coat. Laura was seven, and everybody said that she was the prettiest. Her hair was blonde and curly (like her mother's) while Elizabeth's was dark and straight (like her father's). Peggy's was blonde and curly, too, but Peggy had disappeared around the weatherboarded corner and Elizabeth wasn't sure if they would ever see Peggy again.

Laura, panting, said, 'What? What is it?'

'Peggy's gone.'

Laura stared at her. 'What do you mean, *gone?*'

'I don't know. Just gone.'

'She's hiding, that's all,' said Laura. 'Daddy caught her playing with his fairy egg-cups and he shouted at her.'

Elizabeth bit her lip. 'Fairy egg-cups' was what they called her father's golf-tees. All three of them found them fascinating, and all three of them, at one time or another, had been scolded for stealing them. Elizabeth felt worried. *Worried*, that was it, in the same way that mommy got worried, whenever it was night-time and snowing really hard and daddy hadn't come back from New Milford.

'We'd better find her,' she said.

They trudged through the snow together, around the side of the house. It was half past three, and already it was growing dark. The tennis courts were deserted, their nets sagging and clotted with snow. The only footprints on the

4

snow were the fork-like footprints of robins, and the dabs of the family cat.

'Peggy!' they called. 'Peggy, we're coming to get you!'

Silence. The wind rose, and whirled up a snow-devil. 'She didn't come this way,' said Laura, emphatically.

'She must have, I saw her.'

'But there's no footprints.'

'Of course not. The snow's covered them up.'

They struggled across the patio, and around the conservatory. All along the guttering, icicles hung; and at the very end of the conservatory, where the guttering usually flooded, a grotesque ice-figure hunched beside the house, a frozen hooknosed witch, clinging to the downpipe. Whenever the sun came gleaming through the trees, the witch's nose dripped, and the girls danced around her in terrified glee, singing, 'Nose-drip, nose-drip, witchy-witchy, nose-drip!' But tonight the witch was gunmetal grey and gleaming and her nose was hooked in a cold, impossible curve; and Elizabeth and Laura circled her in genuine dread.

Supposing she spoke? Supposing she struck them stone-cold dead, right where they stood? Walking the stiff, quick walk of the seriously frightened, the two girls managed to reach the steps that led down to the rose-lawn, unscathed, unclawed, their coats unbloodied and their livers intact.

'Peggy,' said Elizabeth, so softly that Laura could scarcely hear her.

'That's no good,' said Laura. 'You've got to scream at the top of your voice. Peggy! Peggy! *Peggy-peggy-peggy-peggy-peggy*!'

Laura's voice rose up into a piercing scream, a scream that echoed and echoed across Sherman, and echoed from the top of Green Pond Mountain, invisible in the snowstorm, and from Green Pond Mountain to Wanzer Hill, and all across Lake Candlewood, until the snow suddenly snuffed it out forever.

The two girls waited, and listened. No reply. Elizabeth

5

turned around, and stared at the Nose-Drip Witch, but she remained where she was, moulded out of ice, around the downpipe. Somehow she looked rather forlorn. Perhaps she was thinking that spring would soon be here, and she would melt away.

They went to the shed. It stood under a tall fir tree. It was small and dark, although its roof was covered with an extravagantly thick coating of snow, so that it looked like a frosted fruit-cake. There were no footprints around it, and Elizabeth could hardly manage to pull open the door, because of the snow. Inside, the shed was gloomy and smelled of creosote and dried grass. Elizabeth could just make out the antlers of the lawnmower handles, and spades, and shovels, and stacks of earthenware flowerpots. The windows were thickly curtained with spiderwebs, in which all kinds of colourless and skeletal shapes dangled and danced.

'Peggy?' she whispered.

'*Peggy, where are you?*' shrieked Laura, making Elizabeth jump.

They listened. They could faintly hear music coming from the house. 'You Must Have Been a Beautiful Baby'. The kitchen window was warmly lit and behind the red gingham curtains they could see their mother crossing and recrossing from table to sink to oven, carrying cakes and pies and mixing-bowls. Further along, the library windows were lit up too, though much more dimly.

'I think we ought to tell mom,' said Elizabeth.

'She can't have gone far,' said Laura. They both knew that they would get into trouble for having lost their little sister. 'Drat her! She's such a *menace*.'

'Yes, drat her!'

Together, they pushed the shed door shut, and fastened it. Then they continued their plodding circuit of the house. It was a huge, rambling place, the largest house this side of Sherman.

There were eleven bedrooms and four bathrooms and three huge reception rooms. The girls' father was always complaining that he spent more of his life carrying logs to the various fireplaces around the house than he did writing or editing. 'My passport should read "stoker", not "publisher",' he used to say. But their mother had fallen in love with the house because of its huge galleried drawing-room, in which they could raise a fifteen-foot Christmas tree, just like those movies in which everybody comes home for the holidays and the children are dressing the tree with tinsel and ribbons, and there's some kind of romantic misunderstanding but everybody ends up dewy-eyed and toasting each other in punch and singing 'Hark The Herald Angels Sing'.

Their mother had come from a broken home, that was all they knew. Until she was eight, Elizabeth had thought that a 'broken home' was a house with a massive crack down the middle. Now she knew that it meant something else, worse, and that was why they had just one grandpa, whereas most of their friends had two.

Elizabeth and Laura reached the southern end of the house. There was nothing here but the swimming-pool and then a narrow triangle of lawn and then the woods. The snow was falling even more thickly now, and Elizabeth's toes were beginning to hurt, even though she was wearing her boots with the sheepskin linings.

'Well, *I* don't know where she is,' Laura declared.

'I'll bet she went back indoors,' said Elizabeth. 'She saw mommy baking, I'll bet, and she's probably licking the frosting-bowl and all the raw cake.'

They made their way back to the house. A gust of wind blew pungent woodsmoke around them, like a fuming cloak.

'I'll bet she's eaten *all* the frosting,' said Laura, cross already. 'I'll bet it's strawberry and I'll bet she's eaten all of it. I'll bet she's even sucked the spoon.'

Elizabeth didn't say anything. She felt it would be spiteful to say anything. But she knew that Peggy was mommy's little special darling, and sometimes when mommy was laughing and playing with Peggy it made her feel old and tall and rather plain, and not exactly *unwanted* but resentful of having grown up.

They reached the snow-covered steps that led back towards the front door, and it was then that they saw the footprints.

'Footprints!' said Laura.

'They're ours,' said Elizabeth. She remembered how Pooh and Piglet had walked around and around in the woods, becoming more and more alarmed at the discovery of their own ever-multiplying tracks in the snow.

But Laura frowned and said, 'No, they're not, look, they're too small and it's only one person.'

The footprints were already clogged up with falling snow, so that they were little more than dimples. When they looked more carefully, however, the girls could see that they came around the front of the house and down the steps. After she had disappeared around the corner, Peggy must have hidden behind the bushes until Elizabeth and Laura had passed her by, and then doubled back.

But where was she now?

Standing on top of the steps, the girls tried to make out the line of the footprints across the luminous white garden. They were slurred, the footprints of a small hurrying child, and there was no doubt where they were heading. Across the garden, diagonally, and straight towards the swimming-pool.

The snow was so thick that it was impossible to tell that there was a pool there, except for the two white-painted metal ladders, about fifty feet apart, and the metal mountings for the diving-board. Father had thought about emptying the pool for the winter but the pump had broken down, and then there had been trouble with the drainage because of all the rain, and by

8

the time the first frost started it was too late. At least, he had *said* it was too late, but he had been frantically busy with his new series of books called *Litchfield Life*, and he hadn't had very much time for the house, apart from bringing in logs for the fires, logs, logs and more logs.

The girls had skated pebbles across the frozen surface of the pool, and once they had sent Elizabeth's Shirley Temple doll windmilling out on an Arctic expedition. It was after Elizabeth had stepped on to the ice to rescue Shirley that their father had forbidden them to go anywhere near the pool during the winter; or else he'd slap their legs.

But Peggy must have gone near the pool. Her footprints led directly towards it; and about five feet away from the nearer ladder, there was a faint greyish depression, which was quickly being filled by falling snow.

Elizabeth opened her mouth in completely silent horror. Cold snowflakes whirled against her lips and melted on her tongue.

'Go find father,' she whispered. '*Go find father!*'

Laura stared at her. Those wide blue eyes. Then Elizabeth stumbled down the steps and across the lawn, ploughing and hopping through the knee-deep snow. She didn't even look back to see if Laura had gone. Her throat felt completely raggedy-red, as if she had every sore throat of her entire childhood, all at once. '*Peggy!*' she screamed. '*Peggy!*'

She reached the brink of the pool and almost overbalanced. Only the slightest line in the snow showed where the edge lay. She hesitated, gasping and panting. There was no doubt about it. Peggy's footprints headed unerringly across the surface, and then stopped.

Elizabeth turned around, trying to swallow her sore throat away. Laura had vanished, so father must be coming. The silence was overwhelming. She could have been the only person in the whole world. She looked back at the faint depression in the snow, and said, 'Please God, please God, please help me,' in the highest and tiniest of voices.

She grasped the top of the metal ladder, and cautiously trod down into the snow. Much further down than she had expected, the sole of her boot met the surface of the ice. She took a deep breath and gradually put her weight on it, still holding on to the ladder. The ice seemed to be thick enough. She stood on it with both feet, and gave a cautious little hop, and still it seemed to hold her.

She glanced back at the house. There was no sign of father yet. She would have to find Peggy herself. She didn't want to. She was sure that Peggy must have drowned; and she was terrified that the ice would break underneath her and that *she* would drown, too, long before father could get here. But she knew that she had to, Peggy might be clinging on to the edge of the ice, underneath the snow, and how would she feel for ever and ever if she didn't try to save her?

Holding on to the ladder for as far as she could reach, Elizabeth shuffled out across the surface of the pool. The snow was almost a foot deep, so that it came right up to her knees, and over the top of her boots.

She let go of her ladder, and started to slide-step towards the depression in the snow where Peggy's footprints disappeared. She found herself whispering Pooh's song under her breath. '*The more it snows (tiddely pom), The more it goes (tiddely pom), The more it goes (tiddely pom) on snowing.*'

She heard the ice complain – an odd, squeaking noise, like two pieces of broken glass rubbing together. She paused, her arms held out wide to keep her balance. She had almost reached the depression in the snow, and if the ice had broken here, then it could easily break again. She cleared away the snow with her feet, and then knelt down and cleared it away with her gloves. Just under the snowflakes, water was slopping, already gelid, more like grey tapioca pudding than water.

Carefully, she cleared all around the hole in the ice, and it was no more than two feet across.

Behind her, she heard her father shouting, 'Lizzie! Elizabeth! Get off the pool! Get off the pool!'

But she didn't turn around. She had glimpsed something stirring, just beneath the surface of the ice. Something that bobbed and dipped and slowly revolved.

'*Lizzie!*' her father was calling her – much closer now. His voice sounded almost hysterical. '*Lizzie, don't you move!*'

But now Elizabeth was frantically clearing away the snow from the surface of the pool, and wiping the ice with her gloved hands, around and around, like a speeding driver trying frantically to see through a fogged-up window. When it was clear, she stopped, and stared, and said nothing. Because it *was* a window – a window through which Elizabeth could look down into another world, dark and dreadfully cold. A window through which she could see her drowned sister Peggy, her skin as white as milk, her eyes wide open, her lips pale blue. Her curls floated and the fur trimming around her hood floated, languid and slow, as if they were weed, or Arctic sea-anemones.

Most poignant of all were Peggy's little hands, in their pink woolly gloves, which were clasped together, up against her chest, as if she were saying her prayers.

The more it snows (tiddely pom).

Her father had reached the edge of the pool. She could hear him, but she didn't turn to look at him. If she turned to look at him, she knew that she would have to obey him.

'Lizzie!' he called. 'Is Peggy there? Where's Peggy?'

Elizabeth didn't know what to say.

'Lizzie, sweetheart, is Peggy there?'

'Yes,' said Elizabeth. Her voice was deadened by the snowflakes.

'Jesus,' said her father. He stepped out on to the pool, and balanced his way towards her. His circular glasses were partially fogged-up, and his grey fisherman's sweater sparkled with snowflakes. A thin, brown-bearded man in his late thirties, intent on rescuing his drowned daughter.

'Lizzie, where is she?' he barked. 'Come on, Lizzie, for God's sake!'

Beneath the ice, Peggy smiled and slowly revolved. Elizabeth knew for certain that she was dead. She felt an intense pang of sorrow – so painful that it almost doubled her up. Peggy's face was so near, just inches below the ice; yet she was already so far away. For her, it would always be five past three on Friday, 23 February 1940, and never any later.

Peggy's face was directly below her. Elizabeth paused, and touched the ice with her fingertips. Then she leaned forward and pressed her lips to the frozen surface of the pool, just above her sister's lips.

Her sister stared at her, but didn't blink. The snow fell all around her, as if it wanted to lay a blanket over her, as if it wanted to cover her up.

'*Lizzie!*'

Her father was picking her up by one arm, swinging her around. She felt her shoulder socket being wrenched.

'Lizzie, get off the goddamned pool and back in the house!'

She stepped back, just as her father started kicking at the ice with his boot heel; but she didn't climb out of the pool. She stood close behind him, watching him in helpless anguish as he kicked and kicked and kept on shouting, 'Peggy! Peggy! Hold your breath, darling! Keep holding your breath! Daddy's here!'

It took him only a few seconds to kick out enough ice to reach her. He caught hold of her sodden fur coat and swirled her into the slushy water where the ice had first broken. Her body circled and dipped, one of her arms floated free. 'Come on, Peggy, come on honey,' he told her, and managed to pull her halfway out of the water, and then roll her on to the ice.

'Blankets!' he roared. 'Somebody get me some goddamned blankets!'

He picked Peggy up, cradled her, balanced himself, and somehow managed to skate and slither to the edge of the pool. He heaved himself up on the ladder. He groaned, 'Oh, God!' Peggy's arms flopped and swung, and water dripped glittering from her fingertips. Her face remained buried in her father's sweater, as if she didn't want anybody to look at her, because she was dead.

Elizabeth's mommy was running from the house, her white baking-apron flapping. '*Peggy*!' she was shrieking. '*Peggy*!'

Elizabeth climbed rigidly out of the frozen pool. Her shoulder hurt where her father had swung her around. Her father was already surging through the snow, back to the house, with Peggy in his arms. Mommy hurried close behind him, crying 'Peggy!' over and over.

Elizabeth was crying, too. She struggled her way back through the snow, shivering and cold and shocked, her face a blur of tears. By the time she reached the house, father had already wrapped Peggy in blankets and laid her on the back of the station-wagon. Exhaust smoke filled the driveway, tinged hellishly red from the rear lights. Elizabeth's mommy came out of the front door, her face like a mask of somebody else pretending to be Elizabeth's mommy.

'Darling . . . we have to take Peggy to the hospital . . . Mrs Patrick is coming over to take care of you. We'll call you later.'

Then they were gone. Elizabeth stood for a while in the driveway, watching the snow fill in their tyre tracks. Then she went back into the house, which was warm and suddenly quiet, and smelled of baking. She closed the front door and went to the cloakroom to take off her boots and her socks and her sodden coat.

Laura appeared, her cheeks watermarked with tears. 'Peggy's dead!' she gasped. 'I said drat her, and she's dead!'

The two sisters sat on the stairs, side by side, and cried until it hurt. They were still crying when the front door opened and Mrs Patrick arrived from Green Pond Farm. Mrs Patrick was their nearest neighbour, and she had known the girls since they were born. She was big and Irish, with a fiery complexion and fiery hair, and a nose like an old-fashioned hooter. She took off her coat, and then she gathered the girls up into her arms and shushed them and shushed them, until at last they were aware that her thick green home-knitted cardigan smelled of mothballs and that her brooch was scratching their faces. Much later, Elizabeth was to write in her diary that the consciousness of ordinary irritations is the first step towards coping with grief, and when she wrote that, she was thinking specifically of Mrs Patrick's cardigan, and Mrs Patrick's brooch.

When the girls were in bed that night, the telephone rang. They crept in their nightgowns out on to the galleried landing, and listened to Mrs Patrick in the hallway. The house was much chillier now: the fires had died down and their father hadn't been there to stoke them. Somewhere, a door was persistently banging.

They heard Mrs Patrick saying, 'I'm sorry, Margaret; I'm really so very sorry.'

They looked at each other, their eyes liquid, although they didn't cry. It was then that they knew for certain that Peggy had left them for ever; that Peggy was an angel; and strangely, they felt lonely, because now they would have to live their lives on their own.

Two

The following Thursday morning their mommy took them to Macy's in White Plains. The sky was brown with impending snow and Mamaroneck Avenue was brown with slush. Snow-covered automobiles crept this way and that, soft and sinister, like travelling igloos. Their mommy bought them black coats and black hats and charcoal-grey dresses with black braid trimmings. The store was overheated and while she was trying on her coat, Elizabeth felt as if she were going to suffocate. But somehow, the sombre ritual of buying mourning clothes was the first normal and understandable thing that had happened in a nightmarish week, and when they left the store with their packages Elizabeth felt very much better, as if a fever had passed.

Every day since Peggy's drowning had been different, frightening and off-balance. On Saturday and Sunday, nobody had spoken. On Monday evening mommy had silently hugged them and rocked them backwards and forwards and stroked their hair, feeling just like mommy, looking just like mommy. But then she had abruptly dropped them off her lap, and left the nursery without turning back, and noisily locked herself in her bedroom. A few moments of silence had passed while they stared at each other in perplexity. Then they heard her cry out like a wild mink caught in a gin-trap.

The sound of their mother's pain had been more than they could bear, and they had started crying, too, while father stood outside the bedroom door ineffectually calling, 'Margaret . . . Margaret . . . for goodness' sake, Margaret, let me in.'

On Tuesday night, without warning, their father came home

catastrophically drunk and started blundering around the house and slamming doors, screaming at mommy that she blamed him for everything, for giving up his job at Scribner's, for moving to Sherman, for buying the house, for failing to empty the goddamned pool. Why didn't she come right out with it, and say what she felt? Why didn't she simply accuse him of murdering his own daughter? Jesus Christ, he might just as well have plunged her head under the water with his own bare hands and held her down until she drowned.

After that, suddenly, the night went quiet. Elizabeth and Laura lay in their beds side by side and listened and listened, and didn't even dare to whisper. Eventually, they heard sobbing, and it went on for almost a half-hour. It might have been mommy's, it might have been daddy's. It could have been both.

They said a prayer to Peggy, although it was more like a conversation than a prayer. They found if difficult to believe that she had actually gone for ever.

'Dearest Peggy, what's it like being dead? Do get in touch somehow, even if it's just a whisper or writing your name on the frosty window. We think about you all day every day and we still love you just as much. We won't let anybody throw Mr Bunzum away, we promise. We cry about you all the time but we know you must be happy.'

Lots of unfamiliar people came and went. Adults who murmured and blew their noses and avoided your eyes. Almost magically, the house began to fill with flowers, daffodils and irises and even roses. There were so many flowers that mommy had to borrow vases from the neighbours, and still the blossoms seemed to swell. In February, with the snow still blinding the windows, all of these bright and fragrant flowers made the week seem even stranger, like a Grimm's fairytale.

Mrs Patrick came in every day that week and brought them lunch, which they ate in the kitchen. They liked Mrs Patrick's lunches because they were pot-roasted chicken and thick vegetable soup and Swedish meatballs, good farm food, fragrant and plain. Their mommy had always baked pretty little cookies and cakes, because granma had taught her when she was a girl. But when it came to stews and casseroles, she seemed to lose interest halfway through, and all her meals were odd-tasting and kind of unfinished, too salty or too herby or too floury, as if she had experimented with some new recipe and then grown bored. Her roasts were always grey and over-cooked and sorry for themselves, and for a long time the girls thought that her greens were an intentional punishment, like losing your allowance, or having your leg slapped.

Once or twice, while they ate, mommy came into the kitchen and talked abstractedly to Mrs Patrick. 'You lost your little Deborah, didn't you, Mrs Patrick? Oh God, I never understood what it was like to lose a child, not until now. It's like having your heart torn out by the roots.' Her cigarette smoke trailed endlessly across the room, towards the range, where the heat made it shudder for a moment and then suddenly snatched it away.

Mommy's presence made the girls uneasy, because they felt that they shouldn't show too much of a healthy appetite, what with Peggy having just drowned. Sometimes mommy said, 'Don't make so much noise with your knives and forks.' Then they picked at their food, hungry but reluctant to eat, and Mrs Patrick looked at them ruefully, but didn't shout at them.

On Wednesday morning, emboldened by the need for affection, and by plain gratitude, Elizabeth said pardon but what was Mrs Patrick's real name? Mrs Patrick looked at her in bewilderment, and said, 'Why, you goose, it's Mrs Patrick.'

Later Elizabeth wrote in her diary that – even in real life – some people are given major speaking parts, while others are only background characters. Even life has its extras; and Mrs Patrick was an extra, and knew it. 'Perhaps God will pay her some overtime, for looking after us.'

*

Mommy was the prettiest woman that Elizabeth and Laura had ever known. It was only later in life that Elizabeth realized that half of her brain was missing.

Mommy was petite and eye-catchingly narrow-waisted, with a clear, fine-boned face and a slightly side-sloping smile that every man friend of the family seemed to take personally, and which every woman friend of the family seemed to take as a threat.

Father always said that mommy looked like Paulette Goddard in a curly blonde wig, only prettier. Her eyes were as blue as that first piece of sky that shows when a rainstorm clears, and she always dressed in crisply-starched cottons or pastel silk sweaters. She had a snappy, flirty way about her – even with Duncan Purves, the doleful owner of the local auto shop, and with the Reverend Earwaker, the pastor of Sherman's Methodist Episcopal church, who believed that the radio was the very larynx of Satan, and who had once spoken the ritual of exorcism throughout the Jell-O programme (much to the fury of his wife, who was a Jack Benny fan).

The girls always loved to hear the story of how father and mommy first met. He had been working at Charles Scribner's Sons, the publishers, as a fiction editor: and she had been working as a cigarette girl at El Morocco – temporarily, of course, while auditioning for parts in Broadway musicals. Father was having dinner with Louis Sobol of the *New York Journal*, who was supposed to be writing the ultimate Café Society novel – a *roman-à-clef* that would out-Gatsby *The Great Gatsby*. In spite of the fact that Louis Sobol was capable of turning in five 2000-word gossip columns every single week, he had written only two paragraphs of his novel in seven months, and he was pleading for more time. 'I've got the *clef* licked; I just don't have the *roman a* sorted out.'

Father had called mommy over for a pack of cigarettes;

which she had opened for him, so that he could take the first one, and then struck a match. Unfortunately, she had dropped the lighted match into her cigarette tray, and before she could retrieve it, the whole tray had burst into flames. The girls loved this bit, because father and mommy always acted it out together, rushing around the living-room to show how father had snatched a magnum of Krug '21 from a neighbouring table, violently shaken it up, and hosed mommy's blazing tray with foaming champagne. Louis Sobol had written about it in his column the following day, calling it 'the costliest fire-fighting exercise in Manhattan's history'.

Mommy's picture had appeared in the paper; and she had caught the eye of Monty Woolley, the famous theatrical producer, who had signed her up for the tiniest of parts in *Fifty Million Frenchmen*. If you happened to sneeze when mommy came on, you would have missed her appearance altogether. But the next day, mommy had called into father's office with a bottle of champagne to thank him. Touched, *enchanted* almost, father had invited her out for cocktails, then for lunch. The rest was all piano-music-and-roses.

Puffing at her cigarette for punctuation, mommy would say, 'That was my only Broadway role but of course (*puff*) if I hadn't fallen in love with your father (*puff*) I could have had many, many other roles (*puff*). Monty Woolley several times said that I had all the potential of a great screen actress. He said my face always lit so well (*puff*). But I made my choice and my choice was to marry and have children,' (*puff*, followed by an emphatic crushing-out).

Mommy would repeat this explanation in a light, gushing, well-rehearsed lilt which Elizabeth at first found romantic but later found unsettling, as if she and Laura and Peggy were directly to blame for the fact that she had given up her acting career. As if she and Laura and Peggy had deliberately plotted together to isolate her for the rest of her life in Sherman,

Connecticut, baking cookies and listening to the radio and reducing rib-roasts to bundles of rags.

Laura, however, never tired of hearing mommy's 'screen actress' story, and would lie for hours in front of the fire swinging her legs and leafing through mommy's newspaper cuttings and agency photographs. 'Miss Eloise Foster, the former cigarette girl who gained notoriety by setting El Morocco alight, was one of the chorus line's brightest sparks.'

Elizabeth often caught Laura posing in front of the cheval-glass in their bedroom, with a table lamp in her hand. 'I think my face lights well, don't you?' she used to ask.

Elizabeth never answered, but sat on her patchwork quilt and opened her diary, or *Lorna Doone*, or a book of Hans Christian Andersen stories.

Her favourite Hans Christian Andersen story had always been *The Snow Queen*. Just like Kay and Gerda, the children in the story, she would warm pennies in front of the fire on winter mornings, and press them against the windows, to make peepholes through the frost. And she always imagined herself as the Snow Queen herself: 'Exquisitively fair and delicate, but entirely of ice, glittering, dazzling ice; her eyes gleamed like two bright stars, but there was no rest or repose in them.'

That Thursday evening, after they had gone to Macy's for their funeral clothes, Laura sat in front of the mirror making faces at herself, while Elizabeth read *The Snow Queen* yet again.

She had read the story aloud to Peggy and Laura, and sometimes to Mrs Patrick's son Seamus, too, over and over, until it had magically transformed itself from a fairy story into a strange kind of reality – into the vivid memory of a parallel life, which they had all secretly been leading, as well as their lives in Sherman, Connecticut.

When Elizabeth read *The Snow Queen*, her sisters listened like children in a dream, because they knew it off by heart. They knew that a magician! a wicked magician!! a most wicked magician!!! had once made a mirror that made everything beautiful look ugly. The loveliest landscapes looked like boiled spinach. The handsomest persons appeared as if standing upon their heads. But the mirror shattered, and broke into trillions of splinters, each of which retained the peculiar properties of the entire mirror. One of these splinters fell into the eye of a boy called Kay, and another pierced his heart.

Up until that moment, Kay had been living an idyllic life with his sister Gerda and his grandmother, but now he became cynical and rude and rash. One winter's day, when the snow was flying pell-mell through the streets, he hitched his toboggan to the back of a large white sledge, in which rode a tall, strange woman, dressed apparently in rough white furs. But her furs were snow, and she was the Snow Queen, and she kissed him with her icy lips and wrapped him in snow until he was only a heartbeat away from extinction. The Snow Queen took Kay to her palace in Finland, where she burned blue lights every evening; and there she made him sit on a frozen lake, which was broken into thousands of near-identical pieces. There she told him that if he could form the word Eternity out of ice, she would give him the whole world, and a new pair of skates besides. But he could never do it.

Gerda, meanwhile, went searching for her brother, seeking help from birds and flowers. Peggy and Laura's favourite was the story that was told to Gerda by the hyacinths, about three fair sisters, and they liked to imagine that *they* were the three fair sisters, and played endless games in which they dressed up in their mother's evening gowns and incessantly combed their hair.

Gerda sought the help of a little robber-maiden, and the wise advice of the Lapland woman and the Finland woman. She fought an army of vicious snowflakes, the Snow Queen's guards; and eventually she found the Snow Queen's palace, with walls that were formed of the driven snow, and its windows of the cutting wind. She sang a hymn to Kay, who wept, and when he wept, the splinter of mirror was washed out of his eye. Together, they returned home. The clock said 'tick-tock!' and the hands moved as before. The grandmother meanwhile sat in God's good sunshine and read from the Bible these words, 'Unless ye become as little children, ye shall not enter the kingdom of heaven'.

Elizabeth was re-reading *The Snow Queen* because it reminded her so much of Peggy. It made her feel as if Peggy might still be alive, somewhere, in that parallel world of driven snow and chilling winds. But she was worried about the hyacinth story. It had been worrying her all week. In fact, it had worried her so much that she hadn't dared to look at it, until today. She read it again, and as she read it she felt guiltier and guiltier and when she had finished she closed the book tight, and held it close to her chest, her cheeks flushed with unhappiness.

'There were three fair sisters, transparent and delicate they were; the kirtle of one was red, that of the second blue, of the third pure white; hand in hand they danced in the moonlight beside the quiet lake; they were not fairies, but daughters of men. Sweet was the fragrance when the maidens vanished into the wood; the fragrance grew stronger; three biers, whereon lay the three sisters, glided out from the depths of the wood, and floated upon the lake; the glow-worms flew shining around like little hovering lamps. Sleep the dancing maidens, or are they dead?'

What if Peggy had remembered that part of the story, when she was out in the garden, in the whirling snow? What if she had tried to dance on the surface of the swimming-pool, like the three fair sisters dancing by the lake?

Worst of all, what if it were all *her* fault that Peggy had drowned?

She glanced up at Laura; just to make sure that Laura didn't suspect anything; but Laura was too busy practising her movie-star pout in the mirror.

Elizabeth lay awake for hours that night and heard the clock in the hallway strike midnight. From father and mommy's room she could hear murmuring conversation, quiet and sad. There had been no sobbing today, thank goodness, and no shouting, and no slamming of doors. Father and mommy were both too tired. Mrs Patrick said they looked like ghosts; although she wouldn't tell them whether she'd ever seen any real ghosts to compare them to.

The murmuring conversation died away. Elizabeth counted to 1001. Then, she eased herself out of bed.

With Hans Christian Andersen's fairy book hidden under her dressing-gown, Elizabeth tippy-toed along the landing, and down the stairs. She had to tread very carefully, because every stair creaked. She had read in a mystery story, however, that burglars always made sure that they trod on the very, very edges of the stairs, close to the wall, or close to the banisters, and if you did that, you scarcely ever made a sound. In fact, really good burglars could actually *run* upstairs, totally silently.

In the living-room, the remains of the day's fire were still glowing, ashy and orange. Elizabeth crossed the threadbare red rug and stood in front of the hearth for a moment, debating with herself if she ought to try burning the fairy book, but in the end she decided that it would probably take too long – and what would happen if father came downstairs and caught her before she had finished? Father had been furious when he heard that away in some country called Germany some people called Nazis were burning books. He said that burning books was as bad as burning babies.

She went through to the kitchen. Although the floor was tiled, and the windows were already misted with cold, it was warm here, because father had stacked up the range for the

23

night. Ampersand the cat was sleeping in his basket next to the range, but when Elizabeth came in he opened one slitty eye and watched her as she walked around the table to the back door.

As quietly as she could, she levered back the bolts and turned the key. Then she stepped out into the silent, snowy night. She crossed the lawn to the shed. Her footsteps made a felty, squeaking noise in the snow. The moon was masked by cloud, but the garden was luminous enough for Elizabeth to be able to see where she was going. Her blue velveteen slippers were quickly soaked, and she was shivering. Yet her guilt was so overwhelming that she *had* to hide the book, as urgently as a murderer has to hide a gun.

If her parents ever discovered that she had read Peggy *The Snow Queen* . . . Well, she couldn't imagine what would happen, but whatever it was, it would be terrible. They might even end up with a broken home.

She knelt down beside the shed, and scooped back the snow with her bare hand. During the autumn, she had discovered a crevice underneath the floor of the shed, and she had used it to hide some of her love letters. They hadn't been *real* love letters, of course, she had written them all herself, but she would have been mortified if anybody had found them – especially the one from Clark Gable which ended 'I promise you that I will wait with bated breath until you have reached 21.'

She wedged the fairy book into the crevice, and pushed it as far under the shed as she could reach. Then she carefully scraped back the snow, and patted it so that it looked reasonably undisturbed.

There was a prayer in *The Snow Queen* which she had long ago learned by heart, because the first time she had read it, it had seemed so sweet and pretty. Tonight, however, it seemed tragic, and she stood in the snow in her dressing-gown with tears streaming down her cheeks, barely able to pronounce the words because her throat was choked up so much.

24

Our roses bloom and fade away,
Our Infant Lord abides alway;
May we be blessed His face to see,
And ever little children be!

She shivered in what she estimated was just about a minute's silence, and then she hurried back across the garden. Ampersand wearily opened his one slitted eye again, and watched her tippy-toe through to the living-room. Humans, I don't know where they find the energy.

She climbed the stairs, keeping close to the wall, burglar-style. It was only when she reached the landing that she realized that father was standing in the shadowy doorway of his bedroom, watching her. She said, 'Ah!' in terror, and almost wet herself.

'Lizzie?' he asked her. 'What have you been doing?' But his voice was gentle, and she knew at once that he wasn't going to be cross with her.

'I thought I heard something,' she stuttered, her teeth clattering with cold.

He came out of the shadows. He wasn't wearing his spectacles, and his eyes were swollen and plum-coloured with tiredness.

'What was it?' he asked her. 'What did you hear?'

'I don't know. Maybe an owl.'

He laid his hand on her shoulder. 'Well, it might have been. You know what they say about owls.'

She shook her head.

'They say that owls bring messages from dead people,' he told her. 'They can fly from the land of the living to the land of the dead, and back again, all in one night.'

Elizabeth looked up at him, wondering if he were serious. 'It wasn't an owl. It was just nothing.'

He hesitated for a while, keeping his hand on her shoulder.

Then he said, 'I'm going down to the library, do you want to come? I haven't been sleeping too well. You can help yourself to a soda if you'd care to.'

'Okay, sure,' she said, as sweetly as she could, in case he changed his mind. She suddenly felt pleased that she was nine, and rather grown-up. She betted he wouldn't have asked Laura to help herself to a soda, and join him in the library, right slapbang in the middle of the night, for goodness' sake.

The two of them went downstairs together, and this time the stairs creaked and it didn't matter. Elizabeth went to the Frigidaire, crammed with platefuls of Mrs Patrick's leftovers, and found a frosty-chilled bottle of Coca-Cola. She returned to the library to find that her father had drawn his big leather chair up close to the fireplace, and that he had poured himself a large cut-crystal glass of whiskey, and set it in the brown-tiled grate.

'Sit down,' he said; and so she dragged up his old piano-stool, the one with the frayed tapestry seat and all the music inside it, strange musty-yellow music that nobody would ever play, like 'Climbing Up The Golden Stairs' and 'Break The News To Mother'.

Elizabeth swigged Coca-Cola from the bottle and watched the fire embers dying away. She wondered if father were going to talk, or whether he would sit here in silence, drinking whiskey and staring at nothing at all.

'I guess you miss Peggy pretty sorely,' he said, at last.

Elizabeth nodded.

Her father said, 'The Reverend Earwaker keeps telling me that the Lord giveth and the Lord taketh away, as if that's supposed to make me feel better. I don't know. I wouldn't have minded *what* the Lord had taken away from me – my arms, my legs, my eyes . . . But not little Peggy, not my little Clothes-Peg. He didn't have to take her away.'

'I expect she's happy,' ventured Elizabeth.

26

Her father glanced across at her and gave her half a smile. 'Yes,' he said, 'I expect she is.'

'Laura and I say prayers to her, every night, and talk to her, too.'

'Good,' he said. 'I'm glad of that.'

Elizabeth said, 'You're not sorry you had her, are you?'

There was a lengthy silence. One of the last logs lurched in the hearth, sending a whirl of sparks up the chimney. 'That's a very mature question,' said her father. 'I'm not too sure that I know what the answer is.'

'Sometimes I think that mommy's a bit sorry she had any of us.'

'Your mommy? Your mommy's not sorry she had you, any of you! Nothing of the kind!'

'But if she hadn't had us, she could have been a movie actress, couldn't she?'

Her father had pressed his hand over his mouth for a while, as if he were making quite sure that no words came out until he was sure what he was going to say. Then he explained, 'Your mommy is one of these people who always needs to think that their life could have been different.'

'But it could have been, couldn't it? She was on Broadway.'

'Yes,' her father agreed, 'she was on Broadway.'

'And she could have been a famous movie star?'

She could tell by her father's expression that he was tempted to say no. She was almost tempted to say it for him. He couldn't look at her: *wouldn't* look at her, in the way that he wouldn't look at mommy whenever mommy started talking about El Morocco and Monty Woolley and *Fifty Thousand Frenchmen*. Elizabeth suddenly realized that she had known for quite a long time that mommy had never been gifted with whatever it takes to be a famous movie star, the style, the idiosyncrasy, the voice, the kind of face that cameras fell in love with.

But mommy's lost movie career was one of the articles of

27

faith of Buchanan family life, and they both understood that it was heresy to question it.

Father looked down into his drink and said, 'Whatever you do, Lizzie, don't regret things that you never did. Don't ever pine for anything. Not men, not money, not things you think you should have had.'

Elizabeth drank more Coca-Cola, and gave her father a sage nod of the head. She was beginning to enjoy herself. This was grown-up talk, in the middle of the night.

Her father said, 'Don't pine for Peggy, either. She's gone now, and no amount of pining can bring her back. Don't worry: she won't be alone. We're going to put Mr Bunzum in the coffin, to keep her company.'

Elizabeth stared at him in horror, and then burped, because of the Coca-Cola. 'You can't do that!'

Her father frowned at her. 'Why not, Lizzie? Mr Bunzum was Peggy's favourite toy.'

'But he'll *suffocate*! And he never liked the dark! You know he never liked the dark!'

'Lizzie, sweetheart, Mr Bunzum is a toy rabbit.'

'But you *can't*! Peggy wouldn't want you to! Mr Bunzum's real! Mr Bunzum isn't even dead yet! He had real adventures, I can prove it!'

Her father put down his whiskey glass. 'You can *prove* it?' he asked.

'Wait.' Elizabeth hurried upstairs, burglar-syle so that the stairs wouldn't creak. She crept across her bedroom, so that she wouldn't wake Laura, and then she opened her desk. She took out three well-worn exercise books, and then hurried back downstairs again. Her father was still sitting in the same place, although he had picked up his whiskey glass again. She handed him the books and said, 'There.'

Because he was tired, and because he wasn't wearing his glasses, her father found it difficult to focus at first. But when he held the first exercise book at arm's length, he was able to read out 'Mr Bunzum Goes To Hollywood'.

'You wrote this?' he asked Elizabeth.

'I wrote all of them.'

Her father set down his glass, licked the tip of his finger, and opened the first page. He stared at it for a very long time, and swallowed. The dying light from the fireplace reflected from the tears that were welling up in his eyes.

'Chapter One,' he read out. 'Mr Bunzum Sees A Movie.'

He paused for a while, and then he read, 'Mr Bunzum was a person who lived in a big white house in Sherman, Connecticut, with his friend Peggy and Peggy's two sisters Elizabeth and Laura. Mr Bunzum's problem was that he was a rabbit, which made life very difficult for him, i.e. he was the proud owner of an excellent red Packard but could not drive it because every time he drove it the cops stopped him and said "you're breaking the law, whisker-face." Also he could not eat in restaurants because whenever he walked in for lunch and said "lunch?" they thought that he *was* the lunch.

'But Peggy loved Mr Bunzum so much that she dressed him and fed him and took him everyplace he wanted to go, for which Mr Bunzum was internally grateful. Mr Bunzum for his part loved Peggy too and the two of them were the firmest friends that anyone had ever known.

'Mr Bunzum – ' But here, Elizabeth's father was stopped right in the middle of reading by a terrible sob. He bent forward in his chair as if he had the world's worst stomach ache, and he was grimacing with grief. He sat there shaking and sobbing, and he wouldn't stop. In the end there was nothing that Elizabeth could do but tippy-toe upstairs again. She climbed back into the chilly sheets of her bed and lay in the darkness with her heart beating, and prayed to Jesus that she had done the right thing.

She saw the moon come out. She thought of *The Snow Queen*,

and the maidens dancing by the lake. She could smell the flowers on their biers; and they were Peggy's funeral-flowers. She heard Laura's blocked-nose breathing; and the clock downstairs striking two. Then suddenly she was dreaming, and she couldn't think how.

In the morning, she found her exercise books back on her desk, with Mr Bunzum lolling on top of them. There was a note beside them, on her father's Candlewood Press notepaper. The note read, 'I have read all of Mr Bunzum's adventures and agree with you that he is a real person, still alive, and not to be buried. You are a writer of wonderful talent and imagination, and one day much grander publishers than me will be proud to publish your books. – All my love and XXXX, your father.'

Three

When father opened their curtains on the morning of the funeral, they could see that the snow was falling thick and hurried. He was already dressed in his black trousers and his black jacket and his starched white shirt. He looked very tired and old, as if he had aged a hundred years in a week. His face looked *papery*, Elizabeth thought. He had trimmed his beard and he smelled of that spicy cologne that mommy had given him for Christmas; but he looked like a fastidious old man, rather than father.

'Breakfast's ready,' he told them. 'Make it quick as you can. The guests will start arriving at a quarter past ten, or thereabouts.'

After he had gone, Laura bounced out of bed in her long pink nightgown and went to the window. 'It's really deep!' she exclaimed. 'We could build a snow-angel!'

'What do you mean, a snow-angel?' asked Elizabeth.

Laura pressed her hands together as if she were praying, and closed her eyes. 'You know, a snow-angel. Like the angels in the graveyard, only snow.'

Elizabeth climbed out of bed and stood beside her. The snow was whirling down so furiously they could scarcely see the garden. 'Yes, we could,' she said. 'And we could make it look just like Peggy.'

Laura looked up at her, her eyes still sticky with sleep, her blonde curls tousled. 'Do you think that Peggy will be an angel?'

'Of course,' said Elizabeth, although she didn't feel completely certain about it. 'She never did anything mean or nasty, did she? And she was only five. You know what Jesus said about suffer the little children to come unto Me.'

'Why did they have to suffer?' asked Laura. 'I thought Jesus was supposed to be kind.'

'Everybody has to suffer sometimes,' Elizabeth told her. 'That's what Mrs Dunning said at Sunday school.'

'Succotash has to suffer, too,' said Laura.

'What?'

'That's what they say in the funnies. "Suffering succotash!" '

They put on their slippers and their cuddly woollen robes, Elizabeth blue and Laura pink, and went downstairs to the kitchen. It was so gloomy that Mrs Patrick had switched on the lights. It wasn't a quiet breakfast. Fifty people were expected for lunch; and Mrs Patrick was punching seven kinds of hell out of a huge batch of bread-roll dough; while a brown cauldron of chicken chowder was quietly blabbering to itself on top of the range, next to a boiling stuffed ham sewn up in muslin, which rhythmically rose and fell in its seething pot like somebody's boiling head.

Mrs Patrick was listening to the radio, too. There was news from Europe, where the Russians were having horrendous difficulties invading Finland. Leland Stowe of the Chicago *Daily News* was recounting what he had seen. 'In this sad solitude lie the dead . . . uncounted thousands of Russian dead. They lie as they fell – twisting, gesticulating and tortured . . . beneath a kindly mask of two inches of newly-fallen snow.'

Mrs Patrick suddenly realized that the girls were listening and switched the radio off.

'What is it?' hissed Laura.

'It's the war,' said Elizabeth. They knew that there was a war in Europe but Elizabeth found it difficult to imagine what Europe was like. At school they had learned that there were kings and queens in Europe, and palaces. They had also learned that Europe was very much smaller than America, and much more densely populated. Elizabeth had a mental impression of a glittering ballroom crowded with thousands of people in golden crowns and ermine robes, angrily jostling and pushing each other. No wonder they had wars.

'You shouldn't fuss your head thinking about the war,' said Mrs Patrick, dredging flour across the tabletop. 'It doesn't concern us, not one whit. It's *their* quarrel, the British and the French and the Germans. If Mr Roosevelt has any sense at all, he'll keep us well out of it. Not that *any* politician has any sense.'

Father came into the kitchen. His glasses steamed up almost immediately, and he had to take them off.

'Come on girls, hurry up now. You don't have all day.'

'Where's mommy?' asked Laura. 'I haven't said good morning yet.'

'Mommy's okay, you can see her in a minute. Just finish your breakfast and get yourselves dressed.'

As they climbed back upstairs, they felt a chilly, unsettled atmosphere in the house. There was very little wind, and so the fires had taken a long time to draw. The whole house was hazy with acrid woodsmoke, which made them cough, and being nine and seven they really made a performance of their coughing, rolling around on their beds in their long woolly underwear, spluttering and hacking and wheezing like terminal tuberculosis patients, until father called out to them to shut UP, will you, and get yourselves ready.

'But it's so *smoky*.'

Father was about to say something angry, he hated laying all those goddamned fires in any case, but stopped himself. Instead, he shielded his eyes with his hand in a very curious way; and then took his hand away again, and said, 'Listen . . . this is going to be a difficult day. It's going to be a difficult day for mommy and it's going to be a difficult day for me. I know how

33

close you both were to Peggy, and that you can still talk to her. But when you're grown up like mommy and me, you can't do that any more, don't ask me why. So for us, Peggy has gone away, completely gone away. We've lost her.'

The girls lay on their beds in their underwear watching him solemnly. He licked his lips quickly (mouth turned dry) and then he said, 'Today mommy and I have to put our youngest little girl into the ground. That isn't going to be easy for us; and I hope you'll understand how we feel, and try to be patient and helpful.'

Laura said, 'Suffer the little children to come unto Me.'

'Yes,' said father, with his eyes glistening.

'And suffer the succotash to come unto Me.'

Father said, 'What?'

'It's all right,' Elizabeth interrupted. 'We promise we'll be helpful.'

Elizabeth brushed Laura's hair, a procedure which was always accompanied by a monotonous chorus of 'ow', 'ow', 'OW', '*ow*,' as she cleared out the tangles. Then they dressed in their mourning clothes and stood side by side and looked at themselves in the cheval-glass. Elizabeth thought that they looked as if *they* were dead, too. Their faces were waxy and their eyes were large, and the luminous snow-light surrounded them with a blurry, almost ghostly aura.

It was then that they glimpsed a shadowy movement in the mirror, which made them jump. They turned around and saw mommy standing in their bedroom doorway. She was dressed in a severe, boxy suit of black moiré silk, with a small upswept black hat and a dense black veil that completely masked her face.

For a split second, they were very frightened. Mommy was so black, so silent, so faceless. 'Mommy?' said Laura, in alarm.

Mommy moved and when she moved she was just mommy. She came into the room and laid a black-gloved hand on each

34

of them. She smelled of cigarettes, and perfume and something else aromatic, which they weren't old enough to identify as gin. 'Don't worry, Laura sweetheart, I'm quite all right. You both look *beautiful*. Are you ready to come downstairs now? Granpa and granma have just arrived; and so has Aunt Beverley.'

'I haven't washed my teeth yet,' said Laura.

'You're all dressed up in black and you haven't washed your teeth? You'll get toothpowder all over your collar.'

'I have to wash my teeth, you can die from dental caries.'

Mommy didn't argue. Elizabeth couldn't see her face, because her veil was too dark, but she could guess what she was thinking. When mommy had gone downstairs, and Laura was industriously brushing her teeth with her Donald Duck toothbrush, Elizabeth came into the bathroom and hissed at her, 'Don't talk about dying any more. Mommy doesn't like it. It'd bad enough Peggy being drowned.'

'But they told us at school. And you can die from not washing your hands, after you've been to the bathroom.'

'Oh, certainly. And you can die if somebody drops a cow on your head.'

They went downstairs. The front door was wide open and a few mischievous snowflake-fairies were flying over the threshold and dancing across the orange-and-yellow Shaker rug. An icy draft was streaming in, ruffling the fringes of the lampshades, and scattering black-edged condolence cards across the floor, but at least it was clearing away the woodsmoke and brightening up father's sulky fires.

Aunt Beverley was taking off her sleek brown mink and talking eight million to the dozen, as usual. Aunt Beverley was a very tall mannish woman in her late thirties, with a long neck, and a big, bloodless, bony head. Mommy always said that Aunt Beverley believed herself to be much more beautiful than she really was. She must have spent untold eye-watering hours plucking her brows into geometrically-perfect arches, and pinning up her hair into a glossy black tidal wave.

But her ears were too big and lobular, and her nose was too complicated, and her funeral-dress might have been Pauline Trigere but it hung on her frame (in Elizabeth's opinion) like a photographer's black cape over a camera and tripod.

'Well, the roads were *so* darned impossible that we nearly turned back at Cannondale. I can't tell you, Margaret, it was Napoleon's retreat from Moscow, all over. Humphrey was adamant that he didn't want to die in Connecticut. He said his grandparents died in their beds in Braggadocio, Missouri, and his parents died in their beds in Braggadocio, Missouri, and he certainly didn't intend to be frozen to death in the middle of winter in a rented automobile in some prissy Yankee dormitory in Connecticut. And, why! Look who's here! My dear little Lizzie; my dear little Laura!'

Aunt Beverley bent down and kissed them both with her sticky scarlet lips. She smelled of cigarettes and freckle cream. She wore four rows of sparkling jet beads, and a ruby-and-emerald brooch in the shape of an apple tree. Mommy had known Aunt Beverley for ever and ever – since *Fifty Thousand Frenchmen*, when Aunt Beverley had been wardrobe mistress. Elizabeth knew that there was something different about Aunt Beverley. She wasn't at all like mommy, or like any of the women who lived in Sherman. She was bossy, and wickedly gossipy, and drank whiskey. Even the men seemed to be afraid of her. She wasn't their *real* aunt, of course, she just liked them to call her aunt. She had never married: she was still 'Miss Lowenstein', although she never seemd to be wanting for male escorts. Humphrey was the latest: a bulbous-eyed man in his early forties with thinning hair and a little clipped moustache.

'I'm very sorry for your loss,' he told mommy. Then he said, 'Wonderful house.'

'Thank you,' said mommy.

Father came up and said, 'Glad you could make it.'

'Wonderful house,' Humphrey repeated.

'Seventeen-sixty-one,' said father.

'As much as that? I thought Connecticut prices were coming down.'

'Excuse me?' said father.

Outside, in the snow, more cars were silently arriving, in plumes of exhaust. Big black Buick Eights and Chrysler Imperials and Packard sedans, nose to tail. There was a sporadic slamming of doors, and then the funeral guests began to make their way towards the house. Elizabeth and Laura had to stay in the hallway to greet them, while Seamus collected their coats and hung them up. Seamus was seventeen with carroty hair and a face like one of his mother's rising loaves. Mommy said that Seamus had been stricken with meningitis when he was six, which had left him fanciful and odd; but Mrs Patrick said that he had been kidnapped by leprechauns for a month or two, that was all, and that when the leprechauns had brought him back he had seen sights and danced dances that no human being had ever seen or danced before, and that was what made him the way he was.

Elizabeth liked him and didn't mind it when he sat in the corner listening intently while she read *The Snow Queen*, but she was always a little afraid of him. He would say things like, 'Brilliant umbrella, sir,' over and over again. Or, 'Forward with fences, that's what I say, forward with fences.' Or else he would quote whole pages of *The Snow Queen*, with extraordinary emphasis, like somebody speaking in Finnish. Laura adored him and thought that he spoke just as much sense as anybody else.

At a quarter to eleven, father told Elizabeth to close the door, because everybody was feeling the draught. The living-room was crowded with guests, and the fires were crackling, and Seamus was taking round trays of sherry and cheese straws.

37

Just as she was about to close the door, Elizabeth saw a whale of a Cadillac arriving through the snow. It parked a little way away from the rest of the cars, and for two or three minutes there was no sign of anybody climbing out. 'Lizzie!' her father called her. 'Close the door now, will you, for goodness' sake?'

'Somebody's coming,' said Elizabeth.

Her father came up behind her and peered through the crack in the door. The snow was falling so furiously that it was almost impossible to see anything at all. The door of the Cadillac opened and a stocky wide-shouldered man in a wide-brimmed hat climbed out, and started to trudge to the house.

'Well, I'll be damned,' said her father, and he never, ever said 'I'll be damned', at least not in front of her. 'It's Johnson Ward.'

'Who's Johnson Ward?' asked Elizabeth.

Her father laid a hand on her shoulder. 'A writer, sweetheart. You've met him before but you probably don't remember. He's one of the greatest writers that ever was, in my opinion. He wrote a very famous book called *Bitter Fruit*.'

Elizabeth didn't know what to say about that. She had met a few writers – a nervous, chainsmoking young man called Ashley Tibbett, who had written some essays about rural life in the Litchfield Hills, books so skinny that they looked as if they didn't have any pages between their covers. And Mary Kenneth Randall, a serious, harsh-voiced woman with thick ankles and thick sombre clothes and hair like a scouring-pad, who had written two huge novels about objectivism, whatever that was.

But as far as Elizabeth had been able to tell, writers didn't care for children very much. Writers talked about nothing except themselves, and they seemed to regard children as competition. Ashley Tibbett hadn't even been able to look at them, and Mary Kenneth Randall had given them a particularly vile cough-candy and patted them so hard on the top of

38

the head that her wedding ring had clonked against their skulls.

Johnson Ward reached the porch and he was big and smiling and twinkly-eyed and he stamped his feet and banged his leather gloves together.

'Johnson,' said father. He looked quite small by comparison, almost as if he had shrunk in the wash. Johnson Ward took off his glove and squeezed father's hand tight, and then clapped him on the back.

'Hullo, David. I hope you don't object to my coming. Michael Farkas told me what had happened. I'm really so sorry. Your little Peggy was a dream come true.'

'Yes, she was,' said father. 'Yes. We're going to miss her.'

'And this must be Lizzie,' said Johnson Ward. He took off his hat, and when he took off his hat, Elizabeth saw that he wasn't so very old. His hair was the shiny light-brown colour of peanut-brittle, and neatly combed into a parting. He had a peanut-brittle coloured moustache, too. His face was broad and generous and friendly, with an easy smile and a captivating way of crinkling up his eyes. He reminded Elizabeth of Clark Gable, sort of, except that he was taller and heavier, and his ears didn't stick out, as Laura always said, 'like the kitchen cupboard with its doors wide open.'

'How do you do, sir,' said Elizabeth, in a whisper.

Johnson Ward squatted down in the porch so that his coat-tails dragged in the snow. He was very *clean*, with a crisp white collar, and he smelled of cigars and spices.

'You don't have to call me "sir",' he told her, taking hold of both of her hands. 'We're friends, you and me, even if you don't know it. The last time I saw you was when your baby sister was born, and you were four. Do you know what we did?'

'No, sir,' said Elizabeth.

'Well, I'll tell you what we did, we spent the whole afternoon in the garden popping balloons, that's what we did. We jumped on them. We sat on them. We pricked them with pins. We even bit them, do you know that? Now, that's what I call brave, biting a balloon. But there's one thing I'll never forget; and that is, what a lady you were. Even at four, you were a lady, and I can see today that you're still a lady; and that you always will be.'

Elizabeth didn't know what to say. She remembered bursting the balloons but she didn't remember Johnson Ward. All the same, Johnson Ward grasped her hands warmly and tightly, and she decided she liked him. Elizabeth's father said, rather sharply, 'Say thank you to Mr Ward, Lizzie.'

'Thank you, Mr Ward,' Elizabeth whispered.

'No, no, thank you, *Bronco*,' Johnson Ward insisted.

Elizabeth hesitated. How could a grown-up writer with a Cadillac and a moustache call himself 'Bronco'? That was a cowboy's name; a name that little boys used, in schoolyard games.

'Come on, now,' Johnson Ward urged her.

Elizabeth swallowed. The cold draught had made her throat feel dry. 'Thank you, Bronco,' she told him.

Father closed the front door and Johnson Ward took off his heavy coat. 'I'll bet you miss your little sister sorely,' he said.

Elizabeth nodded. Most of the time she didn't find it too difficult to think that Peggy was dead. But now and then, for no particular reason, her eyes would fill with tears, and her throat would tighten up, and her voice would sound as if she had a thistle stuck in her larynx – that's if she could speak at all. At those times, she felt a cold and blasphemous suspicion that Peggy wasn't in Heaven, after all; that she wasn't sitting on some sun-blessed cumulus cloud, with white wings and a white nightgown and a golden halo around her head. At those times, she suspected that Peggy had simply left them for ever, and was lying chilly as ice in her coffin, and that was all.

At those times, she thought about Hans Christian Andersen's fairy tales, too, lying concealed beneath the shed.

As they crossed the hallway to the crowded living-room, Johnson Ward laid his hand reassuringly on Elizabeth's shoulder. 'When my older brother Billy died, I was so cut up that I couldn't eat and I couldn't write and I couldn't even think. You know what that's like, when you can't even *think*? Your head's no more good to you than an empty cooking-pot. You can bang on your skull with your knuckles for all you're worth, but there's nothing inside, only echoes. Those were bad, bad times for me, those were.'

He stopped, and looked down at her. 'But do you know what happened? I went to Havana, for the principal purpose of getting drunk. I gambled at the casino, and I smoked big cigars the size of telegraph poles, and I got drunk. And I was sitting in the Plaza de Armas, with a mouth that felt like a cat's favourite cushion and a headache that felt like an iron Derby that was half a size too small, when a Cuban boy came up to me, and stood staring at me. He was wearing a white shirt and khaki pants and sandals with open toes. He stood and stared at me and I sat and stared back at him. And do you know what he said? He said, "Bronco, don't you recognize me?"

'Well, I stared at him even harder, and maybe there was something familiar about his eyes, but that was all. But then he said, "It's Billy, your brother."

'You can imagine that I went shivery all over, just like somebody had emptied an ice-bucket down the back of my shirt. I said, "It can't be. Billy's dead." But he stepped a little closer and he looked at me just the way I'm looking at you now, and he said, "It's Billy. I just want to tell you that everything's fine."

' "Fine?" I said. "You've turned into a Cuban and everything's fine?" '

' "Couldn't be sweller," he said. And he turned around, and walked across the plaza, and that was the last I ever saw of him.'

41

'Was he a *ghost*?' asked Elizabeth, in awe.

'Uh-unh. I don't think so. I think he was just Billy.'

Elizabeth wanted to ask Johnson Ward if it might be possible to find Peggy, too, amongst the crowds around the Plaza de Armas, or anywhere else for that matter. But before she could do so, mommy came across the room, black-veiled, tilting slightly.

'Johnson!' she exclaimed, and flung her arms around him.

'Hello, Margaret. Please accept my condolences, and Vita's, too.'

Mommy turned her head this way and that. 'You didn't bring Vita?'

'Vita's not too well. Nothing serious, but she couldn't face the journey.'

'I'm sorry,' said mommy, in a tone of voice that suggested that she wasn't sorry in the slightest. 'How's the writing coming along?' She pecked at the air with two black-gloved fingers, in a charade of somebody trying to find their way around the keyboard of a typewriter.

'Slow,' said Johnson Ward. 'You know me. Three words a day if I'm lucky.'

'I'm surprised you can still find anything to write about, after *Bitter Fruit*.'

'Well . . . *Bitter Fruit* did have a little of everything in it, didn't it?' Johnson Ward smiled.

Elizabeth's mommy swayed, as if she were trying to keep her balance on the deck of a ship. 'You know what the trouble with you writers is, don't you?' she demanded.

'I'm sure you're going to tell me, Margaret, whether I know or not.'

'The trouble with you writers is that you think you're realer than we are.'

'We do?'

'Of course you do! But that's where you're wrong! I'm real

42

and all these people are real and David's real and Elizabeth and Laura are real. The only ficstitious – the only *fictitious* – character in this room is *you*. You're not real. You're not! But you won't admit it.'

Johnson Ward grasped mommy's black-gloved elbow, partly as a gesture of sympathy, and partly to hold her steady. 'Why don't I mingle?' he said. 'Maybe some of these good people's reality will rub off on me.'

'You're a sham, Johnson,' mommy declared. 'A certified fraud.'

Johnson Ward left mommy frowning at the wall as if she had never seen it before. He circled around the room, shaking hands with some of the people he knew, and smiling to some of those he didn't know. He clasped the Reverend Earwaker's hand and whispered something in his ear, and the Reverend Earwaker nodded, again and again. Elizabeth thought Johnson Ward was wonderful and couldn't keep her eyes off him. He had not only said she was a lady, he had treated her like one, too. And although Mommy had been horribly rude to him, he hadn't seemed to mind at all.

On the other side of the room, Laura was chattering to Aunt Beverley, telling her how she still wanted to be a movie star, even famouser than Shirley Temple. Aunt Beverley was saying, 'Of *course*, candy-cake. You're *twice* as pretty as Shirley. If your mommy says it's okay, I'll take you to see Sol Warberg, he's a very, *very* famous producer.'

At one minute after eleven o'clock, the doorbell chimed. The murmuring conversation died away. Everybody knew who it was; they glanced at each other, discomfited. Elizabeth's father went to open the door with the scissorlike stride of a man who wants to get something over and done with, as soon as he can.

Black as two half-starved crows, Mr Ede the mortician and his assistant Benny, tall and painfully thin, stood side by side in the snow-clogged porch. They both removed their black hats,

43

and Mr Ede's hair, which had been carefully combed across his narrow skull to cover up his baldness, flew up in the air and waved around in the wind.

'Are all of your guests arrived, sir?' he asked, peering beadily into the hallway and swivelling his head. Father turned around to look at their assembled friends and relatives, and there was a look on his face that was close to panic. Even Elizabeth could understand what the mortician really meant. *Are you ready, sir? It's time to put your daughter into the ground.*

Through the open doorway, across the white and ghostly garden, she could see the huge black hearse waiting, its windows so filled with flowers that she could only make out one glinting silver handle of Peggy's coffin.

She repeated the little prayer from *The Snow Queen*. 'Our roses bloom and fade away . . . our Infant Lord abides alway . . .'

When they returned from the funeral, the guests were silent and pinched with cold. There had been some painful sobbing at the graveside as Peggy's small, white, silver-handled casket had been lowered, and mommy had thrown five white roses on it, one for each blessed year of Peggy's life. A keen north-north-easter had cut across the exposed northern slope of the cemetery, so that the snow had blown into their eyes like shattered glass.

As soon as Mrs Patrick opened the front door, mommy rushed past her and fled upstairs, a distraught black shadow. The girls heard her locking her bedroom door. Uncomfortably, the rest of the guests crowded back into the living-room. The double doors to the dining-room had now been opened, and the table spread with food and drink – chicken chowder and breadcrumbed ham and a joint of red-rare beef and spicy meatloaf, as well as a glazed turkey and a whole poached salmon with pimento-stuffed olives where its eyes should have been. It looked to the girls like a cartoon salmon, as if it might suddenly talk to them.

In a giant silver bowl borrowed from the Sherman Country Club, Mrs Patrick had brewed up a hot brandy punch with plenty of sugar and lemon juice and cloves and sauternes wine, which Seamus ladled out to every guest 'to melt you out.' The punch was very strong, and before long everybody's cheeks became warm and flushed, and the conversation grew louder and less inhibited. People even started to laugh. There was a lot of talk about the war in Europe. Butter and meat rationing had just been announced in Britain. Most of the men thought that the United States ought not to get itself involved. 'What's happening in Europe is Europe's business. And – who knows? – Adolf Hitler may well turn out to be just the tonic that Europe needs.'

Johnson Ward, his mouth stuffed with potato salad, said, 'What about freedom? That's what we're talking about here. Freedom of speech, freedom of thought. Those Nazis are against freedom, and if they're against freedom, then I'm against *them*.'

'Freedom of speech, indeed,' said Mrs Gosling from the Sherman Women's Club. 'I've heard about your book, Mr Ward, and from what I hear about your book, the only freedoms *you're* interested in are drinking, dancing, driving too fast and adultery.'

Johnson Ward shrugged. 'I disapprove just as much of bridge, home-made gingerbread and embroidery,' he replied. 'But, believe me, I'll defend them to the last drop of blood.'

When all the guests had been served, Mrs Patrick called Elizabeth and Laura to bring their plates, and she dished out slices of turkey and hot hashed potatoes with thick brown gravy and cranberry sauce. She told them to go to the kitchen if they were thirsty, for milk or lemonade, but Laura said prettyplease to Seamus, who had always liked her, and cajoled him into pouring them two half-glasses of punch.

They sat on the cushioned window seat overlooking the tennis court, swinging their legs. Elizabeth thought that the turkey was quite nice, but it didn't taste the same as Thanksgiving, and she soon felt picky and full-up and bored. Laura was just as bad. She complained to Mrs Patrick that there were holes in her turkey, and even when Mrs Patrick told her they were fork-holes, that was all, she still had to cut round them and submerge the holey pieces deep in her gravy, to hide them.

After all that eyelash-fluttering at Seamus, she and Laura both thought the punch was disgusting. It tasted even more poisonous than Mary Kenneth Randall's cough candy. They made extravagant retching noises until Mrs Patrick told them to stop it. When nobody was looking they emptied their glasses back into the bowl.

They hung around the living-room for a while, but the air was becoming almost unbreathable with cigarette smoke, and the conversation was even more boring than the dining-room. Eventually, Elizabeth and Laura wandered to the library, where granpa was talking to father. Granpa looked exactly like father except he was kind of yellowish, as if somebody had cut father's picture out of the newspaper and left it on the windowsill for too long.

'How are doing, my beautiful young ladies?' he asked, taking Laura on to his bony knee, and jiggling her up and down. 'You're feeling pretty low today, I'll bet.' Elizabeth was glad that she was too big to sit on granpa's knee any more. He reeked of camphor ice, which he used for his roughened, cracking skin, and tobacco, and death. The girls were always quite sure that they knew what death smelled like. They had only to think of granpa.

'Let me tell you something,' said granpa. 'Every time a child dies and goes to Heaven, there's another star up in the sky. You go out one clear night and look for yourself. You'll see our little Clothes-Peg, sparkling bright as can be.'

'Bronco said that I might meet her in Havana,' said Elizabeth.

Granpa frowned at father. 'What's the child talking about, Havana?'

Father gave an uncomfortable smirk. 'Bronco – that's Johnson Ward, the writer. You remember *Bitter Fruit?*'

'Darn dirty book, from what I recall,' said granpa.

'Go on, girls, run along now,' father urged them. 'Granpa and I have things to talk over.'

So it was that they dressed in their coats and their woolly hats and their gloves and their extra socks and their big wobbly-sounding black rubbers and let themselves out of the kitchen door, into the snow. Ampersand the cat glared at them in suppressed fury as the freezing draught ruffled his fur.

Laura carried a Macy's shopping bag, one of the bags in which they had taken home their funeral clothes, slung around her neck like a backpack. They marched around to the tennis court, singing Winnie-the-Pooh's cold toes song. The wind had suddenly dropped, and it had stopped snowing, although the sky was as grey as a Barre granite gravestone. The silence was huge. Elizabeth felt that if she screamed at the top of her voice, she could have been heard in Quaker Hill.

They traipsed to the very centre of the tennis court. Elizabeth looked around. 'This'll do,' she decided. They began scraping up snow with their gloved hands. Then Laura discovered the nursery slate which father had requisitioned last summer for chalking up his tennis scores, and she used it as a makeshift shovel.

Elizabeth said, 'It must be exactly the same size as Peggy, and it must look like her. Otherwise God won't know it's her, will He?'

'God's supposed to know everything,' Laura retorted. Her cheeks were fiery red and there was a bright drip on the end of her nose.

'I know He's supposed to, but He must have so many different things to worry about. You know, like the weather, and the Russians.'

It took them almost a half-hour to create the snow-angel. Elizabeth knew it was the right height because Peggy had come up to the second button on her coat; and so did this snow-angel. Laura rummaged in the Macy's bag and produced Peggy's brown beret and Peggy's bright red kilt and Peggy's brown tweed Saturday coat, all of which she had borrowed from Peggy's closet. They dressed the snow-angel and then they stood back to admire her.

'Her face is too white,' said Laura. 'And she doesn't have any hair.'

'Statues always have white faces,' Elizabeth told her. 'All the statues in the graveyard had white faces.'

'She'd look much better with a pink face, and hair,' said Laura.

'Well . . . let's go look in the shed.'

They walked back across the garden, and tugged open the door of the spidery, spooky shed, and ventured inside. It was so dark now that they could scarcely see anything, only the faintest of snow reflections shining through the spider webs. They groped around, giggling. In one corner, Laura found an old canvas bag, which had once been used to wrap up the roots of a cherry sapling. They also found some soft, oily cotton, which the gardener had used for cleaning the lawnmower.

'This'll do, this'll do,' Elizabeth hissed.

Singing, '*how cold my toes, tiddely-pom*' in an off-key, falsetto duet, they returned to the tennis court. Elizabeth took off the snow angel's beret and carefully fitted the canvas bag over her head. Then Laura arranged the fluffy cotton on top; and Elizabeth replaced the beret. *Now* their snow-angel looked more realistic.

'What about eyes?' frowned Laura.

'We could sew buttons on.'

'It's too cold for sewing. We could use stones.'

'I have a better idea,' said Elizabeth. 'We could heat up the poker in the kitchen range, so that it's red-hot, and burn two holes for eyes.'

'Yes!' agreed Laura, excitedly. 'A red-hot poker! A red-hot poker!'

They went back to the kitchen, much to Ampersand's disgust. Laura kept guard while Elizabeth heated up the poker. Then they rushed out with it and Elizabeth jabbed it into the snow angel's canvas face. With a sizzle and an acrid smell of burning, two black-circled eyes appeared.

'And a mouth, too!' said Laura, jumping up and down. 'Quick! Make her a mouth!'

When they had finished, they stood and admired their snow-angel, and then Elizabeth said, 'We ought to pray.'

They knelt in the snow even though it was wet and bitterly cold, and Elizabeth squeezed her eyes tight and said, 'Dear Lord, this is our memorial to our dear sister who we loved. Please see it and bless it and make Peggy into an angel.'

'Amen,' said Laura, and sniffed.

By the time the girls had tugged off each other's boots and hung up their snowy coats and hats, the funeral guests were beginning to leave. Father and mommy were kissed and hugged again and again, and there were sorrowful faces and tears and slapping of backs and extraordinary yelps of grief, many of which might have been inspired by Mrs Patrick's punch. All the same, it was a sad, disassembled moment.

As they stood at the foot of the stairs, however, dutiful and pale in their mourning dresses, Elizabeth and Laura could sense a general feeling of relief. Peggy had been laid to rest, thank goodness, and her soul had been commended to God – whether she reappeared as a twinkling star or a Cuban girl in the Plaza de Armas or as nothing more than a gradually fading memory, less and less distinct as the years passed by.

Dear Peggy, thought Elizabeth. I hope you can hear me. I hope that God has seen our snow-angel, and taken you up into heaven.

They all returned to the living-room. Father said, 'Thank God that's over.' Through the open doorway, they could see Mrs Patrick noisily clearing up the dishes. Mommy lifted her veil and her face looked puffy and bruised, as if she had been punched. 'I need a drink,' she told father. Without a word, he went to the cocktail cabinet and poured her a gin. He was about to close the cabinet again, but then he turned to Elizabeth and Laura, and smiled. He poured each of them a tonic water with rock-syrup and a maraschino cherry; and winked. 'Cocktails, at your age? Whatever next!'

Mommy said, 'I don't know whether I'm glad it's over or not. I feel as if she's been tugged right out of my arms, just ripped away from me. My beautiful littlest baby.'

Tears streamed down her cheeks and she made no attempt to wipe them away. Elizabeth took a handkerchief out of her sleeve and cautiously handed it to her. Mommy stared at it for a while as if she couldn't think what it was, then dabbed her eyes.

'I don't understand how life can be so cruel,' she said. 'I gave up everything! I gave up my youth! I gave up my career! Wasn't that enough, for God's sake?'

Father said nothing but stood on the opposite side of the room, watching her cautiously. She wandered around the living-room, drunk and distracted, touching the walls for support, and also to reassure herself that she was still here. Then she went through to the dining-room, and sat down opposite Mrs Patrick.

'You've been such a help, Mrs Patrick,' she said. 'A Godsend! I don't know what I would have done without you.

No! I mean it. I don't know what anybody would do without you.'

'It's all shoulders to the wheel in times of trouble,' said Mrs Patrick, scraping plates.

Seamus came up, unsteadily balancing a trayful of punch glasses.

'You, too, Seamus,' mommy blurted. 'You've been wonderful.'

'Times of terrible,' said Seamus. 'Salt mole lord's eye.'

Mommy groped a cigarette from one of the boxes on the table, but didn't light it. She sat with her head bent for a long time, not smoking, not drinking. Father said quietly to Elizabeth and Laura, 'Perhaps you'd better think of taking your bath.' There was a sense of danger in the room; a feeling of adult unpredictability.

Suddenly, mommy raised her head. She stood stock still for just a moment, and then she approached the window seat and stared at her own reflection in the night-blackened glass.

'*David*,' she said, in the oddest of voices.

'What is it?' asked father.

'David, there's somebody out there, in the snow.'

Father peered into the dining-room. 'Margaret? That's just your reflection, darling.'

'No, no it isn't. There's somebody out there! David, there's a child, standing in the snow!'

Father said, 'How can there be? There are no other children for miles.'

'There is! David, there's a child!'

Without warning, mommy's voice suddenly swerved up to an hysterical pitch. She turned around and stared at all of them with her eyes wide and all of the blood emptied out of her face. Father tried to go to the window but she came stalking back into the living-room, pushing him out of the way. She reached the kitchen door. 'It's *Peggy*!' she screamed at him. 'Don't you understand? It's *Peggy*! She's come back to me!'

51

Elizabeth was overwhelmed with dread. She clasped her hand over her mouth and couldn't do anything but gasp for breath. Laura squealed, 'Mommy! Mommy!' But mommy was already wrestling with the key in the back door, and before they could say anything else, she had rushed outside. Through the kitchen window they saw her hurrying across the gloomy garden towards the tennis court, her black veil flying behind her. It was like watching a character in a frightening movie.

'Mommy!' wailed Elizabeth, catching her breath. 'Mommy, *don't*!'

'What is it?' her father demanded. 'Lizzie, what is it?'

They ran outside. 'Mommy, *don't*!' called Elizabeth, in terrible distress; but it was already too late. Mommy was screaming, 'Peggy! Peggy!' and running across the tennis court to the small, silent snow-angel in its beret and tweed coat.

'*We* made it,' sobbed Elizabeth, miserably. 'Laura and I made it.' And father said, 'Oh, God,' and broke into a run.

Mommy rushed up to the snow-angel and then she suddenly stopped, and stared at it in horror. She must have encountered its face, its sack-weave face with its empty burned-out holes for eyes and its grinning black raggedy mouth. She swayed from side to side, and then she dropped to her knees in the snow and she let out a scream that was almost inhuman. '*Peggy! Peggy! Oh, my baby! Agggrrrhhhh!*'

Before father could reach her, she had rolled herself over in the snow, and then up on to her knees, and launched herself at the snow-angel in a frenzy of frustration and grief. She pulled off its beret, tossed away its hair, and ripped its face apart with both hands. She clawed, screeching, at the figure's body, digging out snow as if she wanted to dig out its heart. Then she dropped to the ground and lay flat on her back, shuddering, choking, in a jerking, convulsive fit. Elizabeth could see her eyes roll up into her head and her neck swell: and her feet kick so hard against the ground that one of her black high-heeled shoes flew off. Elizabeth didn't have to be told what to do. She turned around and ran back to the house as fast as she could.

'Mrs Patrick!' she screamed. 'Mrs Patrick! There's something wrong with mommy!'

As Mrs Patrick came bustling out, wiping her hands on her apron, Elizabeth ran to father's library and picked up the telephone. Silence. The telephone was dead. Frantically, she jiggled the receiver-rest up and down, and screamed, '*Hallo! Hallo! Help! Help us! Emergency! Hallo! Hallo!*' but the phone stayed dead. Too much snow. The lines between Sherman and Boardman's Bridge must have come down, the same way they had last year, and the year before.

Elizabeth ran back to the kitchen, just in time to meet father and Mrs Patrick, swiftly and grimly carrying mommy into the house.

'Will she be all right?' begged Elizabeth, as they laid her on the living-room couch in front of the fire. 'I tried to call for the doctor but the phone won't work.'

'Just watch her, keep her warm, make sure she's breathing,' father told Mrs Patrick, ignoring Elizabeth altogether. 'I'll go bring Doctor Ferris myself.'

'Yes, sir,' said Mrs Patrick, sorrowfully. She chafed mommy's hands to warm them. 'Oh, Mr Buchanan, this is a tragedy, and no mistake. What a tragedy, God help us.'

There was nothing Elizabeth could do but stand beside the couch and watch mommy twitch and mutter, her eyeballs roaming underneath her closed eyelids like caged bears. Laura came in and took hold of her hand.

'O Holy Mother, smile on us now when we need You,' said Mrs Patrick. 'You were a mother, too, remember, O blessed Mary. You were a mother, too.'

Elizabeth squeezed Laura's hand tight. 'Don't worry,' she whispered. 'Everything's going to be all right,' she said; even

53

though she had a terrible feeling that she had probably told one of the biggest lies of her life.

Heart of Ice

'Her kiss was colder than ice. It went to his heart, although that was half-frozen already. He thought he should die.'

Four

On the day that would have been Peggy's eighth birthday, 15 June 1943, Elizabeth and Laura took their best friend Molly Albee to the cemetery; and they laid fresh white carnations on her grave. They stood with their heads bowed and their eyes squeezed shut, praying for Peggy's soul, and trying as hard as they could to remember what Peggy had really looked like.

It was a hot, treacly afternoon. With her eyes shut, Elizabeth could hear the leaves rustling and the hoarse warbling of vireos in the high maples that shaded the cemetery's southern side.

She could hear a freight train whistling, on the line that ran between New Milford and Danbury.

She also heard a voice whisper, '*Lizzie,*' quite close to her ear.

She opened her eyes, and turned around. Laura and Molly were both standing on the other side of the grave, and there was nobody else in sight – nobody close enough to have whispered in her ear like that. She frowned, and shaded her eyes against the sun. The shingle pathway was deserted, except for a gardener who was patiently edging the grass, and he was more than two hundred feet away. On the far side of the cemetery, where it was still wooded, she thought she saw something flickering between the trees, but it was probably a rabbit, or a wood-pigeon.

Above Peggy's grave, a white angel with a sweet, sad face looked down where Peggy lay. The birds had perched on the angel's head, and her cheeks were streaked with black tears. Elizabeth could never decide if this was disgusting or mystical, or a bit of both.

57

They walked back through the cemetery and out of the squeaking iron gate. A young bespectacled man with sprigged-up chestnut hair was changing the lettering on the church notice-board. He waved to them, and called, 'Good afternoon, ladies!' His name was Dick Bracewaite and they all loved him. The Reverend Earwaker had been ailing lately, with a prostate condition that had proved resistant both to ice-packs and to prayer. Dick Bracewaite had been sent from St Eugene's in Hartford to stand in for him, and the church had never been so well attended, especially by eyelash-fluttering adolescent girls.

The three girls kept on turning around and giving Dick Bracewaite little finger-waves, until they turned the corner into Oak Street, where they collapsed into fits of laughter.

'Oh, I love him! I love him!' said Molly, dancing around and around and swinging her school bag. Molly was big and freckly, with hair like a bomb-burst in a copper-wire factory, and she was in love with everybody, especially Dick Bracewaite and Frank Sinatra.

Oak Street was neat and hot and empty, apart from Mr Stillwell's green delivery truck parked outside the Stillwell Hardware Store; and Mrs Miller's station-wagon parked in the shade of the large post oak that stood beside the Sherman Grocery, and which had given Oak Street its name. Mrs Miller's chocolate-coloured spaniel sat in the back of the station-wagon with its lurid pink tongue hanging out like a brush salesman's necktie.

There was a feeling of timelessness; as if this summer would never end; and Oak Street would always remain the same, 'as common and familiar as my breath' as Thomas Wolfe had put it. But Elizabeth had lately become aware that *she* was changing. She felt a funny sort of swelling balloon-like tension inside her – and a strange feeling of *bewilderment*, as if she ought to know something, as if she really ought to understand something, but couldn't quite grasp what it was. In less than a month's time, she would be thirteen. To her own surprise, she had lost all interest in her dolls. She had tried very hard to play with them. But even those dolls which she had once adored the most, and to whom she had once confided all of her secrets, now seemed to be lifeless and unco-operative and ineffably stupid. Even the tiny, imaginary family which had once lived in her doll's house appeared to have moved out, without leaving a forwarding address.

All that interested Elizabeth now was love and romance; love, and romance, and horses.

She read every novel that she could find, from Emily Brontë to Sinclair Lewis. The more romantic they were, the more tragic they were, the more she adored them. Her particular favourite was *Anna Karenina*, which made her cry, especially when Anna was killed by a train. But she also loved Esther Summerson, in Dickens' *Bleak House*, because Esther was so pretty and sweet to everybody, yet characterful, too. She felt a wonderful creepy thrill when Esther met the grizzled old rag collector, Mr Krook; and an even ghastlier thrill when Mr Krook died by spontaneous combustion, leaving 'a suffocating vapour in the room, and a dark greasy coating on the walls and ceiling' and something that looked like 'the cinder of a small charred and broken log of wood sprinkled with white ashes.'

She thought the idea of spontaneous combustion was both fascinating and appalling, and she looked it up in her father's encyclopedias. There was the Countess Bandi of Casena, in June 1731, of whom only a head, three fingers and both legs were found in a heap of ashes. Then there was the Indian woman who was consumed by flames and whose smoking body was carried between two constables to the District Magistrate near Dinapore.

As soon as she had finished her homework, Elizabeth would open her fat royal-blue notebook, the one inscribed Strictly And Completely Private, and write another short story about love and horses. Her heroines were always confident, clear-eyed girls whose lives were fulfilled except for one thing: their mothers had mysteriously disappeared when they were little. These confident, clear-eyed girls were invariably mad on showjumping, and their long-lost mothers invariably turned out to be world-class showjumpers who had been permanently crippled in tragic riding accidents at the pinnacle of their careers. Unable to face the world, they had closeted themselves away in 'gloomy, Gothic nursing homes'. Elizabeth gave her stories titles like 'Her Finest Hour' and 'Janet Wins The Day'.

When she was writing, Elizabeth felt elegant and happy and attractive. She circled the showjumping rings of the world, her hand raised to acknowledge the amazed applause of the crowds. And, when she dismounted, *he* was waiting for her. Tall, strong and gentle, with 'dark, hyacinthine curls, and eyes like the restless ocean.'

There were villains, of course; but these were always 'sneering and bony-nosed' and met various sticky ends, including two who died by spontaneous combustion – 'incinerated in their own inner iniquity'.

Nobody had read her stories yet; and nobody knew how much she needed them. Ever since Peggy's death, her life at home had been discordant and unsettling. It was like four different radios playing at once. Father would say one thing; and then he would talk to mommy and mommy would say something else altogether; and then Laura would throw a tantrum and they would all end up saying totally the opposite.

What was worse, she herself was changing so much. Her face seemed to grow uglier and uglier every day, with a long nose just like father's, and sticky-outy ears, and a neck that went on and on just like a giraffe. She had grown much taller, too. In fact she had grown so much taller than Laura, and so much taller than anybody else in her class, that she walked every-where with her books clutched to her chest and her shoulders hunched, so that nobody would notice her extreme height. She kept her hair long and straight, held back from her forehead with an Alice band, because she thought it concealed her giraffe-like neck, and she wore her favourite summer dress almost every day. Father had bought it too big for her, in the expectation that she would 'grow into it', and she had cried when she had first tried it on, because it made her feel so old-maidish. But she liked it now. At least her shoulders didn't strain the stitches around the yoke and her wrists didn't dangle miles beyond her cuffs, like they did with her other dresses, and at least the bodice was loose enough to hide her swelling nipples, about which she was deeply embarrassed. The dress was covered in tiny blue-and-yellow flowers, with a double collar edged in blue-and-yellow piping, and Elizabeth always wore her blue enamel pony club badge with it. She was founder, president, chairwoman and only member of the secret and very exclusive Lake Candlewood Pony Club; and she didn't even own a pony.

As they walked the whole length of Oak Street, along the hot afternoon sidewalk, the three girls didn't have to discuss where they were going next. Laura took hold of every telegraph pole she passed, and swung around it, and sang *'Don't sit under the apple tree ... with anyone else but me ... anyone else but me ...'* Laura, who had been eleven in April, was prettier than ever. The sun had bleached her blonde curls so that they shone even brighter, and she was petite and trim and easily the most popular girl in the third grade.

'Do you think Dick Bracewaite ever thinks about girls?' asked Molly.

'Well, of course, silly!' said Laura. 'He's a man, isn't he, and men are always thinking about girls. That's what Aunt Beverley says, and she should know.'

'Oh, sure,' Molly retorted. 'Your Aunt Beverley is practically a man herself.'

'She is not!'

'She is too! My father says you'd only have to cut her hair short and you wouldn't be able to tell her from Robert Taylor.'

Laura swung her schoolbooks and hit Molly on the shoulder with them. The strap came undone, and they scattered across the sidewalk. Molly chased Laura around and around a telephone pole while Elizabeth tried to rescue them. Loose pages were fluttering everywhere. Molly caught up with Laura and yanked off her hair ribbon, and skipped off with it. Elizabeth was still chasing the last stray page, but she managed to snatch it just before it was blown through the iron grid in front of Baxter's Realty, and into the inaccessible basement area beneath, which was already littered with leaves and gum wrappers and cigarette butts.

She shuffled the loose pages back together again, but as she did so, she saw that not all of it was geography homework. Laura had written on one page, 'took me in his arms and kissed me. He was handsomer than Jesus. Their was a holy light almost shining from his eyes. He took off all of his cloths and said that we could be pure like the dissipuls. I took off my cloths too. He said this my darling is what true lovers do. He kissed me again and again and said I was the closest being he had ever known to an angel.'

Laura had caught up with Molly and retrieved her ribbon, and some kind of honour had been satisfied. Now she came back along the sidewalk and saw that Elizabeth was reading her story.

'Lizzie!' she screamed at her. 'That's private!'

She tried to snatch it but Elizabeth held it out of her reach.

'That's private! That's completely private! How *dare* you read it! That's private!'

Dodging away from her, Elizabeth read the next few sentences out loud. ' "We lay on his bed. His pecker was hard. Frank said it was a true sign of love between a man and a woman if the man's pecker was hard. There was nothing bad about it it was almost divine. He said I should touch it and I held it for a while. He said I could kiss it if I wanted to but I was undessided." '

Molly shrieked in hilarity; while Laura furiously danced and jumped all around her. 'Give that back! Give that back! I hate you! I hate you for ever!'

'More!' begged Molly. 'Read out some more!'

' "He bade me close my eyes. I closed my eyes and he stroked my hair and then he stroked my muff." '

'Aaaah!' shrieked Molly, in delight.

Laura screamed 'Give that back or I'll tear up all of your horse books!'

'More!' pleaded Molly.

' "I felt a heavenly sensation. 'I love you, darling,' I mermered. 'I love you too, my sweet one,' he replied. He went up and down all the while complimenting me on my beautiful body. Suddenly he cried out. I opened my eyes and saw a veritable fountain coming from his pecker. He said 'my goodness the time' and quickly dressed. That was love at its truest. I knew next time I would be ready for doing it properly. Frank kissed me and promised me that he would be gentle." '

Elizabeth stopped reading. Her cheeks were hot with embarrassment and shock, and she stared at Laura with her mouth open. Molly had gone into a squealing-fit, and was furiously stamping her sandals on the concrete paving. 'It's so *rude*!' she kept squealing. 'Laura, it's so *rude*!'

Elizabeth said, 'I'll have to tell father.' She felt terribly grave and responsible. She also felt confused. They had been given a lesson on the fundamentals of human reproduction in class. Their biology teacher, Mrs Westerhuiven, was comparatively young and modern, and had actually demonstrated the erection of a male member (with the aid of a photograph of Michelangelo's *David* and her own discreetly-lifted index-finger.) All of the girls at school talked about sex during recess. In fact, they talked about scarcely anything except music and make-up and 'what it's going to be like.' But Elizabeth had never read anything so graphic or lewd as Laura's story. It scarcely sounded like Laura at all.

'Pecker!' squealed Molly. '*Pecker!* I don't believe it! It's *so* rude!'

Laura's eyes were almost blinded with tears. 'You mustn't tell father. Please don't tell father. It's only a story, that's all. I'll throw it away. I'll burn it. Just don't tell him, okay?'

'*Pecker!*' crowed Molly, gleefully. '*Muff!*'

Elizabeth turned the page over, and saw that there was much more written on the other side. 'None of this is *true*, is it?' she asked.

Laura managed to tear it away from her, and crumple it up. 'Of course it's not true! It's only a story! You shouldn't have read it! It wasn't even yours to read! It was private! You write stories and they're private, so why shouldn't I?'

'If it's not true,' put in Molly, 'then who's Frank? That's what *I'd* like to know.'

Laura wiped her eyes on the back of her hand. 'Frank Sinatra, that's all.'

'*Frank Sinatra!*' shrilled Molly. 'Frank Sinatra's *much* too old for you!'

'It's only a story and it's none of your business!' Laura retorted. And with that, she picked up her books, and bustled off, running diagonally across the street and heading toward Candlewood Road, and home. Her blonde curls shone in the afternoon sunlight. Elizabeth and Molly looked at each other, and Molly shrugged, and then they carried on walking along Oak Street. They had almost reached the shining, curved, stainless-steel façade of Endicott's Corner Drugs. Inside, they could see several of their schoolfriends talking and laughing and drinking sodas. Endicott's was the place where all the kids who lived around Sherman came to mess around after school. The parking-lot at the side was crowded with dented old convertibles, Fords and Chevys and a green Hudson Terraplane with 'Marcia' hand-painted all over it. With petrol rationed to three gallons a week (officially, at least) none of the kids ever drove very far, but their cars were essential to their status; and where else could they find to smooch?

'You don't think that story was true, do you?' Molly asked Elizabeth. 'I mean, it couldn't have been, could it?'

Elizabeth shook her head. 'There aren't any boys around called Frank, are there? Not unless she changed his name. It's just that I can't believe all those words she used. And all that description of doing it. I never knew anything about doing it when I was eleven.'

'And "veritable fountain"! What did she mean by that? It sounds disgusting!'

'Spermatozoa,' said Elizabeth, emphatically.

'Spermatozoa? I thought Mrs Westerhuiven said spermatozoa looked like tadpoles.'

'Well, I don't know,' said Elizabeth. 'I'm going to have to talk to Laura later.'

'Mrs Westerhuiven definitely said they looked like tadpoles.'

Inside Endicott's, an L-shaped stainless steel counter ran along the back and right-hand walls, and it was at this counter that a dozen of the local high-school boys and girls were perched, swinging their legs and drinking sodas and milk shakes and eating ice-cream sundaes. There were four tables, too, all of which were already crowded, but Elizabeth and Molly managed to squeeze in at the end of one of the banquettes.

The noise was up to its usual pitch. At the next table, three fifth-grade girls were screaming with laughter; while down at the far end of the counter, two boys were popping their fingers and trying to sing 'They're Either Too Young Or Too Old' in a growling disharmony of recently-broken voices. Another boy accompanied them by raking a sundae spoon down the side of the tall chromium wire cage that held the oranges for Fresh-Squeezed Juice, and tapping with a fork on the porcelain jar of Borden's Malted Milk.

Behind the counter was a huge crystalline pyramid of upside-down ice-cream dishes, and a coffee urn, with a glass showing the coffee level, and glass jars of pecan nut cookies and Baby Ruths and Planters peanut bars, as well as all the shining paraphernalia of milk-shakers and ice-cream scoops.

Judy McGuinness was sitting on a stool right beside Elizabeth, and Elizabeth gave her a nervous smile. Judy McGuinness was head cheerleader and last year's Prom Queen and just about everybody's heroine. She was round-faced and very pretty, in an exotic, Ava Gardner way, with heaps of curly black hair and violet eyes and – envy of envies – a natural beauty spot. Her parents allowed her to wear lipstick out of school and so she always did, a vivid red shade of Stadium Girl. She was dressed in a blue striped blouse and a pair of well-tailored white slacks rolled up to mid-calf, so that everybody could see her critically fashionable odd socks, one purple and one blue.

'Hi, Buchanan,' Judy drawled. 'How's your mom these days? Any better?'

'She's very well, thank you,' said Elizabeth. She hated it when people asked her about mommy.

'Is she home for the rest of the summer?'

'She's home for good now.'

'Well, that's *marvellous*. I didn't know! You must remember me to her. She can remember people, can't she?'

'Of course,' Elizabeth flushed. 'She remembers everything.'

'Really? I thought – '

'She's not *insane* or anything, if that's what you're trying to say.'

Dan Marshall, the school's star swimmer, tanned and toothy, was sitting beside Judy, his hand resting lightly but possessively on her arm. He gave Elizabeth a wink and a 'gee-up' click of his tongue.

'You tell 'em, kid,' he said. In the mirror behind the counter, between the white-painted lettering for Popsicles and Banana Splits, Elizabeth saw herself flush hot and crimson. She hated it when she blushed; and these days she seemed to be blushing all the time.

At that moment, however, Old Man Hauser appeared, wearing a soda jerk's cap and a red bow tie and a white apron double-tied around his waist. Although the drugstore was called Endicott's, Old Man Hauser had owned it for as long as anybody could remember. He was a calm, dry-voiced seventy-three-year-old, with a face that always reminded Elizabeth of a withered swede. Nobody knew what his first name was. He insisted on being called Old Man Hauser. Laura used to think that he had actually been christened 'Old Man', but Elizabeth thought it was pretty unlikely.

'Good afternoon, Lizzie,' he smiled. 'What's it to be today?'

'Two malteds, please,' said Elizabeth. She had never seen him in a soda jerk's cap before, and she couldn't help smiling at him. 'Where's Lenny today? He's not sick, is he?'

'Lenny? Sick? Of course not. But he's wishing he was.'

'I don't undersand. He was here yesterday.'

'Certainly he was here yesterday. But didn't he tell you? He had the greeting. They're sending him off to Fort Dix on Saturday, for training.'

'Lenny's been *drafted*?' Elizabeth was horrified. 'Why didn't he tell me?'

Old Man Hauser shrugged. 'He didn't think they'd take him, on account of his ears. He was sure they were going to classify him 4-F, the same as they did Sinatra. It came as quite a blow when they told him he was 1-A, and fit enough to fight the whole German army single-handed.'

'Oh, no,' said Elizabeth.

'What are you worrying about, kid?' Dan Marshall asked her, with a grin. 'Lenny's going to be fine. You know what they used to call him at school? "Magic Miller". He never got detention. He never got lines. If anybody ought to be worried, it's Hitler.'

'That's the love of Buchanan's life you're talking about, sweetheart,' Judy told him.

'He's home if you want to see him,' said Old Man Hauser. 'I gave him the day off to say goodbye to his folks.'

'Thanks, Mr Hauser,' said Elizabeth, and turned to go.

'You don't want your malteds?' asked Old Man Hauser. 'Here, have a double-dip cone to go. Come on. It's on the house.'

'Hey,' said Dan Marshall, 'I wish I was in love with Lenny. Maybe I could get free ice-cream, too.'

'You're in love with yourself and nobody else,' Judy told him.

'Ouch,' he replied.

Molly stayed at Endicott's because she would go weak at the knees if she didn't have her daily malted on the way home from school, and might even die of malnutrition. Elizabeth walked along the hot, glaring street, trying to lick her chocolate-and-strawberry double-dip faster than it was dripping down her wrist.

Lenny lived in Putnam Street, a quiet, elm-shaded avenue of large Queen Anne houses with turrets and carpentered porches. Originally, these houses had been built for Sherman's more prosperous citizens, its doctor and its lawyer and the owner of the Sherman Sawmills. But now the sawmill was derelict, and there weren't enough people living in the area to support a lawyer, and the last remaining doctor was so old that he needed a doctor himself. Several of the houses were empty; most of them were shabby and scurvy with weathered paint.

Lenny's house – in the very middle of Putnam Street – was in better repair than most, but then Lenny's father owned and ran the local hardware store, and he could buy all his paint and putty at cost. Elizabeth walked across the lawn to the front door. The garden was unkempt and weedy, but some effort had been made to clear the rose beds under the verandah, and round at the side of the house there was a well-tended vegetable patch, where the bright green leaves of bean plants fluttered, and summer squash shone yellow as Chinese lanterns. A station-wagon was parked in the grass-tufted driveway, its engine still sporadically ticking as it cooled down.

From inside the house, she could hear the radio, tuned to the latest war news. '. . . after a sustained air bombardment to knock out its airstrips and underground hangars, the Italian island of Pantellaria was taken by the Allies yesterday in what is proving to be . . .'

She climbed the steps, banged at the heavy doorknocker, and waited. There was a warm sweet aroma of baking in the air, muffins and cornbread. After a while the door opened and there was Mr Miller thin as a rail in his baggy grey trousers and his shirtsleeves and his yellow braces. The sunny street was reflected in his glasses.

'Lizzie!' he smiled. 'Come on in. You're just in time to wish Lenny goodbye!'

'He's leaving *already*?' asked Elizabeth.

'They called this morning, said he had to report this afternoon, at five.'

'But I haven't even had time to buy him a present!'

'Oh, don't you worry none about that. You can always

send him something, if you're minded to, when he gets to Fort Dix. He'll probably appreciate it more. I know I did, when I was in the service.'

Mr Miller ushered her into the house. She had always liked the Millers' house because every room was crammed with the oddest knick-knacks and bits-and-pieces. A picture of Quonochontaug beach, made entirely out of clam shells. An old-fashioned spinning wheel, half of a plough, a lobster pot. Mrs Miller was standing at the kitchen table, prying muffins out of the baking-tray; and she smiled as Elizabeth came in, the smile of a woman who knows when goodness comes into her house. She nodded her head towards the back door, which had been left ajar; and out on the boarded verandah, Lenny was feeding the canaries, looking smarter than Elizabeth had ever seen him, in shirt and necktie. He was a lean, good-looking, but rather reticent kind of boy, like a young Jimmy Stewart. He was summer-suntanned, with a distinctive mole on his upper left cheek, and his hair short and shiny and quiffed at the front.

'Go on, Lizzie, go talk to him,' said Mrs Miller. 'He could use some friendly talk.'

Elizabeth went out onto the verandah. Lenny was obviously aware that she was there, but he continued to coo and tweet to his canaries, and prod a bone-white cuttlefish shell through the bars of their cage.

'Lenny?' ventured Elizabeth at last.

He looked at her. His eyes were red-rimmed, from hay fever, maybe. Lenny had always suffered from hay fever.

'I didn't know you'd been drafted,' she said.

He shrugged, and pulled a face. 'Oh, sure, of course I was drafted. These days, you have to be a loony, or crippled, or dead already.'

'You didn't *tell* me,' she repeated.

He pushed the last fragment of cuttlefish shell through the bars. 'Lizzie . . . you would have found out sooner or later.'

'But you would have gone! And I wanted to give you a present, and everything!'

'Hey, come on kid,' he told her, and stood in front of her with his thin arms folded, and smiled. 'I don't need no presents, not from you.'

Elizabeth couldn't stop her throat from tightening. 'I wanted to give you something, that's all, to remember me by.'

He leaned forward and kissed her on the forehead. 'I don't need nothing to remember you by. How could I forget you?'

She stared at him, wide-eyed. 'You mean that?'

'What kind of doofus do you think I am?'

Mrs Miller called out, 'Lenny – why'n't you take Lizzie down to the orchard and fetch me some of them pie-apples?'

'Okay, ma!' Lenny called back. Elizabeth had never seen him act so obliging. He was always grumbling that his mother and father took advantage of his good nature, and made him run errands whenever his favourite radio show was on; or made him wash the dishes when he wanted to go fishing.

They stepped down from the verandah into the thick hot glare of the garden. The sun was so bright that Lenny had to keep one eye screwed up. Their ankles rustled through the grass; the birds sang an inquisitive, spangled song.

'Aren't you afraid?' asked Elizabeth. There were very few secrets between them. In spite of the difference in their ages (which in anybody older, would have amounted to nothing at all), they both believed in mystery, they both believed in magic. They had once leaned on the railing of the wooden bridge where Lake Candlewood darkly emptied its waters into a lush and overgrown stream, and Lenny had said, 'You may not think it . . . nobody may think it . . . but trolls live under this bridge, sure as eggs.'

'Trolls?' she had asked him, peering into the gurgling shadows. 'What are trolls?'

'You don't know what trolls are? Trolls are what you're afraid of.'

'What do you mean?' she had challenged him.

'Exactly that, stupid. Trolls are what you're afraid of. Anything. Being embarrassed, coming last in maths, making a fool of yourself in front of your parents. Drinking your first beer and puking. Wrecking your father's car. Dying. All that stuff.'

'Dying?' she had asked him; and that was what she was asking him now. Only this time the danger of him dying wasn't just an idle conversation on a bridge. This time, the danger of him dying was real and immediate. She had seen newsreels of fully-laden GIs dropping out of DUKWs into ten feet of water, and never coming up again. She had seen men lying on the roads of Normandy, as if they were sleeping. But who would sleep in the middle of the road on a summer afternoon, when there was a war to be won?

Lenny picked a cooking apple from a tree, twisting it around so that the stalk snapped. There was so much brightness and shadow; and flying insects criss-crossing the garden in random, sunlit patterns.

'I'm not afraid. Well not *too* much. The way the war's going, I'll probably never even get to Europe, let alone fight.'

Elizabeth watched him picking apples and said nothing for a long time.

'I don't know . . .' he said, after a while. 'I'm kind of looking forward to it. I know I'll have to obey orders and all. But at least they won't be dad's orders, or old man Hauser's orders, or Dan Marshall's stupid orders for Moron's Ecstasies.'

'Oh, yuk,' said Elizabeth. A Moron's Ecstasy was Endicott's ultimate sundae, including eight different flavours of ice-cream, bananas, Melba peach, raspberries, mixed nuts, tutti-frutti, pineapple and whipped cream. It cost a whole dollar, and was the current craze among school seniors who wanted to show that they had stomachs of steel.

'Mack Pearson said that boot camp wasn't so bad,' said Lenny. 'The only part he hated was the haircut.'

'Will you write me?' asked Elizabeth. She had the strangest feeling – a feeling that she had never experienced before. She knew that she *liked* Lenny. She had always liked Lenny, and Lenny had always liked her, even when his friends ribbed him for going around with a girl. But now she couldn't keep her eyes off the way that he raised his suntanned hand to the apple tree, and the way the sun shone through his hair, and illuminated his eyes like two perfect circles of palest agate.

He was almost godly; and a soldier, too. He reminded her of a picture in one of her books of an armoured *condottiero*, one of the mercenary soldiers of sixteenth-century Italy. She had fallen in love with this *condottiero* when she had first seen him. He looked so beautiful and so brave. And now she began to understand that she had fallen in love with Lenny. In fact, she must have gradually been falling in love with him for a long time, if love meant that he was flawless, and wonderful, and that she couldn't bear the thought of him going away.

'What's the matter?' he asked her. 'You're looking all goofy.'

She felt her cheeks burn. She hoped that he couldn't read her mind! 'I was just thinking, that's all,' she flustered. 'I was just wondering how long you were going to be away.'

Lenny shrugged. 'We do six weeks' basic training at Fort Dix . . . then who knows? It's all pretty secret. We're not allowed to tell anybody anything. You know . . . "even walls have ears".'

They walked back to the house. Mrs Miller said, 'How about some cookies and some milk, Lizzie?'

'No thanks, Mrs Miller. I'd best be getting home.'

'Give my good wishes to your folks.'

Lenny took her out to the street. 'Guess this is goodbye for a while,' he said, taking hold of her hand, and squeezing it.

'You will be careful, won't you?' she begged him. 'You won't drink too much beer, and puke?' She paused, and then she said, 'You won't *die*, will you?'

He leaned foreward and kissed her, not on the forehead, not on the cheek, but directly on the lips.

'I'll be careful,' he promised. 'And I'll write, too.'

Mrs Miller was calling from the house. 'Lenny! Which pants did you want pressed?'

'Coming, mom!' he called back. Then he said, 'You bet your cotton socks I'll write.'

He turned, and went back down the side of the house, leaving Elizabeth standing on the sidewalk with her eyes wide and her lips still fizzing with the sherbet sensation of Lenny's kiss. He had kissed her on the actual lips! He must love her! Or nearly love her, anyway.

And she loved him – she loved him, she loved him, with all of her swelling heart.

She walked dreamily back along Putnam Street, staying under the dark aromatic shadow of the elms. Already she was inventing a story in her head about a showjumping star who falls in love with a soldier. The soldier is wounded in the Pacific, and sends her a message that he has been killed, so that she won't have the burden of marrying a man so terribly scarred. One day she wins the highest international show-jumping trophy, and makes a speech in which she dedicates the trophy to all the boys who never came back from the war, and especially to her lost love. With tears streaming down her cheeks, she says that she can never love another man, ever. At that moment, her terribly-scarred lover comes hobbling out of the crowd amongst whom he has been covertly watching her, and they are passionately reunited. She promises to use her prize money to restore his looks, and they have six children and fourteen horses and live deliriously ever after.

Elizabeth decided to call her story 'The Spoils of War'.

*

She was nearly at the end of Putnam Street when she saw a small girl in a white cotton frock walking towards her. She was out of the shadow of the elms now, and the street was dazzlingly bright – so bright that the girl appeared almost to be walking in a fog of reflected light, kind of *out-of-focus*.

The girl had a very pale face and intensely blonde braids – braids so blonde that they were almost silver, so that she looked very Scandinavian, Finnish or Lapp. Elizabeth didn't take very much notice of her at first, because she was too involved in 'The Spoils of War'. But there was something about the way in which the girl was walking that suddenly caught her attention. She seemed to be *gliding*, rather than walking, as if the sun-bright sidewalk was covered with ice.

As she approached, Elizabeth slowed, and stared at her. For some ridiculous reason, she began to feel alarmed, although she couldn't think why. She knew just about every single kid in the whole of Sherman, and Boardman's Bridge besides, even kids as young as this one, but she had never seen this kid before. Maybe she was visiting, with her parents. Maybe she was lost.

The girl came gliding nearer and nearer on white-sandalled feet, until she and Elizabeth were face to face. The sun was so strong that Elizabeth had to squinch up her eyes. Even then she didn't seem to be able to focus on the girl's face.

The girl stared up at Elizabeth with perfect composure. 'Hallo, Elizabeth,' she said. Her voice was oddly tinny, as if she were speaking on the radio.

'Do I know you?' asked Elizabeth.

The girl gave her a blurry smile. There was something familiar about her – something *so* familiar that Elizabeth began to feel seriously frightened. How could she be so familiar, when Elizabeth had never met her before?

'Are you lost?' Elizabeth asked her.

The girl shook her head. In some peculiar way, she had managed to pass Elizabeth by, while at the same time never taking her eyes away from Elizabeth, nor turning her head. Elizabeth could feel the sun beating hot on the top of her head, and yet the girl herself seemed to give off the faintest of chills.

'Do I *know* you?' Elizabeth repeated.

The girl was already gliding away. She was swallowed by the shadows of the overhanging elms, until all that Elizabeth could see of her was a white dress and gliding white sandals. How did she walk like that? It was so strange, like a waking dream, right here on the corner of Putnam Street, on a normal afternoon.

Deeply immersed in the shadows, the girl turned around just once. Her pale face was completely expressionless, yet she was obviously trying to communicate something.

But what?

Elizabeth slowly continued her walk towards Main Street, frowning in perplexity. Why had the girl seemed so familiar? It was almost as if Elizabeth had known her all her life; and yet she knew for sure she hadn't.

It was only when she reached Main Street and saw the sign across the street saying Walter K. Ede & Son, Mortician, that she was seized with the most horrific of thoughts. She turned, and stared back down the street, and she was so frightened that she felt as if centipedes were crawling in her hair.

'Peggy,' she whispered. Then she screamed out, '*Peggy?*'

Five

Laura was already in the billiard-room when Elizabeth got back. She was sprawled lanky-legged on the sofa eating a sugared doughnut and leafing through a copy of *Glamour*. She didn't look up when Elizabeth came into the room and dumped her schoolbooks on the end of the coffee table.

'Well?' said Elizabeth.

'Well what?' retorted Laura, aggressively.

'Well – what do you think I ought to do?'

'What do I think you ought to do about what?'

'Your story, of course. That's what.'

Laura gave her a sulky, challenging stare. '*Be* a snitch. Go on. See if I care.'

'But Laura, it was so *rude*. Where did you learn all of those words?'

'I just heard some of the boys talking, that's all,' said Laura. She pushed almost half of the doughnut into her mouth at once. 'They're always saying things like pecker and muff.'

'It's awful.'

'Why should it be awful?' said Laura, with her mouth crammed. 'You say "woodpecker" don't you? And women say they wear muffs in winter, and nobody gets upset.'

'That's different. You shouldn't write stories like that.'

'Says who?'

Elizabeth was about to answer when the door opened and her father came in. He had become thin as a rail and very grey, like a man who has been standing for hour after hour in a shower of fine wood-ash. The girls had grown used to his emaciation and premature ageing; but his appearance was a

77

constant reminder of Peggy's death; as if her shadow had fallen across him for ever. He still spoke just as firmly, and the Candlewood Press was doing reasonably well, and making a bit of money, but losing Peggy had taken so much of the meaning out of his life.

'Hi, Elizabeth,' he said. She went up and put her arm around his waist. His sand-coloured trousers drooped because he was so thin. He scarcely ate, and wouldn't touch drink these days because it gave him nightmares. Nightmares of snow, nightmares of ice. Nightmares of Peggy rising out of the pool. 'How was school? Do you have much homework?'

'Only geography, the Rockies, and that's easy.'

'Listen . . .' he said. 'I had a call this afternoon that granpa's sick. I have to go to New York tomorrow. I really have to. Do you think that you two could stay home and take care of mommy for me?'

'Is granpa going to die?' asked Laura.

Their father shook his head. 'It's his heart. His heart's weak. He has to have tests for his blood pressure.'

'It's all right,' said Elizabeth. 'We'll look after mommy.'

Their father ruffled her hair. 'Thanks, Lizzie. I'll call the school before I leave, and tell them why you're taking the day off.'

'Okay, sure thing,' said Elizabeth.

'Mommy should have a nurse,' Laura protested.

'Laura –' Elizabeth retaliated. But her father said. 'Ssh, she's probably right. It's just that I can't afford a nurse right now. Besides, you know how difficult your mother can be. Too difficult for most nurses.'

He was about to leave when Elizabeth said, 'Father –'

Laura sat up and glared at her furiously, staring daggers. Long-bladed daggers with elaborately-decorated handles, just like the cartoons.

But Elizabeth had no intention of telling her father about

78

Laura's story. She wasn't a snitch by nature; and, besides, she would have found it far too embarrassing. But she did want to tell him that, somehow, she had met Peggy on Putnam Street on the way back from Lenny's house – that she hadn't exactly *looked* like Peggy, but she was almost certain that she was. After all, hadn't Bronco's dead brother looked like a Cuban? It didn't matter what people looked like, surely, so long as it was still *them*.

The body is simply the costume of the soul, that's what Dick Bracewaite had told them, in church last Sunday.

Maybe, if her father knew that Peggy was still walking around, it would put his mind at rest – give him hope, and peace. Maybe it would brush off all those ashes of guilt that made him appear so grey.

'Lizzie, I really have to run.'

'I'm sorry,' said Elizabeth. 'It's nothing.' Nothing that she could possibly articulate, anyway. She was mature enough to realize that if she told him and he didn't believe her, his pain would be even more difficult to bear. And, just at that moment, she wasn't at all sure that she believed it herself.

There were two hours to spare before supper, so Laura went off to call for her friend Bindy on Sycamore Street and Elizabeth sat in the kitchen with Mrs Patrick while Mrs Patrick finished off a chicken potpie. Seamus was there, too, sitting on his favourite stool next to the range, his head leaning against the tiles, softly singing a nonsensical song.

> Sad the man, mind the man, day after day
> Flowers and clouds,
> Flowers and clouds.

The kitchen was filled with warm marmalade-coloured sunlight, which fell in shafts through the steam and flour dust. Elizabeth traced patterns in the flour with her finger.

79

'Your father's a poor suffering soul,' said Mrs Patrick.

'I know,' Elizabeth agreed. She looked over at Seamus, who was still nodding and singing. His voice was a thin, tuneless whine.

'Is he worse?' she asked Mrs Patrick.

Mrs Patrick nodded, and gave Elizabeth a sad and wistful smile. 'Dr Ferris said he'll have more fits. I like to think that it's the fairies. They loved him so much that they want him back, to play with him some more.'

Elizabeth listened to Seamus singing for a little, and then she said, 'Mrs Patrick – do you think it's possible for people, when they're dead, to be other people, and walk around, and meet their old friends?'

Mrs Patrick was about to put the potpie in the oven. She turned around and stared at Elizabeth in the strangest way. The open oven was so hot that Mrs Patrick's forehead was beaded with sweat.

'What made you say that, child?'

'I don't know. Something I saw.'

'What did you see?'

'A little girl, that's all. She didn't look like Peggy and yet she did. And she looked at me so queerly. And she said, "Hallo, Elizabeth", quite plain, as if she knew me.'

'Where was this?'

'On Putnam Street: I was visiting Lenny. He's had the greeting, and he has to go to Fort Dix tomorrow.'

'The dead go to Heaven, child, to sit with Our Lady and Our Lord Jesus Christ.'

'But you said that Seamus would go back to the fairies.'

'There are fairies in Heaven. There is anything a soul could want in Heaven.'

Elizabeth had the feeling that this conversation was going to get her nowhere at all. Mrs Patrick was a Catholic, and while she may have been a very superstitious Catholic, and believed in elves and piskies and all sorts of supernatural larkings-about in hedgerows and underneath toadstools, she was still sure and certain that her Redeemer liveth, and his Blessed Mother, too, and that it was They alone who set us down on earth when we were born and scooped us back up again when we died.

There was no room in Mrs Patrick's theology for a Peggy who was dead but not really dead at all.

'*Sad the man, mind the man, day after day,*' keened Seamus. '*Flowers and clouds, flowers and clouds.*'

Then, abruptly, he stopped singing, and sat up straight, gripping the seat of the stool. His face was bright with inspiration. 'Living snow flakes!' he exclaimed, his thick lips shiny with saliva. 'Dried stock-fish!'

'What holy gibberish,' said Mrs Patrick, shaking her head.

But Elizabeth sat and stared back at Seamus with her mouth open and her fingers tingling with fright and surprise.

Because dried stock-fish was what the Lapland woman in *The Snow Queen* had used to write a letter to the wise Finland woman ('paper had she none'); and living snow flakes had been the Snow Queen's guards ('their shapes were the strangest that could be imagined; some looked like great ugly porcupines, others like snakes rolled into knots with their heads peering forth, and others like little fat bears with bristling hair – all, however, were alike dazzlingly white – all were living snow flakes').

'Seamus,' said Elizabeth. 'Seamus, who told you that?'

But Seamus leaned back against the fireplace again, and carried on singing.

'He's a poor boy,' said Mrs Patrick, chopping carrots.

Elizabeth found her mommy sitting in her bedroom with the linen blind drawn down to keep out the sunlight. It gave the room the appearance of an old sepia photograph. The bed was made but the quilt was rumpled where her mother had been sleeping on it. Sometimes she slept all day, day after day. At other times you could go into her room in the small, intense hours of the morning, and find her standing by the window in her nightgown, staring into the garden.

Today, her mommy had dressed in a cream short-sleeved blouse and pale blue skirt, and pinned up her hair. She was sitting in her blue basketwork chair smoking a cigarette, her head wreathed in curls of smoke as if she were wearing an evanescent crown of thorns. She looked better today: her eyes were more focused.

'And what have you been doing, darling?' she asked.

'We went to the cemetery to see Peggy. Then we had ice-cream at Endicott's. Lenny wasn't there, though. They've called him up.'

'You really like Lenny, don't you?'

Elizabeth blushed and nodded. *Like* him? Whillikers, she adored him! 'He's always so considerate.'

'You should always go for a *considerate* man,' said her mommy, taking a last hard draw on her cigarette, and then crushing it out. Immediately, she picked up the pack of Philip Morris and shook out another, and lit it with fussing, jiggling hands. 'To hell with handsome,' she continued. 'Do you know what I mean? You need the kind of man who doesn't stifle you. The kind of man who lets you be yourself. Doesn't . . . *disappoint* you all the time. Doesn't dish you up nothing but tragedy. Doesn't trap you with children in the back of beyond.'

Elizabeth said nothing. She was used to this endless complaining about her mommy's lost career. What was more, she quite liked the idea of 'the back of beyond'. It sounded like somewhere mysterious and odd, where extraordinary things could happen. Maybe she ought to sign all her letters: 'Elizabeth Buchanan, White Gables, Sherman, The Back of Beyond'.

'I'm beginning to feel like getting out,' said her mommy. She half-turned towards the shaded window, her cigarette poised. 'It's summer, isn't it? I'm beginning to feel like getting out. Going for a walk, maybe. Sitting on the verandah. Clothes-Peg loved the summer, didn't she? She never liked the cold.'

Elizabeth said, 'I think I may have some good news.'

'Good news? Good news about what?'

'About Peggy, of course. I think Peggy is kind of still with us, in a way.'

Her mommy turned slowly back from the window, and stared at her. 'What are you saying, Lizzie?'

Elizabeth began to grow hot and flustered. She had thought that this was going to be easy – easy and joyful – a way of lifting her mommy out of her misery and her discontent. She wasn't prepared for the hostile, intense look in her mommy's eyes, the quiver of disapproval in her voice.

'I was walking back from Lenny's house and I saw a girl who wasn't Peggy but she was.'

'What are you saying? What the *hell* are you – ? *What are you saying?*'

Elizabeth felt trapped, suffocated by mommy's cigarette smoke. She knew she was right, she knew for certain that she had passed Peggy on Putnam Street, yet she wished and wished that she had kept it to herself.

'I saw a little girl . . . she was dressed all in white, she seemed to *shine*.'

'That's nonsense, such nonsense. What are you trying to do, give me another breakdown? Do you know how *long* it's taken me to – ? '

'Mommy, I know. And I didn't mean to upset you. But she was so much like Peggy. She was, I can't explain why! And then Seamus said things from *The Snow Queen*, which was Peggy's favourite.'

Her mommy smoked furiously. Then she burst out, 'For God's sake, Elizabeth! You're as mad as him! Or maybe you're not! Maybe *I'm* still mad! Ha! It would serve me right, wouldn't it, for marrying your father, for coming here, for having children! And my career – in ruins! In tatters!'

'Mommy, you're not mad, and Seamus isn't mad, and neither am I. Even if you don't believe me, even if you think I'm being horrible to you, it's true. I saw a girl today on Putnam Street and she wasn't Peggy but she was.'

Mommy looked as if she were about to say something furious, but then – quite unexpectedly – she let her head tilt forward, and her shoulders slope, until she was sitting in her chair like one of those old women you see in nursing homes, with all the spirit and stuffing knocked out of them, resigned to tedium and tantalizing memory lapses, and dwindling visits from relatives whose eyes are shifty with guilt or greed.

'Mommy?' said Elizabeth, worriedly.

Her mommy looked up, and managed a smile, 'Oh, Lizzie . . . if it could only be true. If only I could hold her again, just once.'

Elizabeth reached out and touched the back of her hand. It felt dry, dried out, as fragile as a leaf-skeleton.

If only there was some way of explaining what she had seen, and the way she had felt when the girl in white had walked by. But all she could do was lean forward, and kiss her mommy's forehead. Her mommy's skin tasted of nicotine and Isabey perfume, and somehow that taste reminded Elizabeth so much of Peggy and the times that they had all been together, all three sisters, that she was even more convinced that it was true – that Peggy *was* still with them, in some inexplicable way, and for some unimaginable purpose.

Dick Bracewaite was sitting in his small study writing his Sunday sermon when Laura appeared in the open french windows, as if by magic. He sat back and smiled at her. Then he picked up his pen and screwed on the cap.

84

'Laura! You quite made me jump!'

She stepped in through the french windows, her blonde curls shining in the late afternoon sunlight. Behind her, the lawns of St Michael's were freshly watered, so that they glittered, and the flowerbeds were thick with the creamy curds of fullblown roses. Laura walked around the back of Dick Bracewaite's chair, and as she passed behind him he half closed his eyes and breathed in, so that he could catch her aroma. Girl, and summer, and ice-cream.

She sat down in the wooden armchair close to his desk, on a worn-out tapestry cushion. She peered at the pages of back-sloping handwriting. Her eyelashes had been bleached by the summer sun, but they were still long, and they trembled as she read what Dick had been writing.

'What language is that?' she asked him.

'That's Latin. *Aut tace, aut loquere meliora silentio.* I'm using it in my sermon this Sunday.'

'What does it mean?' Her thin suntanned wrist rested casually on the edge of the desk and he felt a compulsion to reach out and stroke it, and then to close his fingers around it, as he had several times before. Look, he had told her, your wrist is so thin that I can close my finger and thumb around it, like a bracelet.

Or handcuffs, she had replied, staring up at him with those misty, misty eyes.

'It means, Stay silent,' he said. ' "Stay silent, or say something that is better than silence." '

'What could that be?' asked Laura. She adored Dick unreservedly, heart and soul. He knew everything and then some. He was so strong and grown-up. He *smelled* like a man, of plain red soap and tobacco and something else indescribably *musky*. He wasn't like father at all, all books and nervousness and wood-ash. He spoke his mind. He had gingery hair on the back of his freckly, suntanned arms, and he had a meaty, handsome face, his cheeks burned crimson and burnished by the sun, and eyes as green as the sea. He wore brown tortoiseshell spectacles with circular lenses, but far from making him look weak, they gave him an even more masculine appearance, like a professional boxer who just happened to need reading-glasses. His chestnut hair was shinily tonicked and combed straight back from his forehead, with an endearing sprig at the crown.

'Personally, I can't think of anything more eloquent than silence,' said Dick. 'Sometimes you can tell somebody you love them better by staying silent than you can by trying to put it into words. I tell God that I love Him in complete silence.'

He left the next sentence unspoken. Laura was quite sure that he was going to say 'I tell *you* that I love you in complete silence', but he didn't. His fingers were poised above her wrist, and she knew that he wanted to touch her, she could feel it on her skin, as hot as summer sunlight through burning-glass. She looked into his eyes and he looked back into hers, and he gave her everything that made her feel bright and good: complete devotion, rapt attention, and a terrible fear of losing her. Such *fear*! It was unbelievable. It made him even more virile; even more of a god. The tension between them was deliciously unbearable.

'Something happened today,' said Laura. 'I thought I ought to tell you.'

Dick swallowed noisily. 'Something happened? Something bad?'

'It's really dumb. I wrote a story about us, that's all. I dropped it, on the way back from school, and Elizabeth read it.'

Dick said nothing. Outside in the garden, a pigeon was cooing, over and over, and the trees were rustling excitedly.

Laura felt her eyes rush up with tears, but they always did when she knew that she had done something cruel or wrong. She wept not because she was sorry, but because she was frustrated at being found out, and because she was angry at the stupid people who told her off. Hadn't *they* ever lied, or flirted with boys, or stolen lipsticks or candies or change from their mother's purse? Sometimes Laura felt that the whole world was filled with people who were trying to make her believe that they were shining saints, and that she was the only sinner. That was one of the reasons she adored Dick so much. He was a minister, a man of the cloth, and if a man of the cloth thought that she was perfect (and hadn't he said so, *Perfect, Laura, you're perfect*), then she must be right, and everybody else who thought such bad things about her must be wrong.

Dick, at last, grasped her wrist. 'You say you wrote a story about us? What did you say?'

'Just what we did.'

'The kissing? The lying together? You wrote about that?'

Laura nodded. For some reason, the more discomfited that Dick became, the more excited she felt. Dick was worried! Dick was terribly worried! There was perspiration on his upper lip!

He kept squeezing her wrist, squeezing and unsqueezing. He tried to speak but he seemed to be having difficulty with his words. 'Did you . . . what did you write, exactly? Did you mention our names?'

Laura shook her head. She was still weeping but she didn't really feel sad. 'I said your name was Frank, not Dick, because your middle name being Frank and all.'

'And you said that we took off our clothes?'

Laura nodded again. 'I said pecker and muff. Elizabeth said it was rude.'

Dick took a huge breath, as if he were going down for pearls. 'Do you think she knew it was us? You didn't mention the church, did you? My God, my darling, this was supposed to be a secret between us, wasn't it, a secret?'

'Dick . . . I didn't drop the story on purpose. Elizabeth shouldn't have read it. I told her not to read it.'

He said, 'Yes . . . I didn't mean to be angry with you. I'm sorry. But you know that what we did together was pure, don't you? It was innocent, an innocent affection altogether, a good and devoted man for a beautiful child, both born of God.'

Laura tilted her head to one side and looked at Dick narrowly. 'Is that what you want me to tell them, if they ask?'

'If who ask? Who else is going to know, apart from your sister Elizabeth?'

'Well, everybody, if we're not careful. You know what people are like in Sherman. They say that if you tell somebody a secret on one side of the town, and then start walking to the other side of town, the people on the other side of town will already know your secret by the time you get there.'

'Oh, God,' said Dick. He took his hand away from her wrist.

But this wasn't what Laura wanted. She didn't want Dick to be distressed. She didn't want him to shrivel up inside of himself, and cut off all his affection for her. She wanted him now to be bold, and virile, the boxer in reading-glasses. She wanted him to say that he loved her forever, no matter what the consequences. She was only eleven, and yet she had discovered already how weak men can be, how easily led, and while she liked the power it gave her, she despised them for not being braver.

Dick said, 'We'll have to wait. I don't think it's wise for us to go on meeting each other any more. Not until we're sure.'

'But I thought you loved me. You *said* you loved me.'

Dick half-lurched up in his chair took hold of her blonde curly head in both hands and wildly and inaccurately kissed her forehead and her cheeks and her eyes and her chin.

'Laura, Laura, Laura, of course I love you, my darling! You're my angel! You're my darling! We know each other completely, don't we, like Adam and Eve? Remember that afternoon when we were naked and then we wore leaves because we ate of the fruit of the Tree of Knowledge?

88

Remember that afternoon? And wasn't that innocent affection, two people revelling in the bodies God gave them, beauty and beauty?'

He kissed her on the lips, tenderly and slowly, and obviously quite aware that he might never kiss her again. He touched her dress; he touched her knee. He slid his hand up inside her dress, against her bare suntanned thigh. She didn't flinch, she liked what he was doing. But she liked to exercise her influence over him even more, and she stared at him with those misty, misty eyes and her eyes said *stop, pederast* even if she didn't know what *pederast* meant, had never heard the word.

'I – ' Dick began, then remembered the words of his sermon. *Aut tace, aut loquere meliora silentio*. Laura looked at him and arched her head back slightly, in quite a superior way.

Dick sat down. Next to the ecumenical calendar on the wall above his desk was a photograph of himself at St Luke's College, soft-focused, faintly smiling, a portrait of Perfect Unctuousness. Beside it was a faded print of *Susanna and the Elders* by Thomas Hart Benton, a painting of a curvy 1930s nude with immaculately-tweezed eyebrows being ogled from behind a tree by knobbly-faced old men. He had always told himself that he liked *Susanna and the Elders* because it harked back to traditional virtues, and brought Christian thinking into the modern age. But of course the reality was that Susanna herself was so arousing, and a close examination of the painting revealed a shadowy and mysterious cleft beneath her pubic hair.

Laura swung her leg backward and forward and stared at him boldly. 'You *did* say that you loved me.'

Dick was evasive, worried. Who might have read Laura's story, apart from Elizabeth, and whom might Elizabeth tell? The end of the world is not just nigh, Bracewaite; the end of the world is practically upon thee.

'I love you,' he said. 'But all the same . . .'

Laura stood up. She took hold of his hands, both of them, as if she were giving him her blessing. It was wonderful to smell his fear, and his virility, and the fustiness of the church. She had actually seen his pecker, red and hairy, with its purple plum-like glans, and for some reason that gave her a power over him that was greater than any other power she had ever known. And just because she didn't fully understand it, that didn't mean that she wasn't going to exercise it.

'Will you get into trouble?' she asked him.

'Only if people find out about us. And even then – even if they do – only if they get the wrong idea.'

'I don't know what you mean.'

Dick was finding this very difficult. 'I'll only get into trouble if people think that I was hurting you, or trying to have congress with you.'

'What about the veritable fountain?'

He flushed. *Look at this*, he had urged her. *A veritable fountain*.

'We ought to forget about the veritable fountain.'

Laura touched his forehead with her inky school fingertips and didn't know whether to feel sorry for him or not. With Dick, she had learned a lot about men, and the best thing she had learned about them was that she could always attract their attention, no matter who they were, just by running the tip of her tongue across her lips, and sitting with her legs crossed so that her frock rose high. She knew how to be a movie star, already, because if she could do this with Dick, she could do it with any man, and have them *all* panting after her, thousands and millions of them, all over the world.

She looked out into the garden. A little girl in a white dress was standing beside the bushes, solemnly watching her. The sun was so bright that the little girl almost seemed to effloresce. Laura didn't know why, but she thought she recognized the little girl, from sometime long ago.

'Is your gardener here today?' Laura asked Dick.

He blinked at her. 'My gardener?'

'His little girl's standing outside.'

Dick turned around in his chair, but the girl had gone, and there was nothing but the lawns and the bushes and the lazily-buzzing bees.

'You don't really love me, do you?' asked Laura, in a voice much wiser than her years.

Dick looked up at her, and then glanced back at the garden. The sun had gone in, and suddenly the lawns were dull and the roses were dull, and a dry, unsettling wind sprang up. Dick grasped Laura's hand, grasped it so tightly that he almost crushed it.

'Of course I love you,' he insisted. 'It's just that I'm frightened.'

'Frightened? What of?'

'I don't know. Satan; or maybe God. Maybe it's my own vileness.'

Laura kissed him on the forehead, even though his forehead was furrowed and glistening with sweat. The girl in white had strangely reappeared, almost as if by magic, and was watching her while she did so.

'I won't tell,' Laura promised him. 'Even if I get into trouble, I promise I won't tell.'

She pressed her fingertip to her lips. All the same, her eyes were alive with mischief, and Dick didn't know if he ought to be melting from heat, or terror, or adoration.

Six

Elizabeth rang at Bindy's doorbell and stood in the shady porch waiting for her to answer. Mr Theopakis the baker drove past in his big green Oldsmobile and Elizabeth waved at him. Eventually Bindy opened the door, a plump brown-haired girl with spectacles and a stutter, and said 'Hi, Elizabeth. You looking for Laura?'

'We're waiting supper. She should have been home twenty minutes ago.'

Bindy shook her head. 'She hasn't been here.'

'Not at all?'

Bindy shook her head again. 'I haven't seen her since school.'

Elizabeth left Bindy's house feeling hot and worried. If Laura hadn't gone to play with Bindy, then where the heck was she? Supposing she was hiding? Supposing she was frightened that Elizabeth would show her sex story to father, and had decided to run away?

She walked as quickly as she could to the end of Maple, and then back along Oak. Mrs Patrick would be furious if they were late for supper, even though it was potpie and she could keep it warm for them. Mrs Patrick believed that the very least courtesy that cooks deserved was punctual arrival at the table, hands washed, no last-minute dives to the bathroom.

She turned the corner, back towards St Michael's, and the cemetery. She could see almost as far as the Ledger property, on Upper Squantz Road. There was nobody in sight. The afternoon was beginning to fade, and the breeze was blowing even more strongly. Elizabeth had the feeling that something was dreadfully wrong – that she had stepped into a world that looked the same as her own, but had subtly altered.

Somewhere in the world, a butterfly had fallen broken to the forest floor, and everything had changed.

Judy McGuinness and Dan Marshall drove past, and tooted her, and called out, 'Hi, Lizzie, why so busy?'

Elizabeth looked back along Oak, then squinched her eyes against the sun and looked down Central. Sherman was gradually emptying, the stores were closing up. Where could Laura have got to? She hoped that 'Frank' in her story wasn't a real man, and that she had gone to talk to him. Or even worse, to do more of that pecker and muff stuff. It made her blush red even to think about it.

She decided to go back and tell Mrs Patrick that Laura was lost. She was just turning around, however, when she glimpsed a small girl dressed in white, running along beside the white fence in front of the churchyard. She shaded her eyes with both hands, trying to make out the girl more clearly, but in a flicker of a second, the girl had vanished between the trees.

She didn't know what to do. She had the dreadful feeling that it was the same girl she had seen earlier this afternoon, when she was walking home from Lenny's. The girl she had imagined to be Peggy.

She walked up to the church, up the old redbrick path and up to the steps that led to the shiny white-painted front doors. It looked as if the girl had been running away from the church, in which case Dick Bracewaite must have seen her. Maybe he had even been talking to her, and knew who she was.

Elizabeth climbed the steps and opened the church doors. Inside, it was gloomy, and smelled of seasoned wood and dust. There was a tall statue of Jesus standing on a pedestal close to the door, with a large vase of freshly-arranged flowers around His feet, lilies and roses and blood-red dahlias. He looked down sadly at Elizabeth, as if He would have liked to have helped her, but was too preoccupied with His own woes.

'Mr Bracewaite!' called Elizabeth. The sunlight fell through the stained-glass windows, burnishing the pews and the huge brass candlesticks. 'Mr Bracewaite, are you there?'

She walked across to the vestry and cautiously opened the door. All of Dick Bracewaite's robes and surplices were hanging there, and a pair of scruffy black shoes lay tilted on the floor beneath them, as if somebody had taken them off in a hurry. On the table was a copy of *National Geographic* featuring Ibo tribesmen, and a pair of spectacles with only one arm.

'Mr Bracewaite?'

She opened the door that led out into the gardens. Across the sloping lawns stood the white weatherboarded house. It looked unnaturally bright in the dying summer's light. The lawns still glittered with water. Elizabeth walked between the rose beds to the back of the house. The french windows were swinging open and closed, open and closed, like a conjuring trick, their panes occasionally catching the flash of the afternoon sun.

Elizabeth stepped through them into the study. The breeze was ruffling the pages of Dick Bracewaite's Sunday sermon. '*Aut tace, aut loquere meliora silentio.*' Only his tortoiseshell pen kept the pages from blowing away.

'Mr Bracewaite, it's Elizabeth Buchanan! Is anybody there?'

She looked around the study. Although she couldn't quite put her finger on it, she felt as if the room had only recently been vacated, only moments before, only seconds before. Human beings leave a resonance behind them when they leave a room, an eddy of disturbed molecules, an echo. Somebody had only just walked out of here: and there was something else, another feeling.

Somebody had shouted in here. She could almost *hear* the

shout, slapped against the wall like wet wallpaper. She circled the room, listening, listening, and she was sure that she could still sense it.

The french windows swung and banged. 'Mr Bracewaite?' (Scarcely audible now.)

She listened and listened, but there was nothing at all, and she had almost decided to leave when she heard a soft, blurred moaning sound, like a man trying to sing 'Swing Low, Sweet Chariot' into an empty jamjar. She stepped out of the study, and across the narrow hallway. The floor was light oak parquet; and there was a large steel-engraving on the wall of Christ preaching to the five thousand, standing on his boat, his hair curled by the wind, his hand upraised. 'I am the bread of life, he who comes to Me shall not hunger.'

She heard the moaning again, and she hesitated. It was coming from the kitchen. The door was half ajar, and she could see a triangular-shaped section of the floor, with black-and-white tiles, and part of the solid pine table. She could also see a blotchy, mottled shape rather like a penguin's flipper that swung repeatedly from side to side. It took her a moment to realize that it was a bare human foot.

Now she was seriously frightened. There was something lying on the kitchen floor; somebody who was moaning; somebody whose foot was blackened and blistered, as if it had been burned.

She was so terrified that she was tempted for one tightly-swollen moment to run right out of the house and back across the lawns and out into Oak Street and keep on running no matter what. But the sight of the foot was so grisly that she knew she couldn't run away. She had to look.

This is experience, she told herself. *No writer can ever shy away from experience. Without experience, writing has no meaning.* She walked into the kitchen in a slow trance of absolute terror. In later years, she never remembered actually moving her legs when she walked. It was just as if she *slid*, irresistibly drawn by the magnetism of what she was about to see.

A man was lying on his back on the kitchen floor, a man with no clothes on, moaning and shuddering, and surrounded by scattered sausages. On first sight, Elizabeth thought that he was a negro, because his face and the upper part of his shoulders were almost totally black, as if they had been stained with ink. Not only was he swinging his feet from side to side, he was jerkily waving his arms in the air, like a wind-up clockwork drummer who had lost his drum. His arms were black, too, almost down to the elbows, and his hands had no fingers, only a few thick stumps of fingers.

Elizabeth suddenly realised that the scattered sausages were his missing fingers, blackened and swollen.

She swallowed, and swallowed again. The man's *face* looked like a negro's face, but even though his belly was blotched with the same kind of inky-indigo discolorations that covered his face and his feet and his upper arms, it was plump and white, definitely a white man's belly. His thighs were white, too, and thick with gingery hair. She stepped closer. She *slid* closer, until the toes of her sandals were almost touching his hip. He had dense gingery hair between his legs, too, but he didn't seem to have a thing – what Mrs Westerhuiven would have called male reproductive equipment and Laura a pecker. Only diseased-looking gristle, yellow and black.

He *stank*, too. He stank like gas, and dead birds, and sour milk, and every smell that made you really sick.

She didn't look too closely. She was far too shocked, far too embarrassed. She was so frightened that she was making a mewing noise, like a locked-out kitten.

The man stopped pedalling his arms and tried to focus on her. His face was so swollen that he could hardly open his piggy little bloodshot eyes. His lips had burst, revealing livid crimson flesh.

'*Oh Christ Jesus,*' he whispered. One of those hurrying, hurrying whispers.

'What?' said Elizabeth, in dread.

'*Oh Christ Jesus forgive me, forgive me.*'

'What happened to you?' Elizabeth asked him. 'Where's Mr Bracewaite? What's happened?'

The man pedalled his arms again; and Elizabeth realized that he was doing it because he was in so much pain.

'*Forgive me Jesus for all of my sins, forgive me, forgive me.*'

He tried to catch hold of the hem of her dress with one of his terrible fingerless hands, but Elizabeth stepped back, not mewling any more, but trembling uncontrollably.

'I'll call for the doctor!' she screamed at him. 'It's all right! I'll call for the doctor!'

He reached out towards her, black-balloon-faced, a thing out of a child's worst nightmare. 'Jesus Christ forgive me for what I did and spare me from eternal damnation, Father Son and Holy Ghost I never meant to touch her, I never meant to touch her it was love and love alone.'

Elizabeth couldn't speak. She backed to the door, quite unable to take her eyes off this blackened, swollen monster thrashing and begging and praying to Jesus for forgiveness.

She was seized with the terrible thought that he had spontaneously combusted, like Mr Krook in *Bleak House* – burned black, yet left the carpet and the furniture unscathed.

'Jesus forgive me,' the monster begged. 'Lord forgive me, my beautiful Laura, my beautiful Laura.'

Laura? Elizabeth couldn't understand what he was babbling about. What did Laura have to do with this swollen, repulsive man who was rolling about on the kitchen floor? Elizabeth had never seen him before; and actively prayed that she would never have to see him again. Maybe he had seen her once, and heard somebody calling out Laura's name, and assumed that she was Laura. Maybe they looked enough alike

97

for him to have muddled them up: there were, after all, only two years between them. She reached the door. As soon as her hand touched the handle, she flew arms-and-legs across the corridor. Her sandals pattered on the parquet. Then she was out through the study and bursting through the net curtains that covered the french windows and into the garden. She couldn't scream out. She was too breathless to scream out, her chest felt all squeezed in. All she could do was stand on the lawn staring at the windows hoping against hope that the black-balloon-faced man couldn't find the strength to follow her.

The black-balloon-faced fingerless man, oh criminy.

Nothing happened for a long, long time. Nothing happened for almost a minute. The birds chirruped, the roses nodded, and their thick creamy petals dropped into the flowerbeds. She heard traffic on Oak Street, and the sound of a woman laughing.

She had to tell somebody. The man could be dying. He could be *dead* by now, and then she would have him on her conscience. His terrible swollen face would visit her in nightmares, whispering for Jesus to forgive him, and asking her accusingly why she hadn't called for help.

In the end, she made her way step by step back, drew back the billowing nets, and stepped back inside.

'Hallo?' she called. 'Are you still here?'

Silence. Then a sudden banging noise, which made her jump, until she realized it had come from outside, somebody slamming a gate.

She went to Dick Bracewaite's desk and picked up the phone. Almost at once, Lucy the operator gave her usual nasal response. 'Sherman exchange, Reverend, and a very good afternoon to you. What number did you want?'

'Lucy, this isn't Mr Bracewaite, it's Elizabeth Buchanan.'

'Well, *hi*, Lizzie, how are you today? I saw your mom earlier. Good to know that she's getting so much better.'

'Lucy – Mr Bracewaite isn't here but something terrible's happened. There's a man here, in Mr Bracewaite's kitchen, and he's wearing no clothes, and it looks like he's burned or something.'

'This isn't one of your practical jokes, is it, Lizzie?' Lucy demanded, sharply. Elizabeth and Laura had regularly amused themselves last summer by ringing Lucy and saying 'Is that the operator on the line? Well, you'd better get off quick, there's a train coming!'

'No joke, Lucy, cross my heart.'

'All right, then, don't you fret. You just leave the house now, quick as you can, and stand outside to wait for the sheriff and the ambulance. I'll call them now, directly.'

'You'll be quick, won't you? He looked like he was dying. All of his fingers were dropped off, it was awful!'

'Don't you fret, Lizzie. Put down the phone now and go wait outside. Don't try to do nothing for yourself, you can only make it worse.'

Elizabeth hung up. She stood in the study for one long moment, listening for any moans or cries from the black-balloon-faced man. Then she left the rectory and walked quickly around to the roadway. She stood by the railing, confident at first, feeling almost heroic. But as the minutes passed, and the oak trees rustled over her head, and the cloud shadows darkly dreamed their way across the sidewalk, she began to feel light-headed. By the time that Sheriff Grierson's big Hudson Six came wailing around the intersection with Oak Street, its red light flashing, she was seeing everything in negative, and the blackness was spangled with stars.

Doctor Ferris came out of the hospital room and closed the door very quietly behind him. He was a lean man of nearly sixty, with the look of a concert violinist rather than a country doctor. He had a large, deeply-pored nose, in which his glasses had made two reddened impressions, and eyes that were slightly too near together and unexpectedly cold. He was wearing a baggy linen suit, his pockets bulging with everything that a country doctor and a pipe smoker and a whittler and an amateur birdwatcher could ever need. He didn't really play the violin: he only looked as if he did.

Sheriff Grierson was making friendly conversation with Sister Baker, who liked to think that she bore more than a passing resemblance to Lana Turner, although her starchy uniform was filled with the equivalent of Lana Turner-and-a-half. She didn't know that was what Sheriff Grierson liked about her so much. He was a big man himself, wore an XXL of everything, and liked his pie, and women who spread out some, instead of those mean pinched-up looking ones.

Doctor Ferris folded his glasses and said. 'It's the Reverend all right, no doubt about it. I saw the birthmark on his back when he visited me before, for his kidney-trouble.'

'Well I'll be . . .' said Sheriff Grierson. 'Is he going to survive?'

'Doubtful, I'd say. Very, very doubtful. That's dead, all of that black area. Gangrenous. We'd have to operate to see how deep it goes, but you can see what's happened to his fingers and toes. Dropped off. And all the flesh on his face is liable to drop off, too. I'm amazed he isn't dead already.'

'The Lord's will, I guess,' said Sheriff Grierson. 'What do you think happened to him? How'd he get all gangreeny like that?'

'I know *what* happened to him, Wally. The trouble is, I can't understand *how* it happened.'

'What are you trying to tell me? He wasn't murdered, was he? Poisoned or something?'

Doctor Ferris shook his head. 'The Reverend Dick Bracewaite is suffering from severe frostbite. Worst case I ever came across.'

Sheriff Grierson stared at him. '*Frostbite?*'

'I know,' shrugged Doctor Ferris. 'Sounds ludicrous, doesn't it, frostbite on one of the warmest days of the year. But that's what it is. Not just frostnip, either, which makes your affected skin go dead white. This is your real hundred per cent turn-you-black frostbite.'

'How could that possibly be?' asked Sheriff Grierson; and Sister Baker said, '*Frostbite?* Where does anybody get themselves frostbitten in the middle of the summer?'

'I surely don't know,' said Doctor Ferris. 'The only thing I can think of is that somebody abducted him and locked in him a cold-store and then brought him back again, but I think the likelihood of *that* having occurred is just about next-to-nil. I saw him myself mid- to late-afternoon, fourish maybe, and the nearest refrigerating plant that could have froze him to this extent is over in New Milford. Then again somebody could have stripped him naked and poured liquid gas all over him, oxygen or nitrogen maybe, but the Lord alone knows how much gas anybody would have needed to cause this much frostbite.'

'That doesn't make any sense, either,' Sheriff Grierson put in. 'Why go to all the trouble of killing a fellow with liquid gas when you can shoot him or strangle him or knock him on the head?'

'I don't know,' said Doctor Ferris. 'I have to admit that I don't have a single sensible explanation.'

'Did he talk to you at all?'

'He said, "Forgive me" just the two times, and that was all.'

'That's what he kept saying when they were carrying him out to the ambulance.'

'Oh . . . one thing more,' said Doctor Ferris. 'He said, "girder". At first I thought he was trying to say "murder", but he said it again, and it was definitely "girder".'

Sheriff Grierson thoughtfully rubbed the side of his neck. 'Girder, huh? That's not much to go on.'

'Could be referring to a construction site,' Doctor Ferris suggested. 'Or maybe a girder bridge.'

'The bridge over the Housatonic at New Milford is a girder bridge,' said Sister Baker.

'Practically ever darn bridge between here and Canada is a girder bridge,' Sheriff Grierson retorted. 'I don't know . . . I've got a bad feeling about this one. This one feels like a headache with an upset stomach, and it's going to take more than Speedy Alka-Seltzer to cure it.'

'You want to see him now?' asked Doctor Ferris, and Sheriff Grierson nodded.

Doctor Ferris opened the door and led the way back into Dick Bracewaite's room. The windows were closed to keep the temperature high, and the smell of gradually-thawing flesh was overpowering. Two nurses were attending to him: one wrapping his arms and his legs in warm hospital towels, the other bathing his blackened, swollen face. Both nurses wore red rubber aprons, and facemasks.

Sheriff Grierson pressed his hand over his face. 'God almighty,' he said, and then he retched.

'Of course the gangrene didn't smell so bad when he was cold,' Doctor Ferris explained. 'If he's still alive when we've finished thawing him out, we can rub him down with a little boric acid ointment mixed with eucalyptus. Helps to subdue the smell.'

Sheriff Grierson approached the bed. Dick Bracewaite's eyes were closed, and his breathing was catchy and irregular. Sheriff Grierson stood watching him for a while with his hand still clasped over his mouth and nose. He had seen plenty of bodies in his years as sheriff of Litchfield County. He had seen people who had burned to death, people who had drowned, people who had blown their chins off. He had even seen people who had died of frostbite, children and vagrants caught out by a sudden snowstorm. But he had never seen anybody who looked like this: puffed up and black like a slowly-collapsing pig's bladder.

However the Reverend Bracewaite had sustained his injuries, whether by accident, or self-mutilation, or by the hand of somebody who wanted him dead, his very flesh had been killed, even when his soul and his spirit were still alive. His face was dead, his arms were dead, his legs were dead – yet, miraculously, the man himself was breathing.

Sheriff Grierson glanced at one nurse, and then at the other. The first one had wide china-blue eyes.

'Okay if I talk to him?' Sheriff Grierson asked.

'You may if you care to. But he probably won't reply.'

Grierson reluctantly took his hand away from his face. 'Rever'nd Bracewaite!' he called, like a man calling a shy cat. 'Rever'nd Bracewaite! It's Sheriff Grierson here, Wally Grierson. Want to talk to you some, if you're compost mentis.'

Dick Bracewaite opened his tiny, swelled-up eyes. He stared at the Sheriff for a while. Then he whispered, '. . . irder.'

'What?' Sheriff Grierson demanded. 'What did you say? Did you say "murder", or did you say "girder"? Come on, Rever'nd Bracewaite, I have to know!'

But Dick Bracewaite was already subsiding. His chest heaved up and down, and his breathing sounded like somebody scraping rough twine over cardboard. He coughed up a fine spray of blood. He coughed again. Then he stopped in mid-cough, and then he died.

Sheriff Grierson stood up straight. He looked at the nurses in their surgical masks and the nurse with the wide china-blue eyes batted her eyelashes at him.

'Guess that's it,' said Sheriff Grierson, tugging up his belt. 'Guess that's no more Sunday sermons for a week or two.'

The next morning, while the streets of Sherman were still filled with sun-golden mist, the Sheriff drove back to St Michael's and parked outside the white-painted railings. He walked up to the front door of the rectory and rang the doorbell, and waited while the Reverend Bracewaite's housemaid came down to answer it. She was a small woman with false teeth and a brunette wig which looked as if it had originally been made for a woman much bigger and much darker. She wore a floral housecoat and a dry, wrinkled expression of intense dislike.

'Wally Grierson,' she said. 'What do *you* want? Zif things aint troubled enough.'

'Hallo, May,' said Sheriff Grierson. 'I've come to take a look around, that's all. Study, kitchen. You didn't touch nothing, did you?'

'That cheeky young deputy of yours, the one with the spots, he said not to, so I didn't.'

'Thanks, May.'

Grierson stepped inside the rectory. He took off his hat, and looked around.

'Kitchen's this way,' said May, crossly, and shuffled ahead of him. She swung open the door and said, 'Help yourself.'

'You sure you didn't touch nothing?' asked Sheriff Grierson.

'Touch anything? Are you kidding me? Do you think I want to risk the wrath of Wally Grierson, class of '25? Pie-eating champeen, weren't you, two years running?'

'That's enough, May,' he admonished her. 'This is the house of God.'

'This is the house of God-knows-what, you mean.'

She went shuffling off and left him alone in the kitchen where the Reverend Dick Bracewaite had been found dying. He stood still for a moment, taking in the pine table and the cream-painted hutch with its jars of sugar and salt and Sanka coffee and the packets of Flako Pie Crust and Nunso Dehydrated corn. A blowfly droned and droned around the room. The electric clock on the wall had stopped at 5:07.

He had looked over the kitchen yesterday, when he had first

been called here, but he had seen nothing at all which had told him how Dick Bracewaite could have been frostbitten. Only Dick Bracewaite himself, blackened and shaking and lapsing in and out of unconsciousness.

He paced around the kitchen, frowning, looking, touching things. On the upper shelves of the hutch, there stood a row of china jugs, as well as cups and saucers and tea plates. Below them, there stood a row of copper saucepans, but the odd thing about the saucepans was that they were all crowded to one side of the shelf. So were a sugar-shaker and a tinplate tea caddy on the shelf underneath.

Sheriff Grierson went over to the hutch and opened the drawers, one by one. In each of them, all the cutlery and the kitchen tools were crammed over to the left. He stood looking at them for a long time, and then at the stopped clock. The last time he had seen anything like this was when the Dixon house over at Gaylordsville was struck by lightning. Everything metal had tumbled into the living-room, where the lightning had struck, and all the clocks had stopped. A massive wave of magnetic energy, that was what had caused it. But that had been lightning. What could have caused a massive wave of magnetic energy in Dick Bracewaite's kitchen?

He left the kitchen and walked across to the study. The morning was beginning to warm up now, and he could hear the vireos warbling in the trees. He picked up Dick Bracewaite's Sunday sermon and read a few lines. *Stay silent, or say something sweeter than silence.* Well, he thought, Dick Bracewaite was surely going to be silent now. He look up at the photograph of Dick Bracewaite as a theology student, and at *Susanna and the Elders.* Kind of fruity for a Reverend, he thought; but a Reverend could hardly put up a picture of Betty Grable.

He opened the middle drawer of the desk. Just the usual stuff, pens, ink, paperclips, a small silver crucifix on a chain, a half-eaten roll of mint. Life Savers.

He looked in the side drawers, one by one. He found nothing but neatly-arranged envelopes and notepaper, and an ecclesiastical calendar for 1942.

The bottom drawer, however, was locked. He tugged it and rattled it without success, then he looked around for a key. One of the mysteries about Dick Bracewaite's death (apart from the mystery of his frostbite) was the whereabouts of his clothes and personal belongings, like his keys and his wallet. He had been found buck-naked without any discarded underwear around him, no wristwatch, nothing. That could have meant that Doctor Ferris' abduction theory was right, and that Dick Bracewaite had been taken over to New Milford or somewhere else where they had access to a freezer. He could have been stripped, frozen, and then driven back here and dumped on his kitchen floor. Good theory, except that the chronology was all wrong. Too many people had seen Dick Bracewaite too close to the time that Lizzie Buchanan had found him.

Other theory: somehow they had managed to freeze him here in the rectory, and then taken his clothes away with them. Only trouble with *that* theory: no discernible motive and no known means of carrying it out.

Sheriff Grierson searched all around the study for the key to the desk. In the end he took out his clasp knife, listened for a moment to make sure that May the housekeeper couldn't hear him, then slid the blade into the desk, just above the drawer. He wasn't a lockpicking expert, but what he lacked in expertise he made up for in sheer strength. He pried the lock away from the front of the drawer, and with one sharp satisfying crack it was open. Inside he found a document-case, made of black calfskin, with a brass-plated clasp. This, too, was locked, but it only needed one twist from the knife to break it.

Sheriff Grierson stood up and emptied the contents across the desk. He spread them around, and said. 'Holy God almighty.'

He hardly ever swore, and up until now he had never blasphemed. But he had never seen anything like this before – nothing that shocked him so much nor fascinated him so much and at the same time made his stomach churn in disgust.

The document-case had been crammed with scores of black-and-white photographs and pencil drawings. There were a few scenes of rural Connecticut, and a drawing of the church of Christ the King in the centre of New Milford, but the rest of them depicted naked or semi-naked children, mostly girls but some pretty-looking boys, too. The photographs were pale and pearly-grey, like children seen through a fog, beautifully but indecently posed. The drawings were mostly in ochre-coloured pastels or very soft pencil, and executed with a lewd and meticulous attention to detail.

The children had half-closed dreamy eyes, and seductive smiles, as if they were enjoying what Dick Bracewaite was doing to them. What was most shocking of all, though, was that Sheriff Grierson recognized at least five of them: Janie McReady, Jimmy Phillips, Sue-Ann Messenger, Polly Womack and Laura Buchanan.

He stared at the pictures for a very long time. His disgust and shock finally subsided, to be replaced by a terrible and suffocating anger – anger that Dick Bracewaite could have used these children to satisfy his own revolting lust – anger that he himself hadn't found out about it, and stopped it, and protected the community that he was pledged to protect.

He sniffed, and took a deep, steadying breath. Then he shuffled the pictures straight, and slid them back into the document-case. Evidence, exhibit one. But Sheriff Grierson almost felt like letting the perpetrator go free. Whoever had killed Dick Bracewaite, and however they had managed to kill him, they had been doing the community of Sherman a considerable favour.

May appeared in the study doorway and stared. 'Wally?' she said. 'You want a lemonade? You look like you're sick.'

Sheriff Grierson ignored the comment and said, 'Tell me, May, what was the Reverend Bracewaite like with children?'

'Children? Why, he adored children. Do you know what he used to say to me? "A man has no need of angels, when he has children".'

Sheriff Grierson tucked the document-case under his arm. 'He don't have neither now, children nor angels.'

May looked perplexed, but Grierson laid a hand on her shoulder and smiled at her. 'There aint no angels where the Reverend Bracewaite's going.'

Seven

Aunt Beverley arrived on Saturday morning, in a fine summer rain that turned the driveway into molten gold. She had been driven up from New York by a big-nosed man in a startling brown check suit and yellow spats. She said his name was Moe and he was something to do with wartime baseball. He perpetually shifted an unlit cheroot from one side of his mouth to the other, and when he did speak he was mostly unintelligible. Aunt Beverley said he had money to burn.

The atmosphere in the house was tense and strange. In some ways, it was worse than it had been when Peggy had died. Ever since Sheriff Grierson had come around on Tuesday evening to talk to father, and then to Laura and Elizabeth, they had been scarcely able to speak to each other, any of them, because of the absolute awfulness of what had happened.

How could you go on chatting normally about horses or lunch or meeting your friends in Endicott's when all you could think of was your own sister or your own daughter, without any clothes on, being touched and photographed and even doing *that* with the Reverend Bracewaite?

Father had a haunted pinched-up look on his face. He had been forced to postpone his trip to New York, and had paced around his desk all day, waiting for the phone to ring with news of grandfather. He had talked to Laura for a long, long time with the door closed, over an hour, and when Laura came out of the study her eyes were scarlet-rimmed and swimming with tears. Upstairs, in her bedroom, she said that father hadn't been cross with her, but he had been deeply hurt that she hadn't felt able to tell him what Dick Bracewaite had been doing to her. Why hadn't she trusted him? How had he failed her? Why in God's name had somebody else managed to kill Dick Bracewaite before father himself had been given the chance to have his revenge?

Father had made them both solemnly promise not to mention a word to mommy. Mommy was improving every day: they didn't want her to go off the rails again, not now.

Elizabeth had stood pale-faced at the end of the bed and watched Laura sniffing and talking and twiddling with the fringes of her bedspread.

After a while, she said, 'You're not sorry, are you?'

Laura had frowned at her sharply. 'What are you talking about? Why should I be sorry?'

'But you're not sorry that it happened. You *liked* it.'

'Don't be so horrible,' Laura had retorted. She had lifted her bedspread and hidden her face in it. For a while she had tried to make a noise that sounded like sobbing; but after a while she had lowered the bedspread a little so that only one blue eye was visible, and the corner of a smile.

'You *liked* it,' Elizabeth breathed, in complete horror. 'You actually, actually *liked* it!'

But now Aunt Beverley was here to take Laura away for a while. Away from scandal, away from small-town disapproval, and most of all away from men. Seamus opened the front door for her, and took her umbrella, and Aunt Beverley came striding into the hallway, pulling off her beige summer gloves like long strings of raw pastry, and swivelling her large head imperiously from side to side. She was dressed in a beige jacket, a spotted beige blouse, and a beige hat that looked like a tureen-lid.

Elizabeth hadn't seen her since Peggy's funeral, and she thought that she looked even more waxy and made-up and older than ever, although her hair had turned to a vivid ginger.

Seamus dutifully shook out her wet umbrella over her feet.

'Well, thank *you*,' she declared.

'Cuffs and coats,' he replied, with a smile.

Moe brushed rain off his sleeves. 'This is alpaca, it shrinks.'

'Isn't that the loudest suit you ever saw?' Aunt Beverley remarked, stepping across the hallway and taking out her cigarette-case. 'That suit's so loud it keeps people awake at night.'

'How are you doing, Beverley?' their father asked her, holding out his hand.

'Better than *you*, I imagine,' Beverley replied.

'Are you staying for lunch? Mrs Patrick's managed to find us a couple of Cornish rock hens.'

'Well, that's sweet of you, but we'll probably stop off at Danbury, on the way back. Moe has to get to his game.'

Moe said, 'You know something, the Giants are playing the Phillies today, and they're both so bad, I don't think *either* team can win.'

'The Phutile Phillies,' said Laura.

Moe looked down at her, his cheroot travelling swiftly from one side of his mouth to the other. His eyes bulged in appreciation. 'Here's a girl who knows her stuff,' he declared. 'The Phutile Phillies, that's right. They brought in that lardbutt Jimmie Foxx out of retirement and what did they get? Sixteen flops on the trot.'

Father laid his hand on Laura's shoulder. 'Sweetheart . . . are you all packed now? Aunt Beverley wants to get you back to New York.'

'I think I have time for a drink,' said Aunt Beverley. 'Where's your lovely wife today? Isn't she joining us? I thought she was making progress.'

'Margaret's been resting,' father told her. 'She *has* been making progress, for sure. But it hasn't been easy. That's why I don't want her to know about any of this. I've said that Laura's been offered the chance of a screen audition, that's all, just a small part. And of course she's thrilled about *that*.'

Moe lit Aunt Beverley's cigarette and almost lit his own cheroot, but then appeared to think better of it.

'As a matter of fact,' said Aunt Beverley, 'there may be a chance of a real screen test. Robert Lowenstein is making a picture about the Home Front. What's it called, Moe?'

'I Piped My Eye In My Old Apple Pie, how should I know?'

'That's nearly it. *The Apple Pie Patrol*. It's a picture about wives and sweethearts doing their bit. And they're looking for pretty little blonde girls like you, Laura.'

Father looked even more pinched than ever. 'Beverley . . . you know why you're looking after Laura, don't you? I want her away from all that. I want her to have quiet and normality and strictly-supervised bedtimes.'

'You're right,' Moe nodded, with exaggerated enthusiasm. 'That's exactly what I could do with. Especially the strictly-supervised bedtimes.'

He waggled his eyebrows at Aunt Beverley like Groucho Marx, and Aunt Beverley said, 'Shut up, Moe, for God's sake.'

They went through to the drawing-room. Moe circled around and around as he walked, admiring the antique fireplace and the tall colonial-glazed windows that gave out onto the gardens. Aunt Beverley sat down in the largest, most dominant chair and asked for a whiskey. Moe said he had an ulcer, and he was driving, so gin would do. Straight up, no ice, no olive. Father allowed Elizabeth to have a small glass of cherry brandy. There were hickory-smoke peanuts on the table and Moe started to scoop them up as if he hadn't eaten in three days.

Laura sat well away from the grown-ups, on the faded brocade window seat. Behind her the sunlight sparkled on the raindrops, and her golden curls shone, and she looked like an angel of flawless innocence. That, of course, was why the late Dick Bracewaite had found her so alluring.

Elizabeth tried to join the grown-up conversation; but there didn't seem to be very much more that she could say. She sensed, too, that her father needed to talk to Aunt Beverley alone.

'Why don't you go find your mommy, you two?' her father asked them. 'See if she needs any help.'

They went upstairs. Oddly, however, mommy wasn't in her bedroom. Her bed was still unmade, as if she had only recently got up, and her dressing-table was still scattered with combs and lipsticks and an open powder compact. The powder puff had dropped onto the carpet and she hadn't bothered to pick it up. Even odder, though, she had left a cigarette burning in the ashtray.

'Maybe she had to rush to the bathroom,' Laura suggested.

But just as they were turning to investigate, Elizabeth glimpsed something down on the front lawn, something white that bobbed quickly out of sight. She ran to the window; and she was just in time to see her mother hurrying across the driveway, wearing her long white nightgown and carrying her white umbrella. 'It's mommy!' Laura exclaimed. 'And she isn't even *dressed*!'

The two girls pelted downstairs and into the living-room. They caught father and Aunt Beverley with their heads close together, earnestly talking, while Moe was pacing around the billiard-room next door, chalking a cue. 'Daddy! Mommy's run out of the house in her nightgown!'

'Oh, God,' said their father. He took off his glasses and came hurrying after them. Seamus had been coming into the living-room with a tray of iced tea, and he almost dropped it. 'Where's the friend?' he asked, in panic. Moe, perplexed, said, 'What?'

They ran outside. The rain was soft and fine. The sun was so bright that at first they couldn't make out where their mommy had gone. But then Elizabeth saw a flicker of shadow on the corner of Oak Street, and she screamed. 'Look! There she is!' and they all set off in pursuit.

Elizabeth hastily smeared the rain out of her eyes with the back of her hand, and prayed that they would find mommy first, and that this latest escapade wouldn't be noticed. She already had enough patronizing gibes to put up with, and she always heard the whispers, although she pretended that she didn't: 'You see *her*? Her mom's a certified loony.'

However, they didn't even have to run as far as Oak Street. On the right-hand side, just before the intersection, the ground dropped away. There was a creek here, no more than a muddy trickle in winter and dried-out in summer. It was here amongst the scrub and thistles that Margaret Buchanan was standing, her upside-down umbrella on the ground beside her, her hair hanging in rat's-tails, her wet nightgown clinging to her ribcage and her bony thighs. On her face was an expression of such desolation and anguish that Elizabeth had to look away.

Father slid down the path to reach her, and put his arm around her.

'Come on sweetheart, let's get you home. What on earth made you come running out here?'

Mommy twisted his sleeve, and stared at him as if he were the one who was mentally unbalanced. 'I saw her. It was just like Lizzie said. I saw her with my own eyes.'

'Come on sweetheart. You'll catch your death.'

'Don't you say "come on" to me. I saw her with my own eyes. She must be here, not too far away, if Lizzie saw her and I saw her, too. And it *was* her, no question about it.'

'Who was it?' asked father.

'You don't *know*? It was Peggy, my little Clothes-Peg! Peggy's back!'

Father looked at her, his face fractured with sadness, and said nothing; but mommy wrenched herself around and pointed along the creek and screamed at him, 'She's here! I saw her! Why can't you believe me? You should be happy that she's back!'

Elizabeth, shivering, peered through the glittering rain. For a split second she thought she glimpsed a blurred white figure, running behind the rainbows, but it could have been nothing more than a flash of refracted light, or something she wanted to see, rather than something that really was. She looked at her mommy's face, however, and she could tell that her mommy had really seen the same little girl all dressed in white. She could tell it for sure. Her mommy was staring at her, quite steadily, quite calmly, and there was nothing in her face that beseeched her to believe that she wasn't insane, because she didn't have to prove her sanity to anybody.

Elizabeth reached out and took hold of her mommy's hand. She was very cold.

'Come on, mommy,' she whispered. 'Let's go home.'

They all climbed back up the slope to the sidewalk. The rain began to ease off, almost as if somebody was slowly closing off their lawn-sprinkler. They walked back with squelching shoes along a street that was already beginning to steam.

'Your hat's gone strange,' Laura said to Aunt Beverley.

'Is *that* all?' Aunt Beverley retorted, fiercely.

As they walked back along the street, Elizabeth noticed that some of the bushes were sparkling. At first she thought it was only caused by raindrops, but when she brushed one of them with her hand, she realized that they were sparkling with ice. She looked down at her fingers, and she could see the crystals melting on her fingertips, like snowflakes. She brushed another bush, and then another, and she was showered with tiny particles of ice. They glittered on her sleeve, and blew through the summer sunshine like chaff.

Ice, in June, it's magic.

Her mommy looked at her, and Elizabeth touched one of the bushes and whispered, '*Ice*, mommy. It's *ice*.'

Her mommy gave her a tired, affectionate smile. Elizabeth was sure that she understood what it meant. She took hold of her mommy's hand, and the two of them walked back to the house with a shared secret and a shared feeling that the world was made of more than rain and sunshine: it was made of mirrors, too.

She hugged Laura goodbye. Aunt Beverley was already waiting in the car, and Moe kept checking his wristwatch and looking fretful.

'I'll write you every day,' Elizabeth promised. 'I won't mind at all if you don't write back every day, but do send me some picture postcards.'

Laura nodded. She was crying so much that she couldn't speak. At last their father laid his hand on her shoulder and said, 'Come along, sweetheart. Time to go.' He was going too, so that he could visit granpa in New York.

But as Laura climbed into the car, Elizabeth called out, 'Wait! Please! I won't be a second!' She ran back into the house and up the stairs. She hurried along the landing to her bedroom, snatched what she wanted from her pillow, and ran helter-skelter back downstairs again.

Laura was sitting in the back of the car, her face pale and her eyes pink. Elizabeth said, 'Here . . . he always wanted to go to Hollywood. You can take him.'

She passed Mr Bunzum through the window. Laura took him and hugged him close.

'You *will* look after him?' asked Elizabeth.

'He's a rabbit,' said Aunt Beverley, turning round in her seat, smoke issuing out of her nostrils. 'He'll have the time of his life in Hollywood. They're *all* rabbits there.'

Moe gave a vulgar chuckle, and for the first time in her life Elizabeth realized that she understood a grown-up joke. It was extraordinary. It was just like the day she had suddenly realized what '*mairzy doats and dozey doats and little lamsy divey*' actually meant. She stepped away from the car feeling extremely adult.

She stood beside her mommy and waved as the car turned out of the driveway and then turned behind the trees. The sun sparked once from its chromework, and then it was gone.

'Well, Elizabeth,' said her mommy. 'It's just you and me now.'

Elizabeth looked up at her. Mommy gave her a wink.

That Sunday was humid and still and very, very hot. The church bells sounded like buckets of treacle being banged slowly together. Mommy and Elizabeth walked to St Michael's and knelt at their usual pew. The doors were left open in a futile attempt to keep the church cool, but all the ladies flapped their gloves and all the men were quietly boiling in their Sunday suits. The service ws taken by the Reverend Skinner, a white-haired retired priest from Danbury with a shrivelled, monkey-like face. He led the congregation in a special prayer for Dick Bracewaite, and hoped that God in His infinite mercy would find it in His heart to forgive him for what he had done. Not many people said amen to that and Janie McReady's parents got up and walked out.

They sang 'Lead Kindly Light' and 'Nearer My God To Thee'. The Reverend Skinner gave a long and scarcely-audible sermon on the text of idolatry. 'Like a scarecrow in a cucumber field are they, and they cannot speak; they must be carried because they cannot walk! They have devoured Jacob; they have devoured him and consumed him, and have laid waste his habitation.'

Elizabeth, in her yellow-and-white-striped cotton dress, so stiffly starched by Mrs Patrick that it crackled whenever she sat down, discreetly sucked a humbug and thought about the scarecrow in the cucumber field. She imagined him drowsing in the summer sun, and the cucumber field all wobbly with heat. He probably didn't care that he couldn't walk, because he was too darn comfortable drowsing in his field.

But she imagined a crow, too – a huge black crow, lazily flapping its wings on the warm up-currents, always circling the cucumber field, waiting for the scarecrow to close his eyes, and so the scarecrow never could.

Elizabeth was almost dozing off herself when she saw a small white figure walking past the church doors, so bright that her outline seemed blurred. A thrill of excitement ran down the back of her legs, and she was tempted for a split second to touch her mommy's arm and whisper, 'Look! She's here!' But she couldn't be sure that it was the same girl, and she didn't want her mommy to get excited, not if it wasn't the same girl. Yet who else would be walking around the streets during communion, except for Catholics or Jews. She didn't know any Catholics in Sherman; and the only Jews she knew were middle-aged.

She watched the doors for a long time but the girl didn't pass again. After a while she squeezed her eyes tight shut and said a prayer for Peggy's soul, and for mommy's sanity, and for herself, too, because it didn't matter about muffs and peckers, not to her. All she wanted was her sister back home.

After the service they left the church and talked for a while to some of their friends. Mrs Brogan was holding the stage, as usual, a big loud woman in a big loud dress and big feathery hat. Elizabeth and her mommy had to elbow their way past them. They had almost reached the gate when Mrs Brogan called out, in a grating, mock-sympathetic cluck, 'How's your trouble, Margaret, dear?'

Mommy hesitated. Elizabeth could see that she was tempted to just keep on going, to pretend that she hadn't heard, but for all of her illnesses, mommy was made of pricklier stuff than that. She turned around and faced Mrs Brogan and said, in a very high voice, 'Oh yes, Mrs Brogan? And which particular trouble was that?'

Mrs Brogan's face subsided into her double chins. 'I was

referring to Laura, of course. And that repulsive Mr Bracewaite. Such a terrible business. Terrible. I was just saying how tragic your life has been, dear, what with Peggy and now Laura. I don't know how you manage, I really don't. Well – I know there are times when you *can't* manage, but surely we all have those.'

Mommy took two or three steps back towards Mrs Brogan and Mrs Brogan flinched. When mommy spoke, her voice was hushed and deadly serious, like a snake sliding swiftly across a shingle slope.

'I'll have you know that all of my daughters are alive. *All* of them; and all are well.'

Mrs Brogan stared back at mommy for a long time, her lower jaw visibly quivering behind the net of her Sunday hat. Then at last she said, 'No offence was intended, Margaret.'

'No offence was taken, Mrs Brogan,' mommy replied.

They walked home through the heat, hand in hand, one white glove in another. There were times when Elizabeth thought that her mommy was one of the prettiest, most characterful women in the whole world, and this was one of them.

'Do you *really* believe it?' she asked. 'Do you really believe that Peggy is still alive, somehow?'

'Yes. I do now. I'm sure of it.'

'She doesn't look the same. She's older.'

Mommy shook her head. 'I don't think that matters. It's her, whatever age she is, whatever she looks like.'

'But how can we be sure?'

'I'm sure. I'm her mother.'

'But – '

'But what? I may be her mother but I'm insane? I'm not insane. I was never insane. I was grieving for your sister, that's all. Grief is a *kind* of insanity, I suppose. But I'm not so grief-stricken that I can't recognize my own baby when she comes calling for me. God, I gave up everything for my children, my stage career, my movie career, my singing career. I could have had the whole world spraddled at my feet. So don't tell me I don't know my own baby when she comes calling for me. I gave up too much.'

They crossed the street and walked down towards the house. The glare of the sun was so intense that everything was brighter and more richly-coloured than Elizabeth could have imagined possible. *Wizard of Oz* colours, chrome yellow and emerald green and gorgeous crimson.

They had nearly reached the front door when Elizabeth said, '*Spraddled*?'

There was a moment's pause between them, and then they both burst out laughing. Seamus opened the door to find them leaning against the verandah rails, helpless as scarecrows.

That night Margaret Buchanan opened her eyes and stared up at the ceiling. Something had disturbed her sleep but she didn't know what. The window was wide open but the night was so hot and so still that she felt as if she were melting, literally melting, and that all they would find of her in the morning would be a thick pink waxy stain on the sheet, and her nightgown, and her hair.

Outside, the sawing and chirruping of crickets was absurdly loud, but there was no breeze at all, not even a hesitant breath of it. No traffic, no distant airplanes, no homegoing feet.

She sat up in bed and wiped her perspiring forehead with the sheet. She listened and listened, with sweat trickling down her sides, but all she could hear was that endless amplified *chirrrp-chirrup-chirrrp-chirrup*, and the crackling of her horsehair mattress.

She climbed out of bed and went to the window. The moon wasn't up yet, and the darkness was absolute. All the same, she stood straining her eyes, as if she expected to see a white girlish figure walking across the lawns in front of the house. She touched the window sash, and she could feel the unevenness of the paintwork with her fingertips. She touched the nets, and she could feel their upraised patterns, flowers and baskets. She often touched ordinary things these days, as if to reassure herself that she was ordinary, too, and that her life wasn't being lived out on some Monty Woolley stage set.

She turned back to the bed and groped around until she found her silver cigarette-case. She opened it up, took out a cigarette, found her lighter, and was about to light up when she thought she heard somebody laughing in the corridor outside her room. A high, girlish giggle.

Her first thought was: *Lizzie, still teasing me for saying 'spraddled'.* But then there was another giggle, and it didn't sound like Lizzie. It didn't sound like Lizzie at all. It was far too young, far too back-of-the-throat, the way young children laugh. Children of five, like Peggy.

She walked round the bed, touching the bedknobs to make sure that she didn't bump into it and bruise herself. She opened her bedroom door, and put her head out, and listened again. The landing was silent, and as dark as the end of the world. Complete, swallowing blackness. Margaret closed her eyes tight, as if that would make her hearing more acute. But all she could hear was the house creaking in the heat, her own heart beating, and the endless crickets.

I'm imagining things. Ever since Lizzie told me that Peggy was still alive, I've been imagining things. That little girl yesterday, who stood in the rain smiling at me, she wasn't real. She was wishful thinking. If she were really Peggy, why did she run away? Peggy would have run towards me, and hugged me, all giggles and curls. She wouldn't have led me into the rain, and made me look such a fool.

She opened her eyes. The landing was still dark and silent. There. It was all my imagination. It was just another of those things that I always wanted and could never have, like a brilliant career on Broadway, with the crowds carrying me shoulder-high through Times Square, while dawn appeared like a greasy-grey hangover, and even the trash-collectors put down their pails and applauded.

She turned back into her room and the girl in white was standing by the window, not saying anything, not moving at all. Margaret couldn't see her face, but the first pale light from the rising moon shone on her dress, and on her hair, so that it gleamed in a silvery halo.

Margaret went cold. She crossed her arms over her breasts and she could feel her nipples hard and her skin covered in goosebumps. She wanted to say something but her lips felt as if they had frozen. She had been quite convinced that Peggy had somehow returned to her, in another guise; but now that she was confronted with this silent, silvery-haired girl, her conviction seemed to drain away, and she felt a chilly sense of fear. Peggy was dead, after all. Peggy had drowned. How could she ever come back, even in another body?

'What do you want?' Margaret whispered.

The girl said nothing. Neither did she move.

'What do you want?' Margaret repeated. She was so frightened that she believed she was going to faint. The darkness was overlaid with more darkness; the stars with even more stars. 'What do you want? Are you real?'

The girl spoke. Her voice was high and clear, and yet it was oddly-accented, too, each word rising in emphasis at the end, almost as if it were a tape-recording played backwards. 'I came to see you, mama.'

Margaret clamped her hand over her mouth. Her eyes filled up with salty tears. At last she managed to take her hand away and say, 'Peggy? Little Clothes-Peg? Is that you?'

'I came to see you, mama,' the girl repeated.

Margaret managed to take one step forward, and take hold

of the bedrail. 'Are you really Peggy?' she asked the little girl. 'Please don't try to trick me. I couldn't bear it if this was a trick.'

'I came to see you, mama.'

Margaret stared at her. 'Are you a doll? Is that all you are? What are you? Tell me what you are, you're frightening me!'

She dropped to her knees on the rug. She was sobbing so grievously that her lungs hurt, and she could hardly speak. The littel girl came away from the window and stood very close to her – so close that Margaret could hear the rustling taffeta of her party dress, and even smell – what? She thought it was funerals at first, the smell of dead flowers, three days after Peggy's funeral, when all the hothouse roses and orchids had started to droop and decay. It was similar, but it was another smell. It was the smell of dead flowers in the changing-rooms of the El Morocco, on Monday morning when you came back to work. Dead flowers mingled with cigar smoke and sour Isabey perfume and weekend-old laundry.

Sordid but exciting. A lost career, distilled into a single smell.

Margaret lifted her head. The girl was very pale, but she was smiling. Her face looked as if it had been caked with white stage powder. 'I came to see you, mama,' she said, although her lips didn't move.

Margaret wiped her eyes with her fingers. 'Peggy, is it really you? Or am I going mad? Please tell me if it's really you.'

The girl giggled. 'You have to say – what you have to say *is* – what it is you want most – in all the whole world.'

'Darling, you know what I want. I want us all to be together. I want to hold you in my arms. I never meant to lose you. I'm sorry I lost you. I'm really so sorry.' Tears were streaming down Margaret's face now, and dripping onto her nightgown. 'Oh Peggy, you don't know how much I missed you, you'll never ever know.'

The little girl stood close to Margaret and stroked her hair. Margaret couldn't actually feel her fingers, but she felt her hair rising up with every stroke, as if it were charged with static electricity.

She felt *cold*, too: she couldn't stop shivering. She would have done anything to wrap a blanket around herself; or find her bathrobe. And yet – only a few minutes before – she had felt so hot that she thought she was going to asphyxiate, like a barbershop customer with his head wrapped in hot towels.

'You can have what you want,' the little girl breathed.

'What?' said Margaret.

'You can have whatever you want. All you have to do is to follow me.'

Margaret sat back and stared at her. She had been very frightened before. Once, when one of her boyfriends had got catastrophically and violently drunk, screaming at her, hitting her, she had seriously believed that she was going to die. But tonight – faced with this pale-faced manifestation of Peggy – her fear was so comprehensive that she felt as if she couldn't move, or speak, or do anything ever again, except kneel on this rug and wait for the whole world to rotate underneath her, so that this moment would no longer be.

Eight

Elizabeth heard the kitchen door slam. She didn't know how she heard it slam, or why she knew what was happening, but she was out of bed and searching for her slippers an instant after it had happened. She dragged her pink bathrobe from the hook on the back of the door, and quickly struggled into it. She opened her bedroom door in time to see her mommy, in her nightgown, fleeing barefooted down the stairs.

'Mommy?' she called, in alarm. 'Mommy? Where are you going?'

Her mommy didn't answer. Elizabeth heard her running across the living-room, her bare feet slapping on the parquet. Immediately she started to run after her. Something was seriously wrong. She could tell. Mommy's bedroom door was still ajar and there was a strange smell of electricity in the air.

Just as Elizabeth was running down the stairs she heard the front door open, locks and chains. By the time she reached the hallway it was wide open, and her mommy had gone. She ran outside, onto the porch, and saw mommy hurrying around the side of the house, towards the swimming-pool.

'Mommy!' she screamed. She was really scared now. 'Mommy, come back!'

She debated with herself for a split second if she ought to call Mrs Patrick, or maybe Seamus, but if mommy were going to do anything stupid, it would take them far too long to get here. She ran down the steps and hurriedly followed her mommy around the side of the house.

The moon illuminated the garden as if it were a stage set,

constructed of artificial bushes and painted trees. Even the sky looked as if it had been painted. The surface of the swimming-pool, instead of looking liquid and sparkling, was pearly white, and steam was rising from it. Elizabeth's mommy was walking towards it, more slowly now, both hands lifted, her nightgown billowing as she walked.

'Mommy, *please!*'

At first Elizabeth couldn't see why her mommy was walking towards the pool so raptly, because she was walking in her line of sight. But then she reached the edge of the pool and stopped, and then took two or three steps to the right, and Elizabeth saw that the Peggy-girl was standing on the far side of the pool, white-faced and smiling. Elizabeth was already halfway across the lawn, but the girl's sudden appearance made her feel as if her knees had turned into jelly, and she stumbled twice and nearly fell over.

The girl wasn't calling or beckoning. She was standing quite still, with her feet together, her arms down by her sides. But there was an expression on her face which was utterly compelling. It was an expression of triumph; but also an expression that was close to ecstasy, like a Michelangelo saint. She was the wrong age to be Peggy. She didn't even look like Peggy. Yet Elizabeth was still quite sure that it was her – and her mommy must have been, too, because she suddenly called out, 'Peggy! Wait! Don't go without me, sweetheart. Not this time.'

The girl took one step nearer, then another. Then she actually stepped down into the pool. Elizabeth was about to scream out and tell her not to when she realized why the surface of the pool looked so milky and opaque, and why it was steaming. The pool was frozen over, and the girl stepped down onto solid ice.

It was summer, the hottest night of the year, and the pool was frozen over.

Elizabeth watched in fright and fascination as the girl glided to the centre of the pool. She seemed to be able to move without putting one foot in front of the other, as if she were skating. Without a word, her mommy stepped onto the ice, too, and walked towards her dead Peggy with stiff, uneven steps. She was barefoot, but if she felt the cold she showed no sign of it.

'I knew they hadn't taken you away from me,' said her mommy. 'I knew you'd come back.' Her voice was high and lyrical, almost like singing, and the chill of the frozen pool made her breath smoke.

The Peggy-girl said nothing at all, but kept on smiling that joyful, triumphant smile, her eyes misted over in the same way that the surface of the pool was misted over. Elizabeth reached the edge of the pool and held onto the cold chrome handrail. She thought of stepping onto the ice, too, but she didn't know how thick it was, and whether it would bear their weight. She remembered too vividly the ice cracking beneath her knees, and Peggy staring up at her, trapped.

Mommy reached out for the Peggy-girl. At the same moment, a white screech owl fluttered overhead, and Elizabeth looked up. A frozen pool, a summer night: it was all too strange for words. The owl circled towards the oaks behind the house, and even though it distracted her for only a moment, Elizabeth missed what happened next. The ice cracked, from one side of the pool to the other, with a terrible grating sound, like a huge sheet of plate glass breaking. Mommy dropped directly into the water – and presumably the Peggy-girl did, too, because Elizabeth couldn't see her.

Mommy screamed and gargled and splashed and went under. Without hesitation, Elizabeth jumped into the pool, half running, half sliding on a tilting piece of ice, and then plunging in her bathrobe and slippers right into the water. She was chilled and shocked, but she managed to kick off her slippers and swim through the slush to the middle of the pool, circling around and treading water.

For one heart-sinking moment, she thought that her mommy had gone under for good. She circled around and around, desperately thrashing her arms, with large lumps of ice bumping into her. She was too cold even to shout out, but at last she managed to take in a huge breath of air, and dive beneath the surface. She looked around, but all she could see were wobbling silver air-bubbles, and the dark shadowy shapes cast by the pieces of ice that were floating on the surface. She kicked her legs, and groped around with her hands, but she couldn't feel anything at all – neither her mommy nor the Peggy-girl.

She swam back up to the surface, and broke through the thick, porridge-like slush. She knew that she wouldn't be able to stay in the water for very much longer. Already she couldn't feel her fingers, and her toes were starting to hurt. She was just about to strike out for the edge of the pool, however, when the slush exploded right in front of her and her mommy came bursting out of the water, wild-eyed, screeching for breath.

Elizabeth shouted at her, 'Mommy! Don't panic!' But her mommy was hysterical. She thrashed her arms around and pedalled her legs, churning up a froth of ice and freezing-cold water. She went under again, but this time Elizabeth managed to catch hold of her nightgown, and pull her back up again.

Her mommy surfaced, and tried to cling onto her – tried to *climb* onto her, scratching her face and pulling her hair in her panic. Elizabeth went under again, and swallowed a stomach-ful of freezing water. But she managed to struggle around until she was underneath her mommy, and then kick herself up to the surface and grasp her around her neck, from behind. She had swallowed too much water to be able to speak, but she started swimming towards the shallow end of the pool, dragging her mommy after her with a strength that was fifty per cent adrenaline, forty per cent determination, and ten per cent downright stubbornness. She wasn't going to die. She wanted to write and ride horses. She didn't want her mommy to die, either. At last, Elizabeth felt her heel scraping on the concrete bottom.

'We're all right, we're all right,' she managed to choke out. 'We can stand up now.' Then slowly zig-zagging like two drunks, the two of them waded the last six or seven feet to the steps and climbed out.

Her mommy knelt on the edge of the pool and coughed up water, her head bowed, her wet hair straggling down. Elizabeth, her teeth chattering, limped all the way around it, peering into the slush to see if she could see the Peggy-girl. She lifted up the long-handled net which her father used for straining bugs and leaves out of the pool, and she pushed it into the water again and again, and churned it around, trying to feel the Peggy-girl's body. There was no sign of her, and Elizabeth was growing too numb and shaky to go on searching. She dropped the net and walked over to her mommy. Her mommy raised her head and looked up at her. Her face was completely empty of colour, as if she were a black-and-white photograph of herself.

'Where's Peggy?' she asked, in a hoarse, haunted voice.

Elizabeth shook her head. 'I can't find her. I'll have to call an ambulance.'

Her mommy turned and stared at the surface of the pool. 'It *was* her, wasn't it?' she asked.

'I think so. We'd better get inside.'

'All right. Don't wait for me. You go run for the ambulance.'

'Mommy – ' Elizabeth hesitated. Her pink bathrobe was dripping, and she felt as if she would never ever be warm and dry, ever again.

Her mommy said, 'It's all right, Lizzie. I love you. I won't do anything silly.'

Elizabeth left her and ran back towards the house. She turned as she climbed back up the steps, and there was her mommy, still kneeling under the moon, the loneliest figure she could ever imagine.

Sheriff Grierson stood beside the empty pool with his big red arms folded and his big red face glistening with sweat. It was just after lunch the following day, and the heat was even more insufferable than on the day before. The flag hung limply from the Buchanans' flagpole, and the whole day looked as if it had been given five coats of clear varnish.

Elizabeth and her father stood close by. He had taken the first train back from New York, and looked tired and disoriented. Elizabeth was wearing her pink blouse and her white canvas pedal-pushers. She had braided her hair and tied it with a pink ribbon.

Sheriff Grierson said, 'I think we're going to have to put this one down to some kind of hallucination, Mr Buchanan.'

'It was real, though,' Elizabeth insisted. 'I saw it myself.'

'Lizzie,' said Sheriff Grierson, with great patience. 'This swimming-pool of yours holds something upward of twenty-five thousand gallons of water. Not just that, its chlorinated water, which has a lower freezing-point than regular water. How could anybody have lowered the temperature of that volume of water sufficient to make it freeze over, on a hot June night with a temperature of 69 degrees?'

'I don't know, sir,' said Elizabeth. 'I just know what I saw. It was all over ice, from one side to the other, and my mommy walked on it, right to the middle.'

'To meet this girl who looks like your sister Peggy?'

Elizabeth nodded.

Sheriff Grierson sniffed and looked around. 'I don't know what to say to you, Lizzie. I surely don't. I know you're a good girl and a truthful girl, and you've never caused no trouble. I also know there's been some funny stuff going on lately, like the way the Reverend Bracewaite met his Maker. I'm inclined to think that you believe you saw what you believed you saw, honestly and sincerely; but that it's much more a question of believing rather than actually was.'

'You think I'm making it up,' said Elizabeth. Her arms and her legs were aching and she felt really angry with Sheriff Grierson for being so obtuse. Of course it was impossible for anybody to freeze a swimming-pool in the middle of summer, let alone enough for people to walk on. But it had happened, and it was Sheriff Grierson's job to find out why, and how – not accuse her of storytelling, and her mommy of being mad.

'I'm not saying you made it up *deliberate*,' said Sheriff Grierson, defensively. 'I'm just saying it came out of your imagination, and you honestly believed it to be when logic might have told you that it wasn't.' He turned to Elizabeth's father and said, 'Could I talk to you alone, for just a while?'

'Elizabeth,' said her father. 'Do you think that you could go see if Mrs Patrick has finished packing mommy's bag?'

'I saw it,' Elizabeth insisted. 'I really did.'

'Please, sweetheart,' her father begged her. 'I won't be long.'

Elizabeth went inside and her father and Sheriff Grierson strolled together around the pool.

'I had hoped that Margaret was over it,' said her father.

Sheriff Grierson laid a comforting hand on his shoulder. 'Obviously she took it harder than you first believed.'

'There wasn't any sign of this girl who was supposed to be Peggy?'

Sheriff Grierson shook his head. 'No footprints, nothing.'

'And what about the pool?'

'Deputy Regan said it was unseasonably cold, all right, but he didn't notice no ice.'

'It could have melted by then.'

'Mr Buchanan, I don't believe that there *was* any ice to begin with.'

'The Reverend Bracewaite died of frostbite. Maybe we're dealing the same kind of phenomenon. Freak weather patterns, sudden localized cold snaps, thought of that? I published a book last year about strange weather conditions in the Litchfield area. In the summer of 1896 it snowed on a quarter-acre field just outside of New Preston and nowhere else.'

'Mr Buchanan, *think* about it,' said Sheriff Grierson. 'It's just not possible. And apart from that, there's this story your wife and Lizzie have been telling us about some mysterious girl who's supposed to be your late daughter Peggy but doesn't actually look like her.'

Elizabeth's father looked back towards the house. 'Well . . .' he admitted. 'I know that it's hard to believe. But I've studied all kinds of local phenomena – ghosts, and mysterious attacks, and things falling out of the sky – and while some of them are bound to be bunkum, some of them are bound to be true, too.'

Sheriff Grierson gave him a comforting pat. 'Come on, Mr Buchanan. There's no harm done. But your wife's still suffering the effects of grief, and Lizzie's always been a little bit of a dreamer, hasn't she?'

'I guess,' said Elizabeth's father. Then he said, 'Anyway, Margaret's going back to the clinic this evening. They're going to give her some tests, see what they can do to help her.'

'How about Lizzie?'

'I think she'll be all right, once her mother's gone. She'll have to be.'

They began to walk back up the lawn. 'Split your family up some, all of this, hasn't it?' asked Sheriff Grierson.

Elizabeth's father said, 'After Peggy went . . . I felt that the family slipped out of my grasp. I didn't know where we were going any longer, or what I was supposed to do. Sometimes I blame myself for everything. For Peggy drowning, because I didn't drain the pool. For Laura, because I wasn't a strong enough father-figure. For Margaret, for driving her half out of her mind. Now I feel as if I've let Lizzie down, too, because I can't believe her.'

'You're wrong to blame yourself, Mr Buchanan,' said Sheriff Grierson. 'I've seen this kind of thing happen to families before. It's the natural effect of a tragedy, that's all. Things will work out for you, don't you worry about that. You just have to square up to your problems, look 'em dead in the eye, and then try to lick 'em in a fair fight.'

'I don't know. It's been worse than losing a child. It's almost as if – when Peggy died – she left, but something else moved in with us.'

'Don't get your drift,' said the Sheriff.

'It's hard to explain. But I feel as if we lost a daughter and gained a curse. There's something living with us that brings us bad luck.'

Sheriff Grierson said nothing. It was plain that he still didn't understand what Elizabeth's father was talking about. He didn't care for superstition, and he didn't like anything inexplicable. He believed in God but he didn't believe in curses, or bad luck, or imaginary girls who could walk on the surface of swimming-pools. He was still irritated enough by what had happened to Dick Bracewaite, he was personally angry at Dick Bracewaite himself, for having been so inconsiderate as to be killed in a way which defied explanation.

Doctor Ferris was waiting in the hallway for them, looking more like an out-of-work violinist than ever.

'How is she?' Elizabeth's father asked him.

'She's fine,' said Doctor Ferris. 'Tired, anxious, but no physical problems, except that she's underweight. I gave her something to help her sleep.'

'You really believe that the clinic's the answer?'

Doctor Ferris snapped his bag shut. 'It's obvious she can't

stay here. This house and all of its surroundings obviously have the effect of bringing on these morbid hallucinations. She needs professional care, well away from here, otherwise she's going to grow steadily worse. I don't like to second-guess the specialists, but it wouldn't surprise me if electric shock treatment weren't considered desirable.'

'Electric shock?' asked Elizabeth's father, anxiously.

'As I say, I don't like to second-guess the specialists. But electro-convulsive therapy has been shown to be quite successful in the treatment of severe depressives. Or, failing that, leucotomy.'

Elizabeth's father looked lost and dejected. Sheriff Grierson said, 'If there's anything else you need, Mr Buchanan, you know where to reach me. Doesn't just have to be police business, neither.'

Elizabeth's father gave him a wan smile. 'Thanks, sheriff. We'll manage.'

Sheriff Grierson tipped his hat, revealing a sweat-stained underarm. Then he walked back to his car, with Doctor Ferris following behind. As they drove away, neither of them saw the white face watching them from the upstairs window, just above the porch. Nor did Elizabeth's father, as he stood watching them go. When he eventually turned around and walked back into the house, the face was gone.

Laura was woken up by somebody whispering, very close to her ear. She opened her eyes with a start, and found herself staring at the empty pillow next to her. She blinked. She could have sworn that she had heard somebody whispering. She didn't know *what* they had been whispering, but it had been one of those distinctive, saliva-sizzling whispers, conniving and secretive.

She sat up in bed. This was her first morning in Los Angeles, and the breeze was flooding warmly into her bedroom, so that the net curtains billowed and flapped. Her room was white-washed, small and plain, with a carved oak Spanish-style bed and a carved oak bureau, on top of which stood a large blue bowl of freshly-picked oranges. On one wall a blue-and-white rug was hanging; on the others there were straw fans and paintings of orange groves. There was a pungent smell of eucalyptus in the air, combined with the smell of freshly-watered terracotta pots.

She climbed out of bed and stepped out onto her narrow balcony. Aunt Beverley's house was perched on the brink of a cliff overlooking Santa Monica Bay. She had bought it 'for peanuts' from the actor George Albert. Although it was quite rundown, and needed redecoration, it was cool and airy with tiled floors and whitewashed cloisters, and a small enclosed courtyard with a blue mosaic fountain and a showy purple bougainvillea on its eastern wall.

Laura looked down at the beach. The ocean was masked behind a thin photographic mist, through which an occasional wavelet sparkled, but it was still early yet, only ten after seven, and by nine o'clock the mist would have burned off. Laura was missing Lizzie really badly, and her father and mommy, too; but she thought this was Paradise, and although she had cried into her pillow before she went to sleep last night, she already had the feeling that she belonged here. She liked going around with Aunt Beverley, too. Aunt Beverley took whatever she wanted and went wherever she wanted to go, and spoke her mind. She might look like a man, and swear like a man; but she was stronger and funnier and ruder than any man that Laura had ever met, and whenever she was with her, Laura felt adventurous but safe. Aunt Beverley seemed to know absolutely everybody in Hollywood, and she was disparaging about all of them. She called Charlie Chaplin 'the Sniffer' because he sniffed around every pretty girl at every party he went to. Elia Kazan – 'Gadge' to his closest friends – she referred to as

'Madge' because she thought he was so self-indulgent and effete.

Aunt Beverley was a fierce woman and no mistake, and you could see it in the eyes of the people she talked to.

Laura was still standing on the balcony in her too-big red-and-white striped pyjamas when she heard that whispering again. It seemed so close that she turned around, startled, but there was nobody there. It could have been the ocean, shushing. It could have been the breeze. Yet she was sure that she had heard somebody close to her ear, trying to tell her something. Whisper-whisper-whisper, the way schoolgirls do.

Her room was empty, apart from Mr Bunzum, tilted lopsidedly on the pillow. Poor old Mr Bunzum had made it to Hollywood at last, and still couldn't drive his excellent red Packard, poor old whisker-face, mainly because he was nothing but a stuffed rabbit, and didn't really own an excellent red Packard anyway. Laura lifted up the net curtains and stepped back into her bedroom and strained her ears. She could hear a woman singing 'Praise the Lord and Pass the Ammunition' in Spanish. She opened her bedroom door and looked down into the courtyard, and saw a plump black-haired woman down on her hands and knees, scrubbing the blue mosaic. The woman looked up and smiled and called, *'Buenos dias!'* Laura quickly closed her door in embarrassment.

It was then that she turned and saw the faintest outline of a girl, standing on the balcony. The girl was aged about ten or eleven, the same age as Laura, with tousled curls. She was wearing the simplest of white dresses. Her face was turned away, and for some reason Laura thought that she was crying. She was scarcely visible, no more than a half-transparent disturbance in the morning air, although Laura could see her more distinctly when the breeze dropped and the net curtains fell across the window.

Laura stood still, her hands tingling with fright. The breeze blew up the curtains, and for a moment the girl's outline disappeared; but then they fell again, and the girl faintly materialized. She turned towards Laura. Her eyes were little more than smudges, and her cheeks were white, but Laura could see that she was deathly serious. What was more, Laura knew her – she knew her so well that her heart almost stopped on the spot.

The girl was Peggy. She didn't actually look like Peggy. She was much older than Peggy had been when she drowned. But Laura was absolutely certain that it was her.

'Ohhhhhh . . .' the girl whispered, her voice fading and swelling like a faraway radio station. 'Mmmmmmhhaaave leffft my boots behind . . . mmmmmmhhhavvve lefffft my gloves behind . . .'

Laura, aghast, said, 'What? What have you left behind?'

'. . . lefffft my boots behind . . .'

Laura knelt on the edge of the bed, reached over, and picked up Mr Bunzum. She held him tight against her heart, and slowly approached the curtains. The breeze blew them up again, and the girl momentarily vanished in the sunlight; but then they sank back, and Laura could see her again, very faintly, scarcely more than a watermark in the air. Anybody who walked into the bedroom by chance, and hadn't heard her whispering, would probably have failed to see her altogether.

'Peggy, what is it?' asked Laura. 'Tell me what you want.'

Peggy whispered something but Laura couldn't hear what it was. The ocean was shushing too noisily on the shore, and two or three automobiles drove past. The maid was still singing 'Praise the Lord and Pass the Ammunition'.

Laura said, 'Peggy, are you crying?'

The whispery voice grew stronger, and for a moment it rushed over Laura's ears like water rushing over pebbles.

'Oh . . . I have left my boots behind . . . I have left my gloves behind.'

'What boots, Peggy? What gloves? What are you talking about?'

But the curtains lifted, and the girl vanished. Laura dropped Mr Bunzum and pulled the curtains back across the window, but the image didn't return.

'Peggy?' she called. 'Peggy, are you there?' She stepped out onto the balcony. She put out both hands and felt the air, in case Peggy was there but couldn't be seen, like *The Invisible Man* or something. But there was nobody there, nobody there at all, and all she could feel was the warm morning wind.

She went back into the bedroom. She almost tripped over Mr Bunzum, and she was just about to pick him up when she realized that he looked very strange. Normally he was a brownish sort of rabbit, in a dirty yellow waistcoat, but now he was sparkly and white. Very cautiously, Laura picked him up, and realized at once what had happened to him. He was sparkly and white because he was frozen solid. Not just cold, but frozen hard, and giving off fumes of intense cold.

Laura dropped him in alarm. He fell onto the Mexican tiled floor and shattered into seven separate pieces – arms, legs, body and head. Even one of his ears snapped off.

Laura sat on the bed staring at him for a very long time. She didn't understand this at all. But there was one thing she knew for certain. Peggy wasn't dead; not in the usual sense of being dead; and somehow Peggy had managed to find her all this way away in Santa Monica.

She stood up after a while, went to the bureau and took out her pen and the pad of writing-paper that father had given her. Carefully, so that she would always remember it, she wrote down the date and the time. Then she wrote the words that Peggy had whispered to her.

'Oh, I have left my boots behind. I have left my gloves behind.'

The words seemed familiar, like something that somebody

had once said to her when she was very small. Yet here, in the warmth of California, they seemed so incongruous. Who needed boots and gloves on a morning like this? Nobody but Mr Bunzum, and he was broken now.

Garden of Death

' "Dead she is not," said the roses.
"We have been down in the earth;
the dead are there, but not her." '

Nine

She stepped off the train and there he was, waiting for her, in his big brown coat and his wide-brimmed hat, still looking like Jimmy Stewart but filled out now, and broad-shouldered, a man instead of a boy.

The locomotive let out a deafening, dolorous wail. Lenny came towards her with both of his hands held out, and grasped both of hers, and kissed her. 'Lizzie . . . you look like a million.'

'You too,' she said. 'I couldn't believe it when the phone rang and it was you.'

'I'm just sorry that it was such bad news. Is this all of your luggage?'

He picked up her tan calfskin bag and together they walked across the depot to the parking-lot. It was a dazzling-bright Thursday morning in October 1951. The train from New York had taken Lizzie back into the reds and russets and shimmering yellows that had illuminated every October of her childhood, and she had sat by the window reminiscing about Laura and Peggy and the days that she had spent in Sherman, all the way from White Plains to New Milford.

Outside the station the sidewalks were ankle-deep in crisp, scurrying leaves. Lenny guided Elizabeth over toward a shiny red Frazer Manhattan convertible.

'What do you think?' he asked her, opening the boot and stowing her case. 'I bought it last summer.'

'It's beautiful. I love the colour.'

'Sure. I chose it specially to match your lipstick.'

He helped her into the car and then climbed behind the wheel. 'I think I ought to warn you that your dad's pretty bad.

He can't walk and he can't talk. He can make a few signs, but that's about as far as it goes.'

Elizabeth nodded. She had tried to prepare herself for seeing her father, but every time she thought about him, she remembered him the way he was, carrying in logs for their innumerable, every-hungry fires; or carving the turkey at Thanksgiving; or bouncing Laura and Peggy on his knees. She remembered him standing in winter with his back to the hearth, his glasses on the end of his knees, reading to them with all the rapture of an actor from one of the latest publications from Candlewood Press, one of his books about local witches or strange customs or the ghosts of those who had lived in Litchfield when it was a country of isolated farmhouses and dark, tumbledown coaching inns.

She couldn't think of him immobile, speechless, his intellect trapped in a useless body.

They drove through New Milford toward Sherman, over the Housatonic bridge. The river reflected the pecan-red trees and the royal blue sky and the ducks that were already flying south. Elizabeth opened her purse and took out her cigarette-case. 'Smoke?' she asked Lenny.

'Trying to cut down. Not very successfully. Sure, you can light me one.'

Elizabeth was never quite sure when she had grown out of being an awkward, gawky adolescent and turned into the trim, elegant young woman she was today. All of her diaries were crammed with miserable ramblings about spots and periods and hair that would never do what she wanted it to do. Yet here she was, at the age of twenty-one, with dark upswept hair, a finely-boned face, and long slim legs. She was wearing her best camel coat from Bergdorf Goodman, a pleated plaid skirt and a red twinset. In her coat lapel sparkled the diamond brooch that her father had given her when she had graduated with honours from Connecticut State University. It was fashioned like a rose, and it had once belonged to her mother.

'How are you liking the big city?' asked Lenny, as Elizabeth passed him a lighted Philip Morris.

'Oh, it's wonderful. My apartment's pretty cramped. There are three of us sharing. But after Sherman . . .'

'Don't tell me. The doziest community since Sleepy Hollow.'

They turned toward Boardmans Bridge, and the sun flickered between the trees. 'Are you back for long?' asked Elizabeth.

Lenny blew smoke. 'I'm just visiting the folks; and sorting myself out, too. You heard about what happened, I guess?'

'Yes. I'm sorry. Isn't there any chance of you getting back together again?'

'Unh-hunh. It was all a mistake, right from the start. One of those wartime idiocies. You don't think about the future, because you think that you're probably going to die anyway. In fact I was sure I was going to die. Even now I still can't believe that I got through it.'

'What about your business? Are you going to carry on working for her father?'

Lenny shook his head. 'He and I mutually agreed that we hated each other's intestines, and that it would be better if we parted company. I'm not sorry about that. I hated Pittsburgh. Besides, the old man gave me five thousand dollars relocation money, which is a polite way of saying that he paid me off.'

'What are you going to do now?'

Lenny tapped his forehead with his fingertip. 'Think, that's what I'm going to do. I'll still work in insurance, but I'm sure that I can come up with some really neat scam, like family-package insurance or special-rate cover for older drivers.'

'I was amazed when you went into insurance. I always thought you were too romantic.'

'Romantic? Me?'

'Don't you remember kissing me, before you went off to Fort Dix?'

'Did I? That was pretty damn forward of me.'

'You wrote me, too, almost every week.'

'That was only because you kept on writing *me*. And sending me those saucy pictures.'

'I used to think that we were going to be married someday.'

'You and me?' Lenny laughed out loud.

Elizabeth glanced at him sharply; and was surprised to discover that, even now, he was capable of hurting her. She had sobbed for days when she heard that he was married. She thought that she would never recover. She still felt jealous – so much, that she could almost taste it.

They were driving around the northern end of Lake Candlewood now. On every side the hills were blazing with crimsons and oranges and yellows, like a forest fire. Elizabeth could smell the trees and the woods and the logsmoke aroma of October, and she closed her eyes for a moment and wished that everything had turned out differently, and that the years hadn't passed yet, and that her father and mother would both be waiting for her when she arrived home, smiling and waving and chatting to her.

Lenny said, 'You tired?'

She opened her eyes. 'No. Just remembering.'

'Remembering's a very bad habit. I wouldn't do it if I were you.'

They drove along Oak Street and then turned into the driveway of Elizabeth's house. Lenny carried her suitcase to the front door. She looked around. The lawns were stained with black patches of moss, and the steps were clogged with wet, unswept leaves. The house itself was beginning to look sad and dilapidated, in need of a fresh coat of paint. It looked almost as if nobody lived here.

Lenny rang the bell and after a long pause Mrs Patrick came to the door, with her hands smothered in flour. She looked tired, and even though it had only been early July since

Elizabeth had last seen her, she seemed to have aged about ten years.

'Lizzie! How good to see you!' she smiled. 'Come on in. Your bedroom's all ready. The fire's lit.'

Lenny carried Elizabeth's case inside. 'Listen,' she told him. 'I really want to thank you for meeting me. Are you going to stay and have a drink?'

Lenny took her hand between his. 'Not now. You have to see to your dad. But I'd like to see you later, if I could. Give me a call, or come around. I know my folks would love to see you, too.'

He gave her a kiss on the forehead, and left. Mrs Patrick closed the door. The house was chilly and smoky, and there was a faint smell of damp everywhere.

'Have you heard from Laura?' asked Elizabeth. Laura was still living in Hollywood, with Aunt Beverley.

Mrs Patrick shuffled ahead of her in rundown slippers. 'She sent a wire. She said she was truly sorry but she wouldn't be able to come home till Thanksgiving at the earliest.'

'I see. Does everybody else know what's happened?'

'Oh, yes. Mr Ament saw to that. He's taking care of the bank, too, and making sure that the bills are all paid.'

Mrs Patrick stopped at the foot of the staircase. 'You'll be wanting to go up to see him.' There were tears glistening in her eyes.

Elizabeth put her arms around her and hugged her. 'Oh, Mrs Patrick, I'm so sorry. You look exhausted.'

'Oh, don't worry about me. I've had a lifetime of hard work, I'm used to it. It's your poor father you should be worried about. I never saw anybody so stricken. Now be careful, you don't want to get flour on that lovely coat of yours, do you?'

Elizabeth wiped her eyes with her handkerchief. 'He's not alone, is he?' she asked.

Mrs Patrick said, 'The doctor was here a half-hour ago, and

the nurse gets here at half after twelve to feed him and bathe him. So he's well looked after. It's hard to tell what he might be thinking, though, or even if he's thinking anything at all.'

Seamus appeared at the top of the stairs, carrying two empty log baskets. Of everybody Elizabeth had known during her childhood, Seamus was the only one who hadn't changed at all. It was almost as if his abduction by the little people had given him a charmed and ageless life. His mind had unravelled even more, like a home-knitted sweater caught on a nail, but that made him seem even younger, and even more endearing.

'Hallo, Seamus,' said Elizabeth. 'I see you're keeping the home fires burning.'

'Blue lights,' grinned Seamus. 'Blue lights every evening.'

'How has he been?' Elizabeth asked Mrs Patrick.

Mrs Patrick shrugged. 'He has his moments, poor darling. Now I must get back to my dumplings.'

Seamus came down the stairs. 'Crows and ravens,' he said, his eyes sparkling, as if he were saying something really mischievous. 'They jumped round the carriage, but they never barked.'

Elizabeth stared at him. 'What did you say, Seamus?'

'They jumped round the carriage, but they never barked.'

'Why didn't they bark, Seamus?'

'It was forbidden.'

Elizabeth slowly nodded. 'Yes, Seamus. You're quite right. It was forbidden. Now how did you happen to know that?'

'Crows and ravens,' smiled Seamus, very pleased with himself. 'They jumped round the carriage, but they never barked.'

'Seamus!' called Mrs Patrick, from the kitchen. 'Stop babbling that nonsense and put some more wood on the fire! And make sure it's dry!'

Elizabeth went upstairs. At the top of the first flight, she stood and looked around her. The house was no longer hers. It had shrunk and grown shabbier, and somehow her presence had left it now, even her childhood presence. Laura's too.

She supposed that it happened to all children in the end, and to all houses. Once she had graduated from High School, and gone to university, she had come home less and less frequently, and two Christmases ago she had moved out altogether to share an apartment in Hartford with one of her best friends, Leah Feinstein. Now she had her job with Charles Keraghter & Co, and she shared a third-storey walk-up apartment on West 14th Street with another assistant editor and a girl who worked on set design for Radio City.

She had written to Lenny all through the war – sending him cards and drawings and badly-knitted socks and the sexiest photographs of herself that she dared to have developed (in her swimsuit, mostly, with the shoulder straps let down). All of that golden dream had died when Lenny had married. But something else had kept her in touch with her childhood: the whispers she constantly heard; and the fleeting glimpses of a little girl in white. Sometimes she didn't see the girl for weeks on end. But then suddenly she would see her running through the crowds on Seventh Avenue; or standing on the corner of Times Square; or staring at her from a passing bus. It always unsettled her; and gave her a bad day, as if the barometer were down. But she missed her if she didn't see her. For some reason, the little girl made her feel watched-over, and protected.

Laura had admitted that she had seen her too; but to Laura her image had appeared much more vaguely. A shade, a quivering reflection, rather than a real girl. She and Elizabeth had written and talked about it again and again. Laura had even suggested they go to a medium. Aunt Beverley knew a man called Gilbert Maxwell who was supposed to have talked to the spirit of Frank Gaby, Universal Studios' *Mr Dynamite*, who had hanged himself in 1949. But Gilbert Maxwell charged $250 a session, even to his friends.

They rarely talked about it now. They found that they argued about it too much; or that they tried to read too much into it. Elizabeth had thought about exorcism, but then how could she exorcize her own sister? She didn't even know what happened to spirits, when they were exorcized. What if they suffered? What if they were trapped forever, in some airless suffocating prison?

She walked along the landing. She had loved this house so much when they first moved here. But now the rooms were empty and there was nothing here but shadows and terrible regrets.

She reached her father's room, knocked, and opened the door. Even though the blinds were drawn, the room was filled with sunshine, because it faced south-westward. Her father hadn't changed it since her mother had gone to the clinic. The cheval-mirror stood in the same corner; the hat boxes were still piled on top of the closet. Her father lay in the large sawn-oak bed that they had bought from a farmhouse in Washington Depot. The heaped-up pillows were white and starched. His face was drained of colour and featureless, like chewed-up papier-mâché. His arms lay inert on the cream bedspread, his hands veiny and emaciated.

'Father?' she said, and approached the bed. His eyes followed her but he showed no sign of recognition. 'Father, it's Lizzie.'

She leaned over the bed and kissed him. His breath smelled of meat. His nurse must have been shaving him because he had random crops of white bristles that had eluded the razor. His mouth sloped open at the left corner, and he was dribbling.

Elizabeth took hold of his hand and squeezed it. He blinked and swallowed, but he probably blinked and swallowed all day and all night. It didn't signify anything. She sat on the edge of the bed so that he could see her. He was definitely looking at her, but he was incapable of telling her that he could see her, and that he was pleased that she was here.

'Oh, father, why did this have to happen to you?' she asked him. 'You were always so energetic, always so lively. But they can cure you, can't they? They can give you exercises. They can teach you how to talk. I was talking to Jack Peabody at work, and his grandfather had a stroke. You remember Dennis Peabody, who used to work for Scribner's? He was paralysed for almost six months, but now he's writing articles for the *Saturday Evening Post*, and walking to the deli and everything.'

She smiled at him but she felt more like crying. That any man's life should come to this; after years of fun and dancing and publishing books and talking and going to parties. Alone now, or all but alone, in a vast dilapidated house without any family at all, incapable of movement or speech. The tears slid down her cheeks and there was nothing she could do to stop them. Her father watched them and said nothing.

'I've been working real hard,' Elizabeth told him. 'They've given me this really complicated book to edit. *Reds Under The Bed*, by Carl Scheckner III. It's all about the Communist threat, and it's full of references and footnotes and indexes and everything and I have to check them all. I have a senior editor called Margo Rossi and she's such a Tartar! If I'm one minute late back from lunch she practically flays me alive.'

Her fingertip circled the back of her father's hand.

'I want to tell you something, though, father. I couldn't have done any of this without your help and without your support. You taught me so much. I know how much you hurt after Peggy died and mommy got sick; but you were always there, weren't you? And you always told me that you loved me.'

Her father made a thick rattling sound somewhere in his throat, as if he were trying to speak. His eyes opened and closed, opened and closed, but there was no pattern to it, no secret semaphore, nothing but helplessness, Elizabeth sobbed, 'Don't give up, father. Please don't give up. I'll do everything I can to help you get better.'

She sat and watched him for nearly ten minutes; and he lay there and watched her back. She tried to tell him about work, and what her friends had been doing, and the weekend she had gone upstate to Mohonk Lake. But his inability even to show her that he recognized her was more than she could bear, and she choked up, and had to sit with him in anguished silence.

She was thinking of leaving him when his eyes rolled slowly to the right, as if he had seen something in the far corner of the bedroom. She thought at first that what he was doing was completely involuntary, but then his eyes rolled back to her, and repeated the movement to the right.

She turned around, and let out a '*hah!*' of total shock. In the corner, only feet away from her, was the little girl in white. She was standing in the sunlight, and she seemed to be quite real, although Elizabeth couldn't understand how she had managed to enter the bedroom and walk across to the opposite corner without being seen and without being heard. Her face was as white and as smooth as polished marble. Her eyes were impenetrably dark. She wore the same simple dress that she had worn before, although she seemed to have put on more petticoats. Her hands were clasped in front of her, and Elizabeth noticed that her nails were bitten down. Somehow this made her seem all the more frightening. Whoever saw a ghost with bitten-down nails?

'Who are you?' asked Elizabeth, standing up and taking a cautious step backwards.

'I came to see papa,' the girl replied. She spoke without opening her mouth, and her voice was extraordinary, with a metallic, distant quality to it, like somebody sliding a brass ring along a brass curtain-pole.

'Are you Peggy?' asked Elizabeth. She was so frightened that she could scarcely speak properly.

'I came to see papa. I've left my boots behind. I've left my gloves behind.'

'Are you really Peggy?'

The girl gave Elizabeth an unfocused smile. 'Don't be so worried, Lizzie. You don't have anything to fear. Nobody will ever hurt you, ever.'

'You've been following me. You've been watching me.'

'Yes.'

'Then why haven't you ever talked to me before? I wanted so much to talk to you.'

'Better to stay silent, unless you have something to say. I didn't want to upset you.'

'I saw you in Macy's. I saw you in Central Park. I've seen you everywhere! You came here before, didn't you? You froze the swimming-pool.'

'The winter froze the swimming-pool.'

'But it was summer, and you almost drowned us, mommy and me.'

'You didn't drown, though. She didn't want me to take you.'

'What are you talking about?' Elizabeth demanded. She was close to hysteria. 'I don't understand what you're talking about.'

'– want me to take you,' the Peggy-girl repeated, her voice more distorted.

She slid towards the bed. As she passed the cheval-mirror, the surface misted over. She stood and looked down at Elizabeth's father and her face was filled with curiosity and regret.

Elizabeth said, 'Don't touch him.'

The Peggy-girl smiled without looking at her. 'He'll be cold soon enough.'

'He's not going to die,' Elizabeth retorted. 'He's going to live, and he's going to get better.'

The Peggy-girl slowly shook her head. 'Even he doesn't believe that.'

'How do you know? He can't even speak.'

'He has something in him that can say what he wants. We all do; although many of us don't know it, and many of those who do know it prefer to stay silent.'

'You're not making any sense.'

The Peggy-girl stared at her. 'Of course I'm making sense. Why do you think some people rest in eternal peace while others never do?'

She turned back to Elizabeth's father. She reached her hand out to his forehead, but Elizabeth snapped. 'No! Don't touch him!'

Elizabeth bustled around the end of the bed and tried to seize Peggy-girl's wrists. But instead of grasping them, her hands plunged *into* them, like plunging into freezing slush. She could feel them, but she couldn't get any kind of grip. She pulled her hands back in shock.

'Just let him alone!' she demanded, breathy and scared. 'I don't care who you are or what you are, just let him *alone*!'

The Peggy-girl stepped to one side, and this time Elizabeth snatched at her sleeve. But the Peggy-girl seemed to have scarcely any weight, or substance. Instead of resisting, or trying to pull herself away, she completely collapsed. Her head dropped into her collar; and then her whole dress folded up, billowy and insubstantial, and before she knew it Elizabeth was struggling with nothing more than an empty bag of collapsing cotton. She clung to it, tried to stop it from collapsing any further, but it rolled up into something the size of a handkerchief; and then Elizabeth found that she was holding in her hand nothing but a snow-white rose, made of frost. It melted in front of her eyes, until the only evidence that it had ever been there was a faint chilly feeling in her fingers.

Elizabeth turned to her father in astonishment. He was watching her, but of course he couldn't speak. She looked wildly around the room, trying to see if she had been deceived by some elaborate trick. But the room hadn't changed; the sun still shone; and there was no place at all where the Peggy-girl could have concealed herself.

Shaking, Elizabeth sat down on the edge of the bed and took hold of both of her father's hands. Her heart was still beating at high speed, and she badly needed a drink. But she looked him intently in the eyes, and said, 'You saw her, didn't you? She was really here? A little white girl in a little white dress.'

Her father moved his eyes from side to side.

'Is that a yes?' asked Elizabeth. 'If that's a yes, moving your eyes from side to side, then do it again.'

There was a very long pause, and then her father did it again.

'You saw her, didn't you? The little white girl in the little white dress?'

Yes.

'That was the same little girl that mommy saw, when she ran out into the rain. She turned the bushes all icy, even though it was summer.'

Yes.

'That was the same little girl that froze the swimming-pool, the night that mommy and I almost drowned. I saw her quite clearly. We both saw her. Mommy was never mentally sick. I wasn't making up stories. We really, really saw her, just like we did just now. I've seen her again and again. I've seen her in New York. I've seen her everyplace that you can think of. Laura's seen her too.'

Elizabeth was crying as she spoke. She wiped her eyes with the back of her hand, and then she said, 'Nobody believed us. Nobody believed either of us.'

Elizabeth's father remained impassive, his face still fixed in a vapid sneer.

Elizabeth said, 'Do you believe that was Peggy? I know she doesn't look like Peggy, but do you believe that she is?'

Yes.

'Have you ever seen her before?'

Another long pause. Then, *Yes*.

'You've seen her before? How many times?'

No response.

'Twice? Three times? More than three times?'

Yes.

'More than ten times?'

No response.

'And how long ago did you see her? Before mommy went to the clinic?'

No response.

'Before mommy had her operation?'

No response.

Thank God for that, thought Elizabeth. At least he hadn't let mommy undergo a leucotomy knowing all the time that she had been telling the truth – that she *had* seen a little girl who was Peggy's soul or Peggy's spirit or whatever part of Peggy still persisted in the waking world.

'Where did you see her?' asked Elizabeth. 'Here in the house?'

Yes.

'Anywhere else?'

Yes.

'Further than Sherman?'

Yes.

'How far?' asked Elizabeth, and now a small dreadful thought was beginning to occur to her. 'As far as New York?'

Another pause. Then, *Yes*.

Elizabeth and her father stared into each other's eyes. She could see now that he had so much that he wanted to tell her, so much that he wanted to explain and discuss. There were so many questions that she wanted to ask him, too – questions that were far too complicated for a *Yes* or a *No*. Like – why did he think Peggy should still be here? Why did she look like another girl altogether? Why was she so cold? What was she made of? Ice, or flesh, or cotton, or smoke, or nothing at all? Were they imagining that she was here? Was she happy or was she sad? Was she trapped somehow between the living world and whatever lay beyond?

'Are you frightened of her?' Elizabeth wanted to know.

No response. But then a very quick *Yes*.

'You *are* frightened of her? Or not?'

Again, the same reply.

'You're frightened?'

Yes.

'But not of her? Of something else?'

Yes.

'What is it that you're frightened of? Is it a person?'

No response. Then *Yes.*

'It isn't a person but it is a person? I don't understand.'

Elizabeth's father lay back staring at the ceiling. She had the impression that he was making an enormous effort to do something, or to say something. His hands began to quiver, and his throat swelled up, and he started to utter a thick, low, growling sound.

'Father – don't,' Elizabeth begged him. 'You don't have to strain yourself, please. I'm going to stay for at least a week – we can spend a whole lot more time talking about it.'

But her father growled louder and louder, an upsetting dog-like *grrrrrrrrr* which grew louder and louder.

'Grrrrdd,' he managed to say at last. 'Grrrdduh.'

Elizabeth shook her head in dismay. 'Father, please, I don't understand.'

'Grrrrdduh!'

He let out a thick, phlegmy whine, and then he relaxed. He kept flickering his eyes from side to side as if to say *Yes, Yes, Yes.* By uttering 'Grrrdduh' he had somehow managed to tell her what was frightening him.

'Grrrdduh?' asked Elizabeth.

Yes, Yes, Yes.

He kept on flickering his eyes from side to side until they were interrupted by a quick, flurrying knock at the door. It was a plump blonde woman in a nurse's white uniform. 'Hallo, Miss Buchanan,' she said, smiling. 'My name's Edna Faulk. I'm here to take care of your father.'

Edna went across to the bed and leaned over Elizabeth's father, still smiling. 'Good afternoon, Mr Buchanan! How would we like to have a little wash before lunch?'

Elizabeth looked into her father's eyes one more time. There was no expression in them at all. He had totally lost the ability to show her how he felt. She wished that she could understand what he was trying to tell her, but she knew that it would need hours or even days of careful questioning. What wasn't a person and yet was a person? What was 'Grrrdduh?'

'You won't mind leaving us for a while now, will you, Miss Buchanan?' said Edna Faulk. 'If you'd care to come upstairs and share some lunch with your father, well, you're very welcome, but I must warn you that we're rather messy, aren't we, Mr Buchanan? We're very messy pups at mealtimes, believe me!'

'I'll come back later,' said Elizabeth. She couldn't bear the idea of watching her father being fed. 'I have some people to meet.'

She kissed her father on the forehead. He looked up at her but she couldn't tell if he were angry or contented, happy or miserable. As she left the sunlit room, she turned around one more time, and she found herself wishing that he hadn't survived. At least, if he had died, he would have found Peggy in heaven, rather than here.

Ten

She walked along Oak Street and saw how much Sherman had changed. Most noticeably, the large post oak had been cut down, leaving nothing but a wide flat-topped stump. There were still seats around it, but without the green cavernlike shade that its overhanging branches used to offer, the street looked bald and ordinary, a Litchfield street like any other.

The Stillwell Hardware Store had gone, to be replaced by Zee-Zee Appliances, with a window full of Frigidaires. Mr Pedersen had died of throat cancer three years ago, and the Sherman Grocery had given way to Waldo's Supermarket. The creekbed where Elizabeth's mommy had pursued the Peggy-girl in the summer rain had been all covered over with hardcore and asphalt now, to make a fifty-car parking-lot. Baxter's Realty was still here, and so was Endicott's soda-fountain, although Old Man Hauser was in a home now, deaf and blind and incontinent, and the drugstore was run by a young, lugubrious pharmacist called Gary with a flat-topped crewcut and red bow tie and heavy black-rimmed spectacles.

The war had changed Sherman first, and most dramatically, because it had taken away its self-absorption and its innocence. In previous generations, the town's children would have stayed, for the most part, and carried on the town's traditions. But Dan Marshall the school swimming star had been hit by a mortar bomb on the beach of Peleliu Island only six minutes after the US 1st Marines landed there in September 1944. His death was famous because the war artist Tom Lea had painted his head flying through the air. Dan's girlfriend Judy McGuinness, the Prom Queen, had joined the Navy as a Wave and had married her boss, Rear-Admiral Wilbur Fetterman, and then divorced him, and now she lived in Charleston, South Carolina, with a Kaiser-Frazer concessionaire called Hewey Something-or-other.

Molly Albee was married and living in Providence, Rhode Island, with three gingery babies and a husband who repaired boats. Altogether three of Elizabeth's friends had died in the war; others had disappeared; but even those who had returned had brought back with them the outside world, with its cool and its be-bop and its cynicism, and its hugeness, too; and once Sherman knew that it was just a minuscule part of something huge, it was no longer Sherman, the warm-hearted centre of everybody's world, but just another place.

Television had changed it next. Those between-wars family evenings by the Zenith radio were gone for ever, those evenings when shared imaginations would conjure up Amos'n'Andy, Burns and Allen, and *One Man's Family*. Now everybody watched Milton Berle and *Hopalong Cassidy* and the kids all sang 'It's Howdy Doody time, it's Howdy Doody time, Bob Smith and Howdy too, say Howdy-Doo to you'. Not only that, but they could see automobiles and floor-wax and which twin had the Toni, they could *see* what was happening in New York, and Washington, and even London, England, and the loss of innocence was complete.

Elizabeth walked along Putnam Street with its Queen Anne houses and this, at least, hadn't changed. She reached Lenny's house and walked up to the porch. As she knocked on the heavy doorknocker she had the most extraordinary sense that the last eight years hadn't passed at all, and that she was back where she had been in 1943, knocking on the Millers' door to tell Lenny goodbye.

Mrs Miller answered the door. She was whiter-haired, but still comfortable and well-rounded, and she must have been cooking, too, because the house was fragrant with the smell of meatloaf.

'Lizzie Buchanan, well I never! Don't you look the picture! Come along in!'

Lenny and Mr Miller were sitting in the living-room, next to a crackling log fire, drinking coffee and reading the papers. Up above their heads the canaries still twittered and chirruped in their cages.

Mr Miller was even thinner than Elizabeth remembered him. Stomach trouble, that's what Mrs Patrick had told her. But he took off his spectacles and stood up and embraced her like a long-lost daughter, and Lenny stood up too, all proud to have her call on them.

'You want a cup of coffee?' asked Lenny.

'Actually, no. But I could use a cigarette.'

'Mom doesn't like me to smoke in the house.'

'All right, then, let's smoke in the garden.'

They strolled down to the end of the garden, through the orchard. The long grass was thick with fallen apples. Elizabeth leaned against one of the trees and blew out smoke and said, 'Sherman's changed, hasn't it? I didn't really notice until today.'

'Everywhere's the same. It's not just the places, though. It's the people.'

'Do you think we're all so different?'

Lenny shrugged. 'That day you came to say goodbye, that seems like a whole world away. I was a rookie, still wet behind the ears, and you were just a schoolkid.'

'So, what if I *was* a schoolkid? I'm still very annoyed that you didn't realize that I was desperately in love with you.'

Lenny gave her a sly grin. 'I did realize. Especially later, when you sent me those swimsuit pictures. You were very cute, Lizzie. But let's face facts, you *were* a tad young for me, weren't you?'

'I wasn't too young to have my heart broken.'

They walked some more, right to the very end of the Millers' property, where it tangled into silver birches and traveller's joy. The more Elizabeth talked to Lenny, the more she found herself liking him. She had always liked his looks – those kind of hurt, self-deprecating eyes, and that very straight nose, and that cleanly-defined jawline. His face had strength and sensitivity.

'You're not married yet?' he asked her. 'I'm surprised at that. You were always writing those romantic stories.'

Elizabeth blushed and said, 'Well . . . just because a girl is romantic, that doesn't mean that she can always find the right man.' She finished her cigarette, and crushed it out on the ground. 'I dated a couple of guys when I was at high school. John Studland, you remember him?'

'Dark curly hair, tall. Did a terrible Charlie McCarthy impersonation.'

'That's the one. He was nice. He was really nice.'

'Nice?'

'All my boyfriends were nice. I dated a boy in Hartford called Neil Bennett. He was nice, too. He was so nice that I almost married him. He gave me a diamond engagement ring and everything.'

'What was the matter with him?'

'*Too* nice. I like men with a bit of danger.'

'Oh, yes?' laughed Lenny. 'Like who?'

'I don't know,' Elizabeth blushed. 'I haven't met one yet. Well, I've met one or two authors who seem a bit dangerous. Felix Rushmore, the man who wrote *The Tongue Tells No Stories*; and Haldeman Jones, who wrote *Babylon*.'

'And you think they're dangerous, these two guys?'

Elizabeth shrugged. She felt embarrassed. 'They live right on the edge, if you understand what I mean. They experience everything they can, like poverty and violence and the dope culture, and they put it all there on the page.'

Lenny flicked his cigarette butt into the trees. 'I bet they never ran up a beach with a tin hat and an M-1 rifle and Jap machine-guns going *dogguh-dogguh-dogguh* all around them.'

Elizabeth looked at him narrowly. There was something in his face which appealed to her strongly. A woundedness: a vulnerability. 'No,' she said, thrusting her hands into the pockets of her coat. 'I bet they never did that.'

She asked him home for supper and he said okay, sure, he'd love to. She was quite surprised because he had seemed so defensive, at times even mocking. She walked back to the house on her own because she wanted to pay a few visits – first to see Molly Albee's mother and then to Sycamore Street to see Bindy Morris, who used to be a friend of Laura's. She suddenly realized as she walked along Putnam Street that she badly missed Laura – especially here, in the old home town, where they used to be so happy together.

She stopped on the corner of Putnam and Oak. This was where she had first seen the Peggy-girl, on that hot afternoon when Lenny had left for boot camp. She stood there for a while, looking around. Three or four automobiles went past but none of them was driven by anybody she knew.

She was walking back along Oak when she saw a girl in a white dress standing on the stump of the sawn-off oak, about two hundred feet away; simply standing there with her arms by her sides. She had her back turned, but Elizabeth was pretty darn sure who she was. She started to walk quickly towards her, even though she didn't really want to. She had to. She had to find out who this Peggy-girl was, and what she wanted, and why her father was afraid of her.

She walked faster and faster, her heels rapping on the sidewalk. The girl in white remained where she was, not moving, her dress ruffled by the breeze.

'Peggy!' called Elizabeth, as she came nearer. 'Peggy!'

The little girl didn't respond; although a small dog jumped

up at Elizabeth and barked at her and began to trot alongside her.

'Peggy!' Elizabeth called again.

She had almost reached the stump when the little girl turned around. She wasn't smiling and she wasn't serious. She didn't have a face at all. She didn't have a *head* at all, only her empty hair.

Elizabeth stopped and stared, her whole skin-surface prickling with fear. The faceless girl remained where she was.

'What are you?' Elizabeth whispered. 'What do you want? If you were really Peggy, you wouldn't frighten me like this, would you? Or maybe you would. Maybe you think it was *my* fault, that you fell in the pool and drowned? Maybe you've always blamed me?'

The little girl leaned towards her. Elizabeth took one step back, and then another. How could a little girl exist without a face? Sheer cold panic began began to rise up inside her and there was nothing she could do to stop it. This was so irrational, especially here in Sherman, as familiar as her own breath. This was so darn *frightening*.

The small dog looked at her quizzically, and then at the Peggy-girl, and nervously yapped. The Peggy-girl leaned further and further over, until she was leaning at an angle at which nobody could have kept their balance, Elizabeth took two more steps back, and said, 'No, Peggy, please don't. Please don't scare me.'

At that instant, a dry autumnal gust of wind blew across Oak Street. It tossed up gum wrappers and empty cigarette packs and showers of leaves. It blew Elizabeth's hair across her face, and fluffed up the dog. Then it caught the Peggy-girl, and blew her around and over, so that she curled and swooped and then she was nothing more than a swirl of soft white fabric, like a blown-away silk scarf, which flew up into the air, and across the street, fluttering and tumbling. But as a stronger gust of wind caught it, it flew apart into dozens of separate pieces, and Elizabeth realized that they weren't silk, but paper, dozens of sheets of paper. She hesitated at first, but then she hurried across the street and gathered up six or seven of them. They were all thin, barely more than tissue, more like Bible-paper than anything else. They were all blank, too, although one edge was slightly plucked and ragged, as if they had been torn from a book.

Riddles, she thought. *Peggy's asking me riddles.* A girl with no face; a girl who can be blown apart by the wind, into dozens of sheets of blank paper. She's asking me riddles, and yet she's trying to tell me something, too – something which she didn't have time to tell me back at the house. I have the feeling she wants to warn me, besides. All of these appearances seemed to have a pattern, and a concealed meaning, like the signs of a coming storm.

The wind got up even more that evening and by six o'clock it thundered. Edna the nurse gave father his supper and tucked him in for the night. Huge fat raindrops pattered on the windows, and the gardens outside were suddenly tungsten-white and then plunged back into blackness.

Seamus stood by the kitchen window staring out. 'Blue lights every evening,' he remarked.

'That's right, Seamus,' said Elizabeth. 'Blue lights every evening. But how do you *know*?'

Mrs Patrick was buttering the potatoes. 'He talks such babble these days.'

'No,' said Elizabeth, 'I don't think he does.'

'What do you mean?' Mrs Patrick demanded. 'Blue lights every evening, he's always saying that. So where's the sense in that?'

'It comes from a story,' Elizabeth explained. 'It was the Snow Queen, who lived in Finland, and who burned blue lights every evening. It was a fairy tale way of explaining the Aurora Borealis.'

Mrs Patrick looked baffled, so Elizabeth added, 'The Northern Lights. You've heard of the Northern Lights?'

'I've heard of all kinds of things,' said Mrs Patrick. 'That doesn't mean to say that I believe them. I've seen all kinds of things, too.'

Elizabeth said, 'You haven't seen a girl, have you? A little girl, aged about ten, all dressed in white?'

Mrs Patrick looked at Elizabeth seriously. 'There's been enough trouble in this family, don't you think, without imagining more?'

'Well, I suppose.'

'Are you going to visit your mommy tomorrow?' It was obvious that she wanted to change the subject.

Elizabeth nodded.

'Let's pray she recognizes you,' said Mrs Patrick. 'These days she can't always tell the difference between people and furniture.'

'There are quite a few people like that,' she told Mrs Patrick. 'You should meet my boss.'

'He's a harsh man, is he?'

'She's not a man, she's a woman. But, yes, she's harsh. You could use her tongue to sandpaper the floor.'

'Well, you know what I think,' said Mrs Patrick. 'Every act of harshness you commit when you're alive, that's one more birch for your back when you get to Purgatory.'

The doorbell rang and Seamus went to answer it. When he had gone, Mrs Patrick said, 'Don't go troubling the poor boy, will you, asking him questions and suchlike? The things he says, they may sound as if they have some meaning, but they're nothing but moonshine. Goblin conversation, that's what his father used to call it.'

'All right, then,' said Elizabeth. 'But I don't actually agree with you. I believe that Seamus knows very much more than you think. He has a funny way of telling us about it, that's all.'

'Whatever he knows, he can keep it to himself, as far as I'm concerned.'

'You're not frightened, are you?'

'Who said anything about being frightened?'

'When I mentioned the little girl, you definitely didn't look happy.'

'What are you saying, child? I've never seen such a little girl, never.'

'You're sure about that?'

'Are you saying you don't believe me?'

'Of course not, Mrs Patrick. But *I've* seen her. I've seen her as close and as clear as you are now. And if *I've* seen her, I'm surprised that you haven't.'

Mrs Patrick opened her mouth as if she were about to say something, but then she closed it again. At that moment there was a knock at the open kitchen door, and Lenny came in, wearing a smart blue suit and a blue polka-dot necktie.

'Something sure smells appetizing,' he said.

'It's only plain and simple,' said Mrs Patrick.

'You won't catch me complaining,' smiled Lenny. 'I'm a plain and simple kind of guy.'

Mrs Patrick looked at Elizabeth with a heavily meaningful expression. 'I'm pleased about that. Some people have a way of being far too fanciful, don't you think?'

They ate supper in the breakfast-room, because the dining-room was far too chilly and there was no fire. Mrs Patrick served her bean-and-vegetable soup, made with Great Northern beans, followed by roast chicken and apple tart. Lenny had brought a bottle of red wine and they toasted each other's health, and made a wish for better days.

After supper, Elizabeth and Lenny went into the living-room, where they sat on the big worn-out velveteen couch and talked about everything that had happened to them since the war. Seamus came in and stacked more logs on the fire, and the flames sparkled in Elizabeth's wine glass.

'You were at Guadalcanal, weren't you?' asked Elizabeth.

Lenny sipped his wine and looked away. 'I don't talk about it, generally.'

'Was it bad?'

'I try not to think about it. I lost a whole lot of friends. I was totally convinced that I was going to die, and that's a feeling I never want to have again, ever.'

To change the mood Elizabeth found the big brown-leather photograph album, and showed him pictures of herself at High School, on vacation in California, and posing on campus at Hartford.

'I like this one of you crossing your eyes,' Lenny grinned. Then, 'Who's this? That can't be Laura, can it?' He was pointing to a colour photograph of a stunning young blonde girl sitting beside a swimming-pool in a red swimsuit.

'That's Laura all right. That was when she got her first movie part. She played a chambermaid in *Hotel Ritz*. All she had to say was, "Make up your room, sir?" '

'She's grown up real pretty.'

'Let's put it this way, she doesn't lack for boyfriends.'

'Has she been in any more movies?'

'Just little bits and pieces, chorus girls, hatcheck girls, waitresses, dancers, that kind of thing. This year, though, she thinks she's going to get her big break.'

'Well, luck to her,' said Lenny. 'With those looks, she deserves it. And who's this?'

Elizabeth leaned against his shoulder and peered at the photograph he was pointing to. It showed herself in New York, standing on the corner of Central Park South, opposite the Plaza hotel. It was summer and she was wearing a yellow poplin blouse and a white calf-length skirt. Just behind her a young girl was standing – close enough to look as if she might have been asked to appear in the picture, but not so close that she and Elizabeth seemed at all intimate. The girl was very white-faced, and she was dressed all in white. She must have moved when the photograph was taken, because her face was blurred, and her eyes were nothing but two dark smudges.

Elizabeth felt a cold prickling in the palms of her hands. 'I don't know who that is,' she told Lenny. 'Just some girl.'

'But, look,' said Lenny, 'she's in this picture, too.'

He lifted the book so that Elizabeth could see it better. And, sure enough, he was right. The same white-faced girl was standing in the background. She was further away, her face half turned, but it was unquestionably the same girl. The strange thing was, this photograph showed Elizabeth's father, about a month before he suffered his stroke, standing outside the New Milford Savings Bank.

'She sure gets around, this girl, doesn't she?' said Lenny. 'Look, she's in this one, too; and this one; *and* this one.'

The little girl was turning to look at Elizabeth as she stood by her father's De Soto outside the country fairgrounds in Danbury; she was running across the street, her hair flying, as Elizabeth posed outside the florists in the middle of Oak Street; she was standing in the distance with a blurry frown on her face when Elizabeth was sitting on the beach at Hyannis with her college friend Mimi.

'Is this just a coincidence, or what?' laughed Lenny. 'She's everywhere. She's in every single darned picture. In Sherman. In Danbury. In New York. On Cape Cod. She's even here in California, when you went to see Laura. And you're trying to kid me that you don't know who she is?'

'I swear I have no idea. I don't know how she got in all those pictures. I mean, I don't see how she could have done.'

She closed the album and put it down on the polished oak

coffee table. 'I don't understand it. I've looked through those photographs dozens of times, and I've never seen her before.'

She kept staring at the album. She felt like picking it up again, to see if the Peggy-girl was really there, but she had the strongest intuition that she would be, and so she left it where it was.

Lenny said, 'It's impossible. This album starts around 1946, right? If that was the same girl in every picture, how come she never got any older, and how come she was always wearing the same dress? Come on, admit it. It's a trick. It's something you do to tease people.'

'Lenny, I promise you, it isn't a trick, and it isn't a joke.'

He picked up the album and opened it. He looked at the first page and said, 'There – she's not in these pictures, is she?' He turned over the next page, and then the next. He stopped, and pressed his fingertips against his forehead, like a man who has a sudden twinge of migraine.

'What's the matter?' asked Elizabeth.

'She's not in any of these pictures, either. I could have sworn – '

He leafed through page after page, turning them quicker and quicker. Then he sat back and stared at Elizabeth. 'She's gone.'

Elizabeth carefully took the album, laid it on her lap, and looked through every single page. At last she closed it, and stared at Lenny in utter dread. 'It's true, isn't it?' she asked him. 'First of all she was there, and now she's not.'

'There must be some kind of an explanation,' said Lenny. He looked around the room, and up at the chandelier. 'Maybe it was an optical illusion, you know. Reflected light, something like that.'

'You know it wasn't.'

He hunched forward. 'Yeah, I know it wasn't. I'm going nuts, that's what it is. I'm going nuts and you're going nuts. It's sexual deprivation that does it.'

Elizabeth took hold of his hand. 'There's something I have to tell you. I saw that little girl today.'

'You saw her? Where?'

'She was standing in my father's bedroom. I don't know how she got there. I just looked up and there she was. She talked to me. I could hear her, as clearly as I can hear you. She said she was going to protect me. Then she collapsed. Well, not really collapsed, but folded up, *shrivelled* up, and disappeared. Right in front of my eyes, I swear it.'

Lenny eyed her for a long time, and then he said, 'You ever hear of reefers?'

'Of course I've heard of reefers. But I've certainly never smoked one, if that's what you're trying to suggest.'

'Okay, I'm sorry. I'm finding this hard to get to grips with, that's all. Tell me all about this girl.'

'There's nothing much to tell. She appeared, and talked to me, and then she tried to touch father. That's when I got angry, and I tried to grab her arms, but she folded up right in front of me, while I was holding her wrists. In the end, all I was left with was a flower, made out of frost, which melted.'

Lenny was staring at her as if she had just said something in a foreign language. 'You were left with a flower, made of frost?'

Elizabeth, embarrassed, slammed down the album. 'You saw those pictures for yourself! She appears, and then she vanishes, no warning, nothing! I saw her again on Oak Street, after I came around to your house! She was standing on the oak stump, as real as anything except that she didn't have a face. Hair, but no face, as if – I don't know, as if her whole head was made of glass.'

'No face, nothing at all?'

'Nothing. I was scared to death.'

'And that was today?'

'When do you think? That was this afternoon, when I was walking home from seeing you. I saw her, Lenny, she was real.

Solid enough to touch! But she kind of blew away, like sheets of paper, like pages torn out of a book.'

'She was real enough to touch and yet she blew away?'

Elizabeth was infuriated. 'You don't believe me, do you? You think that I've lost my mind, like my mother! You think it's a trick, or a joke, or some kind legpull! Well, if that's what you think it is, Lenny, look into my eyes, because I'm crying for my sisters and I'm crying for my parents and most of all I'm crying for me, and if this is a legpull it isn't a very funny one, is it?'

Lenny quickly seized her hands and said, 'Whoa, come on, Lizzie, don't get so steamed up! I'm sorry, I believe what you're telling me. I really do. Come on, I saw it for myself, I saw the photographs, except that was I sure that I must have been dreaming, or having some kind of an optical illusion. I mean that doesn't happen, right? People appearing in photographs and then they're gone. That doesn't happen.'

Elizabeth picked up the album and held it tight against her breasts. 'This time, it *has* happened. This time, it's real.'

Lenny swallowed. Then, almost reverently, he said, 'I've seen men dying. I've seen the shadow of death pass over their faces. I've seen men talking and laughing when they were shot to pieces and should of been dead, and I've seen men sitting on the ground dead without a single mark on them, as if they just decided to stop being alive. But I never saw anything like this before, and I don't know what to think of it, so what I'm doing is, I'm trying as hard as I can to believe that it isn't true, and that I was tired, and my brain was just kidding me along, or maybe you were.'

'It's real,' said Elizabeth. Then, much more quietly, but no less emphatically. 'It's real.'

'Then what do we do? Laugh it off? Call for a priest, or what? What the hell do you do when something like this happens?'

'I suppose we have to try to work out what it means.'

172

Lenny frowned, and raked back his hair with his fingers. 'You really think it means something?'

'It must do. I think it's Peggy. In fact, I'm sure of it.'

'Peggy? Your little kid sister? The one who drowned?'

Elizabeth nodded. 'I know it doesn't look much like her, but it *feels* so much like her. I don't know how, and I don't know why, but she won't go away. It's almost as if she's looking after us, because she made us so unhappy when she died.'

Lenny took out a pack of Luckies, and offered one to Elizabeth. 'On some of those Pacific islands, you know, they believe that you can go into this hypnotic trance, and talk to your dead relatives. These witch-doctor types even advertise their services on billboards. Come on in and chew the fat with your dead Uncle Frank, or whoever.'

He lit her cigarette, and then his own, and blew out smoke. 'That's in the Solomons, though – Choiseul and Bougainville. You don't expect to talk to your dead relatives in Sherman, Connecticut.'

Elizabeth said, 'I'm worried about her. I'm worried that she's trapped in some sort of terrible betwixt-and-between – you know, not quite living and not quite dead. Souls are supposed to let go, aren't they. They're not supposed to haunt you. I read somewhere that ghosts are the souls of people who can't let go, people who can't quite die, because they've left something unfinished here on earth.'

Lenny sat back. 'What did your sister leave unfinished?'

'Her life, of course.'

'But nothing specific?'

'Not that I can think of.'

Elizabeth turned to him. The firelight was dancing in his eyes, and he looked as sensitive and handsome as she remembered him, from all those years back, when he was all packed up to join the army. 'You believe me, don't you?' she said.

'Sure I believe you. Why would you make up something like that? Besides, I saw the photograph album.'

'Shall we look at it again?' asked Elizabeth.

'Unh-hunh,' said Lenny, quickly shaking his head. He laid his hand on top of the album cover so that she wouldn't open it. 'I don't think we need to, do you? Either she's there, or she's not there. If she's there we'll go crazy; if she's not there, we'll start to doubt what we really saw – what we *know* we saw.'

He paused, and smoked, and then he said, 'One day on Guadalcanal I was sitting outside my tent eating my midday meal when one of my best buddies came and sat down next to me. I swear this is true. Ray Thompson, his name was, tall sad guy from St Louis, Missouri.

'I didn't look at him too closely. On Guadalcanal there were so many flies that you concentrated one hundred per cent on what you were eating. We all developed this kind of flick-bite way of eating, twitching our spoons to shake the flies off, and then quickly swallowing it before they could settle again. That was a stinking place, Guadalcanal, let me tell you. There were spiders as big as your fist and wasps as long as your finger, and tree-leeches, and centipedes that left a rash when they walked over your skin. Most of us caught malaria or dengue, and we all had dysentery.'

'I don't know how you could bear it.'

'I'll tell you how we could bear it, we didn't have the choice. You want some more wine?'

She passed over her glass. 'You were telling me about your friend.'

'That's right. Ray and me sat together and talked about home and girls and this and that. I noticed that Ray wasn't eating but I guessed that he'd eaten already, because General Vandegrift was always complaining that we were too damned thin. Mind you, who wouldn't be, with malaria and dysentery? For no reason at all, Ray says, "When you get back, tell Carole that I've left the money under the driver's seat." I turned around to ask him what he meant, and he was gone. I didn't know where he went. I was pretty sick by then, I could have been hallucinating. But I never saw Ray again; and about two days later somebody told me that he was dead. Not only that, they'd found him in a clump of kunai grass a quarter of a mile away from the camp, about an hour before he came to talk to me. An hour *before*. He talked to me, I swear it, but he was dead.'

'Then it does happen,' said Elizabeth, feeling awed.

'I think so. Something lives after you. I don't know what, or for how long, or why. But I believe it does. I still see men who died on Guadalcanal. I see them driving in automobiles. I see them in supermarkets. No man leaves his loved ones, and the life that he worked so hard for, just because he's dead.'

'What about the money?'

'The money under the car seat? I don't know. I wrote to his wife and told her but she never wrote back. Kind of an unsatisfactory ending, huh?'

At first, Elizabeth found Lenny's talk about his dead friend to be convincing and sympathetic. But after he had finished another glass of wine, and started to tell her that everybody lives after death, and that all of his Marine buddies could still be found, if only he knew where to look for them, she began to think that there was something wrong with him, something irrational. She knew for sure that she had seen Peggy, but how could Lenny believe that all of his dead friends were still walking around. Over 1300 Americans had died on Guadalcanal. Surely they hadn't all returned home, dead, to pick up their lives where they left off?

'If somebody wants something bad enough,' Lenny declared. 'Then, death alone isn't enough to stop him having it, believe me.'

Eleven

Elizabeth went down to the cellar and brought up another bottle of wine.

'Were you really that struck on me?' Lenny asked her, as he poured it out.

Elizabeth laughed. 'You were the love of my life.'

'Maybe I should have paid more attention to you.'

'You were going to war. You were a man. Why should you have paid any attention to a gawky thirteen-year-old girl?'

He sat back and lit another cigarette. 'You weren't gawky. You were cute. I always remember you as cute.'

'I *felt* gawky.'

'Well, you've certainly changed now. I hardly recognized you when I met you at the station.'

'Thank you,' she said, and found herself blushing. She still found it difficult to accept compliments without colouring up.

'Can I ask you something personal?' said Lenny. 'Do you have a steady beau?'

'I have plenty of men friends, if that's what you mean.'

'No, no, I'm talking about somebody steady. The kind of guy who takes you home to meet his parents, and who starts discussing children, and where you're going to send them to college.'

She smiled at him and shook her head. 'No, nobody like that. Not now, anyway. After Haldeman Jones, I dated a writer called Kenwood Priest for a while, and Kenwood kept talking about buying a house in the Finger Lakes region and living the life of a recluse, just the lakes and the trees and the whippoorwills, but that wasn't for me. I spent my whole childhood in Sherman. I want traffic, and people, and police sirens.'

'Kenwood Priest, what did he write?'

'Oh, some thin, sensitive book called *The Lost Young Men*. I'll always remember the last line. "For there is no going forward for us, and no going back, and we must stand on the shoreline of our growing-up, with the seagulls keening overhead, until the surf comes in and overwhelms us at last." '

'Hmm,' said Lenny, swallowing wine. 'Sounds kind of mushy to me.'

They paused in silence for a moment, with the fire crackling and the wind blowing hollow in the chimney, and then they both looked at each other and burst out laughing. It was probably the wine, or tiredness, or the extreme strangeness of what had appeared in the photo album. But they laughed until the tears ran down their cheeks.

'Oh God, stop,' begged Elizabeth. 'My sides hurt.'

But Lenny went on hooting and gasping and clutching himself, until Elizabeth seized hold of his wrists and shook him and said, 'Stop it, Lenny! *Stop it!* You're giving me a stomach ache!'

He stopped laughing and looked up at her. She let go of his wrists, but he lifted his hand and touched her hair, soft and fine and shiny in the firelight.

He didn't say a word, but he lifted his face and kissed her, first on the cheek, then on the lips. Their tongues touched, and spoke in silence more words than either of them had said since they had first met each other again. Both of them kept their eyes open, and looked deep and unfocused into each other's eyes, their lashes still wet and sparkling from laughing.

They kissed, and kissed again. Lenny held Elizabeth tight in his arms, his fingers running slowly down her back. Even through his jacket she could feel how lean and wiry he was. All those months in the Pacific had taken the flesh off him, and he had never put it back on again, even after five years of civilian life. He stroked her hair, he stroked her shoulders. His hand slid around the side of her sweater and cupped her breast.

She pulled away. 'Please – I don't think I'm ready for that yet.'

Lenny smiled, and shrugged. 'That's okay by me. Just following my natural urges.'

'You don't mind?'

He leaned forward and kissed her again. 'Of course I don't mind. It's quite enough excitement for one evening, finding out that the girl I always used to like has grown up into the most attractive woman I ever met.'

Elizabeth blushed again. 'Flatterer.'

'That's not flattery.' He touched her cheek with his fingertips. 'You really are one of the most beautiful women I ever saw.'

'Only one of them?'

He grinned, and gave her one more kiss. 'Listen,' he said, 'I have to be going. I'm taking mom to Hartford tomorrow, and I want to make an early start.'

'It's been good to see you,' said Elizabeth, squeezing his hand.

'How about dinner Saturday night? You'll still be here?'

'I'd love it.'

She found Lenny's coat and he shrugged it on. He stood in the draughty hallway holding her close, holding her right inside his coat, like warm wings wrapped around her. Until she stood so close to him she hadn't realized how tall he was. He smelled of tobacco and musky cologne.

'I know things have been bad for you,' he told her. 'I just want you to know that I'm here to help you out now. Old playmates, huh? You should go through your dad's papers, you know. See what kind of insurance he's got, life insurance, pension, disability insurance. His savings won't last for ever.'

'Thanks, I will.'

'Goodnight, then, sweet Elizabeth,' he said, and they kissed – a long, lingering, exploratory kiss. Elizabeth's hand brushed accidentally against his front and she felt how hard he was, and that feeling was imprinted on her nerves for hours to come, in the same way that a dazzling light is imprinted on the eye. By the time the rear lights of his Frazer had disappeared behind the trees, she knew that she was dangerously infatuated with him. But then, she supposed that she always had been.

She went around the house, damping down the fires and drawing back the dusty velvet drapes. She didn't like coming downstairs in the morning to find the house in darkness. The house was silent and filled with heavy regret. All the house could do now was to wait for Elizabeth's father to be moved to hospital, or to die, and then it would welcome a new family. The days of the Buchanan household were gone for ever: Elizabeth, Laura and Peggy, their giggling echoing in the corridors, their slippers scampering down the stairs.

Elizabeth poked the living-room fire until the last log collapsed deep into the hearth, and set up the fireguard around it. Then she walked through to the kitchen, drew back the gingham curtains, and ran the tap for a glass of cold water to take to bed.

She didn't look out of the window at first, but then the moon suddenly appeared from behind the clouds, almost a full moon, fuzzy and pearly-blue. She was filling her glass, and she dropped it into the sink in fright. Right in the middle of the tennis court stood a small white figure in a coat and beret, a small white lonely figure as still as death.

'Oh, my God,' whispered Elizabeth. 'Oh, my God, no. Don't let it be that.'

Swallowing with fear, she went to the kitchen door and lifted down the old duffel coat that her father always wore when he went out to fetch firewood. She pulled it on, unlocked the door, and stepped out into the frosty night. This time there was no cat to watch her with slitted, disapproving eyes; Ampersand had died three years ago, under the wheels of a furniture truck.

She crossed the lawn in a hurried, uneven lope. The figure hadn't moved. It stood exactly in the centre of the tennis court, facing the house. In the moonlight she could see already that its face was a kind of dirty grey, and that its eyes were smudgy and dark.

She slowed down as she reached the tennis court itself, and she approached the figure with extreme nervousness and caution. Eventually, however, she was near enough to touch it, although she didn't. She didn't have to, because she knew what it was made of.

It was the snow-angel that she and Laura had made for Peggy. It was dressed in Peggy's brown beret and Peggy's red kilt and Peggy's brown tweed coat. It had a misshapen fertilizer sack for a face, and two black holes for eyes, burned with a red-hot poker.

It was the snow-angel, made of snow, even though it hadn't snowed since early April.

Elizabeth stared at it, her breath smoking, her heart beating far too fast. What did this mean? What did all of this mean? Had somebody built it for her, to taunt her? Or had they built it to frighten her father?

Maybe it was nothing more than a strange, random occurrence – one of those supernatural phenomena like faces that appeared in mirrors and empty rooms that filled up with blowflies and voices that sobbed in the night. Maybe it had no rational meaning at all.

All the same, it frightened Elizabeth badly. She felt as if she was being given a warning. Who else knew about the snow-angel, apart from father and mommy, herself and Laura? Nobody. Nobody at all. But father was paralysed, mommy was still in her clinic, only semi-rational most of the time, and Laura was three thousand miles away in California. What was even more bewildering than who might have built it was *how* they had built it. It was unseasonably cold for October, but not cold enough to snow. Yet, inexplicably, here was a snow-angel, just as the pool had frozen over in the middle of June and the Reverend Dick Bracewaite had died of frostbite on a sweltering summer's afternoon.

'The winter did it,' the Peggy-girl had told her, in father's bedroom. But what did that mean? 'The winter did it.' There was no winter anywhere; no trace of winter; not real winter; not yet.

Elizabeth circled around the snow-angel. She could even *smell* the coldness of it. It stared at her mockingly with its charred, lopsided eyes. She stood still, and looked around the gardens. There was a thin, chilly wind blowing, which set the dry leaves rustling across the lawns. More clouds began to run across the moon, and the darkness thickened. Only the snow-angel remained luminous and bright.

Elizabeth was tempted to find a shovel and knock the figure down. But then she thought, no, I'll go get Mrs Patrick out of bed, and I'll ask her to come here and see it for herself. Then at least I'll have a witness, and I'll know for sure that I'm not going completely insane.

She hurried back to the house, went inside, and locked the kitchen door. She left the house by the front door, crossed the driveway, and hurried down the street, turning off at the shingle-graded track that led down to Mrs Patrick's farmhouse. There were no lights down the track and only a single light visible at Green Pond Farm, and almost the only way in which she could tell where she was walking was because of the skinny silver birches which lined the track on either side, each as white and thin as a sudden shriek. Her feet crunched on the shingle. Invisible animals scurried through the undergrowth; sleeping birds stirred.

Three-quarters of the way down the track, she thought she heard another sound – the sound of somebody singing. She stopped and listened, but all she could hear was the wind in the branches and the crackling of dead leaves. She turned back and looked towards the house. It looked very large and dilapidated from here, almost abandoned. She thought of the photograph album with all of those images of the Peggy-girl in it, and she thought for a chilling split second that she could see the Peggy-girl standing beside the front of the house, but then she realized that it was nothing but the white-painted garage door, framed into a shifting, irregular shape by the leafless bushes that grew beside it.

She carried on walking – through the gate and past the pigsties. The Patricks didn't keep pigs any longer, but they still smelled of pig. She went up the steps of the front verandah and pressed the doorbell.

While she waited, she listened to the night. She could hear a train rattling very far away; and the sound of branches creaking. She was sure she could hear someone singing, someone very high and clear. At first she thought it was the Patricks' television, but it had such clarity that it didn't sound like television, and apart from that the words were very strung out, with long silences in between, as if somebody was walking and singing at the same time, and sometimes forgetting to sing.

She almost caught it, but then the front door opened, and the screen door squeaked. It was Dan Philips. Mrs Patrick's younger brother, who mostly ran the farm these days, him and his wife Bridget. His fiery red hair was mostly grey these days, but he was just as ruddy and bulbous as the rest of the family, and he looked just like Mrs Patrick dressed up as a man.

'Why Lizzie Buchanan, is that you?'

'Hallo, Mr Philips. Has Mrs Patrick gone to bed yet?'

'She's not here. Seamus had one of his turns about an hour ago, worst one so far. The doctor came and they've taken him down across to New Milford, so that they can keep their eye on him.'

'Oh, I'm so sorry. He's going to be all right, isn't he?'

Dan Philips shrugged. 'We're all saying our prayers, Lizzie.'

Elizabeth hesitated for a moment, and then she said, 'I know this is a terrible imposition, Mr Philips, but do you think you could spare just five minutes to look at something?'

'I don't know ... I'm supposed to be waiting on the telephone.'

'It won't even take five minutes, I promise you. It's something in the garden, back at the house. It's kind of a phenomenon, and I need a witness.'

'It's a what?'

'A phenomenon. Something really strange. The trouble is, it's not going to last, and I don't think anybody is going to believe me, unless somebody else takes a look at it.'

'I'm sorry, Lizzie, I'm not sure. If my sister calls – '

'It really won't take a moment, Mr Philips. I promise you.'

He gave her an odd, questioning look. 'It wouldn't be a flying saucer, would it? I was reading about them flying saucers in the paper. Some guy from Wyoming got himself kidnapped.'

'Nothing like that. Please.'

He thought hard for a moment. Then he said, 'All right, then. I'll take the phone off the hook so they'll know that I'm still here.'

He went back into the farmhouse and returned a few moments later, shucking on his green raglan overcoat.

'I really appreciate this,' Elizabeth told him, and meant it.

They walked up the track together. The wind had died away, but the temperature had dropped dramatically, two or three degrees below freezing, and they found themselves walking unusually quickly, not because they were pushed for time, but to keep themselves warm. Their breath fumed; and all around them they could hear the soft crackling of hoar frost, as it froze the branches and the fallen leaves.

'Snappy night,' Dan remarked, pushing his hands deep into the pockets of his coat. 'Never knew it so cold as this, this time of year.'

Elizabeth said nothing, but hurried on.

They reached the house, and walked around the darkened conservatory towards the tennis court. The grass was thick with frost now, and they left glittering footprints behind them.

'What is it you want me to see?' asked Dan, puffing.

Elizabeth crossed the tennis court. The snow-angel had gone. She looked around everywhere. She stared at the ground to see if there were any trace of shovel marks, or scattered snow. But there was nothing, only the hard sparkling frost. No snow-angel, no beret, no coat, no kilt. No sacking face with poker-burned holes for eyes.

'It *was* here,' she said, in frustration.

'Maybe if you tell me what I was, I might be able to help you look for it,' Dan suggested.

'I don't think you'd believe me. That was why I wanted you to see it for yourself.'

'Well, if it's gone, I don't see that it makes too much difference.'

Elizabeth peered into the darkness, and gave an involuntary shiver. She felt that there was something concealed in the night, some cold and heartless presence, something that was more than just a white-faced manifestation of her drowned sister. Something that was *huge*.

Dan looked at his wristwatch. 'I'm sorry, Lizzie, I'm going to have to get back.'

'All right, I'll tell you what it was. It was a figure made of snow.'

There was a long pause, and then Dan Philips said, 'We haven't had any snow.'

'That was why I wanted you to see it.'

'When you say "a figure"?'

'It was a little girl, all made out of snow. She wore a beret and a coat and she had a sack for her face.'

Dan slowly surveyed the garden, his hands on his hips, sucking in his lips. Then he said, 'Nope. If it was here before, it surely aint here now.'

He was just about to turn to go when Elizabeth thought she glimpsed a small white shape on the very far side of the garden, underneath the overhanging trees.

'Look,' she said. 'Isn't that somebody there?'

Dan peered at it with his eyes slitted. 'Could be. You want to take a quick look?'

They walked down the sloping garden. It was very dark now, and Elizabeth stumbled twice. The second time Dan caught her elbow, and said, 'Have a care, now. You don't want to go breaking your ankle. Even a phenomenon aint worth that.'

They reached the trees; but the small white shape had vanished, if it had really been here at all.

'I'm sorry to have dragged you all the way up here for nothing,' said Elizabeth. 'I just hope you don't think that I'm going out of my mind.'

'Don't believe that's for me to say, Lizzie,' Dan Philips replied.

He turned to go; but as he turned there was an ear-splitting fusillade of crackling noises from the trees. He said, 'What the hell?' and Elizabeth couldn't stop herself from gasping.

The crackling went on and on. Right in front of their eyes, branch by branch, twig by twig, the oaks turned frosty white. They looked as if they were being sprayed by a firehose on an icy day, building up fantastic lumps and columns and sparkling stalactites. In fact, the temperature had plummeted so low that they were being coated in frozen moisture out of the air.

Soon the trees scarcely looked like trees at all, but extraordinary twisted temples, glistening with cold, with gargoyles and balustrades and spires. Whole branches splintered and came lurching off, overburdened with ice. Trunks split in half. And all the time the temperature dropped and dropped and kept on dropping. The lawns all around them were thickly encrusted with frost, and the grass was so intensely frozen that it snapped when they stepped on it.

'What is it?' Elizabeth screamed. 'Why is it getting so cold?'

'Don't ask me!' Dan shouted back at her. 'But I think it's time you and me beat the retreat!'

They started to run back up the lawn. But they hadn't gone more than six or seven paces when Elizabeth looked back over her shoulder and saw the white-faced Peggy-girl standing just in front of the frozen trees. Both of her arms were raised, as if she were hailing them, or calling them to come back. Elizabeth snatched at Dan's sleeve. Both of them stopped running.

'She's *here*,' said Elizabeth, her voice white with panic.

'That's no snowman,' he protested. 'That's only a girl.'

'I know it is. But they're one and the same.'

'One and same? Lizzie, I'm sure I don't know what the two-toned tonkert you're talking about. But I think your best course of what to do next is to put as much distance between you and this house as you possibly can.'

He started to run again, but Elizabeth didn't follow him. The Peggy-girl was gliding across the grass towards her, leaving no footprints whatsoever. Her hair was rimed with ice, her dress was stiff as frozen washing, her eyes were horrifyingly dark. Elizabeth took one half-staggering step away from her, but she couldn't make her legs work properly. All she could do was stare back at this apparition and pray that it wouldn't touch her.

The Peggy-girl came close, almost close enough to touch. 'You remember the night you made the snow-angel?' she said, although her lips didn't appear to be moving.

'I remember,' said Elizabeth, still aghast.

'That was the night you kept me here for ever.'

'I don't understand. You'll have to tell me what you want. I can't help you if I don't know what you want.'

'You can't help me anyway,' said the Peggy-girl. Elizabeth could scarcely hear her over the crackling and snapping of the trees. They sounded like a rifle-range.

Dan stopped halfway back to the tennis court. 'Lizzie! Who is that, Lizzie? Come on, honey, I think it's best if I get back to Green Pond, and you get back in the house.'

Elizabeth ignored him. She didn't want to turn her back on the Peggy-girl. She had the strongest feeling that if she did, the Peggy-girl would jump onto her back and cling on tight and freeze her to death. She didn't want to die the same way that the Reverend Bracewaite had died.

'Come on, Lizzie!' Dan shouted.

But Elizabeth gave him nothing but a quick backhand wave, indicating that he should wait for a moment. 'I have to know what you're doing,' she said to the Peggy-girl. 'Why are you following me? Why are you here?'

'Don't you want me to be here?'

'Of course I do. But I have to face up to the fact that Peggy's dead. That *you're* dead. I've grieved, I've done my grieving, I've come to terms with it. And now you're here; and everwhere else.'

'I'm here to protect you.'

'I don't need your protection. I don't *want* your protection.'

'Don't you think so?' said the Peggy-girl. 'You don't know what you did.'

'Lizzie!' Dan repeated. 'I really gotta go!'

He came jogging back down the slope. His face was red but his eyelashes were white with frost, and there were icicles hanging from his cap.

'Who's this?' he asked.

Elizabeth said, without taking her eyes off her. 'I call her Peggy.'

Dan looked uncomfortable, but then he took hold of Elizabeth's arm, and tried to pull her away. 'Come on Lizzie, I don't know what's happening here, but you'd be better off out of it.'

The Peggy-girl turned to stare at him with those smudgy eyes of her. 'You mustn't touch her,' she warned him.

'And who's going to stop me, missy?'

The Peggy-girl looked back at Elizabeth. '*You don't know what you did*,' she whispered, almost hissed it.

At that instant, the oaks splintered even more loudly. Dan lifted his head, and frowned, his hand still clutching Elizabeth's wrist. 'Something coming,' he said, in the softest of voices. 'Something very big.'

'Yes, said the Peggy-girl, and her dead-white lips slowly pursed into a humourless, self-satisfied smirk. 'Something very big.'

Even Elizabeth could hear it now: the steady crunching of footsteps through the frozen forest. It could have been a man, or a large predatory animal. Whatever it was, it was approaching them fast, very fast, and its progress through the trees was frighteningly noisy. It was breaking all the ice-petrified branches that stood in its way. Even saplings were cracking in half, and silver birches, and as it neared the treeline Elizabeth could see the branches shaking, and undergrowth exploding in bursts of ice.

'For God's sake what is it?' whispered Dan.

But the second *it* burst out of the trees, a screaming wind started up, with such abruptness that Elizabeth thought at first that it was Dan who had screamed. The whole garden was instantly filled with thick, driving snow, thick whirling flakes of it, and Elizabeth had to raise her hand to protect her face. She saw the Peggy-girl's face for a few moments, with her smudgy eyes and her mean little smile, and then the blizzard whited her out completely. White face, white dress – both were obliterated in seconds by a furious curtain of white.

Dan pulled violently at Elizabeth's sleeve and shouted, 'Come on, let's get out of here!'

She resisted for a moment, trying to see where the Peggy-girl might have gone. She was desperate to find out what it was that the Peggy-girl wanted, why she kept on appearing so persistently.

But then a vast black shape appeared through the snow – so black that it was only visible because of the way in which the snowflakes flew around it. It was black as velvet, black as a casket with the lid closed. Night black: eye-shut black. And it was huge. It towered over them, fourteen or fifteen feet tall, shaped like a woman in a hooded cape, but a cape which was hunched up at the back.

Dan stood staring at it for a moment, his mouth open, his eyes blinking against the blizzard. The shape came closer and closer, and the only sound it made was the felted squeaking of feet on thick snow. The shape brought with it an aura of even more intense cold. Elizabeth saw Dan's eyebrows spangle with ice. His breath turned to dry crystals, and blew out of his nostrils like Christmas glitter. She felt her own hair crackle, and her forehead felt as if she had been pressing it against a cold metal door.

Dan released his grip on her sleeve and started, heavily, to run. Elizabeth tried to run, too, in the opposite direction, but almost at once she caught her foot on the bricks that edged the pathway, and fell onto her knees. She turned around. It was too cold to cry out. Every breath that dropped into her lungs was agony. She saw Dan stumbling back uphill through the knee-deep drifts, and close behind him, the huge black hunched-up shape. Dan didn't turn around. He kept on stumbling through the snow, his head bent in concentration, his arms stiffly swinging to give him balance. He had almost reached the steps that led around the side of the house, but the shape was very close behind him – so close that it momentarily blocked out Elizabeth's view of him.

She couldn't think what it was. Bears could grow as big as this; but bears hadn't been seen in these woods for over a hundred years; and what bear brought its own blizzard with it? It was more like some grotesque kind of pantomime-horse; or the shadow of a pantomime-horse, black as the fabric of the night.

Dan Patrick managed to reach the foot of the steps; but here he stopped. The temperature around him was so low that the bricks in the steps split with a sound like pistol shots, and the rose bushes splintered into shards of desiccated twig. Dan managed to lift one arm. His hand was as white as a statue's hand, and just as rigid. Right in front of his eyes, his fingers cracked off, and dropped into the snow. Then his whole palm split apart, skin and blood and bone all frozen into lumps of human salts. He didn't cry out. His lungs were frozen solid. His coat broke, as stiff as a board, and then his dark blue sweater and his shirt.

The black shape circled around him in a fluid, threatening lope, the snow flying off it in all directions. Elizabeth knelt in the snow and watched in horror as Dan Philips broke into pieces – his ribcage splitting, his stomach dropping out like a big red stone, his lungs crushed into heaps of sugar-pink frost. His skull split with a terrible resonant crack, and his head broke into halves. One half dropped onto the steps and lay in the snow, staring at Elizabeth with one frozen, milk-white eye.

The black shape flowed around the remains of his broken-off stump of a body, which was frozen upright. Around and around it flowed, stirring the snow into whorls and eddies. There was a creaking, straining sound, like a shop window about to shatter. There was a single second of absolute frozen tension. Then the remains of Dan's body exploded into thousands of fragments of ice. All that was left to show that he had been standing there was a few scattered fingers, a divided face, and a mauvish glittering stain on the snow.

Gasping, Elizabeth tried to climb to her feet. She was terrified that the black shape was going to come after her now. She was *sure* it would: it was so cold, so heartless, so predatory. She staggered six or seven steps across the lawns, but she was so cold that she could hardly bend her knees or her elbows, and her lungs felt as if they had been hosed out with seawater. She coughed, and choked, and had to stop, her hand cupped over her mouth. She was sure that she could hear the shape squeaking across the garden towards her, but she didn't want to look behind her to see how near it was. She knew that she was far too cold to get away from it. She was so cold that she almost didn't care.

She heard the air splintering all around her. Oxygen and hydrogen, actually freezing. She felt as if her brain were being clenched. She thought, *God help me.*

It was then that she saw something white moving towards her through the snow. It came closer and closer, and soon it was close enough for her to see that it was the Peggy-girl, in her white summer dress, with thick white burrs of snow clinging to her hair.

'You're quite safe,' she said. 'I said I was here to protect you.'

Elizabeth stared at her, and then wildly turned around. The black shape had vanished, the snowy garden was deserted, and already the blizzard was easing off.

'What *was* that?' she said, her eyes still wide. 'What was it, Peggy? What?'

'Didn't you recognize it?' asked the Peggy-girl.

'What do you mean? It's killed Dan Philips! It's killed him!'

'He shouldn't have interfered, should he? He should have stayed at home.'

'He didn't do anything! He only came to look at the snow-angel.'

'Ah, yes . . .' said the Peggy-girl, wistfully.

'What *was* that?' Elizabeth repeated. Her teeth were chattering so furiously that she could barely speak. 'That shape, that thing in the snow?'

The Peggy-girl closed her eyes, and touched her lips with her fingers. It was a sign, it meant something, but Elizabeth couldn't understand what. She began to limp back towards the house, still shaking with cold, but by the time she let herself in through the front door, the snowstorm had died away, and a much warmer wind was beginning to blow.

Twelve

The first thing she noticed was that all the clocks had stopped. The house was completely silent, except for the occasional lurching of a dying fire. She went upstairs, still wearing her coat, and hurried directly to her father's bedroom. The clock had stopped in here, too, but her father was still breathing. She kissed him on the forehead and he was cold. She would come back up and change him and give him a hot water-bottle; but first she had to call the police.

Sheriff Maxwell Brant arrived fifteen minutes later, with two deputies and a photographer. Almost immediately behind him came an ambulance, its red lights flashing through the trees.

Elizabeth switched on the floodlights that they once used when they played tennis on summer evenings, and Sheriff Brant and his deputies carried powerful flashlights of their own. They approached the steps where Dan had died, their beams flicking from side to side. Elizabeth stayed well back, and said, 'There . . . that's all that's left of him.'

Sheriff Brant was a lean, grandfatherly rail of a man, with short-cropped grey hair and metal-rimmed spectacles and eyes that always looked as if they were focused on the far distance, just over your shoulder. His two deputies were young and callow. One had a wispy brown moustache that looked as if it had taken him a year to grow. The other was spotty, and kept blushing.

The ambulance had brought Dr Ferris from the hospital. He was Seamus Patrick's doctor, too, and he had been attending to Seamus when Elizabeth had raised the alarm.

The Sheriff looked quickly around the garden. All the snow

had melted away, but there was still a smell of chilly dampness in the air, a smell of thawing-out.

'Cold here,' he remarked. Then he walked cautiously forward and examined what was left of Dan Philips.

The right half of Dan's head lay on the third step down, one eye still open. His face had spilt so cleanly in half that it looked as if the rest of it were buried in the brick. The other half, in fact, was lying split-side up in the rose bed, a cross-section of head, complete with reddened sinuses and teeth and a fat purple tongue that was seasoned with compost. There were fingers everywhere, and toes, too, and part of a ribcage. But the rest of Dan was nothing but a glistening, gelid pool, as if somebody had poured three or four bottles of cough syrup onto the grass. The smell of death, however, was just as strong as it always was, when somebody was freshly-killed. Sweet, musky and cloying – the kind of smell that stays in your nostrils for days and which affects everything you taste.

Dr Ferris came up, toting his bag, a cigarette dangling out of the side of his mouth. He hadn't worn the years too well: his face was deeply lined and his hair was stained with nicotine. He looked sicker than some of his patients.

'How's it going, Maxwell?' he asked. He put down his bag and briskly rubbed his hands together. 'Chilly here, isn't it? If I didn't know better I'd say that we're due for some snow.'

Sheriff Brant nodded toward the remains that were lying on the ground. 'Dan Philips, poor bastard. Don't even ask me to guess what happened to him.'

Dr Ferris approached the remains with one eye closed against the smoke from his cigarette and the other suspiciously narrowed. 'Jesus,' he said.

Brant said, 'Maybe it was acid, what do you think? I saw some goop like that before once, back in White Plains, when some realtor strangled his wife and tried to dissolve her body in sulphuric acid.'

'This reminds me of when I was in the service,' put in the spotty deputy. 'We were practising with hand grenades, and one of my pals forgot to let go of his. His belly was nothing but pink paste.'

'Will you please watch what you're saying,' said Brant. 'Miss Buchanan's still here; and I reckon that she's probably had more than enough distress for one night.'

'I'll just go inside if you don't mind,' said Elizabeth. She was feeling trembly and shocked now, and overwhelmed by the strangeness of what had happened. She couldn't stop thinking about that huge dark shape with the snow flying off it, and the crushing crackle of Dan's body falling apart.

'I'll come along with you,' said Brant. 'Ned . . . I'll leave the bits and pieces to you for a while. Carl, take pictures of the whole surrounding area, but tread careful. I don't want any evidence being trampled, the way you trampled over that dog-napping case.'

'Don't worry, Sheriff,' said the photographer. 'You can count on me.'

Sheriff Brant took Elizabeth by the elbow and guided her inside. She took him into the living-room and poked the fire, so that it began to burn up again.

'You want a cup of tea, Sheriff?' she asked him.

'Don't you bother yourself, Miss Buchanan. You've had a pretty serious shock.'

Elizabeth sat down and took out a cigarette. Her hands were shaking so much that Brant had to light it for her. He watched her as she inhaled and blew out smoke.

'Do you think you can tell me what happened?' he asked her, sitting down next to her.

'I don't really know,' she told him. 'We were out in the garden when all of a sudden it turned cold. Bitterly, bitterly cold. It started to snow and Mr Philips and I got separated in

195

the storm. The next thing I knew he was lying there literally in pieces. It was awful.'

'Excuse me, did you say that it started to *snow*?'

She drew on her cigarette, nodded. 'It was really thick. I couldn't see anything at all.'

'Miss Buchanan, we haven't had snow since the middle of March. Apart from that, if there was snow, and if that snow was really thick, like you said it was, where is it now?'

Elizabeth shook her head. She couldn't imagine where it was. She could hardly believe that it had fallen at all. She had wondered if she ought to try to explain to Sheriff Brant about the Peggy-girl, and the black shape that had pursued Dan Philips up the garden, but for some dark, tightly-knotted reason she had decided that it would probably be wiser not to.

Sheriff Brant said, 'Are you all right, Miss Buchanan? You're looking kind of pale.'

'It's just the shock of it, I think. I can't believe it really happened. He just froze – froze solid – and fell to pieces.'

'So you actually witnessed him fall to pieces?'

'One minute he was trying to run, the next he was all broken up. I couldn't see anything. All I could see was poor Mr Philips and all of that snow.'

At that moment, Mrs Patrick came bustling in, still wearing her overcoat. Her nose was red from the cold but otherwise her face was drained of colour. Somebody else came in behind her – Wally Grierson, the previous county sheriff, now retired. He looked like a motheaten old bear these days, big and old and sagging, but his expression was concerned and kindly, and he lifted his hand to Elizabeth in a quick, avuncular wave.

'Oh, Lizzie!' sobbed Mrs Patrick, crossing the room and holding out her arms. 'Oh, Lizzie, what in the Lord's name happened?'

Elizabeth took Mrs Patrick in her arms, and for the first time in her life she found that she was comforting Mrs Patrick, instead of the other way about. It was another moment of coming-of-age; but she would have given up everything she owned to have it any other way.

Wally Grierson was sitting in the kitchen with Sheriff Brant when Elizabeth came in. Mrs Patrick had brewed up coffee, and they were dunking ginger cookies in their mugs.

'How're you feeling?' Wally asked her. 'Pretty darn shaky, I'll bet.'

'Dopey, more than anything. Dr Ferris gave me a tranquillizer.'

'Do you mind if I ask you some questions?'

Elizabeth unhooked a coffee mug from the hutch, and half-filled it with coffee. 'You can if you like. But there isn't much else I can tell you. There was snow, that was all. I don't know where it came from and I don't know where it went.'

Wally sniffed. 'Do you know what Dr Ferris said? He said that for a human body to be so frozen that it actually broke into pieces, it'd have to be chilled down to minus two hundred degrees Centigrade, or more; and, frankly, that's pretty well impossible, out in the garden like that, even in a snowstorm.'

'I can't explain it,' said Elizabeth. 'I can't explain the snow, I can't explain how Mr Philips broke to pieces. I wish I could.'

'Do you know why Sheriff Brant called me over here?' asked Wally. 'He called me over because of what happened to the Reverend Bracewaite, remember that?'

'Of course I remember it. Sure.'

'The Reverend Bracewaite died of frostbite in June. He wasn't so seriously frozen as Dan, not by any means. But what happened to him was just as impossible as what happened here tonight. Intense, unnatural cold, that's what we're talking about. Stranger than fiction, don't you think? But stranger still is the fact that you were the only witness to both of these fatalities.'

'I know. But I don't know why.'

Wally stood up and walked around the kitchen table until he was standing right behind her. 'Lizzie – do you have even half an inkling of what this is all about? If you do, you really ought to share it with me, don't you think?'

She shook her head. She didn't quite feel real. But when it came down to it, what was real? *Stranger than fiction*, Wally had said, and Elizabeth thought of the wind-gusted pages that had scattered across Oak Street – pages of a book that hadn't yet been written, and maybe never would be.

The snow must have been real, the cold must have been real, because Dan Philips was dead and Wally Grierson wanted to know why. She was also beginning to suspect that the Peggy-girl was real. It was true that she was capable of appearing and vanishing whenever she wanted to; and that she could raise up snowstorms. It was true that she could collapse into nothing at all, and appear whenever she wanted to. But she was real. She existed just as surely as Peggy had existed.

Something of Peggy had outlived her drowning. But whatever it was, it was more than little Clothes-Peg. Little Clothes-Peg couldn't have caused a blizzard; or summoned up a dark shape that crumbled Dan into lumps of bloody frost.

Mrs Patrick came back into the kitchen. 'I'll be off now, Lizzie,' she said. 'I won't be in tomorrow if you don't mind but I'll ask Daisy O'Connell to come over for you.'

Elizabeth said, 'I'm so sorry. About Dan.'

Mrs Patrick gave Elizabeth a long, sad, complicated look, as if she were searching her eyes for a mystery. 'Well, you've no need to be sorry. It was a freak of Nature, that's all. The will of God.'

'I don't think so,' said Elizabeth. 'God would never have willed your brother dead; never; not until his time.'

'Maybe his time had come, God bless him.'

Elizabeth stood up and hugged Mrs Patrick tightly. 'Are you

going to the hospital tomorrow? Give my love to Seamus. Tell him I miss him. Tell him we all miss him. Tell him *Eternity*.'

'Eternity?' blinked Mrs Patrick. 'Why should I tell him that?'

'He'll know what it means.'

'Seamus doesn't know what anything means. He's been stricken.'

'Please, Mrs Patrick. He'll know what Eternity means.'

'Very well, then,' said Mrs Patrick. She nodded goodnight to Sheriff Brant, and to Wally Grierson, who nodded his head and said, 'Thank you kindly for the coffee, Katherine. It was appreciated.'

Elizabeth opened the front door for them. The night was crisp and silent, and the moon was low in the sky. As they left, Elizabeth thought: *Katherine*. In all these years I never knew her name was Katherine, and now I do, and all the more vulnerable she looks for it, too.

Wally paused in the hallway, and looked around, and listened.

'Your clocks have stopped,' he remarked.

'I know. All of them did, after the snowstorm.'

Wally approached the long-case clock beside the door. It was father's pride and joy, a Thomas Tompion that he had bought in New Canaan after the success of his *Famous Hauntings of Rural Connecticut*. It was veneered with honey-gloss lacquer that looked almost good enough to lick, like hard-shelled candy.

Wally peered deep into the clock's interior with his head cocked on one side, and then he said, 'Stopped. Stopped at eleven-oh-two precisely.'

He said, 'Pardon me, won't you?' and walked back into the living-room, where a wooden ship's clock stood on the shelf above the fire.

'Stopped!' he called. 'Eleven-oh-three, but that's near enough for me.'

He went through to the kitchen, then the scullery, then the dining-room. Every clock in the entire house had stopped around 11:02.

Back in the hallway, he said to Elizabeth, 'Let me see your watch.'

He took her hand in his hand. His fingers were enormous, compared to hers, swollen and red like sausages. All the same, his touch was infinitely gentle, and when he looked at her watch and raised her eyes, she could see how concerned he was.

'Your watch has stopped, too,' said Wally. 'Exact same time – eleven-oh-two.'

'Why do you think *that* happened?' frowned Elizabeth, shaking her wrist, and then listening to see if the watch was ticking again.

'Some kind of strong magnetic wave, that's what Dr Ferris thinks. The same thing happened when the Reverend Bracewaite died. Even his cutlery was shifted, that's how strong it was – one side of the kitchen drawer to the other.'

Sheriff Brant said, 'Are you finished up, Wally, or what?'

'I'm just coming,' said Wally. He looked down at Elizabeth and said, 'One idea. Give me just one idea. This whole thing has been tormenting me all these years.'

'I don't know,' said Elizabeth. 'I really don't.'

'You said Eternity to Mrs Patrick. What did that mean?'

'It comes from a story, *The Snow Queen*. I used to read it to my sisters when they were small. I guess Seamus must have heard it, too, because he's always quoting bits out of it.'

'Go on,' Wally urged her.

'It can't be relevant,' said Elizabeth. 'Not to what happened to poor Mr Philips.'

'Still, tell me about it.'

'All right, then.' Elizabeth sighed. She was feeling desperately fatigued now, and she could scarcely keep her eyes open. 'It says in the story that the Snow Queen lived in a huge palace, with a hundred halls, some of which were miles and miles long. She spent most of her days sitting in an empty, interminable saloon all made of snow, and in the middle of the empty, interminable saloon all made of snow lay a frozen lake, which was broken into a thousand pieces, like a Chinese puzzle. She called it the Ice-Puzzle of Reason. The Snow Queen had abducted a boy called Kay, and he spent all his time trying to form these pieces into words, but there was only one word which he could never manage to form, and that was Eternity.

'The Snow Queen said, "When you can put that word together, you shall become your own master and I will give you the whole world." '

Sheriff Brant said, 'Come on, Wally. It's almost two.'

But Wally lifted a hand and said, 'Wait, I want to listen to this. Why did you say Eternity to Mrs Patrick?'

'Because if Seamus manages to put back together all of the broken-up pieces in his head, he'll be his own man again, and the whole world will be his.'

Wally thought about that, and then he said, very softly, 'You think he'll understand that?'

'I think so. I was brought up with Seamus. Seamus understands more than most people know.'

Wally said, 'What interests me, Lizzie, is all this talk of snow, all this talk of ice. Look what happened to Dan Philips tonight, and the Reverend Bracewaite. Is this all just coincidence, or are we talking about some kind of connection here . . . I don't know, some kind of missing link between life and stories? What do you think?'

Elizabeth thought of her copy of *The Snow Queen* concealed beneath the garden shed and the guilt that she had felt when she had hidden it. She didn't blush. She was far too tired to blush. But she felt as if an earth-tremor had passed beneath her feet, and temporarily unbalanced her. She felt as if she were very close to understanding what had happened. But she also felt that when she eventually *did* understand it, when the Ice-Puzzle fitted into place, the answer that it gave her would be dreadful beyond belief.

Thirteen

At six-thirty in the morning Elizabeth went into her father's room, knocking before she entered, although she expected no reply. The room was chilly and the light was smudged, as if it had been drawn in pencil and half rubbed-out. Nurse Edna had already woken her father and sponged him and given him a drink. His empty orange-juice bottle stood on the nightstand. Nurse Edna was downstairs now, supervising his breakfast. Cream of Wheat, with molasses stirred in, and two softly baked eggs.

Elizabeth sat on the bed and took hold of his hand. He looked up at her but his eyes said nothing.

'I expect you heard the noise last night,' she told him.

Yes, flicked his eyes.

'Something terrible happened. Mrs Patrick's brother Dan was killed.'

No response.

'The thing was . . . Lenny was here earlier. You remember Lenny Miller?'

Yes.

'Well, he and I were looking through the photograph album. I know this sounds ridiculous but we saw that same girl in every single picture. The girl in white. The Peggy-girl. The girl who was here before.'

Yes. Then *Yes* again, which meant more than yes, it meant *go on, I understand you*.

'After Lenny left, I went around the house, damping the fires and closing the curtains. It was then that I saw the snow-angel. You remember the snow-angel, the one that

203

Laura and I made, after Peggy's funeral?'

She paused, and lowered her head, and stroked the back of her father's hand. 'Well . . . how could you ever forget, after the way that mommy reacted?'

Elizabeth's eyes filled up with tears. She felt so tired and so bewildered and she didn't know what to do. At least her father would listen, whether he believed her or not, because he had no choice but to listen. He was like the wedding guest in *The Ancient Mariner*, thought Elizabeth, the one who 'could not choose but stay'. And her story was just as strange as that of the Ancient Mariner, with just as much ice. 'The ice was here, the ice was there, the ice was all around / It cracked and growled and roared and howled / Like voices in a swound!'

And *The Ancient Mariner* included another chilling parallel to what had happened last night. 'The Nightmare Life-in-Death was she / Who thicks man's blood with cold.'

Elizabeth said, hurriedly, 'The snow-angel last night was made of snow, even though it wasn't snowing, and it was standing in the middle of the tennis court, in the same place where Laura and I made it the first time. I couldn't believe it! I couldn't believe it! I was so frightened. I put on your old coat and I walked down to Green Pond Farm to find Mrs Patrick – I mean, just for her to see it for herself, so that I knew that I wasn't going out of my mind! The trouble was, Mrs Patrick wasn't there. Seamus was taken sick last night, and she was over at New Milford, taking care of him. But her brother said he'd come take a look.'

She paused for a moment, and then she said, in a much quieter voice, 'The snow-angel was gone, but it started to snow. Then this – shape, this black shape came out of the snow. It was more like a place where the snow wasn't, rather than a thing that actually was. I don't know how else to describe it. It was huge, like a huge beast, or a giant woman in a black hood. It chased after Mr Philips, and it froze him. It froze him so hard

204

that he *broke*. I never knew that could happen, but it did. I don't believe it, but I saw it with my own eyes.'

She sat on the bed with tears in her eyes while her father looked at her with nothing on his face but the same vapid snarl. 'I don't know what this all means,' she said. 'I don't know why it's happening, or how.'

Her father swallowed. He started growling deep down in his throat again, and he was clearly trying to say something.

'Oh God, I wish you could talk,' said Elizabeth, squeezing his hand.

'Llllgggrrr,' growled her father, then stopped out of exhaustion and obvious desperation.

'Just a minute,' said Elizabeth. 'Supposing I go through the alphabet, and you move your eyes when I get to the letter you want to tell me?'

Yes.

'I know it'll take for ever, but it's better than nothing.' She started to recite the alphabet, over and over, watching her father's eyes for any sign of a sideways flicker. The first reaction was on the letter L. The second was on I. The third was on B.

When he flicked his eyes at R, she said, 'Library? Is that it? You're trying to tell me there's something in the library? A book?'

Yes.

'What's the name of this book?'

H, U, M, A, N, I, M, A, G, I –

'Human Imagination?'

Yes.

'You think there's something in this book that explains what's happening?'

Yes. T, A, L, K, T, O, A, U, T –

'Talk to the author? I should talk to the author?'

Yes. P, E, G –

'Peggy?'

Yes. I, S, G, E, R, D, A.

Elizabeth frowned. 'I don't understand that. Peggy is Gerda? What does that mean? You're talking about Gerda from *The Snow Queen*, the little girl who tries to save her brother?'

Yes.

'I don't understand. How do you know that Peggy is Gerda? How can she be Gerda? The Snow Queen is only a story.'

A, F, T, E, R, I, F, I, R, S, T, S, A, W, P, E, G, G, Y, I, D, I, D, S, O, M, E, R, E, S, E, A, R, C, H.

'You did some research? Into what? Into ghosts?'

Yes. B, U, T.

'Yes, but what?'

G, H, O, S, T, S, A, R, E, N, O, T, W, H, A, T, Y, O, U, T, H, I, N, K, T, H, E, Y, A, R, E.

'I don't even know what I think they are. Peggy seems to be snow, and paper, and thin air.'

W, H, A, T, M, A, K, E, S, Y, O, U, D, I, F, F, E, R, E, N, T, F, R, O, M, A, N, I –

'What makes me different from animals? My soul, I suppose. People have souls, animals don't.'

I, M, A, G –

'Yes, my imagination makes me different, sure. But surely my imagination is going to die when I do?'

No response.

'You're trying to tell me that my imagination is going to live after I'm dead?'

I, N, A, M, A, N, N, E, R, O, F, S, P, E, A –

Elizabeth slowly shook her head. 'Father, I think I'm going to have to read this book first.'

Yes. T, H, E, N, C, O, M, E, B, A, C, K.

'I'm going to go see mommy today. Is there anything you want me to tell her?'

No response.

'Do you want me to give her your love?'

No response. Then, S, H, E, S, L, O, S, T, L, I, Z, Z, I, E, J, U, S, T, L, I, K, E, M, E.

Elizabeth held her father close and stroked his forehead. He didn't feel like father any more. He felt more like a storefront dummy tucked tightly in a blanket. He smelled of breakfast and sickness.

'I'll give her your love all the same,' she said. Then she sat up and looked at him and said, 'Oh, father. What happened to us?'

She was walking across the hallway to the library when the doorbell chimed. She opened the door to find three men in hats and overcoats standing on the verandah. She recognized one of them as Mack Poliakoff from the *Litchfield Sentinel*.

'Good morning, Miss Buchanan,' he said, lifting his hat. He looked almost exactly like Oliver Hardy, right down to his little clipped moustache. 'We heard you had some trouble here yesterday evening. Wondered if you wouldn't object to talking about it?'

The ruddy-cheeked young man next to him said, 'We don't want to upset you any, but the county sheriff's department sent out a news release, regarding the death of Mr Dan Philips in unusual circumstances.'

'Freak weather conditions,' put in the third man, a tall lugubrious-looking fellow with drawn-in cheeks and eyes like the heads of blue-steel nails.

'I'm sorry,' said Elizabeth. 'I'm very tired and I don't really want to talk about it.'

'We only want to know what you saw,' said Mack Poliakoff, with a fat, encouraging smile. 'Sheriff Brant told us all of the technical details. Pretty unpleasant way to go, from what we understand of it.'

Elizabeth said, 'I'm sorry, I'm still getting over it. Maybe you can call back tomorrow.'

'Oh, come on, now,' said the tall, lugubrious man. 'You claimed there was a snow-blizzard blowing in your backyard yesterday evening, that's what Sheriff Brant told us.'

'There was. That's how Mr Philips froze to death.'

'There was no snow reported anywhere else in the locality,' the man persisted. 'It didn't even snow on Mohawk Mountain. In fact the nearest reported blizzard conditions were in Bottineau, North Dakota.'

'I can only tell you what I saw,' Elizabeth retorted. 'Now, please, I really don't want to discuss it.'

'Just one thing,' put in Mack Poliakoff. 'Sheriff Brant said that you were the sole witness to another freak death by freezing, eight years ago last June. The Reverend Richard Bracewaite, if my memory serves me, at St Michael's church.'

'Yes,' said Elizabeth. 'But I didn't understand how that happened and I don't understand how this happened. I don't have anything more to say.'

The ruddy-cheeked young man said, 'Do you think that *you* could have possibly been the cause or the agent of either of these deaths?'

Elizabeth stared at him. 'What do you mean?'

His ruddy cheeks flushed even ruddier. 'Well . . . there are several recorded cases of people being channels for natural forces. One man in Montana used to get struck by lightning on a regular basis, never harmed him once. And the Hopi Indians believe that certain people have a natural-born ability to draw down rain. Supposing it really did snow here yesterday evening – here in your yard and nowhere else – maybe it snowed because of you.'

Elizabeth said, 'I really don't know. I saw what I saw. I don't have any kind of explanation for it.'

'Is there any snow left? Any trace of it, that we could photograph?'

Elizabeth shook her head. The reporters were making her

feel panicky – almost as if she had killed Dan Philips herself, with malice aforethought. 'You'll have go now,' she told them, and started to close the door.

But Mack Poliakoff nimbly stepped forward and wedged his scuffy Oxford shoe into it. 'Listen,' he said, 'we don't want to make a nuisance of ourselves, but this is a pretty unusual story.'

'Can you tell us how much snow fell?' asked the tall reporter. 'Inch? Two inches? More?'

'Did it cover the whole yard, or just a small area?' asked the ruddy-cheeked reporter.

'How come Dan Philips got froze and you didn't?'

'What was Dan doing there? His nephew was sick in the hospital and he was supposed to be waiting at home for a call from his sister. How come he was wandering around your yard instead?'

'Do you believe any of the witch stories they tell in New Milford?'

'Do you believe in black magic?'

'The Buchanans go back a long way . . . any known witches in the family tree?'

'How long did the snow last?'

'If it was cold enough to freeze Mr Philips, how come it thawed so quick?'

'Do you store any liquid oxygen or liquid nitrogen anywhere at home?'

'How come it snowed as much as that and nobody else noticed but you?'

'Do you mind telling us how old you are?'

'Stand still . . . let me take your picture.'

The three reporters were still pestering Elizabeth when Lenny's car drew up alongside theirs, and he came briskly up the path. He was wearing a smart coat of ginger tweed and a tweed herringbone cap.

'Oh, Lenny!' called Elizabeth.

'Hey you guys, what are you doing here?' Lenny demanded. 'You, fatso, get your foot out of the lady's door.'

'Take it easy, buddy.' said Mack Poliakoff. 'We're asking Miss Buchanan a few pertinent questions for the public interest, that's all.'

'Take a powder,' Lenny told them.

'Listen, friend, we're not doing anybody any harm here, okay? We're simply getting some facts straight.'

'Are you deaf or something? I said scram.'

Mack Poliakoff lifted his camera and took a flash picture of Lenny. Then all three of them retreated back down the path and ostentatiously drove away, spraying up gravel as they did so.

'Creeps,' said Lenny. 'I was hoping I'd get here before they did.'

'You heard what happened?'

'Are you kidding? The whole town heard what happened.'

'It was awful. I can't even begin to tell you how awful it was.'

'Look, you're getting cold out here. How about inviting me in for a cup of coffee?'

Elizabeth nodded. 'I think I could use a cup of coffee myself just about now.'

Lenny was free that day: he was due to meet a dry goods dealer over at Torrington, but the man had the flu and cancelled. Now Lenny offered to drive Elizabeth over to see her mother in the Gaylordsville Clinic, and she gladly accepted. It was one of those dull autumn days with a sky the colour of pale gum, when even the turning maples lose their verve. There was a smell of impending rain in the air.

She told Lenny everything about yesterday evening. As he drove, he glanced at her worriedly from time to time; and when she had finished, he said, 'You're sure you're okay?'

'Oh, fine. Maybe a little woozy, but that's only the tranquillizers.'

'Do you have any idea what you saw?'

Elizabeth slowly shook her head. 'I can't even guess. But in a strange way, this all seems to be connected to *The Snow Queen*. Seamus has been quoting it; father said that Peggy was Gerda; and there's all this ice and snow.'

'*The Snow Queen's* a fairy story.'

'I know. But somehow it's kind of overlapped into our lives. Don't ask me how.'

'It's always been a favourite story of yours, hasn't it?'

'We all used to love it. We read it over and over. It was almost part of our lives. We used to act out the parts; we almost felt that we'd been there; been inside it.'

'There's your explanation, then. Whenever you see ice or snow, it reminds you of *The Snow Queen*.'

'What about Seamus?'

'Seamus is different. Seamus is . . . well, his whole life is a fairy story. The Snow Queen is probably more real to him than you are.'

'Maybe he's right. Maybe she is more real than me. Sometimes it feels that way.'

They reached the Gaylordsville Clinic and Lenny drew into the parking-lot. The clinic was a drab rectangular building set back in the woods that overlooked the Housatonic River. The grounds were deserted, and all Elizabeth could hear as she climbed out of Lenny's car was the chipsping of birds, the stirring of leaves in the mid-morning breeze, and the low conspiratorial chuckling of the river.

The swing doors gave a hollow clonk. Inside, the clinic was plain and functional, with green-painted walls and maroon hessian carpets and framed posters of local beauty spots. Lenny took off his coat and said, 'I'll wait here for you. Take your time.' He sat down in the reception area, picked up a copy of *Life* magazine and took out his cigarettes.

Elizabeth walked along the first-floor corridor to the rear of the building. She had visited her mother frequently enough to know where she could usually find her. She was sitting by herself in the dim, glazed conservatory, a thin haunted figure in a bronze Lloyd Loom chair. Her bony shoulders were covered by a grey woollen shawl; and her face was grey; and so was her dress. She didn't look up as Elizabeth approached her. She didn't look up when Elizabeth took hold of her hand, and kissed the top of her head.

'Mommy? It's Elizabeth.'

She dragged another chair across the tiled floor, and sat down close to her. She tried to smile as brightly as she could, and said, 'Mommy? Look, it's Elizabeth! I've come to see you! I've brought you some of those maple candies you like!'

Her mother stared at her oddly. She was still the same mommy to look at – still pretty in her faded, off-balanced way. But while her leucotomy had relieved her clinical depression, it had taken some vital ingredient out of her personality, something that had always made her *her*. Elizabeth always felt as if she were talking to a carefully coached stand-in, rather than her real mommy.

'Lenny brought me over,' she said, with a smile. 'You remember Lenny Miller? He was married during the war but now he's divorced.'

'War?' asked her mommy. 'Is there another war?'

'No, no, mommy. Same old war. It's been over since 1945.'

'It's only 1943 now.'

'It's 1951.'

Elizabeth's mommy smiled at her archly, and then laughed. 'You always were a dreamer, weren't you, Lizzie? Always making up your stories! 1951! What will you think of next?'

Elizabeth laid a hand on her mommy's knee. 'How are you, mommy? Are they feeding you well? Are you happy?'

Margaret Buchanan nodded. 'I'm fine, sweetheart. True as blue, right as rain. You don't have to worry about me.'

'Naturally I worry about you. I'd come up to see you more often if I wasn't so busy in New York.'

Her mommy flapped one hand dismissively. 'Oh, you don't want to worry about that. Peggy comes to see me every day.'

Elizabeth felt a chilly crawling sensation down her back. '*Peggy* comes to see you?'

'Of course she does, every single day. She's such a sweet child, you know. So thoughtful. So eager to please.'

'When did you see her last?'

'She came yesterday, just after we'd finished lunch. She was talking about you. She said you ought to be careful, you ought to take more care of yourself.'

'You really saw her?'

'Do you think I'm as crazy as the rest of the people they have in here? Goodness me, Lizzie. She sat right where you're sitting now; she brought me hyacinths.'

'Hyacinths? At this time of the year?'

Her mommy looked confused for a moment. She tugged up the sleeve of her dress and started to scratch furiously at her elbow, which was already red-raw with eczema. 'I was sure I *smelled* hyacinths.'

Sitting with her mother in that dim conservatory, listening to the echoes of the clinic, the squeaking of trolley wheels, the coughing, the crying, Elizabeth suddenly remembered what the hyacinths in the garden had said to Gerda in *The Snow Queen*. They had told her the story of the three sisters who disappeared into the woods, and reappeared on biers, floating on the lake, with glow worms reflected in the water. 'Sleep the dancing maidens, or are they dead?'

She also remembered what the answer to the question was.

'The odour from the flowers tells us they are corpses, the evening bells peal out their dirge.'

She looked up. A young dark-haired man was watching her from the far side of the conservatory. He met her gaze for a moment, then turned away.

One of the nurses brought them tea. Elizabeth's mommy talked about New York. She was convinced that Cafe Society was still in full swing, and asked Elizabeth about La Hiff's Tavern and the Colony Restaurant, and who was dancing too close to whom on the postage-stamp floor at El Morocco. It was all still real to her, as if the past fifteen years had never happened: the days of Elsa Maxwell's society parties, where Beatrice Lillie jostled with Averell Harriman and Cornelius Vanderbilt Whitney; where Noël Coward danced with Princess Natalie Paley. Gone now, those days of champagne and tiaras and society column photographs by Marty Black, but still alive in Margaret Buchanan's mind, and keeping her entertained. She was still capable of talking about the house, however, and Laura's career, and she seemed to be aware that Elizabeth's father was paralysed, although she wouldn't mention it directly. Her hypothalamus had been disconnected from her frontal cortex; she was always happy.

Elizabeth smiled and nodded and didn't drink her tea. She thought to herself: is it tragic, to be so happy? Perhaps it is.

A shrill bell rang for lunch and Elizabeth stood up to leave. Her mommy reached out and held her hand, quite tightly. 'Shall I tell little Clothes-Peg that you were here?'

'What?'

'The next time she comes, shall I tell her?'

Elizabeth felt her lungs constricting, as if she were going to suffocate. Panic attack, she thought to herself, stop it. She had seen the Peggy-girl herself, so she must have some reality. What made her feel so frightened was that others had seen her, too, and with each sighting the Peggy-girl took on even more reality, until –

Until the black shape in the snow took on reality, too. The beast, the black-hooded woman. And the thought of that filled her with such terrible fear that she started to shake and tried to tug herself away.

'Lizzie – what's wrong?' asked her mommy.

'I'm tired, that's all, I'm sorry. I haven't been sleeping very well. I feel, I don't know, *jagged.*'

'You need a gentleman friend, that's what you need. You need somebody to take you out; somebody to hoof with. You should try the Kit Kat.'

'Mommy, it's lunchtime. I have to go. Lenny's waiting for me.'

'Lenny? Lenny Titze? Theodore Titze's brother?'

'Lenny Miller, mommy. You remember Lenny Miller. His family live on Putnam Street.'

'Lenny Miller . . .' her mommy mused.

She walked back along the corridor towards the reception area. As she did so, the dark-haired man stepped out of a side-corridor and confronted her. He was broadly built, good-looking in an inexplicably dated way, like a man from a 1920s magazine cover, with slicked-back hair and a casual cotton polo-neck, six o'clock shadow and a smile.

'I saw you talking to your mother,' he said. Warmly, but slightly sly.

Elizabeth stopped, and said, 'Yes?'

'I saw your sister talking to your mother, too.'

'My sister?'

'You do have a sister, don't you?'

'Yes, but she lives in California.'

'I'm talking about a *little* sister. Ten or eleven maybe, always dressed in white?'

Elizabeth stared at him in dread. 'You've seen her too?'

He nodded. 'She comes here almost every day. She comes in, she talks to your mother, she walks away. She's *pretty*.'

Urgently, Elizabeth said, 'I have to go. I have a friend waiting for me.'

'You don't understand.'

'I'm sorry. I think I do understand. But I have to go. Really. I'm late as it is.'

Without taking his hands out of his pockets, the man took a neat step sideways, blocking her off, his loafers scuffing on the carpet. 'Please, wait. You shouldn't do anything rash. Your sister is something different, like me, which is why I ended up here, because I didn't have anywhere else to go. At least I have the company of humans here, even if most of them are mad.'

Elizabeth took two or three deep breaths. 'Excuse me,' she said. 'I've enjoyed talking to you, but I really have to go.'

The man said, 'I'm trying to tell you something, but I'm not making a very good job of it. I'm trying to tell you that your sister is alive, in the same way that I'm alive. I'm not what I seem to be; I'm not really me. I'm what I thought I was. For God's sake, writers make worlds and stir up people's imaginations and then they want them to forget about it? How can you forget about it? George Gershwin wrote music and we were all carried away and then what? Forget it? Forget you ever heard it? Forget it ever excited you?'

Elizabeth stood stock still and frightened. She wanted to hear what the man had to say; but on the other hand she didn't. It was creeping too close to reality; it was closing the gap between what was unthinkable and what was totally terrifying.

The man said, 'I used to believe in the green light, you know? I used to believe in that orgiastic future that year by year recedes ahead of us. We didn't get there today, but that's no matter. Tomorrow we'll run faster, stretch out our arms further . . . And one fine morning – and that's the way we beat on, boats against the current.'

'I'm sorry,' said Elizabeth. 'Will you let me pass?'

'We all have to pass in the end,' smiled the man. 'These days, though, it looks like most people pass alone. When I was younger, it was different. If a friend died, no matter how, I stuck with them to the finish.'

'I wasn't talking about dying,' said Elizabeth.

'Hmh. Nobody ever is.'

Elizabeth waited patiently for him to move out of the way. After a few moments, he did. 'I'm Jay,' he told her, as she passed him by. 'I'm Dave. That's all I have to say. I'm really Jay.' He said it with such earnestness, as if she should have recognized him, or at least pretended to recognize him.

He lifted his hands in mock-surrender. 'There may be hundreds of Jays. Look in any bar. Look in any motel. Trashed, out-of-date, turning up at the same old parties, over and over and over. There are only the pursued, the pursuing, the busy and the tired. We share this world, Elizabeth, with everything we've ever imagined. I mean, let me ask you something: what makes us different from the animals?'

Elizabeth blanched; and shivered.

'Are you trying to say that you're dead?' she wanted to know. There was no other way of asking him.

He stared at her and his eyes glittered. 'What do you think?'

'I think that it takes a dead person to know one.'

Without a word she walked on towards the reception area. She didn't turn around, although she was conscious that the dark-haired man was watching her. Lenny was still sitting crosslegged on one of the chairs smoking, and reading an article about Korea.

Lenny looked up. 'Hey, is everything okay? You look like you've seen a ghost!'

'Please, Lenny,' she said, taking hold of his arm. 'Please take me home.'

*

217

She went up to see her father first. In the grey afternoon light he was looking sickly-yellow, even his eyes were yellowish.

Nurse Edna said, 'I'm worried about his kidneys. I may have to call in the doctor again.'

'Is it serious, do you think?'

'I don't know. His heart's still pumping and his lungs are clear, but if his kidneys fail – '

Elizabeth stood close beside him with her hand over her face because she could smell death.

'Father? How are you feeling? Tell me you're feeling better.'

No response.

'I saw mommy this afternoon. She's not too bad.'

No response.

'She's not too bad, but she's seen Peggy too.'

Yes. And, *Yes*.

'There's something else. I met a man at the clinic. He talked to me.'

No response.

'He said he'd seen the Peggy-girl, visiting mommy. Do you want to know what he looked like?'

Yes.

'He had dark hair, combed straight back. Good-looking but very louche. He said his name was Jay.'

No response.

'You want me to say the alphabet?'

Yes. W, H, A, T, E, L, S, E, D, I, D, H, E, S, A –

'I don't know. He talked in riddles. But he said he saw Peggy talking to mommy, and he said that he was the same as she was. I asked him if he were dead, too, I don't know why. He was talking to me, how could he be dead?'

A, N, Y, T, H, I, N, G, E, L, S, E

'He said that he was always trying to reach the future. If you didn't reach the future today, you could reach it tomorrow, so

218

long as you ran faster and stretched out your arms farther. He said that we're boats against the tide.'

H, E, W, A, S, D, E, A, D.

'You really think so?'

Yes. Then *Yes*. Then *Yes* again.

He closed his eyes, and although Elizabeth waited and waited, he didn't open them again. He must be exhausted. Elizabeth stayed beside him for a while, and then kissed him and stood up. Outside in the garden, under the tarnished tureen-lid of the sky, the Peggy-girl was standing beside the tennis court, looking up at her. Elizabeth made no attempt to go closer to the window, and after a while the Peggy-girl glided away into the bracken.

Elizabeth was still staring out of the window when Lenny knocked softly on the door.

'Are you okay?' he asked her. 'How's the old man?'

'I don't think either of us are very well,' she replied, without turning around.

'I'm sorry.' He came up to her and laid his hand on her shoulder. She reached up and patted it.

'Do you believe that it's possible for imaginary people to come to life?' she asked him.

'When you say "imaginary people" . . . ?'

'I mean characters out of stories.'

Lenny shrugged. 'I don't see how that could be.'

'Father seems to believe it. He thinks that the little Peggy-girl is Gerda out of *The Snow Queen*. He seems to think that dead people can come alive again, as characters out of books.'

'Oh, come on now, Lizzie, he's rambling. He was always interested in ghosts and haunted houses and witch trials, wasn't he? He's rambling; it's gone to his head.'

'I guess so. But what about the snowstorm? What about the photograph album? What about the Reverend Bracewaite and poor Dan Philips?'

'Maybe that newspaper reporter was right. Maybe you have some sort of unusual talent for attracting blizzards.'

'Oh, that was nonsense! And besides, I wasn't there when the Reverend Bracewaite was frozen.'

Lenny pinched the bridge of his nose. 'I don't know, Lizzie, I've been turning it over and over in my mind, trying to explain it. I think there *is* something here, but I think it's more than likely to be Peggy's aura. Do you know what I mean? Because Peggy was so young and so lively, she left something of herself in the house, and that's what you and I have been experiencing. You're her sister, so you're much more sensitive to it than I am. You may even be acting like a receiver . . . you know, sort of a human television, picking up the thoughts and the feelings that Peggy left behind. Maybe I'm a little bit sensitive, too. Look at what happened to me on Guadalcanal.'

Elizabeth turned to look at him. He shrugged again and pulled a face. 'I read about it in *Reader's Digest*, Loved Ones Who Speak From Beyond.'

'Well . . . maybe you're right,' said Elizabeth. 'It certainly seems to make more sense than storybook characters coming to life.'

They were still standing silently together when Elizabeth's father let out a thick rattling sound. Elizabeth immediately crossed to the bed and leaned over him. He didn't seem to be breathing, and she couldn't feel a pulse.

'Call Nurse Edna!' she said. 'Quick, Lenny – call Nurse Edna!'

She turned back to her father and held his hand between hers. She knew already that there was nothing that she could do, that he was dead.

'Oh, father,' she whispered. 'I love you so much. Don't forget me, wherever you're going. And please tell Peggy that she can rest now; that everything's fine.'

A huge wave of grief overwhelmed her, and she sat down on

the bed with tears running freely down her cheeks, rubbing her father's hands, over and over, as if she could warm them.

4

Cold Sun

'I do but tell you my tale – my dream.'

Fourteen

Laura climbed out of Petey Fairbrother's bright yellow Jeepster and slammed the door. 'Bysie-bye, Petey – thanks for the ride!'

Petey grinned at her, one eye squinched up against the sun. 'How about later? Some of the gang are going over to Dolores's Drive-In for hamburgers and shakes.'

'I don't know. It depends. Aunt Beverley has guests tonight. I think she wants me to stick around and socialize.'

'Laura, you know that I can't live without you!'

'How come? You managed it before you met me.'

'Sure, but I forgot.'

She leaned over the side of the car and kissed him on the nose. 'You keep on breathing, you eat three times a day, you don't forget to drink your orange juice, and you don't forget to fall asleep at night.'

'That's living?'

She kissed him again. 'That's better than being dead.'

She walked up the concrete path. She was one of the dishiest girls in college. With her curly blonde hair and her broderie anglaise blouse and her pink-and-green striped dirndl skirt she was the epitome of teen chic. On her first day at college, the seniors had collectively voted her Miss Heavy Breathing 1951. She had been dated every weekend – although Petey Fairbrother had always been her favourite. Apart from being very tall and athletic, with a sun-bleached crewcut as flat as the deck of the USS *Missouri*, his father was Jack Fairbrother the movie director, and he had been able to take Laura on the sets of six or seven new movies.

Laura went up the two concrete steps to the front door and opened it. Inside, she could hear Aunt Beverley talking loudly, and smell cigar-smoke. She dropped her bag in the hallway and peered at herself in the mirror. She thought she was putting on weight. The strawberry malteds were beginning to take their toll. She blew out her cheeks so that she looked even fatter. God, what a podge. She placed her hand on her heart and swore to God that she would cut out milkshakes for ever, or at least a week.

They had moved twice since Laura had first come to California. After two landslips, the house overlooking Santa Monica Bay had needed shoring-up with reinforced-concrete foundations, and a whole new deck. Aunt Beverley had decided to cut her losses, 'screw the view', and bought a house in Westwood. But only seven months later, when they were barely unpacked from the first move, a friend had sold her his two-bedroom bungalow on Franklin Avenue, within spitting distance of Hollywood Boulevard. It was much smaller than the Santa Monica house, and less secluded than the West-wood house, but it had large, airy, whitewashed rooms, and a cramped courtyard tiled in aquamarine and yellow ochre, and a riot of flowers and tropical plants. Laura missed the ocean, but she liked the location better, because most of her friends lived much closer, and she could hang out at Schwab's and the Hamburger Hamlet where all the movie hopefuls congregated.

Laura found Aunt Beverley sitting outside in the greenish glow of her fringed sunshade, wearing a fuchsia romper suit and a crimson headscarf and sunglasses. She was drinking aquavit and pineapple juice, and smoking a cigarette. Opposite her, smoking a cigar, sat a leonine grey-haired man in a custard sports coat and white yachting slacks. He was handsome, in an ancient kind of way, like a stone head of Alexander the Great.

'Oh, Laura, you're back,' Aunt Beverley enthused. 'Chester, this is Laura. Laura, this is Chester Fell.'

'Oh, hi,' smiled Laura, holding out her hand. 'I've heard of you.'

Chester gave her a deep, warm, self-satisfied smile. 'Good to know that I'm not a nonentity,' he replied.

'Chester's casting for his new picture,' said Aunt Beverley. 'He's been looking for *fresh new talent*.'

'I see,' said Laura. She sat on one of the gaudy sun-chairs, spreading out her skirt. She picked up a handful of salted almonds from the dish on the table, and began to nibble them in a picky, affected way, keeping her eyelashes lowered. She knew that Chester was looking at her, and sizing her up, and she liked the power of ignoring him. A California quail fluttered down and perched on the trellis, and watched her eating.

Chester glanced up at it, and said, 'You like an audience, don't you?' His voice was deep and rumbly, like distant thunder.

Laura said, 'I like to act.'

'I saw you in *Shanghai Ritz*, playing the cocktail waitress.'

'Yes,' smiled Laura, still without looking at him. 'I had two lines in that. "Sir wants an olive?" and "Don't you dare touch me." '

'I remember,' said Chester. 'You were excellent. Fresh and innocent, without being clumsy.'

'That's not what the reviews said about me,' Laura remarked.

'What *did* the reviews say about you?'

'They didn't say anything. I was never mentioned.'

Chester laughed. A humourless ha-ha-ha. He brushed cigar ash off his slacks, and then he looked at Laura very seriously. 'You have the right kind of face for the movies, did you know that? The cameras go for exaggerated eyes, short straight noses, distinctive jaws. You ought to see most of our so-called stars when they come off set. They're the weirdest-looking bunch of people you ever saw in your life. But put them in front of a camera, and – they're magic.'

'You're not saying *I* look weird, are you?' asked Laura. She was conscious of Aunt Beverley making her 'shush, don't make a fuss' face, but she was sure that Chester wouldn't be upset. Men were never upset with her, except when she refused to kiss them or go to bed with them or see them tomorrow. She was always in control, and she never forgot it.

'Of course you don't look weird,' Chester flustered. 'All you look is pretty and young and fresh as a daisy.'

'She's such a darn tease,' said Aunt Beverley, through clenched teeth. She clenched her teeth so often that it was amazing that she hadn't bitten her way through hundreds of cigarette holders, instead of two or three.

Chester leaned back in his chair, with his glass in his hand. 'There's no doubt about it, Beverley, this girl has screen potential. Maybe a great screen potential. She's going to need some grooming, of course. Hair, make-up, that kind of thing. But, yes, I see the possibilities.'

'What movie are you casting for?' asked Laura.

'The working title is *Devil's Elbow*. It's an automobile-racing drama. A handsome hero, a dastardly villain, a gorgeous moll. In fact, bushels of gorgeous molls.'

'And what would I be, if you gave me a part? Gorgeous Moll number 386, there on the left?'

'Laura!' snapped Aunt Beverley.

But Chester simply smiled. 'Come on, Beverley, she has a right to ask. This is her career, after a while. You wouldn't let some total stranger interfere with your life, would you, even if you *were* young and beautiful?'

'Chester!' snapped Aunt Beverley.

Laura turned around and grinned at Chester and Chester

winked back. 'I'll tell you what I'll do,' he said, without taking his eyes off Laura. 'Why doesn't Laura play hookey tomorrow morning and come over to the Fox lot for a camera test? Yes? It would only take an hour, and who knows? It could be the start of something really big.'

'I'm not sure,' said Laura. 'I don't really like to miss class.'

'What are you studying?' asked Chester.

'English literature, drama and economics.'

'Egghead, hunh?'

'I want to be a screenwriter, as well as an actress. My father was a publisher, my mother was in musicals with Monty Woolley.'

'Quite a heritage,' said Chester. 'Still, it's up to you. You want to come over tomorrow morning, ask for me, and we'll see what we can do. Maybe we can have lunch, too.'

'Go on,' Aunt Beverley urged her. 'You can read Shakespeare any time.'

'You're studying Shakespeare?' said Chester. 'I hate Shakespeare. I always hated Shakespeare, all those prithees and by the roods, who talks like that? Shall I tell you who I admire? Tennessee Williams, that's who I admire.'

He stood up, and flung out his arm, and affected an extraordinary high-pitched voice. 'I don't want realism! I want magic! Yes, yes, magic! I try to give that to people. I misrepresent things to them. I don't tell them the truth. I tell what ought to be the truth. And if that is sinful, let me be damned for it!'

Laura laughed and clapped. 'Blanche DuBois! Brilliant!'

Chester sat down again, and lifted his glass of aquavit, and gave them a toast. 'Here's to American drama, stage or screen, the tormented people who write it, the harassed people who produce it, and the beautiful people who act in it!'

'Hear, hear!' said Aunt Beverley; but not because she cared a hoot about drama, American, English or Icelandic. Aunt

Beverley cared about only one thing: that Laura should like Chester, or at least not find him repulsive. Aunt Beverley hadn't survived in Hollywood for thirty years by being scrupulously moral. Aunt Beverley had survived by fixing and arranging all the shady and tempting things that newly-wealthy men and women felt the urge to indulge in, and by being all things to all people. When she was young, she had been able to provide many of the forbidden pleasures that Hollywood luminaries wanted in person, and sometimes she still could. The silent movie actress Ida Marina had always called her La Linga Buena (The Beautiful Tongue). Jimmy Dean slyly called her Torquemada. Nobody knew exactly what Aunt Beverley had done for him, but they could guess.

Chester said, 'Let me tell you something, the American theatre is light-years ahead of the rest of the world, and I'm talking serious literature here. It's real, it's gutsy. *Death Of A Salesman*, *The Glass Menagerie*, brilliant. Now the American motion picture industry is going to do the same.'

'This *Devil's Elbow* movie you're producing, is this serious literature too?'

Chester was caught off-balance. He blinked at Laura, and then he said, 'Not exactly. It's real, it's gutsy, but, yes, it does have quite a high commercial content. In other words, I want realism, yes, but I also want the accounts to be showing a profit, at the end of the day, so that I can make something *really* serious.'

Laura looked at him gravely for a moment, and then burst into giggles. Aunt Beverley said, 'Laura, for God's sake! Have some manners!'

'No, no,' grinned Chester. 'I like a girl with a sense of humour. I like that. More than anything else, I like a *pretty* girl with a sense of humour.'

'You are a flatterer,' said Laura, although she didn't blush.

Chester's grin became more secretive, more calculating.

'Yes,' was all he said, but his tone of voice said very much more.

'Well . . .' said Laura, airily. 'I guess it's only revision tomorrow. *Othello*. "She gave me for my pains a world of sighs, 'twas strange, 'twas passing strange, 'twas pitiful, 'twas wond'rous pitiful." '

'There – what was I saying?' Chester interrupted. 'Who says " 'twas"? Who goes around saying " 'twas"?'

Laura giggled again. Aunt Beverley could see that she quite enjoyed Chester's bluster. It gave her a sense of power. 'This could be quite a break for you, sugarpie,' she said, with smoke pouring out of her nostrils like twin volcanoes.

Laura threw a nut up into the air and caught it in her mouth. 'All right, then,' she said. 'What time do you want me tomorrow?'

At three o'clock in the morning, she was woken up by the sound of whispering. Her bedroom was on the right-hand side of the courtyard, underneath the clay-shingled verandah. She was used to the night breeze rustling through the bougainvillea, and rattling the yuccas, but this whispering was different. This was a young girl's voice – low, earnest and intense.

Laura sat up in bed and listened. The night was unusually cool, even for October, and she shivered. The breeze made her shutter-catches tap, and tap, and tap again, as if somebody were surreptitiously trying to open them. She strained her ears, and she could still distinctly hear the whispering, but it was too soft and too far away for her to be able to make out any words.

She eased herself out of bed. All she was wearing was a large white Hathaway shirt which she had begged from Petey Fairbrother. She padded over to the window and adjusted the slats of her shutters so that she could see outside. The courtyard glistened in cloud-reflected moonlight, but there was nobody there. Aunt Beverley's chair was tilted back against the wall, just as she had left it. The fringes of the sunshade ruffled and danced. The bowl of nuts was empty, with fragments of shell all around it: as soon as they had gone inside, the quail had fluttered down to finish them off.

Still the whispering went on. It sounded worried, somehow – almost hysterical. Laura tried listening again, but there was too much background noise. There wasn't much traffic passing through Hollywood at this time of night, but the occasional swish of a distant automobile was almost enough to drown out the whispering altogether.

Laura unfastened one of the door-catches, and swung the door open. It was then that she saw a young girl standing on the opposite side of the courtyard, white as death, with dark-smudged eyes. She bit her knuckle in fright, and stood staring at the little girl, unable to speak, unable to move, but trembling from head to foot as if she were being electrocuted.

Elizabeth had mentioned seeing 'a kind of a ghost of a little girl' in several of her letters – 'a ghost that doesn't look at all like Peggy, but must be Peggy.' Laura, however, had seen nothing of the Peggy-girl since she had first arrived in California – only that vague apparition behind the net curtains, the apparition that had frozen Mr Bunzum. She had begun to think that she must have been dreaming, and that Elizabeth was making up stories, as usual. When she was younger, it had been horses; now she was older, it was ghosts. Yet here she was, the Peggy-girl, as white as Elizabeth had described her, beautiful, sad and chilling to look at. And she was whispering, over and over again, the same anxious litany.

'*Oh! I have left my boots behind! Oh! I have left my gloves behind!*'

Laura slowly lowered her fist from her mouth. She had bitten four teeth-marks deep into her knuckle. She took an awkward, shuffling step forward, then another. She felt the cold smoothness of the glazed tiles beneath her bare feet. ' – *boots behind* – ' whispered the little girl. ' – *gloves behind* – '

'What do you – ?' Laura began, but half-choked on her own saliva. 'What do you want?'

The little girl stared at her with such a dreadful face that Laura could hardly bring herself to step any nearer. It was a face that understood the meaning of death; a face that had lived in Purgatory. It was white with misery; white with horror; white on white on white like layer upon layer of chalk and whitewash.

As Laura went closer, she felt a sparkly coldness in the air, and the breeze started to feel as if it were blowing off a field of snow. 'Peggy?' asked Laura. 'Peggy, is that you? If it is, please tell me. I'm frightened.'

'*Oh! I have left my –* '

'Peggy, what do you want? What are you doing here? Can't you rest?'

'*– gloves behind –* '

Laura took one more step forward and the Peggy-girl wasn't there any more. She had simply vanished, disassembled, as if she had never been there. But Laura could still hear her whispering, and still feel that sharp-sided coldness in the wind.

'Peggy, are you there?' she called her. 'Peggy, where have you gone?'

She took one step back, and the Peggy-girl reappeared, as if the moonlight had altered its shape, like Japanese paper-folding. Laura felt a shiver of bewilderment. She stepped forward again, and the Peggy-girl vanished again; she stepped back, and she reappeared.

It was only then that she realized what she was actually seeing. There was no Peggy-girl standing in the courtyard, either real or ghostly. Her outline was formed by the shadow of the overhanging bougainvillea, falling on the whitewashed wall. Her eyes were two dark smudges of soot, where oil lamps had been hung on the wall during a summer cookout. Her dress and her legs were nothing more than the spiky leaves of a fan-palm in a terracotta pot.

One step back, though, Laura could see her as clearly as if she were actually standing there, with her arms by her sides and that terrible expression on her face. And she could still hear her whispering.

She stepped forward, with one hand held out in front of her. She felt nothing, except the chilly breeze. She took another step, and then another, even when the Peggy-girl was no longer visible.

'Are you there?' she breathed. 'Are you really there?'

' – *boots behind* – '

She reached further and further, until she was almost touching the wall. The cold was almost unbearable. Her breath was vaporizing and frost was forming underneath her nostrils.

'Peggy!' she begged. 'Show me where you are!'

At that instant, the terracotta pot cracked sharply and the two halves fell apart, see-sawing on the tiles. The fan-palm fell sideways, and shattered on the ground as if it were made of emerald-green glass. Laura stepped back in shock – one step, then another. Her lower lip was juddering with cold and her toes were so cold that she could hardly feel them.

Aunt Beverley appeared, wearing a hairnet and men's pyjamas and carrying a heavy-duty flashlight.

'What the hell's going on? I thought you were burglars.'

'I'm sorry, Aunt Beverley. I woke up. I thought I heard something. I – '

'Oh, my planter!' said Aunt Beverley, in exaggerated distress. 'You've broken my beautiful, beautiful planter.'

'I didn't touch it, Aunt Beverley, it broke by itself. It just snapped in half.'

'Planters don't just break by themselves. Oh, look at it! Nick Ray bought that for me, in Tijuana!'

Laura was shivering. 'I'm sorry, Aunt Beverley. It was an accident, really. I'll b-buy you another one.'

Aunt Beverley shone the flashlight in her eyes. 'Why, look at you! You're freezing! Get back into bed, I'll warm up some milk!'

She put her arm round Laura and led her back to bed. 'I don't know why you're so *cold*,' she said. 'I hope you're not sickening for something.'

'I'm fine, I'll be fine, so soon as I get myself warm.'

Laura climbed into bed and pulled the blankets over herself and lay curled-up and quaking with cold. Aunt Beverley switched on the bedside lamp and sat beside her. 'Are you sure you're all right?' she asked. 'It wouldn't do to miss that camera test tomorrow. Or today, I should say.'

'I'm sure. I'm sure. Don't worry, I'll be fine.'

She clutched herself and kept on shivering, and thought of the Peggy-girl standing in the courtyard, as real as anything she had ever seen, yet not there at all. An illusion, a mirage, a combination of plant and wall and shadow. Not even a ghost, but an absence of ghost.

Aunt Beverley stroked her shoulder. The stroking was light, monotonous, but strangely reassuring. 'Are you feeling warmer, sugarpie?' she said. 'I'll heat that milk for you now. What did you think you heard? I don't think anybody can climb into the back of the house, to tell you the truth. The walls are too high and there's all of those thorn bushes and prickly pear.'

'I thought I heard somebody whispering, that's all. It must have been the wind.'

Aunt Beverley stroked her shoulder a little more and then stopped stroking. 'You're tense. You're worried about something. What is it?'

Laura said nothing but stared through the triangular space between her pillow and the blanket. All she could see was the side of her bleached-oak nightstand, with its whorls and its knots. She was sure that two of the darker knots were eyes; and that the grainy whorls around it formed the shape of a face. A little girl's face, a Peggy-girl. A girl who was watching her, whatever she did, wherever she went. Protective, but scary.

Aunt Beverley said. 'When you say you heard whispering . . . did you hear what it was they were saying?'

Laura didn't answer for a very long time; but Aunt Beverley stayed where she was, patiently waiting, and it was then that Laura first began to understand that her Aunt wasn't just a mannish, chain-smoking, hard-drinking Hollywood procuress; she was also a woman of considerable acumen and sympathy; a woman who was sensitive to every kind of human weakness.

'I thought it was Peggy,' said Laura at last; and a tear slid out of her eye and dripped across the bridge of her nose. 'I thought she was trying to tell me that she had left her boots behind, and left her gloves behind.'

An even longer pause. Then Aunt Beverley said, 'Why should she tell you that?'

'Gerda says it, in *The Snow Queen*. She visits the Finland woman, and it's so hot in the Finland woman's house that she takes off her boots and her gloves, and leaves them behind, by accident.'

'Peggy used to like that story?'

'She loved it. But she always got worried when Gerda left her boots and her gloves behind.'

'And that's what she was whispering to you, outside?'

Laura nodded.

Aunt Beverley stroked her shoulder for a while. Then she got up off the bed and went through to the kitchen. She filled a saucepan with milk, and put it on the hob to warm, and walked into the sitting-room to find her cigarettes. She had grown to think of Laura as her own daughter, almost. She knew that Laura was happy here, in Hollywood. It suited Laura's extravert personality, and her need to feel wanted, and important. Laura had always suffered from middle-child-itis: with a talented and serious-minded older sister and a younger sister who had always captivated everybody who saw her. Ever since Peggy was born, Laura had been unshakeably convinced that she was hard done by – that Elizabeth and Peggy were better respected, better treated and better loved. That was why she had sought the attentions of men, no matter who they were, no matter what they wanted her to do.

Aunt Beverley was one of five and knew what sibling jealousy was all about. She had done everything she could to restore Laura's pride in herself. Aunt Beverley's own father had abused her, and she knew how important it was to have pride. One night, when she was twelve years old, her father had crept naked into her room at night, sat astride her pillow, and forced his whole erection down her throat, right down to his crunchy pubic hair. After that, it had taken Aunt Beverley years of self-bullying and semi-suicidal behaviour to regain her self-esteem. She had started chain-smoking only to fumigate her mouth. If she closed her eyes and thought about it, she could taste her father, even today.

She could only touch men if they asked her to punish them; and then she gladly did.

She lit a cigarette and smoked a quarter of it before she crushed it out. As she did so, she thought she heard somebody in the kitchen. 'Laura?' she called. 'You shouldn't be out of bed. Get yourself warm, for goodness' sake.'

She walked towards the kitchen door. A fleeting white reflection crossed the hallway; but it was only a reflection. 'Laura?' said Aunt Beverley. 'Is that you, Laura?'

The kitchen was deserted. Only the green-topped Formica table, with its neatly-arranged salt-and-pepper pots, its A-1 bottle, and its pear-shaped vase of freesias. Only the electric clock, chirring quietly on the wall. Only the gas flaring under the milk.

She frowned. She had a sense that somebody had been here, she didn't know why. She switched off the gas, and carried the milkpan over to the table. She tilted it to pour the milk into the mugs, but the surface of the milk tilted, too, and it wouldn't come out. The pan was blazing hot. The milk should almost have boiled by now. But when she prodded the surface with her finger, she realized why it wouldn't pour out.

The milk was frozen solid, its surface sparkling with ice-crystals.

Aunt Beverley returned the pan to the hob and stood staring at it. The milk was frozen. She had poured it out of the bottle into the pan and lit the gas underneath it, and it was frozen.

She sat down at the kitchen table, took out another cigarette and smoked it until it nearly burned her lips. Afterwards, she went through to Laura's bedroom to tell her about the milk, but Laura was fast asleep, her blankets thrown aside, her Hathaway shirt ridden up so that her bottom was bare. Aunt Beverley stood and looked at her and thought that she was beautiful. She never would have dreamed of touching her, ever. Laura was family; Laura was practically hers. But she loved her, all the same; and she wondered what it was that had disturbed her tonight, because it was chilly and unfamiliar, and it had made its presence felt in every room.

Laura stirred, and clutched at her pillow. Aunt Beverley watched her for almost ten minutes, but as the room darkened before the dawn, she turned and went back to her own bed, where she lay sleepless for over two hours, occasionally smoking, thinking about bad times and happy times, and whether she was right to take Laura down to Fox tomorrow.

She didn't look out of the window, or she would have seen the way in which the bougainvillea threw its shadow on the whitewashed wall; and the way the oil-lamp smudges seemed to stare towards her bedroom like brooding eyes.

She would have seen what looked like a rat, at first, or a small raccoon, lying dead among the jasmine. The Mexican cleaning woman would pick it up tomorrow morning, before Aunt Beverley woke up, and she would throw it in the trash. After all, what did anybody in Hollywood need with a small-sized, dried-up, fox-fur glove?

Aunt Beverley drove Laura to Fox herself; in the powder-blue Chevrolet Styleline she was borrowing on a 'semi-permanent' basis from Max Arnow, the casting director at Columbia. Only God and Max Arnow knew what favours Aunt Beverley had provided in return. Laura had woken up tired, with swollen eyes, and so Aunt Beverley had splashed her eyes with ice-water, and made her lie in her room with cucumber slices all over her face. The puffiness had gone down, but she still looked distracted. Aunt Beverley was smoking like a fast-running locomotive, and kept flicking her ash out of the window.

'Remember to be natural, be yourself,' she repeated.

'For goodness' sake, Aunt Beverley, I *will* be natural.'

'Give him a private moment. Do you know what a private moment is? A private moment is when you act out something that you would only do on your own, with nobody watching. Shelley Winters once told me about this private moment that Jerry O'Loughlin acted out, at the Actors Studio. A young man comes into his apartment, right? It's snowing outside, it's cold. He's wearing a hat and an overcoat and a scarf. He's carrying a box of fried chicken. He takes off his gloves and he puts the chicken on a high stool. Then he just stands there in his hat and his overcoat and his galoshes and he eats the chicken. He's eating because he must, with no enjoyment, without undressing, without sitting down. Shelley said that it was so sad, so lonesome, so pointless, she was crying like a baby.'

'I never ate fried chicken standing up,' said Laura.

'But you must have done something in private.'

'I read in private. I fix my make-up in private. What else? I take showers in private.'

Aunt Beverley gave a grim, J. Edgar Hoover smile. 'I'm quite sure that Chester would sign you up for ever if you decided to do *that* for your private moment.'

Laura leaned against the Chevrolet's door, and tipped her sunglasses down to the end of her nose, and scrutinized Aunt Beverley with a mixture of affection and cockiness. 'You're not *selling* me to Chester, are you?'

'You're going for a camera test, that's all.'

'I don't know. Do you think I should trust you?' They often teased each other this way.

'Do you think you should you trust anybody?' Aunt Beverley retorted. 'Some of the people I trusted the most were the people who betrayed me the worst. You remember Moe? The man who was with me when we first collected you from Sherman? Moe was such a sugarpie. He borrowed eight thousand dollars to put on the horses and lost it, all of it, and practically made me bankrupt. "Trust me," he said. In an iguana's ass.'

They reached the gates of the Fox lot and Aunt Beverley showed her pass. She drove in and parked in the visitors' parking-lot, behind the commissary. It was a cool, bright day, with the yuccas shaking in the breeze like castanets and the sun bouncing off the concrete sidewalks. A Roman slave walked past, wearing sandals and a red tunic, smoking a cigarette.

'Don't forget,' Aunt Beverley promoted her. 'Natural, and private.'

'I won't forget. Natural, and private.'

'And sincere.'

'For goodness' sake, Aunt Beverley.'

'And *innocent*. Chester really goes for innocence.'

They had to wait for over an hour before Chester was free. Eventually he came out of his office in a yellow polo shirt and

240

white ducks, with a towel slung over his neck. He kissed both of them.

'Sorry you had to wait so long. Did they bring you coffee? Accountants! They want me to shoot the crash scenes on the lot, to save money. I said listen, why don't we spend no money at all, and just have a loud bang offscreen, and a cloud of dust, and some kid to throw an old car tyre into shot. All right, it'll cost a dollar seventy-five for the tyre and a quarter to the kid, if you can stretch to that.'

He checked his watch. 'Why don't I take you across for your camera test right now? They're all set up. Beverley, you don't have to hang around here if you don't want to . . . this is going to take at least an hour. Come back and join us for lunch, say, twelve-thirty?'

Aunt Beverley gave him a hearty clap on the shoulder. 'Okay, Chester. I have some shopping to do, anyway. I need a new terracotta planter.' She said it in a long-drawn-out sarcastic tone, and looked directly at Laura as she did so. Chester said, 'Some kind of private joke between you two?'

Aunt Beverley left and Chester took Laura across to one of the smaller soundstages. 'That aunt of yours, she's a character, isn't she?' said Chester.

'She's quite eccentric,' Laura admitted. 'But she's so understanding. She lets me do whatever I like, most of the time, but I always know that she cares.'

'I'll tell you a funny story about your Aunt Beverley,' Chester enthused. He opened the door to the soundstage and winked at her. 'One day, maybe, when you're old enough.'

'It's not one of *those* stories?'

'Unh-hunh,' he told her, shaking his head. 'It's not like any story you ever heard. And everybody's in it. It's a Who's-Who-of-Hollywood story. It's even got Trigger in it.'

'Roy Rogers' Trigger?'

Chester made a face which meant 'you'd better believe it.'

Inside the soundstage, the lights picked out the corner of an 18th-century garden, with a stone balustrade and an urn overflowing with roses. 'This is the garden set for *Lady of Versailles*,' said Chester. 'We're going to do your tests here. Look – this is Rosa, she's going to take you into makeup. This is Bruce, the greatest lighting cameraman since God, and this is Terry, she's going to give you some lines to read.'

'Aunt Beverley said you wanted me to act out a private moment.'

Chester looked nonplussed.

'You know,' said Laura. 'Act out something which I usually do by myself, with nobody else watching.'

Chester shook his head. 'That's Method. I'm not interested in Method. I want actors to act.' He looked at her for a moment, his cheeks puffed out, and then he said, 'Still . . . if you want to share a private moment a little later . . . ?'

She was tested for over an hour – walking, smiling, turning her face this way and that way, looking up, looking down. She had to talk, and laugh, and pretend to weep. She had to scream. She had to show what Chester called 'the whole ga-mutt' of emotions.

'What did you think?' asked Laura, as they walked across to the commissary.

'Bruce will bring me the rushes this afternoon. I thought you looked terrific, but it's what the camera felt about you that counts. If the camera loves you, you're made. If it doesn't, well . . . you said you wanted to write.'

He stopped, and took hold of her hand. 'I'm going to tell you something, though, you're one pretty girl, Laura. Your Aunt Beverley was right about you. You're a doll.'

'Is that what she called me?' asked Laura.

At the same time, however, she glimpsed a small white figure in a white dress crossing quickly between the commissary and the offices next to them. It was only for a second, the briefest of glimpses. She could have blinked and missed it. It could have been a child actress, walking from one soundstage to another. It could have been anybody's daughter, in a white summer dress. But Laura was almost certain that it was the Peggy-girl, watching her – keeping her distance, but watching her.

'Something wrong?' asked Chester.

'I don't think so,' said Laura; but she continued to feel troubled all through lunch, and even Aunt Beverley noticed how often she turned to look out of the window.

When they returned home that afternoon there was a wire waiting for them, telling them that Laura's father was dead.

Fifteen

Two days before the funeral it snowed and went on snowing. The Litchfield hills became eerily silent, under a sky the colour of dark grey flannel. There was little that Elizabeth could do except spend her days indoors, tidying up her father's books and papers.

Her boss Margo Rossi had reluctantly given her two weeks' compassionate leave, although she had insisted on sending up the manuscript of *Reds Under The Bed* so that Elizabeth could finish line-editing it. 'I'm sorry about your father,' she had told Elizabeth, over the phone. 'But there's nothing deader than a deadline.'

Elizabeth used only the kitchen, the library and a bedroom – otherwise she would have had to spend half the day fetching and carrying logs from the snow-clogged yard outside. She had restarted all the clocks, but then she stopped them again. The house was so huge and empty that the sound of ticking made her feel as if her life were sliding by; and the chimes always made her jump.

She wasn't alone all the time. Mrs Patrick called by every afternoon; and several friends had called by. Lenny had taken her out to dinner twice and on Sunday she had cooked him lunch. Their affection for each other grew each time they met. Elizabeth felt so natural with him. Although his wartime experiences and his marriage had made him different – edgy, sometimes, and restless – he was still a part of her early life, when her family had been together, and her mind had been filled with gymkhanas and handsome horsemen and passionate kisses under the cherry-blossom trees.

Lenny was in Hartford this week, although he telephoned her every evening at seven o'clock, just to tell her how much he missed her, and how boring insurance could be. What Elizabeth was looking forward to the most was Laura's arrival. She hadn't seen Laura for over a year now, although they still corresponded two or three times a month and sent each other photographs. Laura was flying to Idlewild and then taking the train. She was expected in New Milford mid-afternoon.

Elizabeth sat at her father's desk, leafing through page after page of business letters. Most were letters to the printers, and the binders, and the bank. There were a few letters from authors, some of them famous. A quick scribbled note from Marc Connelly; a neat 'thank-you' letter from Edna Ferber; and a rambling typed letter from Alexander Woollcott. There was also a letter from a local address, New Preston, signed by Miles Moreton. It read: 'I am delighted that you want to publish my book *Human Imagination: Our Immortal Soul?* and I can certainly meet you for lunch at 12 noon on the 13th.'

Elizabeth suddenly remembered that her father had told her to read *Human Imagination*, and to talk to its author, too. She walked along the shelves, trying to find it. Her father had been chronically untidy, the books were in no kind of order, but at last she discovered a thick black-jacketed book right at the very end of the second shelf. It had a plain typographical dust-jacket, but on the inside flap there was a photograph of a very thin, angular young man with curly hair and staring eyes, smoking a cigarette.

Elizabeth lit a cigarette herself, and sat back in her father's chair and started to read. Outside the french windows, it had started to snow again – huge, tumbling flakes that danced and whirled. The temperature had been steadily dropping since yesterday night, but the Reverend Bullock had telephoned to reassure Elizabeth that the funeral would go ahead, the grave had been dug before the ground froze. That problem hadn't actually occurred to her, and she had stood for a long time in the hallway after she had hung up, thinking of the deep, cold, shoulder-wide trench in the ground into which her father would be lowered, and covered over, as if to mask his face from the sky.

She had found it very difficult to come to terms with the fact that he had died, because the last warmth of her childhood security had died with him. Her mother couldn't take care of her. Now she was truly on her own, and it was snowing.

She smoked, and read, and while she read the day grew darker and darker.

Imagination exists independently of all other brain functions. All other brain functions are concerned with response to quantifiable external stimuli – to cold, to heat, to pain, to caresses. Humans alone possess imagination. Even the so-called 'sixth-sense' that animals possess – for instance, the much-vaunted ability of dogs to be able to anticipate earthquakes – is only a highly-refined response to measurable ground-tremors and changes in atmospheric pressure. Dogs cannot imagine earthquakes, any more than cows can imagine rain. Animals cannot imagine that they are another animal, living in an another age, in another country.

Humans, however, are capable of creating infinite worlds inside their heads. They can imagine that they are other people. They can even imagine that they are animals. One human can create an imaginary world, with imaginary people in it, and write about it, and that world can then be recreated, with certain personal adjustments, inside another human's mind. Imagination is capable of taking on its own existence.

There is anecdotal evidence that the human imagination is capable of outliving the human body and the reactive brain – that 'ghosts' are not the souls of people who have died while leaving some important corporeal business undone, or the spirits of those who are still seeking revenge for some terrible injustice that was done to them during their substantial lifetimes. Instead, 'ghosts' are the living resonance of that most powerful of human qualities, the ability to create out of nothing that which is not, and which never can be, and yet is just as real to the common consciousness as something that actually was.

Who is the more real? Abraham Lincoln or Tom Sawyer? What is more real? Tara, or the Jefferson Memorial? If we can imagine a place or a person with complete conviction, is that not every bit as good as 'reality'?

In 1927, in New Orleans, a Negro pianist called John Michaels claimed to a reporter from the *Times-Picayune* that his dead brother had paid him a visit in the guise of a 13-year-old white boy called Philip LaSalle. His brother had shouted at him and persecuted him and woken him up, night after night, demanding that he got out of bed and worked. Some nights, his brother would even whip him with a riding-crop, and Michaels showed weals on his back to prove it – injuries that it would have been impossible for him to inflict on himself.

After several months of this, Michaels was close to nervous collapse. He was interviewed by two doctors from the Pontchartrain Mental Institution, who concluded that he was sane and that he was telling the truth, although 'the substance of his claim is beyond explanation and completely beggars belief.'

Michaels' brother was a full-blood Negro and had died of viral pneumonia at the age of 32. Anybody less like 'Philip LaSalle' would have been hard to find. However,

247

two years after his death, some of his property was returned to Michaels from his brother's lodgings in Baton Rouge. This property included the novel *Sweet Remembrance* by Chauncey Geffard – a popular story of life on a Southern plantation in the days before the Civil War. One of the principal characters in this book is a privileged young white boy who is given everything his heart desires – a horse, a carriage, and a fine rifle. He mistreats his slaves – whipping the men and seducing the girls – but one of the strands of the novel's plot is the way in which he is gradually transformed by ill-luck and personal tragedy into a sympathetic character.

The white boy's name was Philip LaSalle.

Michaels swore that he had never even heard of the book before his experience; and there was no obvious reason why he might have lied. He made no money from the newspapers or the magazines who came to interview him, and he left New Orleans shortly afterward and went to live under a false name in Mobile, Alabama. On May 8, 1928, he was found moaning and covered in blood in his hotel room on Conception Street, and taken to hospital, where he died the next day. His injuries were consistent with a sustained thrashing with a cane or riding-crop.

Before his death he was interviewed twice by Mobile police, and on both occasions he claimed that his assailant was white, aged about 13, and that his name was Philip LaSalle.

Elizabeth laid the book down on the desk. The afternoon was so dark now that she could scarcely see to read. She switched on the amber-shaded Tiffany desk lamp and looked at the book, her chin in her hand. She didn't know whether she wanted to read any more or not. All she knew was that Miles Moreton was trying to suggest that our imagination could outlive us, and that we could come to life again as anybody we chose to think of – even if that 'somebody' was fictitious, out of a novel.

What was even more frightening was that – fictitious or not –they were still quite capable of hurting people, even killing them, as the swirling black shape in the garden had killed poor Dan Philips.

She stood up, and went to the windows, and watched the snow. They reminded her so much of the snowflakes in *The Snow Queen*: 'Those are the white bees swarming there . . . they have a Queen bee. She flies yonder where they swarm so thickly. She is the largest of them, and never remains upon the earth, but flies up again into the black cloud. Sometimes on a winter's night she flies through the streets of the town, and breathes with her frosty breath upon the windows, and then they are covered with strange and beautiful forms, like trees and flowers.'

She shivered. She knew without a doubt that the Peggy-girl was out in the garden somewhere, standing in the snow, watching the house, waiting, impervious to cold, but her toes and fingers almost black with frostbite.

She turned back to *Human Imagination*. She began reading another case history, about a woman in Bethlehem, Connecticut, who had reappeared to her family in the shape of Jo, from *Little Women*, and who protected them so thoroughly from anybody who threatened to take advantage of them that her widower was unable to remarry, because any prospective partner was unexpectedly drenched with ice-water or showered with broken glass, and her children were ostracized at school because any other pupil who said so much as 'damn!' in their presence found that their ears were viciously boxed by empty air.

Elizabeth thought: this is too much like the Peggy-girl to be true. The violence, the over-protection, the mysterious cold snaps, the strange appearances. Father had been visited by the Peggy-girl and had discovered what she was; and she was this. Peggy's imagination had outlived her. She had no substance now, apart from her bones. But what she did have was presence, and her presence was Gerda, from *The Snow Queen*. Who is the more real? thought Elizabeth. Gerda or me? Gerda or Margo Rossi? Gerda or Peggy Buchanan, that poor little girl who had fallen through the ice while she was playing dancers. Sleep the dancing maidens? No, they're dead. Dead and cold and never likely to breathe again. But the story lives on, Gerda lives on.

Not only Gerda, but the Queen of the white bees, who flies yonder where they swarm so thickly.

She squashed out her cigarette and immediately took another one. At that instant the front doorbell rang, and she jumped. She went to answer it, and it rang again, and she called out, 'All right, all right! I'm coming!'

Standing on the snow-whirling doorstep was Laura, wearing a huge fur hat and a huge fur coat, her face orangey-tanned in the winter light. Behind her a red taxi burbled in the snow, and Jack the taxi-driver from New Milford was lifting her bags out of the trunk.

'Oh, Lizzie,' said Laura, and hugged her. Her fur coat was chilly and prickled with wet. 'Oh, Lizzie, poor father, this is all so sad.'

Elizabeth cooked them a supper of rib chops with celery stuffing, which they ate in the kitchen. Laura said, 'I'd almost forgotten what home food tasted like, I've been living off avocados and alfalfa.'

'You're looking well on it.'

'Thanks. But sometimes I could kill for a plateful of Mrs Patrick's ham and red-eye gravy. With dumplings, of course. And chocolate chiffon pie to follow.'

Elizabeth sat back and looked at her and smiled. 'Oh, come on, Laura. You're a Hollywood girl. I think you always were. How did that screen test work out?'

'Camera test, actually. "I want to see if the lens loves you, baby," But good, I think. If I get it, it'll be the biggest part I've had so far. I'll actually get to say some sensible dialogue, instead of "Dry martini, sir?" or "Ooooh, thank you, Mr Frobisher", which was the sum total of my first two speaking-parts.'

Elizabeth laughed. 'Do you want some more wine? I don't have any chocolate chiffon pie, I'm afraid. I should have bought some apple turnovers, shouldn't I?'

'Not for me. I never eat dessert. I only dream about it. You should see some of those girls who hang around at Schwab's. Thin, you'd never believe it.'

They poured another glass of red wine and sat back and smoked and enjoyed the silence of each other's company for a while. Elizabeth felt that Laura's arrival had already made her father's funeral much more bearable. She had realized, thinking about Laura, that she had been intensely jealous of her, when she was younger, but very protective, too. She still felt protective, because she was older; but she wasn't jealous any longer, and that was surprisingly liberating, and good for the soul.

Laura said, out of the blue, 'I'm not really sure, but I think I've seen Peggy again.'

Elizabeth stared at her. Laura thought that Elizabeth was looking rather too thin. 'When was that?' she asked, cigarette smoke trailing.

'The day before my camera test. Well, the night before, actually. I heard somebody whispering in the courtyard outside my bedroom. I looked out of the window and I was sure that it was Peggy – I mean, the girl who looks like Peggy, but isn't. The only thing was, when I walked towards her, she wasn't Peggy at all, or even the girl who looks like Peggy, she was nothing more than a shape.'

'A shape? What do you mean?'

'She was just the shape between the palms and the creepers and the wall; there was nothing actually there. It was like, what do you call it, an optical illusion. Except that it wasn't, because I heard her whispering.'

Elizabeth was silent and thoughtful for a very long time. 'I told you what happened to Mr Philips.'

'Yes.'

'But there's something more. Father saw the Peggy-girl too. He saw her several times. I don't know what he thought about her. He wasn't able to tell me. But he did put me on to a book that he published, *Human Imagination*, and this book says that our imagination lives on after we're dead. Everything else dies, but imagination's different, because it's something that never was, made real; and so it stays real. Like Oz, and Narnia.'

Laura swallowed a large mouthful of wine. 'I don't get it,' she said.

Elizabeth looked embarrassed. 'To tell you the truth, I don't, either. Not exactly. But father said that I should talk to the author, and the author's local. Maybe we should go to see him, now you're here.'

'Oh, I don't think so,' said Laura. 'I just want to be quiet, and sorrowful, and think of father.'

'Wait up,' said Elizabeth. She went through to the library, and came back with Miles Moreton's book, which she opened at the flyleaf, to show Laura the author's photograph.

'Heyy . . .' said Laura, raising her eyebrows. 'Maybe you're right.'

Later, as they sat by the fire in the sun-room, Elizabeth told Laura everything that had happened on the night that Dan Philips had been killed. Laura sat and listened without

252

interruption and when she had finished, Elizabeth was quite sure that she believed her.

'It's a force, isn't it?' said Laura. 'It's something supernatural. But Mr Bunzum was all frozen, Mr Bunzum broke into pieces. Whatever happened to Dan, that must have been the same thing.'

'Dick Bracewaite, too,' Elizabeth put in, as gently as she could.

Laura gave her a small, unfocused smile. 'Yes . . . poor old Dick Bracewaite.'

'You never told me about that.'

'There was nothing to tell. You want to know the truth? He was a pervert and I was a show-off.'

'He really did it to you?'

Laura nodded. 'Oh, yes, he did it to me. He did everything you can think of, and a few other things besides. The trouble was, I liked it, at the time. It made me feel naughty and special and excited. I knew I shouldn't be doing it, but the naughtier it was, the more I liked it.'

She paused, and looked at the fire. Twin flames sparkled in her eyes. 'The terrible thing was, I didn't feel sorry when they told me he was dead. I didn't feel anything at all. Maybe I should have felt angry. Maybe I should have gone to spit on his grave. But, I don't know. He took advantage of me. He took my innocence. But, in a funny way, I think I took far more from him than he ever took from me. You're like that, at that age. You expect everything. You expect the world. And just for a while you get it.'

Elizabeth said, 'This frightens me, all of this.'

'Why should it?'

'These cold snaps . . . Dick Bracewaite dying, the way he did. Frostbitten, in June! Then Dan Philips. I can't really believe that it's Peggy, yet it must be Peggy, mustn't it? She's guarding us, protecting us, and anybody she doesn't like, she freezes.'

'Do you really believe that?' asked Laura, leaning back against the cushions.

'I don't know. But who could freeze people, just by kissing them?'

'You don't mean the Snow Queen?'

' "Her kiss was colder than ice. It went to his heart, although that was half-frozen already; he thought he should die." '

'But, really, that was just a fairy story.'

'I know. But that's the point. It was Peggy's favourite, and if Peggy's imagination lived on after she was drowned – *everything* would live on, Gerda, Kay, the Lapland woman, the Finland woman, the snowflakes, the Dreams.'

Laura said nothing, but watched the fire.

Outside the window, the snow fell thicker and thicker, as if the sky were determined to silence them, no matter what. And a figure stood in the tennis court, in a white summer dress, with a truimphant smile on her face that would have chilled Elizabeth and Laura right down to their feet, if they could have seen it.

They took a left past Marble Dale and up a sloping tack between the snow-laden trees. The car slid sideways on the ice, but Elizabeth changed down into second gear, and gradually the tyres took a slithering grip and they climbed slowly up the hill.

Today was unexpectedly bright and sunny, so bright that Elizabeth had to wear sunglasses to drive. She had borrowed Mr Twomey's old Studebaker Champion, repainted by hand in a terrible grass green. The car's heater didn't work, so both girls wore gloves and coats and woolly hats.

They took a sharp right turn at the top of the hill, down a snowy incline and up another hill. Here, set above the road behind a natural-stone retaining wall, was a small chalet-style house with a fretwork-decorated verandah, and fretwork-decorated shutters. The sign on the mailbox said Moreton. A black Labrador appeared around the side of the house and barked at them monotonously as they climbed the path to the front door. 'Shut up, dog,' said Laura, and the dog stopped barking, turned around and disappeared around the side of the house again.

'I always knew you had a way with animals,' said Elizabeth.

The dog had obviously alerted his owner, because the front door opened immediately and there was Miles Moreton, much older than he had appeared on his book jacket, his curly hair wired with grey, his eyes pouchy, his fingers stained dark with nicotine. He wore baggy green corduroy trousers and a green checkered lumberjack shirt.

'Come on in,' he called them. 'I didn't know whether you'd be able to make it up the hill.'

The house was grossly untidy, with books and papers stacked in the hall, and not one of the pictures hanging straight, but at least it was warm, with a huge fire crackling, and by the smell of it Miles Moreton had just brewed up some coffee.

Elizabeth and Laura hung up their coats and shifted stacks of paper so that they could sit on the old brown velour couch. Miles distractedly moved books from one side of the room to the other, and then back again. 'I guess you can tell that I'm not used to having visitors. Would you like some coffee? It comes from Basel, in Switzerland. It's the same coffee that Carl Jung used to drink.'

Elizabeth said, 'You're coming to the funeral?'

'Oh yes, I'd be honoured. Your father was a man in a million. He was intelligent, he was sensitive. I never met anybody with such diverse interests.'

'He was interested in everything,' Elizabeth agreed. 'I guess that's why he never made much money. He never published the same kind of book twice. One month it was fly-fishing; the next it was Greek poetry; or obstetrics; or cheese-making.'

Miles found a crumpled pack of Camels on the table and offered them around. 'I wrote that book on human imagination over ten years ago. I'm surprised that your father even remembered it.'

'He had a reason to remember it. He was beginning to have experiences that convinced him that what you were writing about was true.'

'Experiences?'

'Visits,' said Laura.

'You mean – ?'

'That's right,' said Elizabeth. 'He was visited on more than one occasion by our sister Peggy. She drowned in the family swimming pool when she was five.'

'Did she appear as herself?' asked Miles. He was quite breathless with fascination.

Elizabeth shook her head. 'We think that she appeared as Gerda, from *The Snow Queen*. She was always saying that she would like to travel to Lapland, and visit the Snow Queen's palace.'

'Do you have any proof of these manifestations? Any photographs? Any lost artefacts?'

'We've seen her for ourselves. Not just once, but dozens of times.'

Elizabeth told him about the Reverend Bracewaite and Dan Philips, and Laura described her experiences in Santa Monica and Hollywood. He sat and listened and smoked his cigarette right down to the butt, so that it burned his lips.

'There's no question that your sister's manifestations are very similar to other sightings,' he said. 'One of the most common characteristics is this ability to leave the scene of the sighting by changing shape, by becoming something else. The visitors don't simply vanish into thin air, they change into a scarf or a sheet of paper and disappear that way. It's also interesting that she appears to be slightly unfocused. We never imagine fictional characters exactly, down to every last mole on their chins; and this is how your Peggy-stroke-Gerda seems to look. She also seems to appear less vividly in California than she does locally. This is because she imagines that the Snow Queen story is centred on the house where she was brought up; and this is where her imagination is at its strongest.'

'What makes her appear?' asked Laura. 'What do you think she wants?'

Miles shrugged. 'I don't think she actually wants anything, in the sense that people want money or love or forgiveness. It sounds as if she's being very protective towards you both – in fact, over-protective. Wasn't that a characteristic of Gerda in *The Snow Queen*?'

'Oh, absolutely. The whole story is about her travelling to Finland and Lapland to rescue her brother.'

'Quite. And in that case, you're going to have to get accustomed to the idea of being guarded for the rest of your lives.'

'I can understand if she attacked the Reverend Bracewaite,' said Elizabeth. 'But why would she kill Dan Philips? He was there to help me, not to hurt me.'

'I can't say. It might depend on what was going on in his mind.' She looked puzzled. 'Let me put it this way: imaginary characters are apparently able to "see" other imaginary characters, even if they're created by people who are still living. Dan may have imagined himself to be doing something with you of which your sister didn't approve, and so she killed him.'

'Doing what, for instance?' Laura demanded.

'Use your imagination,' said Miles, rather archly.

Elizabeth sat back. 'I never thought of that. But that means . . . well, any man who finds me attractive could be at risk.'

'That's right. You could be very dangerous to know.'

'But I've never had any trouble before now.'

257

'You've been out with men before?'

'Of course.'

'Maybe their intentions were all honourable; or at least benign. Maybe Dan imagined doing something violent. It's impossible to say.'

'What exactly *is* this Peggy-girl?' asked Laura. 'You say she's not a ghost. Does she exist on her own, or do Lizzie and I have to be there to see her? What I mean is, when Lizzie and I die, will *she* die, too? Is she real, or are we imagining her?'

Miles said, 'I don't know for sure. But so far, all the evidence seems to suggest that these spirits have their own independent existence. They survived the death of their own material brains; I'm sure that they can survive the death of the people who knew them when they were alive. As to what that actually *are* . . . my theory is that they are creations of the collective unconscious, that great shared pool of human thought which all of us are tapped into. If you go back in human history, to the time when men first became capable of articulating the things they thought about, you can find dozens of examples of fictional and mythological creations which took on flesh.

'For instance, there was a thing that Viking sailors used to call Shony. It was a manlike creature that used to appear in the North Sea, with shaggy hair and spines. It was supposed to devour seamen who fell overboard; or else it would mimic the screams of a drowning man, and when somebody dived into the water to rescue him it would tear them to pieces. Viking shipbuilders used to redden the keels of their ships by tying a victim to the logs on which they rolled their boats into the water – kind of a sacrifice, so that Shony wouldn't attack them. There was no real evidence that Shony existed, but then something very interesting happened. Sir Walter Scott the Scottish novelist wrote about Shony, calling him by his local name of Shellycoat. Here . . .'

He stood up and sorted through a tilting stack of notebooks

until he found the one he was looking for. 'This is what Scott wrote. "When Shellycoat appeared on the shore, he seemed to be decked with marine productions and, in particular, with shells whose clattering announced his approach." '

'About two years after this was published, a young man was found on the beach near St Andrews, in Fife, with no legs and half of his torso missing. It looked as if he had been attacked by a shark – although there are no sharks in the North Sea. A month or so later, a young woman was found mutilated, and then two dogs. A young anthropologist from Cupar decided to keep watch on the beach. He camped out there day and night for three weeks until one morning he saw a woman coming in his direction, walking her dog. There was a dense *haar*, or sea-mist, so it was difficult for him to see very much. But when the woman was only about two hundred feet away from him, he heard a clattering sound, and behind her "some huge, hunched Thing came out of the ocean shallows, covered with dripping brown weed and mussel-shells." '

'The young man shouted a warning, the woman turned around, saw what it was and ran. The thing was quick, though. It caught her dog and literally tore it in half, devouring one half and throwing the rest on the beach. Then it disappeared back into the mist.'

'My God,' said Elizabeth. 'Did anybody find out what it was?'

From the back of the notebook Miles produced a photocopy of a blurry charcoal sketch. 'This is what the anthropologist drew, less than an hour later.' The sketch showed a woman in a black coat running to the left foreground. Her eyes were deep black smudges of terror. This was a woman who was running for her life. Her hat had flown off and was lying on the beach. Fifty feet behind her was a massive shape, black and bulky, hung with seaweed and encrusted with shells.

'It could have been a hoax,' said Laura.

'Yes, you're right, it could be a hoax,' Miles agreed. 'The anthropologist swore on oath that what he had seen was real, and so did the woman, but they could have invented the thing together; or somebody could have dressed up like Shellycoat just to scare people, although it's hard to imagine how he managed to tear a dog in half. However, two interesting facts came to light. One was that a local lad named Angus Renfield had drowned the previous spring at the same spot, and that his favourite story was Sir Walter Scott's description of Shellycoat. Apparently he used to try to frighten his pals by covering himself in weed and chasing after them along the beach. The other fact was that a fishing-boat returned to St Andrews shortly afterwards with a damaged trawl-net. The crew discovered that a huge hole had been torn or bitten out of it. In one part of the net, they found twenty or thirty mussel-shells, in an overlapping pattern, all interwined with coarse, greasy hair. These shells, if you held them up and shook them, made a distinctive clattering sound.'

'That's a pretty scary story,' said Laura.

Miles lit another cigarette. 'It's impossible to authenticate, although you can still see the shells in the library at St Andrews University. I have a photograph of it somewhere. But this isn't the only instance of a fictional or mythological being coming to life. People have reported seeing Dickensian characters, Joycean characters, Raymond Chandler private eyes. A nurse at a drug clinic in London says she was totally convinced that a man who came for treatment was Sherlock Holmes.'

'Oh, come on,' said Elizabeth. 'She must have been helping herself to the medicinal brandy.' She wanted to laugh but the serious look on his face completely silenced her.

'No, the nurse wasn't drunk and she wasn't imagining things, but somebody was. Somebody was imagining that they were Sherlock Holmes. Somebody dead. Their spirit hadn't survived in the form in which they actually lived. When you think about it, why should it? Your imagination is completely free from the constraints of your body. Somebody had imagined that so strongly that they took on a perceivable form.

'There is vast psychological power in the collective unconscious. Jung knew that, and used it to help people with schizophrenia and other serious mental disorders. It's like one person being knocked down in an accident and dozens of other people rushing to help . . . medics, nurses, doctors, surgeons, anesthetists, blood donors . . . not to mention the community that built the hospital and paid for the emergency services in the first place. The only difference is that the help you receive from the collective unconscious is psychological rather than physical.'

'If this is true, how come the whole world isn't populated by fictional characters?' asked Laura. 'Why aren't we shoulder-to-shoulder with the Hardy Boys, or Huckleberry Finn, or Anne of Green Gables? Just think of it! I could be Scarlett O'Hara when I die!'

Miles poured himself some more coffee. His expression was still serious. 'I don't think all spirits take on the shape of fictional characters. I don't think that very many spirits survive the moment of extinction. In almost every case that I've come across, the deceased person died a traumatic death. They almost always drowned or suffocated, or suffered a long period of oxygen deprivation in some other way. I don't have any idea how it happens, but oxygen deprivation seems to be one of the necessary conditions for the imagination to be released. This is why so many people report out-of-body experiences when they're clinically dead for a short period of time. There have been far too many reports to be dismissed; especially since they're all so similar. The sensation of floating to the ceiling and looking down at your own body . . . the sensation of moving away towards a bright light. Seeing parents and friends who have predeceased you. This is the human imagination leaving the human body, and after that has happened, it can take on any form it wants to, provided it has the will, and the strength, and the need to do it.'

'I'm finding this very difficult to believe.' said Elizabeth.

'I'm surprised,' Miles replied. 'You're a writer yourself . . . you should be quite familiar with the power of the human imagination. Believe me, in the backs of our minds there *is* another world, with other people in it. They exist because we want them to exist. You have only to close your eyes and think of them, and there they are. You can actually see them. You can actually describe them. You can hear them talking and smell their perfume. To all intents and purposes they're *real*. They're really real.'

Elizabeth was thoughtful for a moment. Then she said, 'Is there any way to get rid of them? I mean, if we can make them up, surely we can unmake them, too.'

'You're talking about getting rid of Peggy?'

She nodded.

'But Peggy's your sister,' said Miles. 'She may not look exactly like your sister any longer, but that's who she is. You can sense it for yourself. What if Laura here were in a fire, and her face got all burned, and she had to have reconstructive surgery so that she wound up looking like somebody different? You wouldn't want to get rid of her, would you?'

'This is different. Peggy's liable to kill people. Besides, she's dead already. Whatever this Peggy-girl is, whether it's Gerda or Peggy or somebody else altogether, the Peggy that I knew is lying in the cemetery and she's not going to come back.'

'You're wrong,' Miles replied. 'What's lying in the cemetery is Peggy's material body, that's all. Her essential being, what she actually was, is still with us, and will remain with us.'

'You're saying I *can't* get rid of her?'

'How can you get rid of Gerda from *The Snow Queen*? Burn

every copy and brainwash everybody who's ever read it? Once a character has been devised, he or she can never be *un*devised.'

'But she could ruin my life! If every man I ever meet is liable to be frozen to death, how can I have any kind of relationship with anybody?'

'I guess you could try living as far away from Sherman as possible.'

'Oh, I see! I have to go live in China because my dead five-year-old sister doesn't like me going around with men who have sex on their mind!'

Miles lit a third cigarette. For a moment, his face disappeared behind the smoke. Then he blew it away, and nodded, and said, 'Yes . . . it may actually come to that.'

'And what about me?' asked Laura.

'I guess the same thing applies,' said Miles. 'After all, there's every reason to think that your Peggy killed the Reverend Bracewaite, isn't there, even though you didn't actually see her do it.'

Elizabeth said, 'There's really no way?'

'Not that I'm aware of. Spirit-forming isn't exactly a known science, after all. You have to believe that a fictional character can actually exist before you can work out how to be rid of her, and that's not a leap of faith that many people are prepared to take.'

'I'm not sure I'm prepared to take it myself.'

'You've seen Peggy for yourself.'

'I know. But maybe it isn't Peggy at all, maybe I'm deluding myself. And that black shape that froze poor Dan to death, what could that be?'

'The Snow Queen,' said Miles, matter-of-factly. 'When a spirit becomes a character, she can conjure up all of the other characters that make her what she is.'

'That's what I thought,' said Elizabeth. 'But the Snow Queen wasn't black, like that. The way that Hans Andersen described her, she was white. She wore a cap and coat entirely of snow, and she was tall and slender, and she was dazzlingly white.'

Miles said, 'For sure, that's what he wrote in the story, but he was writing for children, wasn't he?'

'I don't understand.'

'Hans Andersen wrote for adults long before he started writing fairy stories for children. In fact, he didn't particularly enjoy writing fairy stories, but they were so successful that he didn't have any choice. When they were first published, a lot of critics said that his stories were too morbid for children. They read like children's stories, but they're aimed at adults. He was a Scandinvian. You know, gloomy and dire. The Snow Queen was based on one of the daughters of Loki, the great Nordic incarnation of evil. Loki was like Satan to the Norse people. He frightened them so much that they wouldn't make any sacrifices to him, or build any temples in his honour, in case he appeared to thank them. His first wife was called Embers and his second wife was called Ashes. Even today, when Danish housewives hear the fires spitting, they say that Loki is beating his children.

'His third wife was called Augur-boda, which means Anguish-boding. She had three children, the first of whom was Hel, the queen of the underworld, who gave her name to the English word "Hell". Hel was thrown out of the celestial kingdom of Odin, and according to legend she was given "nine unlighted worlds to rule, a queen and empress over all the dead." The people who lived in Hel's palace were criminals and sinners, and anybody who had died without shedding blood. The Norse people had the greatest contempt for anybody who died in bed. You were supposed to be warlike and valiant, and die by the sword.

'Hel was supposed to have been responsible for the Black Death. The Danes said that she mounted her white, three-legged horse and travelled the length and breadth of Northern Europe, spreading disease. She was also supposed to be responsible for any death by freezing or frostbite. In other words, Hel, the daughter of Loki, was the original model for the Snow Queen.'

Laura said, 'She's only a legend, though, isn't she?'

Miles blew out smoke. 'Your sister Peggy is only a fairy story.'

'You're trying to suggest that Peggy has been reincarnated as Gerda; and that Hel has been brought to life, too?'

'You want my serious opinion?'

'Of course!'

'Then my opinion is that it's all impossible, that none of it could happen, and yet it has.'

Elizabeth stood up, and walked to the window, and looked out of the snowy yard. The black Labrador was standing by the frozen birdbath, watching her with garnet-coloured eyes.

'How do we put her to rest?' she asked.

'I don't know,' said Miles. 'I'm an author. I'm a psychologist. A dabbler in this and a dabbler in that.'

'I have to put her to rest. She's going to haunt us for ever, if I don't.'

Miles looked at Laura, and made a face which meant, what can I do, I've told you everything I know. Laura said, 'Maybe you should move out to California, Lizzie. I'm sure that Chester would give you some screenwriting work.'

'No,' said Elizabeth. 'I don't want to run away. Why should I? Loki, Hel, they're only stories, aren't they? Stories can't hurt you.'

'Lizzie,' said Miles, as gently as he could. 'I think you ought to understand that they can; and often have done; and will again; and that of all the stories your sister could have chosen to imagine, *The Snow Queen* is one of the most frightening. The name of Loki may be unfamiliar to you, but the name of Satan isn't, is it, and we're talking about the same kind of manifestation. If Peggy has imagined herself to be Gerda, then she has imagined the Snow Queen, too, because the Snow Queen is essential to Gerda's struggle. Without the Snow Queen, Gerda is nothing more than a little girl who presses hot pennies against frosty windows so that she can see the street outside.

'You've seen the Snow Queen. You've seen her for yourself, and her name is Hel.'

They buried their father with the simplest of ceremonies. A biting north-westerly wind was blowing from Canada, and sizzles of fine snow blew over the open grave.

Elizabeth and Laura were amazed how many people came. Mary Kenneth Randall, the novelist, in a wheelchair, pushed by an ever-complaining black woman. Eugene O'Neill, the playwright, looking old and cold and miserable. Ashley Tibbett, the essayist, emaciated and yellow and dying himself from lung cancer. The humorist S. J. Perelman, who used to challenge David Buchanan to martini-drinking contests at the Algonquin, and usually won. Marianne Craig Moore, the poetess who wrote *The Pangolin*. Frederic Nash, better known as Ogden, but on a day like this short of any witty verses.

Somebody else came, a little late. A huge black Cadillac trundled up to the cemetery gates, as silent as any of the hearses, and a stocky wide-shouldered man climbed out. He wore a black overcoat with an astrakhan collar and he walked with a silver-topped cane. The Reverend Bullock was already intoning the words, 'Ashes to ashes, dust to dust . . .' as the man reached the graveside. He took off his hat and stood bareheaded while David Buchanan's casket was lowered into the frozen ground. His hair was no longer the colour of peanut-brittle, more like rusted steel; and his moustache was droopier; but it was Johnson Ward all right, no doubt about it, the once-notorious author of *Bitter Fruit*.

266

He waited until the ceremony was over, and then he stepped forward and dropped something into the open grave.

Elizabeth circled around the back of the mourners.

'Bronco,' she said.

'Little Lizzie,' he said. 'My favourite balloon-popper.'

He kissed her, and he still smelled spicey-clean. 'I'm so pleased you could come,' she said. 'I haven't seen you since – '

'Yes,' he said. 'Not since we buried your little Clothes-Peg. Maybe we should stop meeting at funerals.' He looked down at the grave. 'That father of yours, he was so dear to me, do you know that? It was a joy to write for a publisher like him, even if he couldn't pay much money. He cared so much for what he did.'

He took out his handkerchief and wiped his nose. 'Do you know what I threw in his grave? The pen he lent me, the first time I ever met him. A woman came up to me in Jack & Charlie's and asked me for my autograph. That was the first time that anybody had ever asked me, and I didn't even have a pen, so Davey lent me his. I offered it back to him, but he said, no, keep it. You can give it back to me when people stop asking for your autograph any more. Well, they don't. They don't even know who I am, half of them. Those days are long gone; and now Davey's gone, too, and he can have his pen back.'

Elizabeth took his arm. 'Surely you're working for us now, aren't you? Margo said you were writing a new novel, all about Arizona.'

Bronco shrugged. 'I'm supposed to be, in fact, I'll probably have to. I've spent the advance already.'

'When's it due?'

'The end of the year. Not much hope of that.'

'How much have you written?'

He lifted his leather-gloved hand, as if he were framing a cinema shot. 'I've written, "The Sun Worshippers, by Johnson Ward". Then I've written, "Chapter One". Then I've written,

"Pearson sat in the middle of a day with no shadow. He had women on his mind. Women and liquor, but mostly women." '

There was a long pause. They were walking downhill from the gravesite now, arm-in-arm. The wind blustered in their ears.

'Is that all?' said Elizabeth.

Bronco gave her a keen, tired, paternal look. 'That's it, little Lizzie, balloon-biter extraordinaire. But don't you tell Rossi, or she'll have my guts for banjo-strings.'

'You're blocked, that's all. You can get over block.'

'Unh-hunh, this isn't block. Billy's been calling.'

'Billy?'

Bronco glanced over his snow-dandruffed shoulder. 'I told you about Billy. He was my brother, the one who died. I met him in Cuba and now he keeps appearing in Phoenix. How can I write when my dead brother keeps pestering me?'

Elizabeth pulled Bronco to a halt. 'Are you serious?' she demanded.

He stared at her and his eyes were wild. 'Of course I'm serious, for Christ's sake. He never leaves me alone. Vita thinks I've gone crazy. *I* think I've gone crazy. I try to write and he sits in my room and stares at me, and interrupts me, and talks to me, and tells me how careless I am, I shouldn't have let him die, I shouldn't have made any money, I don't have any talent, I'm a failure. He's always there, goddamnit.'

'Have you spoken to anybody else about it?'

'I have a gardner. I've talked to him about it. Actually I had to, because he saw me arguing with Billy, and asked me what was wrong.'

'Did he believe you when you told him who Billy was?'

They had reached the funeral cars. Laura and Lenny came over, Lenny clapping his hands against the cold.

Bronco said, 'Funny thing . . . I only told him that Billy was my brother. But he said, "You shouldn't go messing with dead people. Dead people will try anything".'

268

'Somebody must have told him that your brother had died. Maybe Vita.'

'But what would *you* assume if you saw me arguing with somebody in the garden and I said it was my brother? You'd assume it was another brother, wouldn't you? You wouldn't think that it was my *dead* brother!'

Laura came up and took hold of Bronco's arm. 'My favourite risqué novelist,' she said, kissing his cheek.

'My,' smiled Bronco. 'You sure have grown, little Laura.'

Now Margaret Buchanan came down the shovel-cleared pathway in a wheelchair, wrapped in a dark plaid blanket. Seamus was pushing her, although Seamus didn't look well. His cheeks were as pale as kitchen soap and his eyes were red-rimmed. He wore a black woolly hat that gave him the appearance of a big, mollycoddled toddler. He stopped beside them but he didn't say anything. A shining drop swung from the end of his nose.

Margaret wore tiny circular sunglasses and a wide black hat. Her mouth was pinched. 'I don't know why David had to go on such a cold day,' she complained. 'He always used to be so considerate. But now he's gone, goodness! isn't he making a meal of it?'

Laura said, 'Come on, mother. There's some hot food back at the house. You'll feel better when you've had something to eat.'

But Elizabeth took out her handkerchief and went up to Seamus and wiped his nose for him. He didn't look at her. He didn't say anything.

'Are you all right, Seamus?' she asked him, gently.

He gave her a quick sideways glance, but still he said nothing.

'Is there something wrong?' coaxed Elizabeth. 'Have I done something to upset you?'

He paused for a very long time, chewing the cold morning air as if it were gum. 'Daren't say,' he replied, at last.

'Daren't, or won't?'

'I know what happens to them who dares to say.'

'Those who dare to say what, Seamus?'

He rolled his eyes. 'Daren't say, nohow. Just daren't say.'

'Well, what happens to them, when they dare to say this thing that you daren't say?'

'Get kissed,' said Seamus.

'Kissed? Kissed by whom?'

'If I give you more kisses, I shall kiss thee to death.'

Elizabeth shivered. Seamus was quoting from *The Snow Queen* again; he seemed to be obsessed by it; but Elizabeth knew what he was talking about. The Snow Queen's kisses were as cold as a glacier, and her mouth could drain out the very last warmth from anybody's heart.

Seamus saw how alarmed she was, and caught hold of her sleeve. 'You can't blame us! You can't blame us! I do love you, even though I daren't tell!'

Elizabeth stared at him. 'Is *that* what you daren't say? That you love me?'

'Ssssshhhhh!' hissed Seamus, in a panic, pressing his finger to his lips, and spraying spit everywhere.

Margaret turned around and looked up at him disapprovingly. 'It's bad enough with it snowing, without you spitting on me, too. Come on, take me to the car, I'm cold and I'm tired of this wheelchair. I never knew a wheelchair-pusher to fidget so much. Backwards and forwards, all though the funeral. I thought I was going to be seasick.'

Seamus pushed Margaret away, and then Miles Moreton came up, and took off his hat, and offered his condolences. 'I'll miss him, you know, more than I can tell you. He was a brother, just as much as a publisher.'

'Thank you, Miles,' said Elizabeth.

'By the way . . . I hope I didn't frighten you too much yesterday, with all my talk.'

'Not at all. At least you gave us some kind of explanation for what's been going on.'

'I did some more reading about it,' said Miles. 'Apparently there *are* ways in which you can exorcize somebody whose imaginative consciousness has been haunting you. People have tried it, from time to time.'

'Can we talk about this later?' asked Elizabeth. 'I don't want to keep everybody waiting in the cold.'

'It's very simple,' Miles enthused. 'It's merely a question of choosing a character of your own . . . a character who's capable of dismissing the character who's been troubling you . . . and *being* that character, and – '

'Come on, Lizzie!' called Laura. 'We're freezing to death out here!'

Elizabeth touched Miles's arm. 'I'll talk to you later on. Thanks for coming. My father would have appreciated it no end.'

Sixteen

That evening, when all the rest of the funeral guests had left, Elizabeth, Laura, Bronco and Miles sat by the fire and drank three bottles of red wine between them. The house was huge and hushed; and every now and then they heard that distinctive threatening creak which means that there are too many tons of snow on the roof.

'You ever had such weather in autumn before?' asked Bronco, his necktie loosened, his feet propped on the stool in front of the fire.

'Nothing like this,' said Miles. He lit one Camel from the burning end of another, and blew out smoke. 'This'll go down in the record books.'

'Bronco's seen his brother,' Elizabeth told Miles.

Miles narrowed his eyes. 'From the way you said that, I assume that has some special significance.'

'The same significance as seeing Peggy,' said Elizabeth.

'You mean your brother's deceased?' Cigarette smoke trailed between them, and was suddenly lifted by the chilly draught.

Bronco said, 'I met him in Cuba. He didn't look like Billy, not at all, but I knew that it was him. Now he's back again, pestering me all the time.'

'Who does he look like?' asked Miles.

'I don't know, some Cuban.'

'When he was alive, did he read any books or see any movies about Cuban people?'

'Not that I know of.'

'Did he ever visit Cuba?'

'He didn't even visit Poughkeepsie.'

Miles said, 'From what I've been reading, it appears that when a person dies, they have to base their imaginary identity on people they've known or read about or thought about while they're alive. Once they're dead, they *are* their own imagination, that's all they are, and their imagination can't imagine themselves to be anybody else, if you get my meaning.'

'I'm not sure that I do.' said Bronco. 'Particularly after all this wine.'

'What I'm saying is, your brother had to base his appearance on somebody he knew when he was alive – whether that person was fictitious or real. Some people base their after-death appearance on the way they looked when they were alive. This has the fascinating side effect that many spirit-forms look younger or better-looking than they did on the person who died. It seems as if the dead are just as vain as the living.'

'I can't think of anybody my brother would have based himself on. He didn't know any Cubans, as far as I know, and he never read a book in his life, apart from *Practical Mechanics*. He spent all his time listening to jazz records.'

'How about jazz musicians?' asked Miles. 'Any particular ones?'

'I don't know . . . there was some rhumba-type record he used to play. Maybe that was it. I don't know who played on it, though.'

Miles swallowed more wine. 'Do you still have his record collection?'

'Sure, I have everything he ever owned. Even some ridiculous zoot suit he used to wear, with a belt at the back.'

'Well, what I suggest is, when you get back to Arizona, check through his records and see if you can find anything Latin. Once you know who his spirit-form is based on, you can take the necessary steps to stop him from bothering you.'

'And what are these steps'?'

'To put it simply, you have to play the spirit-form at its own game. It's rather like scissors-cut-paper, paper-wraps-rock. You have to choose a character for yourself, fictitious or real, but someone who's capable of negotiating or dealing with the spirit-form who's bothering you. For instance, if your brother is manifesting himself as some Cuban musician, you can take the form of an impresario or a bandleader or a record producer, and tell him that he has to leave you alone or else he's going to lose his job.'

Bronco guffawed. 'And how, precisely, am I supposed to take the spirit-form of some rhumba-playing bandleader?'

Miles remained serious. 'You have to use the glamour. It's one of the oldest and best-documented forms of occult deception.'

'The glamour?' asked Elizabeth.

'That right. We use the word "glamour" today to describe illusory beauty. But actually it's a Scottish variant of the word "gramarye", meaning shape-changing, as practised by witches. What the witches did was to wind a cord made of braided animal-hair around their necks until their breathing was restricted and they were starved of oxygen. In other words, they were in a state of near-death. Their imagination was then free to leave their body and take on any form they wished.'

'That doesn't sound very glamorous to me,' said Bronco. 'Is there any kind of evidence that it actually works?'

'I've found four authenticated cases so far. The earliest was in 1645. The latest was in August, 1936. A man was arrested in Schaumburg, Illinois, for trying to pass a dud cheque. He gave his name to the police as Babbitt, a real-estate agent from the town of Zenith.'

'You mean Babbitt from Sinclair Lewis's novel?' asked Elizabeth.

'The same, or so he claimed. He was examined by two psychiatrists, and both of them claimed that he was perfectly

274

sane. He not only resembled Babbitt, he talked like Babbitt, he knew everything that had happened in the novel – and not only that, he knew things that hadn't happened in the novel but which logically could have done. The police even sent a copy of the man's statement to Sinclair Lewis himself, but there's no record of what *he* thought about it, and of course he died in January so we can't ask him for ourselves.

'The day after "Babbit" was released on bail, the body of a middle-aged woman was discovered in a house close by. She was wearing a man's suit which one of the attending officers recognized as "Babbitt's". He also recognized the signet ring she was wearing, which was much too large for her. He checked her fingerprints and found that they were identical to "Babbitt's".

'If the Renaissance writings on glamour have any truth to them, both of these people had deliberately half-strangled themselves in order to leave their bodies in the shape of fictitious characters . . . for what reasons, we can't even guess. But then nobody would guess what you were doing, would they, Bronco, if they found you dressed as a bandleader?'

'Well, you're right,' said Bronco. 'But this isn't very encouraging news, is it? If you have to risk strangling yourself just to get rid of a bothersome spirit, I think I'd rather put up with the bothersome spirit.'

'These days, you may not actually have to strangle yourself,' said Miles. 'There are several drugs which dramatically lower your rate of respiration. You could actually deprive yourself of oxygen by chemical means, which would be much more controllable. I'd have to find out more about dosages, of course.'

'I'm sorry,' Bronco told him. 'This glamour business doesn't appeal to me at all. Too weird by half, too dangerous. I think I'll try a good old-fashioned exorcism. Bell, book and candle, and a well-bribed priest.'

The long-case clock in the hallway chimed eleven. Miles

finished his wine and said, 'I'd better leave now, Lizzie. Thanks for everything. I really appreciate your inviting me. Your father deserved a good send-off.' He went into the hallway, shrugged on his overcoat and found his hat.

Laura kissed him. 'Goodnight, Miles. It was good to meet you. Come out to sunny California sometime.'

They didn't stay long at the open door. The wind was rising, and the snow was falling as thick as swarming bees. He climbed into his old brown pre-war Ford, pulled out of the driveway, tooted his horn, and made his way through Sherman on the way back home.

He had been deeply saddened by David Buchanan's death, but he had found a great deal of comfort in the funeral service, and he had enjoyed talking to Elizabeth and Laura and Johnson Ward. Most of the time, he lived a very reclusive life these days, writing and researching. On Tuesdays and Thursdays he gave lectures on creative writing at Western Connecticut State, but he never fraternized with any of the faculty, or formed any kind of social relationship with any of his students. Some of the girls fluttered their eyelashes and said, '*Hi*, Mr Moreton', but that was as far as it ever went. He couldn't imagine taking any of them out and trying to talk about Tommy Dorsey and Frank Sinatra and whatever else it was that excited girls these days.

A long time ago Miles had been in love. But it was so long ago that it almost seemed like medieval times, a gilded past of chivalry and high romance. Her name was Jennifer and she had hurt him so much when she rejected him that his bones had ached for months afterwards. Now, unbelievably, he could scarcely remember her. Blonde hair through which the sunlight always seemed to shine, and cornflower-blue eyes, and a ringing laugh, and that was all. Time had worked the glamour on her, too.

Miles was excited by his new research. When he was writing

Human Imagination he had occasionally come across some extraordinary demonstrations of what the human psyche could do, but he had never come across such strong evidence that spirit-forming was not only possible but actually happening here in Litchfield County. He was excited, but he was frightened, too. He was beginning to understand just how tenuous our grip on life actually is: how fragile we are. One slip, one choke, one step in the road, one breath too few, and everything we ever were is gone for good. All of our consciousness has closed itself off, like a camera shutter. Gone, dark, finished. Yet it was clear that some element of what we had once been could sometimes survive our clinical death, in some changed and glamorous form – although whether this form would be happy or not, he didn't like to think.

Of course, what excited him more than anything else was the prospect of writing a new book, and he had thought of the title already: *The Proof of Ghosts*. All he had to do was establish that Elizabeth and Laura were telling the truth; and that Johnson Ward had really seen his dead brother; and he would be famous worldwide. He could answer at last the question that everybody had been asking since sentient life began: is there life after death – and if there is, what form does it take?

His car whined through Sherman and out towards Boardman's Bridge. In the summer he might have turned toward Gaylordsville and driven over the hill to New Preston, but in this weather it was out of the question. There was no other traffic on the road, and the snow was flying down in big, thick lumps, so thick that the windscreen wipers could barely cope. The side and rear windows were blotted out, and Miles felt as if he were covered in a blanket. The heater worked, but the rubber door-seals were perished, and so his ankles were exposed to thin, icy draughts.

Oh well, he thought, as he trundled towards New Milford and the Housatonic bridge, once I've written *The Proof of Ghosts*

I can afford a new automobile. Maybe a new bed, too: and an icebox. But that was the sum of his material ambitions. What he really wanted was to travel. To Rome, to Vienna, to Lisbon. He wanted to see Casablanca, and stand on the edge of the Sahara desert, listening to heat and emptiness and the slow susurration of the human soul.

He had almost reached the Housatonic bridge when he saw a figure beside the highway. To his astonishment, his pale-yellow headlights illuminated the figure of a young girl, no more than nine or ten, standing in the snowstorm in a white summer dress. She was neither walking nor waving, just standing, with her arms by her sides, her eyes as smudgy as smoke.

He stopped the car and waited for just a moment, his hands gripping the steering-wheel, to see whether she might climb in, but when she didn't, he opened his door and climbed out.

'Can't say you're dressed for a night like this!' he called out, one hand lifted to protect his face from the driving snow. The girl said nothing but stood watching him with those smudgy eyes. The snow had clogged her hair like a beret made of dandelion-puffs. Her skin was deathly white, and her lips were faintly purple. Her fingers were tinged with purple, too, as if she were frostbitten.

Miles high-stepped across the snow towards her, sliding once, and nearly falling over. 'Listen,' he said. 'You can't stay here, you'll catch your death. Let me take you home, huh?'

Still the little girl said nothing. Miles laid a hand on her shoulder and as soon as he had done so he wished he hadn't. It was thin and bony and very, very cold. In fact, it seemed colder than the snow. It was like laying his hand on a dead, skinned shoulder of lamb.

'Do you live close by?' Miles asked her. 'I can take you wherever you want to go. If you don't want to go home, I can take you to the cops, they'll take care of you, give you something warm to wear.'

The girl at last turned her face towards him. He was shocked how white she looked. 'Oh, I have left my boots behind,' she whispered.

'What, sugar?'

'Oh, I have left my gloves behind.'

Miles gave her a tight, humourless smile. 'We can soon sort that out, can't we?' He looked around. The highway was deserted. No traffic, nobody walking, not even a sledge. Just a girder bridge and an empty road, and snow that pattered softly down and changed the landscape into somewhere strange. 'Where do you live? Is it very far from here?'

The little girl raised one arm and stiffly pointed north.

'You live in New Milford?'

She shook her head.

'Further? You live further than New Milford? Marble Dale? No? New Preston? No? Cornwall Bridge?'

The girl shook her head again and again but continued to point north.

'You live in Canaan? No? You live in Massachusetts? Vermont? What are you trying to tell me, you live in Canada?'

The snow was falling so thickly now that the car was beginning to look like nothing more than a huge white hump at the side of the highway. 'Come on, honey,' Miles said, in exasperation. 'Let me take you to the cops. They'll know what to do with you.'

The little girl shook her head. Miles had started to reach out to her, to take hold of the arm, but there was some ferociously negative quality in the way she shook her head like that, and there was a look in her dark, unfocused eyes that made him hesitate. This wasn't some innocent little child being standoffish. This was some being that was in full possession of its powers and its senses saying *no, don't touch me – you dare to touch me!*

'Okay, please yourself,' Miles told her. 'All you have to do is get in the car. It won't take us more than a couple of minutes.'

He walked back to the car, and cleared the freshly-fallen snow off the windscreen with the side of his glove. He opened the driver's door, and stood waiting for the little girl to follow him, but she remained where she was, staring at him, frozen to the bone.

'Will you please just come?' Miles pleaded. 'I can't leave you standing here, now can I?'

'She breathed!' the girl called out.

'She breathed? What do you mean? Who breathed?'

'She breathed on the young ones as she passed,' the girl told him.

Jesus, thought Miles, this kid's touched in the head. He was inclined to leave her and find the nearest telephone so that he could call the police. The trouble was, the temperature had dropped so steeply that he was afraid she would die of exposure if he left her out here very much longer, dressed as she was. Supposing he called the police but the police couldn't find her? How could he live with himself if she died?

There was nothing for it. He would have to pick her up bodily and carry her into the car.

He walked back towards her but she lifted her arm again and this time she pointed directly at him.

'She breathed and they died from her breath!'

'All right, sugar,' he said, trying to reassure her. 'I know you're cold. I know you're exhausted. I'm just going to help you into the car, okay? Then we can get you all nice and toasty-warm again.'

The snow was pelting against Miles's back. The temperature was so low that the power-lines cracked and dropped from the utility poles beside the road, thin and rigid and curved. Miles found it almost impossible to breathe: the air was so cold that his lungs literally cringed, because they didn't want to take it in. His nose and his chin were encrusted with ice, and lumpy little beads of ice formed in the corner of his eyes.

'For Christ's sake, kid!' he shouted at the little girl. 'You *have* to get into the car!'

Her face was white and wild. She was staring at him in such a terrifying way that he felt as if sharpened fingernails were dragging down his back. She kept on pointing, kept on pointing, and he realized then that she wasn't pointing at him at all, but something behind him.

'What?' he demanded. He was too frightened even to look.

He heard footsteps. They sounded soft and heavy and intentional. Whommp, whommp, whommp, whommp, soft and heavy and very intentional.

'What?' he whispered. '*What?*'

He turned, and almost lost his balance. Towering above him, only a dozen feet away, was a huge black shape, hooded, cowled, and crackling with unimaginable cold. He couldn't understand what it was, but it was approaching him with such determination that he knew that it meant him serious harm. He shouted out, '*No!*' and started to run away from it, but it kept on billowing towards him, its cape blowing out behind it like the wings of a giant manta ray.

Oh, shit, he thought, and bounded through the snow in giant, cumbersome leaps, swinging his arms from side to side to keep his balance. He knew that he didn't stand a chance of escaping; he could hear it bearing down on him. But there was nothing else that he could do, except to run.

Oh, shit, he thought. *I didn't want to die like this.*

The black shape came rumbling after him. He could *smell* how cold it was, it froze the roof of his mouth, and clogged up his nostrils. He reached the Housatonic Bridge, leaping and jumping through the calf-deep snow, a hurdler, a ballet-dancer. He didn't know where he was trying to go. He didn't know how he could possibly escape. But the thing that was following him was cold and terrible and felt like evil, and he was quite sure that it wanted to tear him apart. Its cape literally thundered through the snowstorm, yards and yards of heavy black material, like velvet funeral curtains being shaken out. Snow flew off its outline: snow flew out of its hidden face.

'Oh God preserve me. God preserve me,' Miles panted. He reached the bridge and gripped one of the crossbars to support himself. His breath was blasting out of his mouth in agonized clouds of ice. He heard the shape so close behind now that his whole being seemed to be shaken by the vibration of its approach.

Somehow, he found the strength to take another step; but when he did so he was abruptly pulled back. The palm of his hand had frozen to the steel crossbar, and he couldn't pull it free. He tugged, and tugged again. He twisted his head around, and the black shape was looming right over him now. For an instant, he glimpsed a huge white horselike face that looked as if it had snakes growing out of it. Then the hood fell back and there was blackness once again.

He gripped his left elbow in his right hand, and wedged his right shoulder against one of the bridge's uprights, and heaved. There was an instant when he knew that he could never pull his hand free. Then the skin tore away from palm of his hand, with a sticky crackling sound, revealing red flesh and tendons, and even glimpses of white bone. He screamed: a small, muffled scream. But he tugged his arm again, and the skin tore away at the wrist, and he was free.

He ran. At least, he thought he was running. In fact he was stumble-trudging across the bridge until he was less than halfway. *Imagination*, thought. *This is all imagination. Not mine, but somebody else's.*

But knowing that it was simply imagination was not enough to save him. He stumbled sideways and his right ankle cracked. It didn't just crack, it shattered, because the bone was frozen. He tried to walk on it, but his sock was filled with nothing but skin and crunchy slush, and the pain was so terrible that he let out a high, piercing shriek, and toppled over, and hit the roadway, shuddering and kicking, even though it hurt him even more.

The black shape rushed up to him; and hung over him; blotting out the whirling of the snow. Miles stared up at it, his vision gradually dimming because of the cold. His optic fluid was chilling; his blood was sluggish in his veins. He tried to speak but he found it impossible. He felt tired beyond all reason, and death would be welcome. At least he could rest, when he was dead. At least he could sleep.

He was still lying in the roadway when the little girl came hobbling up to him, and stood beside him, watching him with an expression that was almost remorseful.

He looked back at her, but he couldn't speak.

'I have to protect my sister,' she said.

He understood; but he couldn't nod.

'I couldn't let anybody hurt her,' the little girl explained. 'I couldn't let anybody lead her astray.'

Miles tried to close his eyes but the lids were frozen open and the snowflakes fell onto his open pupils and burned them with cold. He knew that he was almost dead. All he could feel was a dull, thick pain, from skull to toes.

'Do you want me to say a prayer for you?' asked the little girl. 'Our roses bloom and fade away, Our Infant Lord abides alway; May we be blessed his face to see, And ever little children be!'

She bent over him and stared into his flinching eyes. 'Did you like that?'

There was a moment in which he hoped that she would simply leave him there, and let him die. But then she stepped smartly back, and beckoned to the black shape that was hanging over both of them.

Miles heard a roar like an approaching express train. He screamed out loud, and fragments of half-frozen lung came spraying out of his mouth. He was seized by claws that were worse than claws. They were titanically strong, crushing his pelvis into slush, bursting his stomach, exploding his pancreas, turning his intestines into ribbons of ripped-apart tripe.

He was lifted right into the air, and torn apart. Frozen arms were ripped from frozen sockets; legs were twisted off. In only a matter of minutes, there was nothing left of Miles Moreton but stains on the snow, and offal, and hanks of hair.

The little girl stood reflectively beside the bridge. Then she turned around on her bare frostbitten feet and walked off into the snow. The black shape walked close behind, the snow glancing off its shoulders. It wasn't following her. It wasn't subservient. It was walking in the same direction because they were both returning to the same place: the place to which the little girl had pointed, when Miles first stopped for her.

By first light, it had already started to thaw. A pale sun gleamed in a sky the colour of steam. Deputy Jim Hallett was driving towards New Milford when he saw flocks of huge black carrion crows strutting across the highway, close to the Housatonic Bridge. As he approached, they briefly lurched up into the air, but they soon returned to the slushy road surface. They were tearing at something with their beaks, something from which they were determined not to be distracted.

Deputy Hallett stopped the car and climbed out. The first thing he saw was Miles Moreton's face, staring at him eyeless out of the bloodstained snow.

Seventeen

Laura was sitting in the courtyard, leafing through the latest copy of *Variety*, when Chester appeared wearing a bright lemon-yellow sports coat and carrying an extravagant spray of purple orchids.

'Hey there, I was hoping you'd be home!' he enthused. He came over and kissed her on top of the head and dropped the orchids onto the table. 'I was really cut up to hear about your old man. I hate funerals, don't you? Mind you, my old man died a couple of years ago, cancer, and those morticians really did a number on him. He looked more dead when he was alive than he did when he was dead. My sister saw him in his casket and said, "Look at him, doesn't he look well?"'

He sat down uninvited and took out a cigar. Although it was November the temperature was up in the high 70s, and his tanned forehead glistened with perspiration.

'Beverley must have told you the camera tests were terrific. Sam Persky really loves them. He loves them.'

'Does that mean I get the part?' asked Laura.

Chester clipped the end off his cigar and took out his lighter. 'It means you're shortlisted for the shortlist.'

'What else do I have to do? More tests?'

'Yes, kind of more tests. You and me have to pow-wow.'

Laura put down her magazine and sat up, smiling. Her curly hair was brushed back into an Alice-band and she was wearing a tight blue sleeveless V-necked blouse with wide lapels, and a pair of dark blue calico shorts and sapphire sandals.

'Do you want to talk about it now?' asked Laura.

Chester was busy lighting his cigar. 'Well . . . not now, I'm kind of pushed. I just came by to see that you were still just as delicious as you were in the tests. In case my eyes had deceived me, if you know what I mean.'

'And have they?' asked Laura.

Chester frowned at her as if he didn't understand what she meant. He didn't have a very long span of attention, even for his own conversation. 'Those flowers are for Beverley. Kind of *muchas gracias.*'

'Oh, really?'

'Your Aunt Beverley is the best man-friend that anyone could ever wish for, believe you me. How about dinner tonight? Are you free? Well, who cares. *Be* free. I'll call by at seven o'clock.'

'*Then* we can pow-wow?'

Chester stood up, rising through his own clouds of smoke like a rocket taking off from Cape Canaveral. 'Sure. Then we can pow-wow.'

He left as abruptly as he had come. Laura sat up straight on her sunbed, feeling vaguely uneasy. The courtyard seemed to have grown chillier, and the birds had stopped singing. All she could hear was the traffic. It wasn't so much Chester's unexpected visit that had unsettled her. She didn't know what it was. Ever since her return to Sherman for her father's funeral, she had felt as if she were being watched and followed. She supposed it was probably natural, after a death. Her friend Tilly Makepiece had lost her mother last year, and yet she still heard her singing in the kitchen. Laura hadn't seen any sign of the Peggy-girl since her return, but after she had talked to Elizabeth and Miles Moreton about it, she was sure that her visions had been real, or at least as real as visions could be.

She hadn't yet heard about Miles's death. Until the county coroner returned a verdict on how he had died, Elizabeth had thought it wiser not to tell her, and even then she doubted if she would. Laura had her future to think about. She didn't want to

286

be unnerved by another horrific death, especially when there was nothing that either of them could do about it.

Laura picked up the orchids and took them into the house to put them in water. Aunt Beverley wasn't here this afternoon. She had gone to the Chateau Marmont to talk to Harrison Carroll the movie columnist about something-or-other. Laura opened the kitchen cupboard and took out the largest receptacle she could find, a turn-of-the-century tall brown glass vase which Aunt Beverley had filched from the set of *Winchester '73*.

'I'm Going To Wash That Man Right Out Of My Hair' was playing on the radio in the living-room. She sang along as she lifted the orchids out of their crackly cellophane and arranged them in the vase. This was it, she thought to herself. Dinner with a famous director, a pow-wow about her part, and then fame at last. She couldn't wait for Aunt Beverley to come back, so that she could tell her.

'I'm going to *wash* that do-dee-dum-diddle-dee! I'm going to *wash* that wacka-smacka rooty-too tee!'

She had almost finished arranging the orchids when the radio abruptly went dead. She stopped singing, and listened. Silence. Not even the sound of the yuccas rustling, or the yelp of a distant dog. She waited for a moment, and then she left the flowers and walked through to the sitting-room. It was empty, striped with sunlight, with the white lace curtains silently stirring in the faintest of draughts.

She went across to the radio and switched the knob on and off. The speaker crackled as she did so, but that was all. She banged the side of the cabinet with the flat of her hand, the way that she had seen Aunt Beverley 'fix' it whenever it went wrong; but all she managed to elicit from it was a thin, soft, blowing noise, like the wind behind a tightly-sealed window.

She started to walk back to the kitchen. It was then that she distinctly heard a young girl's voice say, '*I have to protect you, Laura. You know that.*'

Frightened, she turned around. There was nobody there.

'Who's that?' she called out. 'Is that you, Peggy?'

'*I have to protect you, Laura. Sisters have to look out for each other, don't they? Even if you never looked out for me.*'

With a skin-contracting sense of horror, Laura realized that the voice was coming from the radio. She hesitated for a split-second, wide-eyed, then she leaped across the room and switched it off.

'*Oh, I have left my gloves behind,*' the voice continued, undeterred. '*But that won't matter, will it, Laura? I can endure almost anything, for the sake of keeping you safe.*'

'Go away!' screamed Laura, in a panic. 'Go away, leave me alone! You're dead!'

'*I still have to protect you, Laura, dead or not.*'

'I don't want you to protect me! I don't *need* you to protect me! Just go away and leave me alone!'

At that moment, the whole room appeared to tremble. Not the way it trembled in an earthquake, but as if Laura were seeing it through a heat haze. It seemed to *darken*, too, and in some extraordinary way the corners drew nearer. Laura took a step back, then another, but then she couldn't step back any further. She didn't know why. She simply couldn't. Her brain seemed incapable of telling her legs that she had to move.

The lace curtains in the far corner of the room seemed to be stirring more than the others. They started to fold and bulge and rise away from the wall. Laura watched in dreadful fascination as they took on the form of whatever was standing underneath it. There was somebody there. There was somebody hiding behind them. She could see the shape of their head and the shape of their shoulders, and their upraised arms.

There was a little girl hiding behind the curtains. A little girl so white of hair, so white of face, that Laura couldn't see her underneath the lace.

288

'You can't be,' she whispered. 'You can't be here. Leave me alone, please. You don't need to protect me, you honestly don't.'

But the figure behind the curtains said nothing, and now it was growing, and rising from the floor. Right in front of her eyes, the curtains floated in the air, their folds revealing an agonized, childish face, and outstretched arms, and a summer dress, in dusty lace, that was more like a funeral dress.

Laura opened her mouth, but she was incapable of speaking. All she could manage was a sharp barking sound. She saw now that there was nobody hiding behind the curtains, no little girl at all. The curtains *were* the little girl, they had taken on her shape. Even her eyes showed as darker whorls in the lace.

The lace-girl rose and sank in the faint currents of air that blew through the room. Her lips moved, and she spoke, but her voice came out of Aunt Beverley's radio, as before, crackly and distant, like listening to a radio programme from long, long ago.

'I always wanted to protect you, Laura. There are so many things around us. So many frightening things, only seen in dreams.'

Laura managed to say, 'Please, Peggy. Don't scare me like this.'

But the room darkened even more, and Laura saw strange shadows moving across the walls, as if there were someone behind her; a rushing sound like something passing; horses with long, attenuated legs; ghostly men and women.

'They are dreams,' whispered the Peggy-girl. *'They have come to haunt us in the night.'*

Laura turned around, her neck stiff with terror. But there was nothing there, only the open door. She turned back again, and seized hold of a curtain, and flung it violently to one side, to reveal what was underneath. It billowed and fell back against the window, empty and lifeless. At that moment, the room brightened, too, and Laura found herself standing alone. A car

289

horn honked in the street outside, and she heard birds chirping and people laughing. She went over to the radio and tried the control-knob. It was switched off. She switched it on again and it was playing the Chiquita Banana calypso commercial. She switched off again and went through to the kitchen. The flower-vase was covered in a thick furry layer of white frost, and when she touched the orchids, they shattered, as if they were made of fragile glass, and scattered over the tabletop.

She went to the phone and picked it up. 'Long-distance, please. New York.'

She reached Charles Keraghter & Co. but a nasal receptionist told her that Elizabeth was in an editorial meeting, and wouldn't be free for another hour.

'Do you want to leave a message?'

Laura hesitated for a moment, and then looked across at the broken orchids. 'Yes, tell her that her sister called. Tell her that the Snow Queen's paid me another visit.'

'Do you want to repeat that?'

Aunt Beverley came home in time for lunch and they ate shrimp and avocado salad in the courtyard. Aunt Beverley's lipstick was smudged and she was wearing a silk polo-neck blouse in a particularly jarring mauve. She seemed irritable and distracted.

'You saw Harrison?' asked Laura, cautiously.

'Yes. He's being very nosy.'

'That's his job, isn't it, being nosy?'

'There's nosy and nosy. Harrison makes Jimmy Durante look like Porky Pig.'

'What's he after?'

Aunt Beverley put down her fork, lit a cigarette. 'It's all hearsay. He can't prove anything.'

'What's all hearsay?'

'I've done some people some favours over the years, that's

all. Fixed it for people to meet. Fixed it for people to get hold of some difficult merchandise that they might have had a hankering for. He says I might have supplied some difficult merchandise to Vele Lopez.' She defiantly blew out smoke. 'It's all lies, of course.'

She didn't seem to want to say any more, so Laura said, 'Chester called by. He's seen the camera tests and he says they're terrific. He wants to take me out for dinner tonight, so that we can pow-wow.'

For one fleeting instant, there was a look on Aunt Beverley's face that almost approached remorse, but then she shrugged and turned away, 'Make sure he takes you somewhere fancy. Last time he took me out, we ended up at the Hamburger Hamlet on Sunset.'

Laura gave her a brief, dissolving smile. Then she said, 'Aunt Beverley, do you believe in ghosts?'

'Ghosts? What do you mean, ghosts? Of course I believe in ghosts. Every time I look in the mirror, who do you think I see standing behind me, but every man I ever knew?'

'I mean real ghosts, people who have actually come back from the dead.'

Aunt Beverley crushed out her cigarette right in the middle of her shrimp. 'That's a funny question to ask. Are you serious?'

Laura nodded. 'Peggy's still with us. Elizabeth's seen her, too.'

Aunt Beverley thought about that for a very long time without saying anything, her eyes searching Laura's face. 'Do you know what it is she wants?' she asked, at last. 'Ghosts usually *want* something, don't they? Peace, or reassurance, or forgiveness. Mind you, Peggy couldn't have had anything to forgive.'

'She says she wants to protect us. The trouble is – '

Aunt Beverley raised a hand to silence her. 'Don't tell me

what the trouble is. Don't tell me anything. I don't want to know about ghosts, not real ghosts. God knows, I have quite enough of my own. If she wants to protect you, fine, let her protect you. All of us could use some protecting, now and again.'

But Laura persisted. 'The trouble is, it's not just her. There's always something with her, something that freezes everything it touches. You remember your planter that broke? That was frozen. And today, when Chester had left – '

Her eyes filled with tears and she clamped her hand over her mouth. She hadn't realized until now how much Peggy's apparition had distressed and frightened her. Aunt Beverley stood up and put her arm around her shoulders and said. 'There, come on now. You've been under a strain, that's all, what with David's funeral and trying to get this part.'

All the same, she remembered the pan of milk that she had set to boil, and which had frozen solid.

She stayed where she was, stroking Laura's shoulder, and for the first time in her life she began to feel that the past was catching up with her, as if every sin that she had ever committed had been painstakingly set to paper, and stacked away, leaving a crooked chalk initial on the wall to identify it. V for Velez, H for Herman, B for Bartok.

Elizabeth left the conference room at 4:15, when it was still only 1:15 in Hollywood. She felt exhausted and angry. Almost every editorial suggestion she had made to Margo Rossi about *Reds Under The Bed* had been greeted by a single, supercilious raise of one eyebrow, followed by a sweeping and totally contradictory suggestion from Margo herself. Margo had dismantled Elizabeth's attempts at editing the book so completely and so systematically that even George Kruszca, who was normally Margo's Number One Yes-Man, had started to look disturbed.

He stopped Elizabeth in the panelled corridor. He was a big wide-shouldered man with heavy-rimmed glasses and startlingly black brushcut hair. 'Hey . . . that was rough,' he told her.

'Oh, forget it,' said Elizabeth. 'Margo doesn't care for anything I do; and she doesn't care for me personally; and she doesn't mind who knows it.'

They walked along the corridor. George said, 'You have to understand that Margo clawed her way up from the bottom and she resents anybody else who looks as if they're doing it, too. As far as she is concerned, nobody else claws their way up after her. Especially if they're pretty.'

'I thought you were a Margophile.'

George gave her a lackadaisical grin. 'I'm a George-o-phile, if you want to know the truth. I've worked at Keraghty for six years and believe me I know the value of keeping my mouth shut and my head nodding. Or shaking, depending on the question. I have a wife and a baby to keep. What's more important? Telling Margo that she's an 18-carat bitch, or putting strained vegetables in my baby's lunchbowl?'

They reached the elevators. George prodded the button for 7, they stood back, waiting. 'Let me give you a word of advice,' he told her. 'You're clever, you're educated, you're creative, you're likeable. You can be careless, I've seen it, not only in your editing, but in the way you deal with people. But experience should sort that out, and experience is what you need. So don't let Margo bug you. Take whatever she dishes out, and think to yourself that you're working for one of the hottest publishing houses in the country, and the longer you're here, the more valuable you're going to be.'

'You're a man of steel, George,' said Elizabeth, and grinned.

Margo Rossi came stalking on sharp high-heeled shoes along the corridor towards them. She was a tall, svelte woman of thirty-two with dark swept-back hair and Italianate good looks. She had hooded eyes and a long thin nose and the tightest mouth that Elizabeth had ever seen.

'Lizzie,' she said. 'I'm glad to see you're not sulking.'

'I'm a little disappointed, I admit. But I never sulk.'

'Good,' said Margo, baring her considerable teeth. 'That's the first lesson of corporate survival. Admit your mistakes and never whine about them.'

'And bow a lot,' George murmured, under his breath.

The elevator arrived. Margo said, 'You go ahead, George, I want to talk to Lizzie for a moment.'

He hesitated for a second, then stepped into the elevator and stood with his arms by his sides staring warningly at Elizabeth as the doors closed.

Margo said, sharply, 'I understand that Johnson Ward is one of your family friends.'

'Bronco, yes, that's right.'

'Bronco? I never heard him called that before. Is that what you called him when you were a child?'

Elizabeth said, 'I don't know. He asked me to call him Bronco, so I did.'

'I knew that living out West would be the finish of him,' said Margo. 'I suppose you're aware that he was paid a twenty-thousand dollar advance for his latest novel, due for delivery the week before Christmas? I called him yesterday and after a great deal of evasion he admitted that he hadn't written more than six or seven pages.'

'I knew he was having difficulty with it. It's his brother Billy.'

Margo blinked, in that intimidating slow-motion way of hers, her eyelashes sweeping downward like raven's wings. It was a blink that meant, am I hearing this correctly, or do you wish to change your mind before I open my eyes again?

'Billy is dead, Lizzie. He's been dead for a very long time.'

'Yes, but Bronco's been sort of *haunted*. By memories, I guess.

He's always written slowly, and now he's finding it even harder.'

Margo said, 'The difficulty I have with this, Lizzie, is that we have twenty thousand dollars invested in this book and Mr Keraghter is *very* keen to know when we might be expecting some kind of return on our investment. I don't need *Bitter Fruit* all over again, but I wouldn't mind a couple of hundred pages of sour grapes.'

'Do you want me to talk to him?' asked Elizabeth.

'Do I want *you* to talk to him? No, I do not want *you* to talk to him. The last person in the world I need to have talking to him is somebody who sat on his knee and called him Bronco.'

'Margo, I don't think you really understand. This Billy thing is serious.'

'You're telling me it's serious? I have to account for commissioning one of the most costly novels of 1951, and all I have is six pages of novel and a twenty-page letter of excuses.'

Elizabeth looked down at the floor. 'Actually, you don't.'

'Actually, I don't *what*, dear?'

'Actually you have only two-and-a-half lines of novel and a twenty-page letter of excuses. The lines are: "Pearson sat in the middle of a day with no shadow. He had women on his mind. Women and liquor, but mostly women." '

Margo stared at Elizabeth and her mouth squeezed tighter and tighter. 'That's it? That's all he's written? And you *knew*?'

'You're his editor.'

'You're incredible! Jesus, you're *incredible*! I should sack you on the spot.'

Elizabeth turned her face aside. 'I'm sorry. I didn't mean to be arrogant. He's a friend of the family, that's all, and I suppose that makes me more tolerant of him.'

Margo visibly quivered. Then she said, in deliberately clear and measured tones, as if she were speaking to a halfwit, 'Johnson Ward obviously needs help with his novel. I am his editor. I am going to take two weeks away and fly to Arizona to help him get his nose to the grindstone. If he fails to get his brain back together again, I shall make it my business to come back to New York with twenty thousand dollars of Mr Keraghter's money.'

She took a deep breath, and then she said, 'While I am away, you will take over some of George's editorial duties, and you will also edit Mary Harper Randolph's new book, to the best of your ability. Although I was critical of the work you did on *Reds Under The Bed*, it did show promise, Lizzie, and some of your suggestions were almost usable.'

Elizabeth bit her lip. Her mind kept trying to frame the next sentence. With all due respect, Johnson Ward needs somebody who believes him when he talks about Billy. With all due respect, Johnson Ward needs companionship and relaxation, not another Vita on his back. With all due respect, you have as much appreciation of the lazy, scandalous, vain, arrogant and heartbreaking world of Johnson Ward as you have about playing the slide trombone.

With all due respect, you're a bitch.

She said none of these things. Instead, she said, 'Yes, all right,' and pressed the button for the elevator.

'I'm relying on you, Lizzie,' said Margo, in a steelspring, uptilting voice.

'Yes,' said Elizabeth, and waited with her head bowed for the elevator to arrive.

Chester angled his Cadillac into the steeply downsloping driveway of his house on Summit Ridge Drive, and pulled up under the Spanish-style lantern which stood outside the front steps. It was a chilly night, but brilliantly clear, and when Chester opened the door for her and she climbed out of the car, Laura could see the lights of Los Angeles sparkling all the way to the airport. She was wearing a tight white satin dress that

Aunt Beverley had brought her for one of Sidney Skolsky's parties. It left her shoulders bare, and so Aunt Beverley had lent her a mink wrap. Aunt Beverley said that someody seriously disreputable had given it to her, but she couldn't remember whether it was Gaetano Lucchese or Franklin D. Roosevelt.

'Come inside,' said Chester. 'There's somebody I want you to meet.'

Laura almost lost her balance on the slope, and tip-tap-tip-tapped all the way down to the bushes at the bottom. 'Your house isn't straight!' she giggled. 'It's all leaning over!'

Chester laughed and rescued her from the shrubbery. 'I like to live on a hill,' he told her, putting his arm around her and steering her back up to the steps. 'I like to look down on people, from up above. And that's what you're going to be doing, only from higher up.'

Laura managed to focus on his face by screwing up her left eye tight and peering with her right. 'How high up?' she wanted to know.

Chester pointed directly to the night sky. 'All the way up. You're a star.'

He helped her into the house, and across the marble floor of the hallway into his living-room. It was cream-painted, cream-carpeted, with huge cream leather couches. The walls were hung with oil-paintings of huge-breasted nudes, so vast that they looked as if they had been painted to be viewed from at least a half-mile away.

The south-facing wall was all glass, and gave out onto a balcony, from which they could see the whole of Los Angeles stretched out beneath them.

'Welcome to my humble abode,' said Chester.

Laura looked around. 'You're right, it is pretty humble, isn't it?' she slurred. 'Come to that, you're looking pretty frowsy yourself.'

'Groucho Marx!' said Chester. 'You have a talent for comedy, too!'

Laura collapsed into one of the sofas and let the mink wrap slide off her shoulders. 'I have a talent for everything,' she said.

'Champagne?' asked Chester, walking over to the cream-lacquered liquor cabinet.

'*More* champagne?' screamed Laura, and started giggling again.

'Come on,' Chester urged her, taking three tall flutes out of the cabinet, and a chilled bottle of Perrier-Jouët. 'This is a celebration. This is a night for champagne!'

'All right, then,' Laura declared, far too loudly. 'More champagne!'

She felt wonderful. She felt as if she were floating. Chester had picked her up promptly at seven o'clock and driven her to the Players on Sunset Boulevard. The Players was a gourmet restaurant on a second-floor verandah, owned by Preston Sturges, the director. All his Oscar-winning friends liked to gather there: not only for their own company, but for the matchless food, especially the rare beef and the Caesar salads. Laura had eaten lobster, and drunk champagne, and drunk more champagne.

All evening, Chester's face had smiled at her over the candlelit tabletop like the waxing moon, and assured her she was a star. 'When I said shortlist, I was just trying to be cautious, you know what I mean, in case you were disappointed. But look at you now! Shortlist, schmortlist. The camera loves you, I love you. The public's going to love you.'

Now she lay back on the sofa and everything swam around her and she knew that she was going to be famous. 'Ohhhh, Chester . . .' she said, 'Kiss me!'

But Chester simply smiled and shook his head. 'Come on, Laura, you're a beautiful girl. You're the most beautiful girl I've seen in Hollywood in years. But I can't kiss you. This is a professional relationship – director, star. How many people in Hollywood fall victim to scandal? How many actors and actresses jump into the sack with everybody they meet, practically? Far too many, that's my opinion!' He sat down beside her and clinked glasses. 'They're at it like rabbits, for God's sake.'

Laura frowned at him. 'Mr Bunzum,' she said.

'I beg your pardon?'

'Mr Bunzum . . . he was a rabbit. Do you know what happened to him?'

Chester stared at her suspiciously. 'No,' she said, thickly, his throat filled with phlegm.

Laura sat up and pressed her nose flat against his, so that they were staring into each other's eyes at point-blank range. 'Mr Bunzum was frozen to death. Frozen so solid that his arms fell off. Frozen so solid that his legs fell off.'

She leaned away from him, so far back that he thought she was going to topple off the sofa. 'Frozen so solid that his *peter* fell off!'

She whacked the sofa and threw back her head and laughed and laughed. Chester pretended to laugh but he wasn't laughing at all: he was too tense. All the same, watching her, he thought that she was perfect. Beautiful, perfect, her hair golden, her skin shining, her small breasts swelling the white satin dress.

'Listen,' he said. 'There's somebody I want you to meet. Somebody important.'

Laura squeezed the tip of her nose between finger and thumb to stop herself laughing. She let out a terrible snort, and laughed even more, but eventually she managed to calm herself down. 'Somebody important? Somebody *how* important? More important than you? More important than me?'

'Just . . . somebody *very* important. His name's Raymond. You'll like him a lot. He's been thinking of putting some finance into *Devil's Elbow* . . . quite a fair amount of finance . . . in which case – well, we can afford to have you play a starring role. Not exactly lead starring role, Shelly Summers has been cast for that, we have to have some established box-office names, after all. But "also starring", and that's a whole lot better than "forty-seventh floozie on the left" now isn't it?'

Laura stared at him wide-eyed. 'I'm going to be "also starring?" Really?'

Chester swept his hand across an imaginary movie screen. '*Devil's Elbow*, starring Michael Grant and Shelly Summers, also starring Laura Buchanan, Mitch Forbes and Zachary Moskowitz.'

'You're kidding mee!' she squealed.

'I'm not kidding, I promise. But be nice to Raymond, okay? Raymond is the money man . . . if Raymond gets upset, we don't get the extra finance. Then it's bye-bye "also starring".' Chester tried to look tragic, without much success. 'Not only that, it could be bye-bye *Devil's Elbow* altogether.'

Laura sat up and frowned at him. 'Okay, Chester. This is my solemn-num oath. I shall be nice to Raymond.'

Chester raised his glass. 'What a good girl, then. Raymond! Raymond – are you there? Come say hello to our brand-new star!'

There was a pause about as long as it takes for the needle to drop onto a record and the music to begin. Then a very tall swarthy man in a beautifully-cut tuxedo appeared from the dining-area, holding a balloon-glass of brandy. He was ugly in a brutally handsome way, with scar-spattered cheeks and a sloping forehead and slightly bulbous eyes. He carried himself like an athlete, although there was the hint of a limp in his left foot, trailing slightly. An injured athlete. He approached Laura and stood towering over her, and his thick lips lifted in a patronizing smile.

'Is this her?' he asked Chester.

'What do you think?' said Chester, suddenly nervous.

Raymond reached out one of his octave-spanning hands and touched Laura's silky curls. 'I don't know yet,' he said. 'Depends how pliable she is.'

Eighteen

Margo Rossi reached home shortly after midnight. Since September she had been living in a plush but rather stuffy two-bedroomed apartment at the Apthorp, a vast apartment building on Broadway and 78th Street, popular with actors and writers and theatrical producers. Margo's father was big in walnuts, and had paid the lease for her, two years in advance.

She peered at her face in the mirror as she went up in the elevator. She thought she was looking haggard. She had spent the evening at Downey's with a lawyer called Victor Emblem who had been pursuing her relentlessly for six months, sending her roses, sending her teasing little notes, telephoning her at the office. Victor was good-looking in a pallid, shock-haired way, rather like a handsome Stan Laurel, and his sense of humour was highly sophisticated. Victor's idea of a rib-cracking joke was a senior judge saying to a junior colleague, 'Be just! And if you can't be just, be arbitrary.'

She suspected that he liked her because she was confident and tough. That was why she hadn't enjoyed herself this evening, in spite of drinking four green brandy stingers. She was tired of the way in which men responded to her. Either they found her threatening, and turned their backs on her; or else they wanted her to dominate them. Sometimes she felt as if the world were populated by only two kinds of men: masochists or boors.

She let herself in to her apartment and switched on the light, and suddenly became aware of how cold it was, so cold that she could see her breath. The heating was working, because the lobby and the corridors had all been up to their usual intolerable temperature. Mostly, her apartment was so warm that she could scarcely breathe. She knew she hadn't left a window open. Unless somebody had climbed up the fire escape and broken in. She hung up her coat. She cautiously approached the living-room door, which was an inch ajar. The whole apartment was quiet, quiet enough for her to hear her wristwatch ticking.

'Is anyone there?' she called out.

Of course there was no reply. But a draught was blowing out through the inch-wide gap in the doorway and it was freezing cold – not just window-open cold, but intensely cold, meat-freezer cold.

She hesitated. Maybe she should call the super before she went into the sitting-room. There had been a rash of burglars and intruders at the Apthorp lately. Mrs Lindhurst in 711 had been hit on the head with one of her own zinc statuettes; and the Strasbergs had lost a fortune in jewellery. But Margo considered herself more than a match for any scavenging burglar. If she were capable of reducing seasoned editors to tears, there was no reason to think that she couldn't do the same to some uneducated bum who made his living climbing other people's fire escapes.

She pushed open the sitting-room door and swung it wide. It was dark inside, except for the light from the hallway falling across the carpet, and her own attenuated shadow. And wasn't it *cold*! She groped her hand sideways until she found the lightswitch, and turned on the lamps.

The room had been catastrophically wrecked. The lamps still worked, but they lay on the floor with their bases and their shades broken. The tapestry couch had been ripped open, and its stuffing strewn everywhere. Side-tables had been over-turned, ornaments smashed, paintings torn to ribbons. The carpet and the scatter-rugs had been cut to pieces, and the pale blue moiré wallcovering hung from the wall in shreds.

'Oh, my God,' breathed Margo, and walked into the centre of the room like a woman in a nightmare. She picked up a small Dresden figure of a shepherdess, headless and crookless now, and placed it carefully on the one occasional table that remained upright – even though its unlaid surface had been deeply scored. She looked around with her mouth open and her eyes blurring with tears. It looked as if a ten-clawed monster had rampaged around the room, tearing and smashing everything in sight. She had heard of burglars doing damage before now: but she had never heard of anything like this.

She found the telephone lying on the floor, chipped but still working, and dialled down to the super's office. He seemed to take an age to answer. He was either asleep, or watching TV with the volume turned up so loudly that he couldn't hear. Then she heard the bathroom door bang. She covered the phone receiver with her hand and listened hard. She heard it again, but this time it was softly closed, as if somebody were using the handle.

She put down the phone and walked back into the hallway and along to the bathroom. The door was closed but the light was shining from underneath it. She wiped her nose and her eyes with the back of her hand and stood outside the door wondering what to do.

'Who's there?' she called, nervously. 'If there's anybody there, you'd better come out. I've called the police and they'll be here at any minute.'

There was a long silence, an eternity. Biting her lip, she stepped towards the door and clasped the handle. It was ice-cold, so cold that it almost burned her. But she was determined to find out who had wrecked her apartment. She would damn well kill them if she had the chance. She was just about to open the door when she heard high-pitched laughing, somewhere behind her. A child's laugh: a little girl's laugh. She turned around in time to glimpse a white dress and a bare white foot disappearing into her bedroom.

'Hey!' she snapped. 'Hey, you! I want a word with you!'

She ran back along the corridor, kicking off her shoes. She reached the bedroom door and slammed it open so violently that it juddered on its hinges.

The room was even colder than the rest of the apartment. It could have been outside, on a sub-zero day, with the wind blowing off the snow. It was light, too, even though the lamps weren't switched on. The whole room was illuminated by a blue, chilly fluorescence which crawled up the drapes and across the radiators and around the edges of the furniture.

A little girl in a white dress was standing on the opposite side of the room, in front of the long mirror. She had her back turned. She was standing quite still, staring at herself, although Margo couldn't see the reflection of her face.

'What have you done to my apartment?' Margo demanded, her voice quaking. 'What the hell have you done to my apartment? Are you crazy? Are you some kind of lunatic?'

The little girl said nothing. Margo took two sharp steps towards her, but then abruptly stopped. She suddenly realized that the girl was swaying very slightly from side to side, and the reason she was swaying was because her feet were more than two clear inches off the floor.

Margo stared at her, not knowing what to do, not knowing what to say.

'Cat got your tongue?' asked the little girl, in a curiously muffled voice.

Margo opened and closed her mouth. Then she managed to say. 'What are you? What are you doing here? What do you want?'

'I never come to nice people,' said the little girl.

'What are you talking about? I don't understand you. You're floating. How can you float?'

'Anyone can float,' said the little girl. 'It's just a question of desire.'

Margo said, 'I'm going to call the police.'

'What for?' asked the little girl. 'I'll be gone by then, and who will ever believe you?'

'I want to know why you're here,' Margo demanded.

'Don't you ever say "please"? You never say "please" to my sister, do you? You never say it to anybody.'

Margo took a gritty little breath. 'Please tell me why you're here,' she said. 'Please tell me why you've torn my whole damned apartment to pieces. Please tell me why I shouldn't take hold of you and wring your scrawny little neck!'

'Now, now, Margo, that will never do,' the little girl replied. 'You must beg me to tell you, and say "pretty please".'

Although the girl was still floating and swaying, Margo was regaining her confidence. It was some kind of damn stupid trick, that was all. And the little girl, for all of her insolence, was only a little girl. She took the three remaining steps toward her and seized hold of her bare skinny arm. It was intensely cold, much colder than she had expected, but she held on tight and tried to tug the little girl around, so that she could look her in the face.

'Look at me!' she screamed. 'You damn well look at me!'

Instantly, the little girl turned her face away. Margo tried to grab her hair, but the little girl twisted her head around and pulled it free.

'Look at me! Look at me, you little bitch!'

The girl struggled to tug her arm free, digging her elbow painfully into Margo's ribs. But Margo gripped both of her arms now, and forced her to look towards the mirror, so that she could at least see a reflection of her face. When she looked, however, the surface of the mirror was obscured with fronds and leaf-patterns of frost, and all Margo could see was a blur.

Margo tried again to look at the girl's face directly, but again the girl twisted her head away, and whirled her hair so that it covered her like a bedraggled white veil.

'You bitch!' Margo raved. 'You vicious little bitch!'

She gripped the girl around her neck, dragged her nearer the mirror, and rubbed furiously at its frost-flowers with her sleeve. At first she succeeded in clearing nothing more than a few semi-circular scratches, but she rubbed and rubbed until she had cleared a hole in the frost the size of a breakfast-plate. All the time the girl kept struggling and twisting, but even though Margo was disgusted by the coldness of her skin and the ice-cold crustiness of her dress, she clung round her neck and refused to let go.

'You don't want to see me, Margo!' the little girl choked. 'You don't want to see me, I promise you!'

'Let me be the judge of that!' Margo panted.

'Not in the mirror, Margo!' the little girl gasped, trying to pry Margo's fingers away from her neck. 'The mirror is the puzzle! The mirror is the reason! The mirror is the answer!'

But the more she protested and fought, the more determined Margo became. She seized the girl's shoulders and thrust her face towards the patch she had cleared in the frost, and said, triumphantly, *'There!'*

And froze. And released the little girl; and lowered her arms; and stared.

There was a face in the mirror, but it was not the face of a little girl at all. It was a white, deathly face with eyes like black stones, a face which appeared to have white snakes growing from it. It was exquisite and terrible at the same time, and it stared back at Margo through the hole in the frost like some appalling creature staring cruelly and longingly into the world of humans.

The little girl slowly spun away, around and around, so that her white dressed twirled. Yet still the terrible face stared at Margo through the porthole of frost, and it seemed to be saying. *I shall know you now, by sight. I shall know who you are. You will never be rid of me. Every time you rub a circle in a misty window, I shall be staring in at you. Every time you take out your powder-compact on a winter's day and look in its mirror, there I shall be. You are mine, now. You belong to me, for ever.*

Margo turned and stared at the little girl in panic, but the little girl did nothing but giggle and rush out of the room.

Margo looked back at the mirror. She saw the face for one split-instant more, and then the mirror shattered like a bomb, catching her in a vicious blizzard of broken glass. Shards of mirror flew into her face and into her eyes. More shards sliced through her clothing and cut her shoulders, and her arms and her thighs and her breasts. She had opened her mouth to scream, and her lips and tongue were porcupined with scores of tiny triangular pieces of mirror.

Blinded, bloody, shocked, she stood where she was for almost a minute. Then she collapsed onto her knees, even though her knees were filled with fragments of glass, too, and when she knelt they were driven into her flesh even further. She couldn't speak, she couldn't move. She tried to reach up to tug some of the glass out of her tongue, but there were splinters in her fingers, too, and all she succeeded in doing was cutting her mouth even more.

And she was so cold. She was so miserably cold. She was freezing and shaking and she wanted her father so badly that she couldn't bear it. She couldn't even cry because her eyes were filled with glass.

She heard a dreary wind blowing, like the wind across a black winter landscape. She even thought she could feel snow, falling wet and cold against her skin, but that might have been blood. She heard a young girl laughing, eerie and high and chillingly self-delighted.

Raymond was leaning close to Laura. 'How about some more champagne?' he asked her, lifting the bottle out of the ice-bucket. The bottom of the bottle was wet and it dripped onto her ankle.

'Ahh!' she screamed, and then she burst out laughing again.

Raymond topped up her glass, and poured just a little into his own. 'You know something,' he said, 'Hollywood is crowded with hopefuls, and that's all they'll ever be, hopefuls. Hoping isn't enough. You have to have something beyond hope. You have to be totally convinced that everybody wants you ... that everybody wants to look at your face, that everybody wants to look at your body, that everybody wants to possess you.'

'And how about you, Raymond?' said Laura, wiping the tears of laughter away from her eyes. 'Do you want to possess me?'

Raymond cocked the little finger of his left hand and gently touched the tip of her nose. 'You're a very special woman, Laura. One in a million-million. What man wouldn't?'

He looked into her eyes for a long, long time. Then he turned to Chester and said, 'How about something to eat? I've been sitting in meetings all day. I'm feeling hungry.'

'Cold roast chicken, and maybe some salad?'

'Sure, why not?'

Chester called for his manservant, a small dour Mexican with a flat face and beady black eyes like a gingerbread man. 'Hernandez will fix you something,' he told Raymond. 'You want to talk finance?'

'All in good time,' Raymond replied. 'Let me satisfy my appetites first.'

'So what do you actually *do*, Raymond?' Laura asked him.

Raymond started to wind her curls around his finger. He was so close to her that she could smell the cigarettes and alcohol on his breath, as well as another smell, flat and strong and quite unpleasant.

'I'm a clever guy, that's all. People want to make movies, I help them to make movies. People want to do anything, maybe stage a boxing bout, maybe put on a show – I help them to do it.

I find people who have money and don't know what to do with it, and I put them in contact with people who know what to do with it but don't have any. Also, I dedicate my life to enjoying myself. That's a high thing on my list. Tell me, what's the use of being alive if you don't enjoy yourself?'

'No point at all,' smiled Laura. She leaned her face nearer and nearer to him, until their noses were almost touching. 'Tell me,' she said, 'have you been eating garlic?'

For an instant, Raymond's eyes turned as hard as nailheads. His mouth turned to a slit. But Laura fell back onto the sofa, laughing again, and Raymond uneasily softened, and rubbed the palm of his hand against his thigh. 'Sure,' he said, as if he could only just choke the words out. '*Totani e patate in tegame alla Genovese*. Why – you want to make something of it?'

He let out a harsh, repetitive laugh, and Chester joined in, but then abruptly stopped as if he had forgotten what he was doing right there in mid-laugh.

'Squid and potatoes,' Raymond explained. He drank a mouthful of champagne and swished it around his mouth. 'It has to have garlic, otherwise it tastes like squid and potatoes.'

He laughed again, and repeated himself. 'Otherwise it tastes like squid and potatoes, hanh?' Chester was obviously relieved when Hernandez appeared with a large napkin-draped tray, with pieces of cold chicken and a green salad. Hernandez mixed a little dressing from small tear-shaped bottles of oil and vinegar, and then left.

Raymond voraciously ate chicken and stared into Laura's eyes while Chester wandered around the room with his glass of champagne, lighting and relighting his cigar. There was some kind of sleazy jazz playing on the gramophone, quite softly but suggestively.

'Shouldn't I start thinking about a press agent?' asked Laura.

Raymond tore at a leg-muscle with his teeth. 'One thing at a time. But I know plenty. I can introduce you. First of all, you have to start dressing good. Change your wardrobe. Change your hair. Get your face made over.'

'That's going to cost something, isn't it?' asked Laura, although she couldn't suppress her feelings of excitement and flattery and sheer fantastic luck.

Raymond didn't take his eyes off her. 'I can fix all that. Now you're a star, you have to start looking like a star, right?' He swallowed and sniffed, although he still had a greasy shred of chicken hanging from the side of his lip.

Laura reached out to pick the chicken off. He instantly gripped her wrist so hard that it hurt her. Then he clapped his hand to his mouth and wiped the chicken off himself. 'Never do that,' he said.

'Don't be so fierce!' Laura retorted. 'I was only being friendly.'

'You're trying to suggest I eat like a pig, is that it? First of all I smell of garlic, then I eat like a pig?'

Laura pulled her hand away. 'You're too sensitive, Raymond.' But then she gave him a coy, lopsided smile. 'Still, I like sensitive men. Especially sensitive men who give me entire new wardrobes.'

Raymond picked up a napkin from the tray and vigorously towelled his mouth. Then he tilted himself over to Laura and kissed her cheek. 'You like furs?' he asked her. 'Which do you like the best? Fox, mink, what?'

Laura was bright-eyed. 'You mean it? A fur?'

Raymond nodded. 'Full-length mink, that's what you need. Every star who is worthy of the name has to have a full-length mink. And maybe a fox-fur jacket, too, what do you think? And we have to think of jewellery. Diamonds, especially, because they glitter so good when the press takes your picture.'

Laura smiled and nodded and felt as if she were floating away on some gently-rising balloon. The sitting-room was a balloon, soft and rounded and warm and comfortable. Raymond's face was a balloon, too, bobbing up and down in front of her. She thought he was so ugly that he was handsome. She wondered how that could be. How could a man have such a sloping-back forehead and all those craters in his cheeks and still be so sexy?

She sat up and kissed him. He tasted all right. A bit chickeny, but otherwise all right. 'You know what you are?' she said, nuzzling in close to his shoulder. 'You think you're a Latin lover.'

'You think that's what I think I am?'

She nodded her head up and down, up and down. 'You sure do.'

'You want me to prove it to you?' he asked.

She snorted and giggled and flung her arms around his shoulders and kissed him on the nose. 'Latin lovers are always like that, aren't they? Always having to prove themselves!'

Raymond made a *moue*. 'Isn't that the only way that you can find out if your guess is correct?'

Laura nodded giggling again. She couldn't help it, everything seemed so delicious. Raymond kissed her cheeks and her ears and her eyelashes, and then he kissed her on the mouth, deep on the mouth, and his tongue slid in between her teeth, and started exploring her gums, like a walrus exploring a rocky shoreline.

Something happened to Laura then. She never remembered how, or why. But it seemed at that moment as if Raymond were the most desirable man she had ever met, that he was the key to everything exciting and successful. He was rich, and he could make her famous, and that gave him a magnetism that she found totally irresistible. The gramophone was playing 'Downright Dirty Blues', with a slow, strutting rhythm and a trumpet that sounded as if it were physically in pain. Laura nuzzled and kissed Raymond's lips, and then she lifted herself up, lifted her dress high on her thighs, and climbed astride him, reverently holding his pockmarked cheeks in both hands. 'You, *senor*, are the answer to a maiden's prayer,' she whispered, and kissed him, and kissed him again.

His right hand slithered down the back of her white satin dress and cupped her bottom. He allowed himself a small smile, because he could confirm now what he had already suspected earlier – that, in a close-fitting satin dress like this, she wasn't wearing any undergarments. His left hand cupped her breast. He looked over Laura's shoulder at Chester, and Chester nodded his understanding, and walked out onto the balcony, behind the net curtains, and smoked his cigar, and admired the lights of Los Angeles.

Laura felt Raymond's hands sliding her dress higher and higher. It felt so silky and sensual, and he was such a Latin Lover, wasn't he? His hands caressed her bare bottom, his fingertips ran soft as spiders in between the cheeks. She kissed him again, a wet, passionate, all-over kiss. 'Do you know what you are, Raymond? You're . . . god, that's what you are. Not *the* God. But *a* god. The god of Hollywood. The keeper of the keys.'

'You are a very exciting little girl,' breathed Raymond, and his fingers ran around her thighs and found the soft damp fur of her pubic hair.

She felt him struggling for a moment underneath her, but she was floating and floating away, and she didn't realize that he was twisting his fly-buttons open. It was only when his fingers opened the lips of her vulva, and a hot bludgeoning presence made itself felt between her legs that she realized what he was doing. Even then, it didn't seem really real. It was more like one of those dreams she had, when she thought that a boy was on top of her, thrusting and thrusting, and then suddenly he melted into nothing, and it was morning, and the birds were singing, and Aunt Beverley was bringing her a glass of orange juice.

313

Raymond grunted, and pushed himself up into her, only halfway, then grunted again, and buried himself deep inside her, right up to the balls. She was sitting on top of him, but he was far stronger than she was, and it was he who set the pace. He gripped her bottom in both hands and rammed up into her, again and again and again, until she was jiggling around on his lap like a marionette.

She loved it, she hated it, it made her feel sick. It was fantastic. His huge cock ramming into her over and over again, his tongue wriggling deep inside her mouth.

'You're a floppy little fuck, aren't you?' Raymond sweated. He kept on thrusting himself into her, and her vagina was making a monotonous, systematic squelching noise. 'Come on, Laura, I thought you were sexy! I thought you were the screen queen!I I thought you were a star!'

'Star,' Laura mumbled, her arms flapping loosely by her sides.

Raymond rammed her and rammed her again and then he lost his patience. He tipped her off his lap, so that she sprawled onto the sofa. Then he furiously unbuttoned his shirt, although he didn't take it off, unbuckled his belt, and took off his black evening pants and his shorts. Hairy-chested and hairy-legged, still wearing his shirt and his black evening socks, he lifted Laura off the sofa and carried her over to the marble-topped breakfast table. He laid her flat on her stomach, her dress lifted up to her waist, her legs wide apart.

'This is cold,' Laura murmured, to her own reflection in the polished top. Her eyes closed, then opened again. 'What am I doing here? Chester? Is that you, Chester?'

From the balcony outside, there came a suppressed smoker's cough. Chester was watching through the net curtains. He saw Raymond take the tear-shaped olive-oil bottle from the supper-tray, and approach Laura where she lay spreadeagled on the table. He heard her call his name, but he stayed where he was, and continued to watch, and to cough. Raymond stood between Laura's outspread legs. His cock was darkly-pigmented, very hairy, and huge. He took the stopper out of the bottle of oil, and carefully poured a thin stream of it all the way down the shaft. Then he put down the bottle, and massaged the oil into his cock and balls until they shone, and his black pubic hair looked like Frank Sinatra's quiff.

His hands still smothered in oil, he parted the cheeks of Laura's bottom and smeared them around and around. Laura opened her eyes and tried to lift herself up off the table, but Raymond pushed her back down again, and said, 'You want to be a star? Then shut up, and stay where you are.'

Chester smoked and watched through the breeze-blown curtains as Raymond positioned the plum-coloured head of his cock against Laura's bottom. Somewhere not too far away he heard a police siren but he didn't turn around to see where it was. He didn't once take his eyes away from the tense, still scene in the living-room. He coughed, though, when Raymond forced himself forward, once, twice, and then again; and Laura cried out and tried to get up again, but Raymond punched her with his clenched fist in the small of her back to make her stay where she was.

She stayed where she was. Her face was turned towards Chester as though she were watching him accusingly, but he knew that she almost certainly couldn't see him, out in the dark. He smoked and wished that it were all over, but he knew that Raymond wanted him to watch. Raymond was even standing slightly to one side, his right hand on his hip, his shirt drawn back, so that Chester could get a clearer view.

Chester closed his eyes, but he could still see dark, greasy veins, sliding in and out, and stretched reddened flesh. All the same, he still had his eyes closed when Raymond let out a thick, coarse shout of triumph, and shouted. 'You're a star after all, Laura! You're a star!'

After a while he opened his eyes to see Raymond on the sofa with a full glass of champagne, and Laura still lying on the table, her dress raised, the cheeks of her bottom decorated with sperm. He opened the sliding door and stepped back into the room. Laura's eyes followed him but she didn't attempt to move. Chester walked across to the bathroom and came back with a thick turquoise towel. He looked down at Raymond but he couldn't find the words to describe his loathing, not only for Raymond, but for himself, so he said nothing at all. He wiped Laura and then he helped her off the table. She clung on to him and kept swallowing as if she wanted to be sick.

'You want the bathroom, sweetheart? I'll take you to the bathroom.'

When he came back he stood looking at Raymond and he still couldn't think what to say.

'Do you have a problem?' Raymond asked him, at last.

Chester shook his head. 'No, no problem.'

Raymond swallowed more champagne, and sniffed. 'You want to talk some finance now? How much do you need?'

'Whyn't you put your pants on first?' Chester suggested. Raymond's penis was lying shiny and curled-up on his sofa like a slug.

Raymond sniffed his underarms. 'I have a better idea. Let's go for a swim. We can talk about finance in the pool.'

Nineteen

Hernandez drove Laura home in Chester's Cadillac. She had to ask him to stop twice so that she could be sick by the side of the road. Apart from that, she said nothing, but stared out of the window and watched the lights of Hollywood dancing a nauseating rhumba.

'I know what you're thinking,' said Hernandez, as he turned into Franklin Avenue. 'You're thinking, "Those bastards, I'll get even one day." '

He drew into the kerb and shut off the engine. 'Let me tell you something, Miss Laura. If you ever get those bastards, I want to be there when you do. I want a front-row seat, and popcorn.'

She turned her head and stared at him. Her throat and her sinuses were raw from vomiting. She felt as if she had been beaten all over with a billy-club. Hernandez climbed out of the car and opened the door for her. He held out his hand to help her out but she wouldn't take it. He stood and watched her climb unsteadily up the steps to Aunt Beverley's front door. There was a bloody stain on the back of her white satin dress.

Hernandez waited until the front door opened and Laura went inside. Then he returned to the car. 'You get those bastards,' he repeated to himself, as he started the engine. 'You get those bastards good.'

The bastards themselves were paddling around in Chester's bean-shaped pool under a starry sky. The air was cool now, but the water was well over 70 degrees. Chester had brought out another bottle of champagne and cigars for each of them.

'You know, sometimes I think about girls, and I think, "fuck 'em,"' said Raymond.

'What do you mean?' Chester wanted to know. 'You not only think it, you do it.'

'No, you're missing my point. Sometimes I wish they'd help themselves, do you know what I'm saying? They're so goddamned helpless. They're so goddamned eager-to-please.'

'Laura didn't look very eager-to-please.'

'Ah, forget it. Laura drank too much champagne. She would have loved it, else. She would have been begging on her hands and knees for more. There's nothing girls like better than a reaming.'

Chester didn't trust himself to reply to that. He leaned his head back against the side of the pool and puffed cigar smoke into the night. 'We're looking at a shortfall of one-hundred-fifty thousand dollars,' he said. 'You think your pals can come up with that?'

'They'd want to see some projected figures. The trouble is, things aren't as easy as they used to be. Time was, you could move your money from state to state in your back pocket, and nobody would stick their nose into it. These days, every Treasury agent seems to have got religion or something. They don't seem to understand that it's greasing and lubricating that made America what it is today.'

'You should know,' said Chester, although he probably didn't say it loud enough for Raymond to hear.

'I'll tell you what,' said Raymond. 'I'll go talk to some of my people in Reno. There's somebody in particular I have in mind. Somebody who's very interested in movies.'

'Not Bernie Katz. Jesus, that toad.'

'Why not Bernie Katz? Bernie would really go for Laura.'

'I don't know, Raymond,' said Chester, pensively. He had done similar favours for Raymond so many times before, and yet this time he felt deeply guilty. Most of the girls had done plenty of favours before, and didn't mind what Raymond did to them. They just smiled falsely and laughed falsely and looked into the middle-distance while he grunted and humped. But Laura was different. Laura was sweet and bright and if she didn't get mixed up with too many people like Raymond, she might even get to keep her sweetness and brightness, and make something of herself. Not in *Devil's Elbow*, of course. All of the casting had been completed over five months ago, although there was probably still some room for a 356th moll on the left.

They floated around for a while, and Chester began to sense that Raymond wasn't particularly interested in coming up with an offer. He didn't want to beg, but he had most of his own money tied up in *Devil's Elbow*, plus the money of a lot of people who wouldn't exactly be delighted if the picture never got finished and released.

'Listen,' he said. 'Why don't you *talk* to Bernie Katz, at the very least?'

'What can I tell him?' asked Raymond. His voice was very flat.

'Tell him he can play it any way he wants to. If he wants the picture to lose money, it'll lose money. If he wants it to make money, it'll make money.'

'All right. I'll call him, then I'll go see him. I presume I can take Laura along.'

Again, Chester didn't trust himself to answer.

Raymond took a leisurely and absurdly over-stylish swim across the pool, naked and hairy, his body illuminated by the lights beneath the surface. Chester didn't care for people swimming naked in his pool, and he looked the other way, especially when Raymond trod water in the deep end, his short refracted legs paddling like a frog's.

After a while, however, Raymond called out, 'Do you think this water's getting cold?'

Chester had been thinking the same thing. 'Yes,' he said. 'Guess we're just tired. How about calling it a night?'

'This water's definitely cold. Is your heater on the fritz?'

'It was working fine this afternoon. I'll have Hernandez take a look at it tomorrow.'

Raymond swam to the side of the pool, and was about to lift himself out when a little girl suddenly appeared, almost from nowhere, through the bushes. She was very pale, and she was dressed in white, and it seemed to Chester almost as if her long white hair were flying up in the air, rather than hanging down.

Raymond was half-way out of the water but he dropped back in again with a heavy splash. 'Hey, Chester, we've got ourselves a visitor!'

'Hey, sugar, this is private property!' called Chester. 'Besides, you shouldn't be out so late, should you?'

'I'm fine, thank you,' said the little girl. Her eyes were very strange: almost as if she had no eyes.

Raymond said, 'I'm glad you're fine, sweetheart, I really am. But the point is I'm kind of buck-naked here, and getting cold, and I need to get out of this water.'

'Then why don't you?'

'Because I don't have any clothes on, and you're a little girl, and men shouldn't show themselves to little girls. It isn't nice.'

'You're afraid I'll laugh, aren't you, because you're fat and you're ugly. You don't have to be afraid I'll laugh, because I'm very serious tonight.'

'Oh, you're serious? What are you serious about?'

'I'm serious about you not getting out of the pool.'

Raymond said. 'What is this? Come on, kid. I'm freezing in here. If you don't scram I'm coming out anyway.'

Chester stood up in the water. 'It's all right, Raymond, I'll deal with this.' He, at least, was wearing shorts, a voluminous pair of red-and-yellow Bermudas with palm trees printed all over them. He waded over to the edge of the pool where the

320

little girl was standing, and gripped the edge so that he could heave himself out. He was just about to pull himself up, however, when he noticed the little girl's feet. They were bare feet, stained inky-black and purple with frostbite. But more alarming than that, they were floating an inch above the tiled surround.

Chester jerked his head back and stared up at her. 'What the hell? You're – ' She was smiling at him, such a winning smile, her face was white as snow, her eyes as dark as shadows. With a graceful sweep of her body, she bent down and circled her arm over his fingers. He saw something flash, and he felt something brush his knuckles, but at first he didn't realize what it was. The little girl spun around and around, her white dress flying out like convolvulus flower. Chester ducked down in the water again, preparatory to heaving himself out, when he saw that the side of the pool was swimming with blood, and that blood was running down his arms. He raised both hands, and saw that the little girl had sliced through his fingers – sliced so deep that he could see the bones glistening.

He let out a great roar of indignation and fear. 'She's cut me! She's fucking cut me!'

The girl laughed at him, and stopped her spinning, and came back closer. In her right hand she was holding up a long triangular shard of mirror.

'You can't get out,' she told him, in that strange muffled voice. Shirley Temple talking through a handkerchief. 'I won't *let* you get out!'

'Look at my hands,' Chester babbled. 'Look what you've done to my hands!' He held them out in front of him, and they furiously dripped blood into the water, little clouds and tangles of crimson.

Raymond surged towards the side. Naked or not, he wasn't going to allow some crazy child to keep him imprisoned in this pool. He hoisted himself up into the tiled surround, close to where she was standing, his arm raised to protect himself. Without a sound, she swept her arm in a fast criss-cross pattern in the air, and suddenly Raymond's arm and shoulder were cross-hatched with cuts.

He tried to stand up, but she cut him again and again, the wounds proliferating as if by magic. His belly was sliced from side to side. His hairy thighs were drenched with blood. He cupped his hand protectively over his genitals, but she cut the back of his hand open, and more blood poured down between his legs. He dropped to his knees. He was silent with shock. The little girl danced around him, cutting his ears, cutting his cheeks. He swayed, and tried to keep his balance, but then he dropped back into the water, in an ever-spreading fog of blood.

'Raymond!' shouted Chester, and started to walk out towards him. Chester didn't swim too well, even when his hands weren't sliced to ribbons. 'Hang on, I'm coming out to get you!' He turned to the little girl and screamed at her, 'What the hell have you done? You're out of your mind! You're insane! You could have killed him!'

Raymond was floating on his face, around and around, surrounded by blood. As he waded out to him, Chester kept calling, 'Hang on, Raymond! Hang on, Raymond!' and Raymond let out a gargling, choking sound, so at least he was still alive.

Chester found that the water was growing colder and colder, so cold that he couldn't feel his legs. This wasn't just water any longer, this was *slush*, like half-melted ice. The surface was grey and thick, like frozen porridge, and the waves that were caused by Chester's wading were languid and self-suppressing.

'Raymond!' Chester managed to shout; although it was more of a gasp than a shout.

Raymond gargled, and tried to call, 'Help!' but then he disappeared below the surface. Chester saw his hand thrusting up, clawing at nothing at all, then even that was gone.

322

He took a deep breath and dived. He found it almost impossible to submerge himself. The water was mostly frozen, and he might just as well have dived into quicksand. He groped around in the slush, and by chance he found Raymond's leg. He hooked his arm around it, and struck out for the surface. But there was something dreadfully wrong. His fingers met a solid ceiling, cold and complete. The pool had frozen over, to a depth of two or three inches. He groped frantically in all directions, trying not to breathe, but he was out of energy and oxygen.

He tried to punch a hole in the ice, but it was impossible. He wallowed, swallowed a mouthful of freezing water, and let out a shrill, hysterical, bubbling noise. *Hernandez*, he thought. *Hernandez will hear me*. But then he remembered that Hernandez was driving Laura back to Franklin Avenue. There was nobody here but Raymond and him; and both of them were bleeding badly, and both of them were trapped beneath the ice.

He dropped Raymond, let him sink down slowly in the gelid water. Raymond wasn't struggling. Raymond was probably dead already. Bursting for air, Chester hammered at the ice with both fists. Dimly, he could see the patio lights and the vague outline of the house. But then a terrible darkness swept across the pool, blacker than any night. The water was cracking and complaining as it froze even harder. He breathed in water, a whole chilly flood of it, and when he breathed in water he knew that he was going to die.

In the instant before he drowned, however, he saw a face, peering down at him through the ice. It was the most terrifying face that he had ever seen – long and white, with darkened holes for eyes, and fronds that grew out of it; and it was all the more terrifying for being so blurred, through the ice, so indistinct.

He drowned, and sank, but only a little way, because the water was so thick with ice.

Laura stood in the shower for almost twenty minutes, with the water running as hot as she could bear it, soaping herself and scrubbing herself. Eventually she slid back the frosted glass partition and stepped shakily out and wrapped herself in her thick towelling bathrobe, and crept to bed with the shuffling gait of a woman three times her age.

She lay on her side and watched the shadows of the yuccas dipping and dancing on the shutters. Aunt Beverley wasn't home yet, so she couldn't talk. She didn't really know whether she wanted to talk to anybody. The pain and the degradation that Raymond had inflicted on her was more than she could bear to think about. What made it worse was that it was she who had encouraged him to make love to her, she had sat astride his lap, and kissed him, and told him that he was a god. She didn't just feel physically hurt, although she couldn't even touch her bottom and her back felt cracked. She felt stupid, and betrayed, and ridiculous. Had she really thought that Chester was going to bill her as 'also starring'? Had she really been suckered into thinking that Raymond was going to buy her a whole new wardrobe and a full-length mink?

Her head thumped and her mouth felt as dry as Death Valley. The trouble was, she blamed herself as much as she blamed Chester and Raymond. They were both manipulative and lustful, but she was vain, and it was her vanity that had hurt her, as much as Raymond's cruelty. She still blamed herself for what had happened to Dick Bracewaite, even though he had subjected her to sexual indignities far worse than anything that Raymond had done to her. She blamed herself for wanting too much to be wanted. It excited her, when she knew that men wanted her, and that women envied her. It gave her a bright shining feeling that nothing else did. Elizabeth had her writing, and her career. But all she had was this bright shining feeling, whenever she could get it, which wasn't often, and sometimes she needed it so badly that she would have done anything, with anyone, just to feel the slightest glimmer of it, the faintest glow.

She closed her eyes and remembered how it had felt, face down on the table, her legs stretched apart, with Raymond forcing his way inside her. It had been agonizing, and humiliating, but the more she thought about it, the calmer she became, because he had wanted her, hadn't he? He had wanted her badly. He may have thought that he was the master, that he was God, but who was really in control? The wanter or the wanted?

She closed her eyes and slept, without even realizing that she was sleeping, and in her dreams she saw other dreams, like spindly horses, and lords and ladies, and people who rushed silently behind you when you weren't looking.

It was almost two o'clock in the morning when Jim Borcas found Aunt Beverley sitting in his white Pontiac Chieftain convertible, pretending to drive. Jim Borcas was one of Hollywood's most successful producers, and tonight he had been celebrating the completion of his latest movie *The Woman In Sable* at his huge art deco house in Bel Air. Just about everybody who was everybody was there, Charlie Chaplin and Marlon Brando and Alan Ladd. The party had quietened down now. The guests had dispersed around the gardens or gathered in Jim Borcas's den for stag stories and bone-dry 6-oz martinis or retreated to the library to get some serious slandering done. The laughter had died away, the coyotes were calling eerily from the hills. The orchestra had been replaced by a small Tijuana band, Ken Morales and his Pico Brass, and a few bedraggled couples were still shuffling around by the pool like the survivors of a 1930s dance marathon. Six or seven half-deflated balloons bobbed on the surface of the water, occasionally scuttling from one side of the pool to the other when the morning breeze caught them.

Jim had a cigarette in one hand and a half-empty bottle of tequila in the other. He leaned on the car door and said, 'How are you doing, Beverley? Where are you headed?'

Aunt Beverley twisted the steering-wheel from side to side. 'I'm on my way to the beach. I feel like the wind in my brain.'

Jim nodded appreciatively. He was one of the easy-goingest producers in Hollywood, balding, self-assured, friendly to everyone. 'How far have you gone?' he asked her.

'Oh . . . I'm almost there. Just past Brentwood. *Beep-beep!* Look out, you stupid pedestrian! And as for you, sir,' she said, turning to Jim, 'stop hanging onto the side of my car, I'm doing sixty miles an hour!'

Jim blew smoke out of his nostrils. 'How about going for real?' he asked her.

'For real?'

'Sure, we can go swimming.'

'Swimming?' she said, in pretended astonishment.

'Sure . . . the sea's chilly, the moon's full, What more do you want? Move over.'

Aunt Beverley shifted herself over, and Jim climbed in. He started the engine with a soft *whoosh* of power.

'What about your guests?' said Aunt Beverley.

'What about them? So long as the canapes keep on coming and the booze keeps on flowing, what do they care? You know this town better than I do. It's Christians and lions, that's all it is. Christians and lions. And not too many fucking Christians, either.'

He swigged tequila. Then he said, 'Hold this,' and handed her the bottle. 'You want wind in your brain? Is that what you want?'

At that moment, Elia Kazan came up, looking sweaty and concerned. He was closely followed by Jim's accountant, and a woman whom Aunt Beverley didn't recognize. 'Jim, get out of the car, please, you've been drinking all night.'

'We're going to the beach,' Jim insisted. 'Beverley wants to feel the wind in her brain.'

'Jim, I'm serious, get out of the car!'

Jim frowned at Aunt Beverley, and his expression was deeply drunk-serious. 'Tell me, Beverley, why do you want the wind in your brain?'

'Because I did something tonight that I want to forget about.'

'Oh, yes?'

'I arranged for somebody to meet somebody, and I don't think that somebody's going to come out of it too happy.'

'I see! You've got a guilty conscience!'

'If that's the way you want to put it.'

'Well ... there's only one way to get rid of a guilty conscience, and that's to go to meet your Maker, and look Him in the face, and say, "*So?*" '

Elia Kazan said, 'Jim, get out of the car, will you? This is crazy!'

Jim violently revved the engine, so that the Pontiac's suspension dipped with torque. 'Sorry, Gadge. Meet us at the beach, why don't you?'

'You're out of your tree!' Kazan rapped at him.

Jim whooped and screeched and scratched his armpits like a chimpanzee. 'Hoo-hoo-hoo!' and Aunt Beverley joined in with him, laughing in delight.

'King Kong *liiivves*!' Jim called out, and revved the engine again. Tyres howling, horn blazing, they swerved around the ornamental shrubbery in front of the house, and dipped down the driveway towards the road. As they passed the rows of parked cars, they caught the bumper of a pale blue Rolls-Royce, with a terrible crunching, banging noise.

'Jim, be careful!' Aunt Beverley screamed.

'Hoo-hoo-hoo!' Jim retorted, and Aunt Beverley laughed all the more.

'Free!' she sang at the top of her voice. She leaned back so that the slipstream ruffled and thundered in her hair. The Pontiac squealed down Stone Canyon Road, swaying and dipping from one side of the road to the other.

'Power!' shouted Jim. 'Beauty! Madness! Guilty consciences! Tequila!'

'Chimpanzees!' Aunt Beverley shouted back.

They careened through the gates of Bel Air, suspension bucking, tyres screeching, and fishtailed onto Sunset. As the Pontiac slid from side to side, Aunt Beverley thought for a frightening split second that Jim had lost control, and she clung desperately onto the doorhandle. But still she couldn't stop herself from laughing. A passing fruit truck blared its horn at them, and the driver leaned out and screamed, 'Crazy loco bastard!' But Jim yelled back 'Hoo-hoo-hoo!' and deliberately swerved the car from one side of the highway to the other.

'You know what day it is today?' he shouted.

'I don't know!' said Aunt Beverley. 'Thursday?'

'No, no. Today is a very special day! Today is Tlazolteotl's birthday!'

'Who the heck is Tlazolteotl?'

'Tlazolteotl, my darling Beverley, is the queen of all Mexican magic! She has a white face like death, and a butterfly tattooed around her mouth, because that's the symbol of a dead soul. On Tlazolteotl's birthday, any sinful woman has to go to the crossroads to meet her, take off all of her clothes, and bite her own tongue until it bleeds. Then she has to walk home naked.'

'What for?' Aunt Beverley laughed.

'That way, she gets absolution. Takes her clothes off, bites her tongue, Tlazolteotl forgives her.'

'Does it really work?'

'I don't know. Do you want to try it? How sinful have you been, Beverley? You said you were feeling guilty, didn't you? What were you feeling guilty for?'

Jim overtook a slow-moving gasoline truck on the long blind curve around the Bel Air Country Club. The truck driver flashed his headlights and blew his klaxon. Jim waved at him and Beverley waved, too.

'If only he knew who he was blowing his horn at,' said Aunt Beverley.

'He'd probably pray to St Ignatius to forgive him.'

'St Ignatius?'

'Patron saint of the terminally unappreciative.'

They slewed around the next curve, the speedometer needle touching 70.

'Power!' Jim shouted. He took the tequila bottle from her, unscrewed it with his teeth, and spat the cap out of the car. 'Beauty!' he shouted, and took a huge swig. 'Butterflies! Tequila! Happy birthday, Tlazolteotl!'

He handed the bottle to Aunt Beverley. 'Come on – you drink Tlazolteotl a birthday toast, too!'

Aunt Beverley took a mouthful of warm tequila, swilled it around, and swallowed it. It roared down her throat like soft fire, and she gasped, and almost choked. Jim slapped his thigh and whooped with hilarity. 'Hoo-hoo-hoo! Hoo-hoo-hoo!'

The speedometer wavered close to 85. 'Are you ready for redemption?' Jim yelled.

Aunt Beverley had never experienced such fear; never experienced such elation. They were invincible, they were king and queen of Hollywood. Nothing could touch them, nothing could harm them. 'Hoo-hoo-hoo!' Jim gibbered, in a high-pitched monkey's mating call.

'Hoo-hoo-hoo!' Aunt Beverley gibbered back, pushing out her lower lip so that she looked like a chimpanzee.

And it was then that a huge toiling flatbed truck appeared around the right-hand hairpin bend that takes Sunset Boulevard down through Santa Monica Canyon past Will

Rogers park. It was carrying eight steel girders for the new Regency Hotel on Hollywood Boulevard, twenty-five tons of them. It was probably travelling at less than 8 m.p.h.

Jim was saying to Aunt Beverley, 'Whatever it is you feel guilty about, don't. I gave up feeling guilty years ago.' He wasn't even looking at the road ahead.

Aunt Beverley saw dazzling lights and cried, '*Jim!*'

But when Jim looked ahead, the windscreen was totally frosted over, totally opaque with feathers and ferns. He swerved to the right, and hit the nearside embankment, then swerved to the left. The frosted glass was flooded with white light, and he couldn't see where he was going, or where the truck was, or anything at all. Aunt Beverley didn't know if she was looking at Klieg lights or flashlights or the terrible white face of Tlazolteotl, whose mouth was tattooed with the butterfly symbol of a dead soul.

They were less than a hundred feet away from the truck when Jim hit the brakes; but any automobile designer could have told him that a five-and-a-half-thousand-pound automobile travelling at over 80 will take nearly three quarters of a mile to stop, even if the driver isn't bombed on tequila.

Jim cried out, '*Mother!*' (Of all things that a domineering and successful Hollywood producer should cry out, in a moment of danger.)

The Pontiac missed the front of the truck by less than an inch, and for a split second Aunt Beverley thought that they were divine. But then the front wheels hit the opposite banking, with a noise like thunder, and the car flew roaring into the air, and she was thrown out and into the night sky. She felt as if she were being wrenched this way and that like a Raggedy-Ann doll in the hands of argumentative children. She thought of screaming, but decided that she didn't want to. She was worried that she was going to ruin her suit. Out of the corner of her eye, she saw the car dropping into the canyon, and then she knew that she could fly. This was all going to work out well. All she had to do was land somewhere soft, brush herself down, and then walk back to Bel Air. No problem at all.

She heard the Pontiac nosedive into the ground – a deep, resonant bellowing and banging. I hope Jim can fly too, she thought to herself.

And this was only an instant before she fell head first into the glass studio roof of 3373 Rosita Drive, a purple-suited angel dropping from the sky, with a huge explosive crash. The glass –as she shattered it – caught her just beneath the nose, and sliced off the flesh right up to the bridge. It took off most of her chin, and opened up her left cheek all the way through to her tongue.

She hit the angled architect's drawing-board that was positioned right under the glass roof, hit the chair, hit the floor, breaking both arms, breaking both legs, then rolled in a chaos of blood and glass and tracing-paper until she finished up underneath a model of a new poolside bungalow.

A fat Mexican maid in a pink nightdress came running into the studio. The first thing she saw was the broken roof. 'Senor Grant!' she cried. '*Ha habido un accidente!*'

It was then that she saw Aunt Beverley's bare and bloodied feet under the table. 'Senor Grant!' she screamed. 'Senor Grant! *Necesitemos un medico – rapidamente!*'

A tall wiry-haired man appeared, in green-striped pyjamas. 'Jesus,' he said. Then, very softly, 'Jesus.'

'*Esta sangrando mucho,*' said the maid. She crossed herself.

The man crawled under the table and peered at Aunt Beverley closely. Her face was a glistening red mask of blood.

'Miss?' he said, his voice quaking. 'Miss, can you hear me?'

Strange Days

'Can the flame of the heart expire
amid the flames of the funeral pile?'

Twenty

'Here we are,' said Bronco, turning into the driveway and pulling on the brake. 'It isn't much, but it's home.'

It was two weeks before Christmas in Scottsdale, Arizona. There was only one cloud in the sky, a small heat-frittered fragment of white that Elizabeth would have described as a shrimp and Bronco would have called Mr Punch. They climbed out of Bronco's ageing station-wagon, and Elizabeth looked around. Bronco's house was a sprawling, ranch-style property set in ten or eleven acres of its own land, although most of that land was dust and heat-baked rocks. Off to the left of the house was a kitchen garden, with gourds and tomatoes and cabbages growing. The front of the house had been cultivated with spiky bushes and prickly pears and other desert shrubs. In the distance, Elizabeth could see the tawny hump of Camelback Mountain, and two or three circling buzzards.

'I was grieved to hear about Margo,' said Bronco, as he lifted Elizabeth's suitcase out of the back of the station-wagon. 'I never liked her, in particular. But she's got fire in her belly; and that's pretty rare these days. Most of the editors I meet are time-servers or sycophants. Did I ever tell you about the time that Harold Ross punched me on the nose? Those were the days.'

'She should make a complete recovery,' said Elizabeth. 'She'll have scars, of course. But she's been talking to a plastic surgeon, and he's really optimistic.'

'Strange thing to happen, though. A mirror exploding like that. I used to work in a bar once, and sometimes the beer glasses exploded of their own accord. They were moulded out of really cheap glass, under tension. Maybe that's what happened to Margo's mirror.'

'Actually, I'm not so sure.'

They had reached the verandah steps. Bronco squinted at her from underneath the brim of his Panama hat. 'What do you mean, you're not so sure? Do you have some other theory?'

'I don't know. But the police said that the mirror was smashed into hundreds of triangular slivers, and that each sliver was identical. They said the chances of that happening were countless millions to one.'

'It could have been the structure of the glass,' Bronco suggested. 'Sometimes crystals break like that, don't they?' He looked at Elizabeth's expression and tilted his head to one side. 'But you don't think so, do you?'

'I can't be sure,' said Elizabeth. 'But Margo talked about a little girl wrecking her apartment, a little girl in a white dress, just like the Peggy-girl. And in the story of the Snow Queen, there's a frozen lake, which the Snow Queen herself calls the Mirror of Reason, and the lake is broken into a thousand pieces, each of which exactly resembles the other – so that the breaking of them might well be deemed a work of more than human skill.'

Bronco looked at her steadily, but didn't answer. Elizabeth said, 'The day before Margo was hurt, she gave me a very difficult time at the office. I'd been editing that book *Reds Under The Bed*, and she criticized just about everything that I'd suggested, right in front of everybody.'

'You think Peggy was punishing her, for embarrassing you?'

'The same way she punished Miles Moreton, and the same way she punished Aunt Beverley, and those two movie producers who tried to take advantage of Laura.'

Bronco opened the screen door and they went inside. The house was single-storey, but it was spacious and cool, with that distinctive aromatic smell of oak. It was sparsely furnished, but it was obvious that Bronco and Vita had once been wealthy, even if they weren't so well-off now. There were antique armchairs and antique sofas, and an inlaid bow-fronted cabinet filled with exquisite Dresden figurines. Over the wide stone fireplace hung a huge painting by Everett Shinn of a snowy night on Broadway, bustling with horse-drawn cabs and umbrellas and hurrying theatregoers; and on the right-hand wall there were two paintings of New York tenements by John Sloan, the most celebrated painter of the 'ashcan' school.

'Vita's having her afternoon zizz,' Bronco explained. 'She doesn't like the heat; but then she doesn't want to go back east, either, because of her arthritis.'

He showed her through to a large airy bedroom that looked out over several acres of sandy-coloured scrub, with a view of Camelback Mountain. It was prettily decorated with a brass bed and an antique bureau and a French writing-desk with a vase of sweet peas on it. Bronco set her suitcase down on the bed, and said, 'Hope you like it here. Sorry as I am about Margo, I'm real glad they sent you instead. At least you understand what I'm trying to write about.' He glanced shiftily sideways. 'You understand about Billy, too.'

'Have you seen him recently?'

'Three days ago, when I went into Phoenix to buy some typing-paper. I told myself, "Come on, Bronco, Lizzie's coming to help you, you've got to help yourself." So I went into Phoenix to buy some fresh typing-paper. Best quality onion-skin.'

'What happened?'

'I was standing in the stationery store when I looked in this narrow mirror that was advertising pens, and there was Billy, standing out in the street watching me. He wasn't a ghost. Leastways, he wasn't transparent. He was just as real as you or me. Standing in the sunlight, watching me. And do you know what he did? He wagged his finger from side to side, like I was doing something wrong, like I shouldn't be buying typing-paper, like I shouldn't write at all, or even *think* of writing.'

Bronco paused, and lowered his head. 'He talked to me before. He said I shouldn't write any more. One book like *Bitter Fruit* was quite enough. If I tried to do it again, the critics would have my guts for breakfast. Especially since *Bitter Fruit* was so damned long ago. I was a young blade then. Daring, you know? Outspoken. What am I now? Just a dried-up old geezer with writer's block and a nagging wife.'

Elizabeth said, 'He's protecting you. He doesn't want to see you get hurt.'

'Yes, but that's the whole point of doing anything, isn't it? That's the whole point of living. If I never wrote another book, because I was scared of what the critics might have to say about it, I might just as well blow my brains out and have done with it.'

'It's the same with me and Laura,' Elizabeth nodded. 'Every time that somebody upsets us or hurts us, even if they're only *thinking* about it, like Dan Philips must have done . . . Peggy calls up this Snow Queen thing and tries to kill them. I think she *means* well, goddamnit, but you can't live your life in cotton wadding, can you? You have to take risks. You have to be hurt. Otherwise – you're right – you might as well be dead.'

Bronco rested a hand on her shoulder and looked down at her with deep paternal kindness. 'You know something, Lizzie? I always loved you, when you were little. You were wise, you were clever, you had so much imagination. Now you're a woman and I love you still.'

She smiled and took of hold of his hand and squeezed it. She hadn't realized how much she had missed having a father in her life.

'You and I and Laura, we all have the same problem to deal with,' he said. 'We've buried our dead, but we haven't yet laid them to rest.' He looked at his watch. 'Why don't I give you a half hour to rest and freshen up, then we can talk some more? How would you like a drink? I mix a mean Pisco Punch.'

'I'd like that.'

After Bronco had left her, she unpacked her clothes and hung them up in the large Spanish-style closet. Then she took a long shower in the small green-tiled bathroom next to her room, a ceramic fish the size of a grouper grinning at her. She towelled herself and looked in the mirror. She thought that she was putting on a little weight. Too many take-away lunches in the office; too many pasta suppers. She was still reasonably trim, however, and if she worked hard while she was out here in Arizona, and didn't drink too many Pisco Punches, she could probably get back to her ideal avoirdupois.

She had been shocked about Margo – especially when she had found out the details of what had happened. Margo had talked about 'cold, terrible cold, and a little girl in a white dress who floated.' The police and the doctors had put her description down to trauma, but Elizabeth had been convinced that the Peggy-girl had been exacting her revenge. She had been doubly convinced when Laura telephoned, the very next day, with the news that Aunt Beverley was seriously injured, close to death, while Chester and Raymond had been found at six o'clock in the morning, suspended in Chester's totally-frozen swimming-pool like crushed flies in amber. The police had put their deaths down to a 'vicious attack with a knife or other sharp-bladed instrument by persons unknown, followed by freezing due to pool equipment malfunction.' A warning had been published to all owners of Safe-T-Pump heating units to vacate their pools immediately in case of any dramatic lowering of temperature.

Despite her distress, however, Elizabeth was glad that she was here. If she could help Bronco to exorcize Billy, then maybe she and Laura could find a way to rid themselves of Peggy. She was no longer 'poor little Clothes-Peg'. Apart from being dangerous, Peggy's protectiveness was seriously interfering with their lives, right or wrong. Peggy seemed to feel that they needed shielding from everything harmful, from pain, from betrayal, from hypocrisy, from everything that could possibly spoil a fairy tale life: 'grown-up and yet children – children in heart, while all around them glowed bright summer, warm, glorious summer.'

She dressed and went through to the sitting-room. Vita was sitting on one of the sofas in a sackish cocoa-coloured robe, looking pale and freckly and very much older than Bronco. Vita was one of those women who was never completely well. She suffered from migraines and allergies and colds, not to mention a long-running comprehensive 'out-of-sortsness' that prevented her from attending any party or dinner or social gathering which she didn't wish to go to, and even a few that she did wish to go to. She would always want to leave early, especially when Bronco was laughing and flirting and really enjoying himself; and even when he was attentive to her and well-behaved, she carried herself with such bloodlessness that nobody would have been surprised if he had one day strangled her, and thrown her body in the Arizona Canal.

She was a very thin, bony woman, Vita, with an almond-shaped head and contemptuous, almost Oriental eyes. Her hair was scraped back and fastened firmly with a diamanté clasp, although a few strands always contrived to escape her control, and form a wiry dancing-troupe on top of her head. Her nose always looked as if it were undecided: shall I be blobby, or shall I be pinched? and so it was both, or either, depending on how you looked at her. In the 1930s she had been wildly romantic, and deep, and written poems that wrung people's souls; but then she had lost Bronco's first and only baby, and with it, her ability to have any more children. On that morning, eighteen years ago, she might just as well have died. Bronco had once said of her, 'There's no damn accounting for what makes life worth living for one person, yet not for another. I didn't care for babies, not particularly; but for Vita, giving birth was everything.'

As Elizabeth came into the room, Vita drawled, 'So you're here to squeeze blood out of a stone, are you?'

'Hello, Mrs Ward. I'm Elizabeth Buchanan. I'm pleased to make your acquaintance.'

'I made *yours*, my dear, when you were lying in a crib. As did Johnson.' She made no attempt to conceal the implication that Bronco was old enough to be Elizabeth's father.

Elizabeth said, 'I can't remember that far back, I'm afraid.'

Vita picked at the hem of her robe. 'I was sorry to hear about your father,' she said. 'For all of his weaknesses, David was a true gentleman.'

'Weaknesses?' asked Elizabeth, tartly.

'Well, one doesn't like to criticize the dead. But he could have gone so far. That little publishing house . . . really – '

'That little publishing house brought out some great works of literature. Not to mention all of those supernatural books; all of those books on ghosts; and spirits; and hobgoblins.'

Vita gave her a slanting shrug. 'That's precisely my point. David could have done so much better, if he had stayed in New York. And look at Johnson. He's no better. One of the greatest novelists who ever was, sitting out here in the back of beyond, drinking whiskey and waiting for inspiration.'

Elizabeth kept her peace. Bronco had told her that Vita made a sport of needling people, as if she could somehow provoke them into admitting that her present suffering was their fault, instead of hers. All she said was, 'Johnson's been suffering from writer's block, that's all. It happens to hundreds of writers.'

'Oh, yes, and of course it had to happen to Johnson.'

'Why not? *Bitter Fruit* was sensational. Now everybody expects him to produce another novel, the same but different, the same only better. He may look tough, he may talk tough, but he's sensitive, and proud, and he's terrified of failing, that's all.'

Vita gave her a tight, masklike smile. 'I *have* been married to him for quite some time.'

'I know,' said Elizabeth. 'And that's why I'm sure you know what he's capable of writing, given the confidence.'

Vita was about to reply when Bronco came into the room, carrying a champagne bottle and three glasses. 'Hey . . . let's crack open some bubbly,' he said. 'Let's celebrate.'

'Celebrate what?' asked Vita.

Bronco opened the bottle and filled their glasses. 'Better times,' he said. 'Times without memories, times without ghosts.'

'I'll drink to that,' smiled Elizabeth.

Vita said, 'Oh, yes? Well, I'll drink to a long-overdue admission that Johnson's no damned good, and that it's time for him to find himself a real job.'

Elizabeth protested, struggling to keep her temper. 'Your husband needs confidence, not criticism, Mrs Ward. Creating a book . . . that's even more difficult than giving birth to a baby.'

Immediately she wished that she had stitched her lips up, rather than use that analogy, but it was too late. Vita was already arching her head back and rolling her eyes and forming her retaliation on her tongue. 'Implying, I suppose, that if Johnson can write another novel, I should have managed to bear him a child?'

Elizabeth said, 'No, that wasn't the implication. And if I was clumsy, talking about babies, then I apologize.'

Bronco said. 'You don't have to apologize,' and held her hand. 'It wasn't your fault, what happened to our baby. But if you can help me write another novel – well, that'll be something worth doing, won't it?'

342

Elizabeth turned to Vita and tried to tell her in one sympathetic look that she understood what her irritations were, what her fears were. But Vita turned her face away, her mouth drawn in, her cheek twitching, and Elizabeth had to recognize that Vita was impossible.

Bronco gave her a wistful smile and said, 'Come on, Elizabeth, let's bury the dead. Let's think about tomorrow.'

At one o'clock in the morning, when the moon was shining baldly through the shutters, Bronco knocked softly on the door of her bedroom and whispered, 'Lizzie? You awake?'

She lifted herself on her elbow. 'Yes, I'm awake. What do you want?'

'Thought you and me could talk, that's all.'

'No, Bronco, we can't.'

He softly closed the door and sat on the end of her bed. 'It's been a long time, Lizzie, since I held a woman close to me, for all of my reputation.'

She reached out and touched his hand. 'I know that, Bronco. But we can't.'

'You're diplomatically trying to tell me that you don't find me attractive, is that it? You're trying to let an old geezer down gently?'

'It isn't that.'

'Then what is it? You don't want to hurt Vita's feelings? Vita has no feelings, believe me. She used to be a siren, but now she's a Gorgon, and Gorgons are best avoided, you know that, less'n you want to turn to stone.'

She kissed him, and he still tasted of cigars and spice and cleanliness, the way he had when he arrived in Sherman for Peggy's funeral. 'You're a man and you're very attractive, but I'm here to work.'

'Work? That's all you think about? It's the middle of the night!'

343

'There's something else. Any man who threatens me, any man who even approaches me . . . well, think what happened to Dan Philips and Miles Moreton. I'm fond of you, Bronco, I really am. But I'm afraid. Supposing the Peggy-girl comes after you. Supposing she freezes *you*, the way Dan was frozen. I couldn't bear it, Bronco – especially if it was my fault.'

Bronco nodded. 'All right then,' he said, at last. 'But let me ask you one thing: once we've dealt with Billy, once we've dealt with little Clothes-peg.'

She kissed him again. 'Once we've dealt with both of those, then you can take me out to dinner and tell me how much you love me. Do you remember Dean in *Bitter Fruit*, what he said to Cory? "There's no such thing as love, Cory . . . there never could have been, not if what I feel for you is love. Antony and Cleopatra, what did they have? Sweat, and empire-building, and snakes. Romeo and Juliet, don't make me laugh. Calf-love, and nagging parents, and faded flowers. Casanova? Dicksores, and hangovers, that's all." '

They finished the quotation together, in soft and hilarious unison. ' "But what we have is love. Cory. The love that's lit by glowing cigarettes and dome-lights, the love that joins our outlines together, so that we're one single Rand McNally, so that nobody who drives through the dark can ever tell where Cory ends and Dean begins." '

Bronco looked at her, his eyes glistening. 'You've got a memory,' he said.

'How many times do you think that I read *Bitter Fruit*? Only as many times as the rest of my friends, and more.'

Bronco stood up. Elizabeth thought that he was looking very old; but then she was older, too.

'Goodnight, Lizzie,' he told her in a husky voice; and closed the bedroom door.

The gardener's name was Eusebio and he was a Pima Indian

344

from the Gila River Indian Reservation south of Phoenix. His Indian name meant something quite different, like 'Growing-Bean-Hands', but his family had taken the name Eusebio from Father Eusebio Kino who founded a mission in 1687, and who had given the Pima Indians religion, cattle and the ability to grow wheat. Eusebio still talked about Father Kino as if he had seen him only a week ago; the fact that he had died in 1711 seemed unimportant.

Bronco took Elizabeth out to meet him. He was hoeing rows of beans. The morning was mild and warm with a slight wind blowing from Sonora. Eusebio was small and stocky, with a face that looked like a large crumpled mushroom. He wore a faded blue smock and a wide-brimmed hat, and open-toed sandals.

'Eusebio this is Miss Buchanan, she's staying here for a while.'

Eusebio looked at Elizabeth with one eye closed against the glare. 'You like it here?' he asked her.

'I think it's beautiful.'

Eusebio shook his head. 'You try to scratch a living out of this land, then tell me it's beautiful. This land has nothing. No water, no life. Nothing at all. This is a land for dead people.'

Elizabeth watched him scratching at the dust for a while. Then she said, 'As a matter of fact, I was going to ask you about dead people. Or one dead person in particular.'

'Oh, yes?' said Eusebio. He had a half-smoked cigarette perched loosely behind his right ear, and every time he leaned forward with his hoe, it looked as if it were going to drop out, but it never quite did. As if talking about the dead weren't unnerving enough, Elizabeth thought.

'You saw Mr Ward's brother, Billy,' said Elizabeth.

Eusebio nodded, without interrupting his hoeing.

'In fact you've seen him more than once . . . and you've seen him at times when nobody else has seen him, apart from Mr Ward.'

345

There was a long silence. Eusebio continued to work, but Elizabeth could tell that he was doing nothing more than going through the motions. The sharp sound of his hoe blade echoed flatly in the warm morning air. 'I take the peyote,' he said. 'The peyote shows you spiritual sights, like tomorrow, and the dead who take on different shape.'

'What's the peyote?' asked Elizabeth.

Bronco said, 'It's a drug. The Indians extract it from the tubercules of the mescal cactus. When you eat it, it gives you extraordinary hallucinations, and makes you sensitive to all kinds of impressions, especially colours. You can see plants grow. You can see the clouds go speeding past. You can see dead people, too; or so Eusebio says. The Indians used it as a medicine, but also to bring them visions. It's mentioned in some of the surviving Aztec manuscripts, and there are old Spanish documents that report its use all the way from Yucatan to Oklahoma. What interests *me*, however, is that it was used to slow down respiration, so that anybody who took it could see their dead relations. We could use it as a way of achieving the glamour, the shape-changing, without having to strangle ourselves.' He put his hand around his throat. 'I don't really relish the idea of strangling myself.'

'Do you really think it works?' asked Elizabeth.

'I don't know. But Eusebio had been taking it when he saw "Billy". My guess is, if *we* took it, we could take on fictional identities, too, and tell "Billy" to leave me be.'

'What do you think, Eusebio?' asked Elizabeth.

He shrugged. 'A spirit is not like a man. A spirit is hard to control. You can't say to a spirit, do what I say, because I'll punish you, you wayward spirit. What does a spirit care?'

'But supposing we took the peyote ourselves, Mr Ward and me, and became spirits, and took on different shapes?'

'Depends what they are, these shapes.'

'Well, if he's a Cuban musician, supposing we were record producers, or something like that?'

Eusebio's mouth cracked into a mirthless laugh. 'You sure have dreams and fancies, don't you?'

Elizabeth said, 'That isn't a joke. Mr Ward's brother has been worrying him and stopping him from writing! We have to stop him, one way or another!'

Eusebio stopped working and leaned on his hoe. 'You must find out the truth first, Mr Ward. You must find out who your brother has chosen to be. You can't take risks, in the spirit world. Not even little risks. If you appear there, and you don't have the power, you could be killed. Worse than that, your brother could catch your spirit-character, and never let you return to your body. You would be dead, and yet alive, and nobody could revive you.'

'He'd be in a coma, you mean?' asked Elizabeth.

Eusebio thought for a moment, then nodded. 'What you call a coma, yes. People who breathe, but never move or talk. They are visiting the spirit-world. Sometimes they achieve great things in the spirit-world, while their families and their friends sit by their bed and despair. There are three worlds, and there always have been. The world of the living. The world of spirits. And the world of the truly rested, the empty world, which is the world of absolute peace.'

'That's where I want Billy to go,' said Bronco, emphatically. 'The world of absolute peace. Then maybe *I'll* get some absolute peace.'

Eusebio took off his hat and wiped his forehead with the back of his hand. His hair was straight and greasy, and curled-up in the back. 'Mr Ward . . . I can bring you some of the peyote. But take my warning, okay? You find out who your Billy really is, before you start to go after him, or you could pay the price.'

They walked back to the house. In the distance, Camelback Mountain wavered and shifted in the morning heat.

'What do you think?' said Bronco. 'Do you think we're crazy?'

Elizabeth took hold of his hand. 'Probably,' she said.

They were still walking, hand-in-hand, when Vita appeared on the verandah, wearing a flowery brown dress that made her complexion look paler and muddier than ever, twirling a parasol.

'Johnson!' she called, in a high, imperative voice. 'Johnson, we're fresh out of cinnamon!'

Bronco squished Elizabeth's hand, and let it go; but the meaning wasn't lost on her; any more than the difficulty of what they had to face.

They searched all afternoon through Billy's room. His gramophone-record collection, his clothes, his books, his half-completed diaries. Some of the bits and pieces they found were unbearably sad, especially the photographs: a young man laughing, a young man squinting at the sun.

'We'd only moved here four months before he was killed,' said Bronco, leafing through some jazz magazines. 'I bought a motorcycle . . . I'd always wanted a motorcycle, but there wasn't much point in having one in New York. Billy asked me if he could ride it, and like a fool I said yes. He came off at the very first curve, doing sixty miles an hour, and hit a telegraph pole. Broke his neck, killed him instantly.' He was silent for a long moment. 'It was all a long time ago. I think I could have forgotten it, if Billy would let me forget.'

'Didn't he ever read any books?' asked Elizabeth, more to break the mood than anything. 'There's only magazines here.'

'Sure, he did sometimes. Maybe I should look in my study.'

They walked across the living-room to Bronco's study. Vita was reclining on the sofa with a glass of weak Russian tea, reading *McCall's*. The blinds were drawn, which meant that she was suffering from a migraine. Bronco blew her a kiss, which she vaporized in mid-air with one of the most withering looks that Elizabeth had ever seen.

'This doesn't look very much like writing a novel to me,' she remarked.

'Oh, it will be,' Bronco assured her. Elizabeth didn't trust herself to say anything at all. She had never met a woman so hostile and sarcastic – yet a woman who never stopped complaining that she was so helpless, so sick, so starved of sympathy.

They went into the study. It was an L-shaped room illuminated with white, watery, reflected light. Its longer walls were lined with hundreds of books, some leather-bound, some paper-jacketed, some exquisite, some torn. Facing the window stood a large leather-topped desk. An Underwood typewriter was neatly positioned in the centre of the desk, and a stack of typing-paper was neatly positioned next to it. It was a still-life which completely illustrated writer's block, without the need for a caption.

Elizabeth said, 'You take the top three rows, I'll take the bottom three.'

They patiently made their way along the bookshelves, their heads tilted to one side so they could read the titles on the spines. Elizabeth had never come across such an eclectic selection of books in her life: *Spanish Drama Before Lope de Vega* was squashed in between *The Mesolithic Settlement of Northern Europe* and *The Beast In Me – And Other Animals* by James Thurber.

At last, Elizabeth came across a thin book called *Nights in Havana*. She tugged it out, and held it up. 'Ring any bells?'

Bronco took it and leafed through it. 'It's certainly not mine. Here's a note in Billy's handwriting. And look – ' he held up a ticket for a Duke Ellington concert in New York. 'He must have been using this for a bookmark.'

Elizabeth said, 'If Miles was right about the glamour, we

should read this book, and see what character Billy has chosen to be. Then we should choose characters of our own ... characters who can tell him to leave you alone – or *persuade* him to leave you alone, at the very least.'

Bronco nodded. 'Why don't you read it first, while I try to get some writing done? Do you fancy a Pisco Punch?'

'No thanks. A little too early for me.'

Bronco stared philosophically at his typewriter. 'You're right. I shouldn't have one either.'

Elizabeth reached up and kissed him on the cheek. 'Oh, go on, have one, if it helps to get you started. If there's one thing I'm determined not to do, it's to give my boss your twenty thousand dollars advance back.'

While Bronco pecked hesitantly at his typewriter, Elizabeth sat on the verandah outside his window and started to read *Nights in Havana*. It was a novel set in Cuba in the early days of Batista's dictatorship. The hero was a young idealist called Raul Palma who was trying to free his father, who was imprisoned on suspicion of murdering one of Batista's right-hand men. Only one person knew who had really killed him, a beautiful prostitute called Rosita, and she was too frightened to speak out. The plot was hackneyed; but the scenes of Havana's sleazy night-life were unforgettable, the pimps along the Paseo, the brothels and the bars, and always the constant throb of sub-tropical heat and mamba music. The character of Raul Palma was inspirational, too. He was lean, he was good-looking, he was driven by reckless political commitment. Elizabeth liked Rosita, too – childish and beautiful but soiled by poverty.

By the time she had reached the climax of the novel, Elizabeth was sure that Billy had taken on the character of Raul – and, if that were true, she was convinced that Rosita could persuade him to leave Bronco alone. Raul was ready to risk his life for Rosita, shielding her with his own body from the vicious, corrupt chief of police, Captain Figueredo.

She had almost finished the novel when she heard Bronco calling her. 'Lizzie! Lizzie, can you hear me? Come here, quick!'

She closed the book and went inside. Bronco was waiting for her by his half-open study door. His face was ashy, and lined with tension. 'Tell me you can see what I see.'

He opened the door wider so that she could step inside. She did so, very hesitantly. She passed so close to Bronco that she could smell his cologne and the rum on his breath. Sitting beside Bronco's desk, his chair tilted back on two legs, sat a young sallow-faced man in a faded grey shirt and voluminous black trousers. His eyes were bright and glittery and very amused, although he wasn't exactly smiling. He was handsome in a cheap, matinée-idol way, with black greased-back hair and a large gold pendant around his neck.

Elizabeth approached him cautiously. The young man followed her with his eyes, although now and then she glanced quickly at Bronco, as if to make sure that he wasn't up to any funny business. The atmosphere in the study was stifling. The air was so humid and hot that Elizabeth found herself perspiring, and she had to wipe her forehead with the back of her hand.

'This is Billy,' said Bronco, tensely. 'This is my brother, back from the dead.'

'*Buenos dias, senorita*,' said Billy, although he didn't get up.

Elizabeth nodded. There was some unearthly quality about this young man that frightened her very much. Although he was sitting in Bronco's chair, he wasn't quite sitting in it, he looked as if his image were *superimposed* on it. His voice didn't quite synchronize with his lips, either, and there was a strange unsteadiness in the way he moved.

'Something is worrying you,' Billy suggested.

'You worry me. You should leave your brother alone. He has work to do.'

'I am protecting my brother. Besides, who are you to tell me what to do?'

'Your brother doesn't need protecting. Your brother can protect himself.'

The young man laughed, a blurry, indistinct laugh that had no real humour in it. 'My brother will be hung, drawn, quartered and stretched out to dry. My brother will be safer if he keeps his peace.'

'Perhaps your brother doesn't want to be safe.'

Billy shook his head. 'I have to protect him. He never took care of me; but I must take care of him.'

Elizabeth looked down at Bronco's typewriter. So far this morning he had typed only a single sentence: 'They knew what time the bus would arrive.'

Elizabeth turned back to Billy. 'You're Raul, aren't you? Raul Palma.'

The young man's eyes darkened, and his face turned serious. 'Maybe you should mind your own business. Johnson is my brother, not yours.'

'Maybe you should leave him in peace.'

Billy stretched out his left hand and placed it on top of Bronco's typewriter. 'So long as my brother risks his dignity, then I will be here to protect him. You can't make me abandon my duty.'

His hand trembled, and his eyes stared at Elizabeth in fury. She took one step back, then another. As she did so, the sheet of paper in the typewriter began to darken, and curl at the edges. The next thing she knew, it had spontaneously burst into flame.

Still Billy stayed where he was, his lips clenched tight, daring Elizabeth to challenge him, daring her to cast him out. Amid the paper-smoke that burnt the nostrils, Elizabeth turned away, and took hold of Bronco's arm, and led him away out of the room, and closed the door.

Bronco said, 'You saw him, didn't you? You saw what he's been doing to me?'

'Yes,' said Elizabeth, and held up *Nights in Havana*. 'He's Raul Palma, a revolutionary in the time of Batista. That means that you and I will have to take the peyote, and hunt him down in Havana, and persuade him to leave you alone.'

'You really think it's possible?' asked Bronco, taking the book and flicking through the pages.

'I don't know,' said Elizabeth. 'But if we can't get rid of Billy, then we can't rid of Peggy; and we have to. We really have to.'

'Gotcha,' Bronco nodded.

Twenty-One

The afternoon was eerily silent. Vita had gone to bed to nurse her migraine. Elizabeth was sitting out on the verandah, correcting proofs, while Bronco lay some distance away, stretched out on a basketwork sun-lounger, reading *Nights In Havana* and sipping Pisco Punch.

The sky was faultlessly blue. The ground was faultlessly white. The air was totally transparent, like a polished lens. In the distance, the heat wavered and flowed, so that it looked as if Camelback Mountain were floating in a glassy lake. The only sounds that interrupted the silence were the cracking of ice in Elizabeth's drink, and the soft rustle of paper as Bronco turned another page.

Elizabeth lowered her proofs onto her lap and looked towards the horizon. She was frightened of what she and Bronco were going to do; yet in a way she was quite excited by it, too. Surely the living could exert their influence over the dead? And surely real people could exert their influence over imaginary characters – people who wouldn't even have existed, if it hadn't been for human imagination? She had often wondered where fictitious characters 'came from'. Somebody at a literary dinner party had once argued that they were all of those people who had never been born . . . either because their potential parents had failed to meet, or because their sperm had come second in the race towards the egg, or for whatever reason. 'Imagine that you never got to be, simply because your father argued with your mother about the way she cooked the dinner . . . and so they didn't make love that night . . . and that was your chance gone for ever. Unless, of course, you could make your presence felt in some fiction-writer's imagination. A life on the printed page is better than no life at all, after all.'

Eventually, Bronco closed the book, picked up his drink, and took a swallow. 'Pretty crappy novel, hunh?' he remarked.

'The characters were good; especially Raul.'

'Yes. I can see why Billy liked him. He didn't give a bent cent for anybody, did he? Mind you, I liked Captain Figueredo, too. What a bastard he was.'

'How about Rosita?'

He eased himself off the sun-lounger and walked along the verandah until he was standing next to her. 'Ah, well, Rosita . . . now you're talking.'

'I think I should try to be Rosita and you should try to be Captain Figueredo.'

'You're really game to try it?'

'What choice do we have?'

Bronco sipped his drink and stared out over the dry, bleached landscape. 'You think we should do some research? Like, study some maps of Havana, maybe, or learn the Cuban national anthem?'

'I know the Cuban national anthem. "Al combate corred bayameses . . ." '

'How the hell do you know that?'

'I had a Cuban friend at school. Her father had something to do with the abrogation of the Platt Amendment. That was when the United States gave up control over Cuba's internal affairs. She was very proud of him.'

Bronco smiled at her. 'I like you, Lizzie. You're the only person who knows more irrelevant rubbish than I do.'

Elizabeth said, 'Why don't you ask Eusebio to get us some peyote for tomorrow morning? Laura should be here by nine tonight . . . I'd like her to be here when we try the glamour. It's not that I don't trust Eusebio, I do. But if anything goes badly wrong . . . well, I think I trust Laura a little more.'

355

Bronco sat down beside her. 'How come you're so young and I'm so old?' he asked her.

She smiled at him kindly because she was very fond of him. She knew what he was trying to say to her. She knew what longing and what frustration he was trying to express. They would have been the happiest of partners, if their ages hadn't been so disparate, if they hadn't met when his career was waning and hers was just beginning to flourish. The life they could have led. The talks they could have talked. She gripped his hand and gripped it and gripped it, trying to communicate to him that she knew, she knew.

They collected Laura from the airport at sunset. The sky was luridly streaked with orange and mauve. The sisters flung their arms around each other and held each other tight, and cried, but they cried out of happiness more than grief, and the feeling that fate had brought them back together again, where they had always belonged.

Laura was wearing a pretty yellow-and-grey dress with puffy sleeves and a crossover bodice, and a big yellow hat. Elizabeth said, 'Look at you! Just like a movie star!'

'Don't,' said Laura. 'That's a sore point with me, after what happened.'

Bronco took off his hat to her. 'Laura, sweetheart . . . good to see you. Glad you could come. How's Beverley?'

'She's going to recover . . . I mean, she's going to live. What she's going to look like, though – I've only seen her in bandages. The surgeon told me that she lost her nose.'

'What about Jim Borcas?'

'Paralysed, with facial burns. He swears that the windshield frosted over. Ice, that's what he said, so that he couldn't see where he was going. The police say that he was drinking too much tequila.'

'So nobody believed him?'

'Would you, if you didn't know about Peggy?'

'Will he get better?'

They were walking across to Bronco's station-wagon. It was growing dark already, and there was a strong aroma of mesquite and aviation fuel in the air.

'Jim Borcas? No, I don't think so. He can't walk. He can't speak clearly. He can't even swallow.'

Bronco said. 'This convinces me, you know. This really convinces me. We have to learn how to do this glamour thing, and make it work.'

Elizabeth stroked his hair; and it was a gesture that Laura didn't miss. 'Come on, Bronco,' she said, 'let's get home first, and let Laura settle in. Then we can talk about the glamour.'

They were driving east on Indian School Road. The night was velvety-black now and warm, and the lights were sparkling everywhere. Laura said, 'I know that Peggy was wrong. Chester and Raymond didn't really deserve to die. But, by God, when I heard what had happened – I was pleased, I have to tell you, I was pleased.' She hesitated for a moment, and then she said to Elizabeth, 'You didn't tell Bronco what happened?'

Elizabeth shook her head. 'I told him they were rough with you, that's all.'

Bronco said, 'I don't need to know what happened, sweetheart. If anyone lays one finger on you, all I can say is, they deserve the very worst. I'm sorry about Beverley, too, but I think she got her just deserts. That woman has been playing a dangerous game for many, many years, believe me. It was bound to catch up with her, sooner or later.'

Elizabeth reached over the back of her seat and took hold of Laura's hand, and held it all the way to Bronco's house. Tonight, they all felt a strong need for physical contact.

Bronco served up barbecued chicken for supper, and a big

357

salad of palm hearts and avocado, with his own special dressing, and plenty of cold white wine. Vita ate a little, then excused herself, and went to bed, pleading nausea. Bronco watched her go, and then relaxed. 'She doesn't take kindly to female company,' he explained. 'Mind you, if it's a man, no migraines then, she's all over him like wallpaper paste.'

'She's probably jealous,' Laura suggested.

Bronco shrugged. The candles flickered in his eyes. 'It doesn't really matter what she is. The truth is, I should never have married her. She used to follow me around, when I was at NYU, and she would do everything for me . . . cook my meals, press my trousers, type my essays, you name it. I needed a partner for dinner? There she was, all dressed up, corsage and all. I was lonely, one night? She was always ready to warm my bed. She made herself indispensable, that's what she did. I didn't marry her because I wanted to marry her. I married her because I didn't have the heart not to. In other words, I was a moral coward; and I can never forgive myself for that.'

'This is the author of *Bitter Fruit* talking?' asked Laura. 'The low-down dirtiest book that ever was?'

Bronco laughed. 'I think you'll find that's pretty dated now. All that swing, and trucking, and so-called loose behaviour.'

Elizabeth said, 'We'd better talk about the glamour, hadn't we, before we drink much more wine?'

'Do you think this cactus stuff is really going to work?' asked Laura.

'The peyote?' Bronco was filling up his glass. 'I don't see any reason why it shouldn't. The Indians have been using it for centuries. Elizabeth and I are going to eat a little and see if we can take on two of the characters that appear in Billy's novel.' He held up *Nights In Havana*. 'If it works, we're going to find him and try to persuade him to take off somewhere else, and stop bothering me.'

'What if he refuses?'

'I don't know. We'll have to think of something else.'

Elizabeth said, 'Like I told you, we want you to watch over us while we do it, just to make sure that nothing goes wrong.'

Laura pulled a reluctant face. 'All right, but I can't say I'm very happy about it.'

'Just think about Aunt Beverley,' said Elizabeth. 'You wouldn't want that to happen to anybody else.'

'I guess not. But it frightens me, all the same.'

That night, Elizabeth slept badly, and dreamed of walking through the snow. She was standing in a vast, black-vaulted hall, and snow was falling thickly all around her, and carpeting the floor. The experience was very intense. She could feel the cold. Then, gradually, the light began to fade, until she was standing in total blackness. She reached out with both hands, but all she could feel was the snow falling. She shuffled forward like a blind woman, groping in the air in front of her. She heard a thin, lamenting voice close to her ear. 'Oh, I have left my gloves behind . . . oh, I have left my boots behind . . .' over and over again.

'Peggy?' she said, with a sudden thrill of terror. Then she woke up.

She sat up in bed, cold and shivering, as if she had really been shuffling through the snow. Her nightlight was still dipping and flickering in its terracotta bowl. She looked down at her right hand, and found that she was clutching something that looked like a dead, desiccated rat. She cried, 'Agh!' and tossed it away from her. It fell beside the desk, and when it fell she realized what it was.

She climbed out of bed and picked it up between finger and thumb, and looked at it with awe. It was a child's fur glove, very old and very dried up, as if it had been soaked and then left by the fire. It was probably nothing grander than rabbit fur, and it was very roughly made, with big, childish stitching.

359

What gave Elizabeth such a feeling of dread, however, was that she knew whose glove it was. It had been left behind by Gerda when she was trying to find the Snow Queen's palace. Until Peggy had drowned, it had existed only in a story, an imaginary glove, left by mistake in some hot imaginary hovel, in a fairytale Finland that nobody could ever find in any atlas. Yet now it was here, in Scottsdale, Arizona, on a winter's night in 1951, the actual glove.

She had read of cases in which people woke up suddenly from very vivid dreams to find that small objects had materialized on their pillows. A woman in Montana had dreamed of her childhood in New Orleans, and woken up to discover that she was holding a handful of Spanish moss. An elderly man had dreamed of his wife, who had died twenty-six years before in a hotel fire in Pittsburgh, Pennsylvania. He had opened his eyes to find her wedding ring lying on his pillow, so hot that it had scorched a circle on the pillowcase.

But a glove from a fairy story? She stood staring at it for a very long time. She wondered if Peggy were trying to intimidate her, to discourage her from entering the spirit-world. If she were, then maybe she was frightened herself of what Elizabeth might do. On the other hand, maybe she wasn't frightened at all. Maybe she was trying to protect Elizabeth from an experience more terrible than Elizabeth could begin to imagine. Maybe this was the most potent way in which she could say, '*Don't.*' After all, if there were powers in the spirit-world which were capable of changing an imaginary glove into a dream glove, and then into a real, wearable, measurable, touchable glove, then what other powers were there, and how could she and Bronco possibly hope to influence them?

She drank a glass of water, and then she went back to bed. The nightlight cast the most peculiar shadows on the wall – spindly men and women, and stretched-out horses – the silent caravan of dream-people, on their way to other people's sleep.

She stayed awake until the nightlight burned itself out, and the first wash of dawn appeared on the wall. Before she fell asleep, she thought she heard a child crying, somewhere in the yard outside; but she covered her ears with the blanket, and told herself it was only imagination.

They set up two canvas cots in Bronco's study, side by side, so that when they lay down in them they could reach out and hold hands. Eusebio stood by the window, staring out at his vegetable patch, a tiny screwed-up cigarette stuck to his lip. He showed no interest whatever in Bronco's books, or his pictures, or any of his souvenirs. He was absorbed by the soil, and what he was growing, and the way the cloud-shadows moved across the ground.

Elizabeth was so nervous that she had been sick. Now she sat pale faced on the side of her cot, waiting for Bronco to finish his preparations. She had dressed as nearly as possible to look like Rosita, the prostitute in *Nights in Havana*, in a tight scarlet dress with big yellow flowers on it, and a deep V-shaped décolletage. She had swept her hair up in a 1940s wave and fastened it with two sparkly clasps that she had borrowed from Laura, and painted her lips the same vivid scarlet as her dress. She had borrowed a pair of red high-heels that had once belonged to Vita. They were a size too large but they made her walk in a shoddy, teetering way that went with the character.

She lit a cigarette and puffed it rapidly while Bronco fastened his belt. He had taken his old white Navy uniform out of storage. It reeked of mothballs, and it was so tight around the waist that he could barely button it up, but all the same he looked the part of a seedy Cuban chief of police, especially with his hair greased flat and his moustache waxed so that it pointed upwards at ten to two.

361

'What do you think?' he asked. He was red in the face from doing up his belt.

'Drink less wine, eat fewer enchiladas,' Laura remarked.

'You look fine,' said Elizabeth. 'It says in the book that Captain Figueredo's uniform is "ill-fitting and stained with sweat".'

Bronco lifted his arm to see if his uniform was stained with sweat, too, and the stitching ripped.

'There, you look seedier still,' Laura teased him.

'Are you ready, *senor*?' asked Eusebio, dourly. He plainly thought that this was all madness, and was impatient to get back to his beans and his corn and his collard greens.

'Oh, wait up one minute,' said Bronco. 'You never see a police chief without a gun.'

'You don't need a gun, do you?' Elizabeth asked him. 'It's only imaginary, after all.'

Then, however, she thought of the rabbit-fur glove lying on her desk. For some reason, she hadn't wanted to tell Bronco and Laura about it, particularly Bronco. She knew how desperate he was to exorcize Billy from his life, and she hadn't wanted to unnerve him. 'All right,' she said. 'You'd better have a gun. There are some pretty tough types in this novel.'

Bronco went to his gun-closet in the living-room, unlocked it, and took out a long-barrelled Colt .45 revolver. He loaded it, and pushed it into his belt.

'Now you really look the part,' said Laura, as he came back in.

Eusebio stepped forward with a small parcel of greaseproof paper, and unwrapped four dried slices of cactus. 'These are the mescal buttons,' he said. 'You must think of who you want to be, think about them strong, so you don't think nothing else. Then you chew the button slow and even, let the juices flow down your throat. They make you nauseous, you understand? Some people never get the peyote dream because they sick too soon. Let the dream come into you. Let it rise up inside you. You will be feeling plenty strange. You will see the peyote plant. You will *become* the peyote plant. Everything become vegetable. Then vegetable will open and out you will step . . . spirit-form, yes?'

Bronco picked up one of the mescal buttons, and sniffed it. 'We can't smoke these, no?'

'No,' said Eusebio, shaking his head. 'No smoke, chew.'

Elizabeth lay back on the cot. Laura knelt down beside her and held her hand.

'You'll watch me, won't you?' said Elizabeth.

'Every moment,' Laura promised her. 'If it looks like anything's wrong, I'll wake you up immediately, I promise.'

Eusebio handed her one of the buttons. 'Think of your spirit-shape first, then start to chew. Try to hold back your sickness. The peyote changes your breathing, same as strangling, same as hanging. Too much peyote and you don't breathe at all, and you die.'

'Thanks for the reassurance,' said Bronco. 'Let's just get on with it, before I change my mind.'

Elizabeth settled herself down. Then she reached across, and held Bronco's hand. They were taking this journey together, and she wanted them to stay together. She looked at him, and tried to smile, and he winked back at her, and said, 'God be with us, what do you say?'

Elizabeth nodded.

'Close your eyes now,' Eusebio instructed them. 'Close your eyes and think of your spirit-form. Think of its appearance, think of what it looks like. Make out that it's somebody you know, somebody real. Make out that you can touch this spirit-form, and talk to it. Make out that you know it better than you know yourself. Then slide inside it, one person inside another, like two photographs, one on top of the other one. Then you can be that spirit-form, then you can know what they know, and talk like they talk, and go to places where only *they* can go.'

Elizabeth closed her eyes, although the room was still so bright that she could see the scarlet veins in her eyelids. She tried to forget that she was lying on a canvas cot, holding hands with Bronco, with Laura leaning over her, and Eusebio impatiently sniffing and fidgeting in the corner.

She tried to imagine that she knew Rosita; that she had met her in New York. She tried to imagine her face, and her voice, and the way she walked. According to *Nights in Havana*, she always wiggled her hips when she walked, and shook out her black curly hair, and when she could get it she ceaselessly chewed Wrigley's gum. She tried to imagine that she could actually hear Rosita, smell her perfume, feel her skin. Rosita had a tiny tattoo of a flying owl on her left shoulder, carrying a bell in its claws. 'Death's fatal bellman', that was what the Cubans called owls. It was a symbol of mortality – live your life to the utmost, because tomorrow the ground may open up and swallow you, or a drunken client may slash you with a cut-throat razor.

Hesitantly, she dropped the mescal button into her mouth. It tasted bitter and dry, and she almost spat it out at once. But she knew that she had to help Bronco to hunt down Billy, and that she herself had to exorcize the Peggy-girl, and if this was the only way to do it, then she would have to chew this hard, disgusting slice of cactus until she took on Rosita's spirit-form, until she *became* Rosita.

'Slow – chew *slow*,' she heard Eusebio telling her, quite crossly.

She thought: I'm chewing as slow as I can. This cactus is absolutely disgusting, it's hard and it's fibrous and this sickening bile-tasting juice keeps squidging out of it. How can I be Rosita when I'm chewing this stuff?

There was a moment when she almost vomited. The juice was so foul that her stomach contracted, and she gripped Bronco's hand and let out a loud cackling retch. She kept her eyes closed, though, and lay back again, and even though she knew that Laura was kneeling beside her, stroking her forehead, she began to feel less like herself and more like –

– she didn't know. She felt as if she were poised in the desert, with the sun blazing down. She felt as if she would never move again. She heard drums softly beating, and voices chanting, and the sky rotated around her like a smoky kaleidoscope. She felt as if lying here motionless were her natural state. There was no need to move to have insight. She felt as if time were slowing down, slower and slower by the second, until her thoughts were moving like treacle, and a second lasted for hour. No need to move.

Yet the drums kept on softly beating, they were mamba drums; guitars began to strum. She was opening, she was flowering. She felt almost as if she were being born.

She journeyed an infinite journey across the desert, sliding sideways on her own unconsciousness. Days and nights went past, like a fanblade flickering in front of a shaded electric lamp. She heard women talking and laughing: she heard men shouting and fighting. She saw a cockroach on a plaster wall. She bought the dress because she wanted to buy the dress, it reminded her of flowering gardens, where fountains splashed, and cherubs stood blind-eyed and toupeed with moss. She got drunk on American whiskey and screamed with laughter. Then she was falling downstairs and jarring her back. She screamed and swore. She was sure that she would lose the baby. Later, bewildered and exhausted, she sat in an armchair watching a man in a dirty sweat-stained vest dealing cards. His name was Esmeralda and he never looked up once. On the other side of the room a dark-skinned girl of no more than fifteen years old was dancing for him, swaying her hips. She was naked except for 7-inch high-heeled shoes and a cluster of rainbow-coloured combs in her hair. All the time she was dancing she was stretching her vagina open wide with two fingers, glistening and crimson. Still the man didn't look up. The cards were more important. Fate was more important.

She sat up. She had a hangover and her mouth was dry. Next

to her, Captain Figueredo lay snoring. They must have finished that whole bottle of whiskey and fallen asleep. He stank like a pig, like he always stank. He never washed his penis, either. A girl had to be drunk to suck on that. Opera music was playing in the next room, on a scratchy gramophone record. She looked around. She had the extraordinary impression that she was in two places at once. She was sitting up in her own bed in her room in the Hotel Nacional, but at the same time she was sitting in somebody's office, with a half-transparent desk, and ghostly shelves that were filled with books. She could see the faint shadowy outline of a man standing by the window, and when she turned to climb out of bed she saw another shadowy outline that looked like a girl, kneeling close beside her.

She rubbed her eyes, but the shadowy outlines remained. The whiskey, she thought. The whiskey was bad. That fucker Perez. She had paid him $6 for that bottle of whiskey, and what had it done to her? The opera went screeching and warbling on and on, and she felt like going through to the next room and snapping the record over her knee.

'Jesus,' she said, shaking Captain Figueredo's arm.

He breathed in sharply, and then let out an extraordinary bellowing snort. 'What? What's the matter? What time is it?'

'I don't know, afternoon. The whiskey was bad. I keep seeing double.'

Jesus Figueredo rolled himself into a sitting position. He blinked towards the window, and then he said, 'You're right. I see double too. I see books, and a table, and a man.'

'Perez must have sold me some of that bootleg stuff.'

'I'll kill him. I'll bite off his fucking kneecaps.'

Rosita stood up. She felt nauseous, and strange, but there was something more. She felt as if she could hear people speaking in her ear – sometimes loudly, sometimes scarcely audible. She shook her head so that her long black ringlets shivered, but she could still hear them.

'What do you think?' she asked Captain Figueredo. 'What do you think, the whiskey's made us crazy?'

Captain Figueredo stood up. He licked his lips like a lizard, as if he would have given anything for a drink, and paced around the room. 'We're here,' he said, after a while. 'And yet, we're *here*, too. Bedroom, library – library, bedroom. We're in *both*.'

'What does it mean? Does it mean we're still drunk?'

'No. I don't think so. It means . . . we've done something. I know I've done something, but I can't for the life of me remember what it is.'

'It has to do with . . .' Elizabeth began. But her memory was so fragile and fleeting that she didn't have time to articulate it before it twisted out of sight, and off it went, like a freshly-opened but unread love letter being caught by the wind. She hesitated for another reason, too. She was concerned that Captain Figueredo might not want her again, if she turned out to be difficult. He always paid well, and brought his friends, and that was what survival was all about. She had a reputation as the girl who would do anything, from dancing the mamba to letting you fuck her with the leg of a kitchen chair.

Captain Figueredo pressed his hand over his eyes, and counted to ten in a loud, obvious whisper. Then he opened his eyes again, and looked around. 'It's still here,' he said. 'Books, people. Nothing's changed at all . . . except that man was standing further to the right.'

'Maybe he's waiting for something. He looks the impatient type.'

'He's not impatient. He's frightened of me. He's just a peon, look at him.'

'I'm going mad,' said Rosita. 'Fuck that Perez.'

'Don't you fret about Perez,' Captain Figueredo reassured her, clapping his hand on her back. 'Perez is a dead person from now. Besides – '

He hesitated, thinking, thinking. He touched his forehead with his fingers.

'What is it?' asked Rosita. 'You have a headache, what?'

'I . . . I don't know who I am.'

'What do you mean? Don't frighten me!'

'I am Jesus Figueredo. I *am* Jesus Figueredo. But why? I feel like I was somebody else, and now I'm me.'

'It's that fucker Perez.'

'No, no,' said Captain Figueredo. 'It's more than that. I *am* somebody else; and you are, too. Don't you feel it?' He looked around the room, at the bare-plastered walls of the Hotel Nacional, but at the bookshelves, too, and the people who were watching them but weren't really there.

Rosita knew what Jesus was trying to say. She *did* feel like somebody else. She also knew that she was supposed to do something important – more important than meeting Manuel at the Mamba Bar, more important than collecting her money from Dr Cifuentes.

At almost the same moment, both of them looked down at Rosita's bed and saw the book. It didn't look like a real book. It was semi-transparent, like the pencil-sketch of a book which an artist might have added to a finished painting. But they could read the title clearly enough, *Nights in Havana*.

'Raul Palma,' said Rosita.

Captain Figueredo nodded in agreement. Then he checked his wristwatch. 'You know him better than me. It's nearly four o'clock. Where can we find him now?'

'The San Francisco brothel maybe. Or the Super Bar on the corner of Virdudes.'

'What does he do at the San Francisco brothel?'

'He has friends there. You would say co-conspirators.'

Captain Figueredo dragged a filthy handkerchief out of his pocket and blew his nose. Then he stuck his finger up his nostril and twisted it around. 'We'll try the Super Bar first. Are you ready? Do you want to wash?'

Rosita moved through two worlds at once, out of the bedroom and into the bathroom. She could see ghostly furniture that wasn't there, and windows letting in light where there were solid walls, and pictures hanging in mid-air, and potted palms in the middle of doorways. She went to the bathroom and switched on the light over the mirror. She peered at herself and thought she looked haggard. She lifted her dress in front of the basin and washed herself with her hand. She watched herself in the mirror while she did it. She saw somebody else in her eyes but she didn't know who it was.

She wondered when she would ever learn, and of course the truth was that she *had* learned, but failed to act on it. She was free to leave Havana whenever she wanted to. She had no children; she had no family now that her father had died. But she had grown used to being Rosita. The wolf-whistling that followed her all the way along the Paseo was all the acclamation she required, and she didn't mind the men she called 'clients' half as much as she pretended. Most of them were shy and courteous, with voluminous pee-spotted undershorts and bad breath. Some of them were rough and drunk, and left her cheeks with stubble burns. But on the whole they invaded very little of her total body-space, only her mouth and her vagina, a few cubic centimetres which she rented out to pay for her food, and her apartment, and her Ford (which was waiting for a replacement gearbox), and the rest she kept for herself. When anybody asked her about prostitution, she always said, 'Men sell their whole bodies and brains to banks and insurance companies, all day, every working day, for a lifetime. I give my body for twenty minutes only, then I can do what I like, go for a walk, have a drink, meet my friends. Who is the prostitute, tell me?'

*

They drove to the Super Bar in Captain Figueredo's Buick but they drove like people in a dream. The buildings and trees that unravelled past them seemed more like a painted frieze than actual scenery. The sidewalks were crowded with the usual pimps and dirty-postcard sellers, yet they all appeared to be frozen in time. The sky was bronze and threatening, and a strange four-engined seaplane churned through clouds with propellers like eggbeaters.

The day was so humid that the Buick's windows were steamed up on the outside. Captain Figueredo laid his hand on Rosita's thigh, and said, 'There are not many things in this life which give me succour, Rosita.'

'No,' she replied. 'And I won't, not again, if you don't start to take showers.'

'I am a pig, I know it,' he said, gloomily.

They parked outside the Super Bar and Captain Figueredo gave a ten-year-old boy a nickel to watch his car. Inside the bar it was dark and smelled of stale cigars and disinfectant. A tall black man with a pointed head was polishing glasses behind the bar. Three men in black shirts were sitting around a table, their chairs tilted back. Another man was sitting on his own beside a tank of tropical fish.

Rosita had hung around the Super Bar for years. Yet this afternoon it was more than the Super Bar, it was a sitting-room, too, with phantom sofas and ghostly chairs, and people who walked from side to side like rippling sheets of cellophane. The barman called, 'Rosita!' but she ignored him, and walked directly across to the fishtank.

The young man on the barstool crushed out his cigarette and smiled. He didn't look at Rosita, however – he looked over her shoulder at Captain Figueredo. 'Well, Bronco ... I was wondering when you'd come looking for me.'

Captain Figueredo leaned against the bar and wedged the

fingers of both hands together. 'Bronco,' he repeated, and nodded, and smiled. 'Thank you for telling me.'

'You didn't know who you were?' asked the young man, in mock astonishment.

'I suspected, but I wasn't sure.'

The young man turned to Rosita. 'And you?' he queried. 'Do *you* know who you are?'

Rosita's mind flickered on and off like a silent movie. She could see Laura. She could see Eusebio. It was daylight in Scottsdale. At the same time, she could see Raul Palma, and the darkened interior of the Super Bar. She could hear mamba music and people laughing.

'It's confusing, for the living,' said Raul. 'They don't know who they are. Ficititious, or real. For the dead, of course, it's very much easier.'

Captain Figueredo said, 'You have to stop bothering me, Billy. You have to go your own way, and leave me alone.'

Raul blinked at him. 'You're my brother. How can I leave you alone?'

'I have to live my own life. I have to make my own mistakes. If I suffer, too bad. If I write a new book and the critics hate it, well, I'll just have to sulk, and do better next time.'

Raul said, 'I don't want them to hurt you, Bronco. They can and they will, no matter what you write.'

'So what do I do? Spend the rest of my life driving to the Scottsdale pharmacy, to pick up placebos for Vita? Stare out of the window at Eusebio weeding his greens? You're not protecting me, Billy, you're killing me!'

'You want a drink, *senor*?' asked the black man behind the counter.

'Whiskey, straight up,' said Captain Figueredo, without looking at him.

'What about the lady, *senor*?'

'I don't see any lady.'

'Whiskey for me, too,' said Rosita. 'Whiskey with a twist.'

Raul turned around on his barstool and looked at her with one eye closed. 'I don't know why *you* came along,' he told her.

'I came along because Bronco's my friend. He needs you to leave him alone.'

'You don't think he needs my protection?'

'That's the last thing he needs. He's a writer. He has to take risks. Every time a writer starts a new book, it's like throwing himself off a cliff. If he kills himself, well, that's just bad luck. But it's the risk that makes writing important. If you protect him, he won't be able to write, and if he can't write, you'll be killing him just as surely as you were killed, when you came off that motorcycle and hit that tree.'

'Do you know what?' said Raul, with the slowest of smiles. 'You're so damned wrong. You want my brother to write because you're his publisher, and you know you're going to sell a whole lot of copies. Doesn't matter if it's crap, which it will be. Doesn't matter if it never matches up to *Bitter Fruit*. Doesn't matter if Bronco's brought low, and humiliated, and gutted by the critics, and winds up shooting himself. God, you're so interested in profit, you don't see it, do you? He'd be far better living out the rest of his life with Vita, no matter how dull his life might seem to be, than writing his stupid bombastic book, and opening himself up, so that all of the buzzards and jackals can tear at his flesh. I want him to *live*, Lizzie . . . you don't know how precious life is, till you've lost it.'

Captain Figueredo said, 'You've been asked nicely, Billy. I love you. I *loved* you. But leave me alone.'

Raul swallowed the last of his whiskey. 'I'm sorry, Bronco. Even big brothers don't always know what's best for them.'

Rosita went up to him and draped her arm around his shoulders. 'Supposing I make it worth your while?'

Raul looked her up and down. 'You? What could you ever do for me, except give me the clap?'

'Supposing I help you ... you and the others who hate Batista?'

'Supposing you go back to bed with your sweaty chief of police?'

At that moment, another voice demanded, *'Johnson? What are you doing?'*

Rosita could see somebody standing just behind Raul's barstool, the dim apparition of a woman. It was Vita; because they had never really left Bronco's house; they were here, in the Super Bar; and yet they weren't.

Captain Figueredo tipped his drink down his throat, and banged down the shot-glass, and asked for a refill. The black man obliged.

'Johnson!' the voice repeated. *'You're leaning on the sofa, will you stop it, and stop drinking, too, you know what you're like when you drink before lunch!'*

Rosita said, 'Raul, this is really important. You have to allow Bronco to live his own life. If he's hurting, he'll seek you out, you know that. But you can't protect him from his own experience. You can't.'

'Johnson!' the voice shrilled out.

Captain Figueredo drew his Colt .38 out of his belt, raised it, and cocked it. *'Arriba las manos,'* he told Raul.

Raul didn't make the slightest effort to raise his hands. 'You're joking,' he said, steadily. 'What am I supposed to have done? Subvert the government? Consort with seditionaries? Drink too much whiskey? Run guns, hobnob with tarts?'

'Johnson, put that thing down! You know I don't like those things in the house!'

Shadows shifted, lights moved and dimmed and moved again.

'Raul – he's serious,' said Rosita. But then she took hold of Captain Figueredo's arm and said, 'Jesus, don't. This is not the way.'

'You see?' mocked Raul, spreading his arms wide. 'Even Rosita thinks you're got it wrong! The poxiest tart in Havana!'

Captain Figueredo pointed his revolver directly at Raul's heart and pulled the trigger. Raul's white shirt burst into a fury of blood and tissue, and he was knocked back off his barstool and crashed against the fishtank. Glass shattered, water and fish gushed all over him.

Rosita sat with her hand over her mouth, too shocked and deafened to speak. The black man behind the bar said, '*O Gloria Patri*.' Raul lay sideways on the carpet, not moving, totally dead, while parrot-fish twitched and gasped all around him, and a thin stream of rancid fish-water poured into his ear.

'Jesus, what have you done?' Rosita mouthed; but she wasn't really Rosita, she was Elizabeth. The Super Bar shrank and faded – it almost *fled*, as if it were being hurried away by stage technicians. Suddenly everything was bright and ordinary, and they were standing in Bronco's living-room in Scottsdale, with the morning sunlight dancing behind the blinds.

Laura caught hold of Elizabeth's arm. 'Lizzie – are you all right?' she cried out. She practically screamed it. 'What happened? What happened? What did he do? *Don't look!*'

But it was already too late. Elizabeth looked down and there was Vita, sprawled awkwardly on the Papago rug, one knee lifted, the other twisted, one hand pathetically raised. Eusebio was kneeling next to her, trying to unbutton her dress, which was sopping with blood, and more blood pumping with every heartbeat.

Bronco was standing beside the sofa in his overtight Naval uniform, his arm outstretched, his revolver still smoking. His eyes were wide with disbelief. Elizabeth stared at him, and he stared back, and for one split second she was still Rosita and he was still Captain Figueredo.

'Ambulance,' said Eusebio, but nobody moved, because

they were all too stunned. '*Ambulance!*' he repeated, and Laura walked stiffly back to the study and picked up the phone.

Bronco dropped the revolver on the sofa and approached Vita in a slow circling movement, his hands half-lifted in despair. 'Vita,' he said.

Elizabeth said, 'Bronco – you didn't do it on purpose. I was there, you were shooting at Raul.'

'And who's going to believe me?' Bronco flared up. 'Who's going to believe that I was Captain Figueredo?'

Eusebio eased Vita's head onto the rug, and looked up at Bronco, and said, 'Dead. There's nothing you can do.'

'I was shooting at Billy,' said Bronco, miserably. 'I wasn't shooting at Vita, I was shooting at Billy.'

'It's unfortunate,' said Eusebio, but without any trace of forgiveness in his voice. Vita had been good to him. Vita had given him extra cans of food for his family, and baby-clothes, and, once, a pocket-watch.

'I was shooting at Billy, Eusebio! As far as I was concerned, Vita wasn't even *there*!'

'Yes,' said Eusebio. 'But she was there. Objects can go from the dream-world to the spirit-world, and into the real world, too. This object was small, and it was travelling very fast, and with bad intent. There was nothing to stop it but your love for your wife.'

Bronco looked down at Vita, his mouth puckered, his eyes crowded with tears. 'I didn't mean to,' he said. 'I really didn't mean to. I was shooting at Billy, not her.'

Eusebio stood up, and shoved his hand through his stiff, wiry hair. 'You can kill imaginary people just as dead as real people. Your Billy will never trouble you no more.'

He went to the study, and came back carrying *Nights In Havana*. 'Read it now,' he said. 'Read how your brother dies.'

While they waited for the ambulance, Elizabeth went to her

room and read the last few pages of *Nights In Havana*. Bronco was kneeling next to Vita's body, abstractedly fingering her hair. Laura was waiting by the front window, for the first sign of a flashing light.

' "You see!" said Raul, spreading his arms wide. "Even Rosita thinks you've got it wrong! The poxiest tart in Havana!"'

'Captain Figueredo pointed his revolver directly at Raul's heart and pulled the trigger.'

Elizabeth looked up, at the rabbit-fur glove that was lying on her desk, and she was filled with the coldest sense of dread.

Twenty-Two

Bronco was arrested for shooting Vita, but released on $50,000 bail posted by Charles Keraghter, his publisher. He was still shocked and stricken with guilt, but when she left him, Elizabeth had already seen a straightening of his back, and a calculating look in his eye, like a man who wants to get back to work. For the first time, he talked about his new novel as if he could actually *see* it, as if it were alive, and all that he needed to do now was to type it out.

'Do you think that Billy's gone for good?' she had asked him.

'He's gone all right. I can sense it.'

'You meant to shoot him all along, didn't you?'

Bronco had nodded. 'I knew that he wouldn't be persuaded: Billy never was. But it makes me feel all the more remorseful about Vita. Whatever she was, she didn't deserve that.'

They embraced, and Elizabeth had felt in his embrace the certain knowledge that if time and chance had been kinder to them, they would have been lovers. 'Call me,' she urged him. 'Call me whenever you've finished a new chapter. Call me whenever you *haven't* finished a new chapter.'

Bronco said nothing at all, but held her, and looked into her eyes, and tried to live out all the years they had never spent together in a long, concentrated look.

'Goodbye, Bronco,' she said, kissing him.

Elizabeth and Laura returned to Connecticut from New York late on Monday afternoon the week after Christmas. The house was all shuttered up. It took them until Wednesday to warm the place through, lighting fires in almost every room, and keeping them heaped up with logs. At least Seamus had cut them a plentiful stack to keep them going through the holidays. Even when the sitting-room and the library were reasonably habitable, however, draughts still moaned through the window frames and under the doors, and they spent most of Tuesday sitting in their overcoats in the kitchen, next to the range.

On Wednesday morning they walked down through the freezing north-westerly gale to Green Pond Farm to see Mrs Patrick. Seamus was there, too, but he had the flu, and his mind was wandering more than ever. Talking and sniffing by turns, he sat by the fire wrapped up to his neck in a thick blanket, his hair sticking out every which way. Every now and then Mrs Patrick had to put down her embroidery and take a large handkerchief to him, so that he could blow his nose.

She made coffee, and they sat around the kitchen table while she worked. She seemed to have aged even more; her cheeks were like withered apples, reddened and roughened by the wind. Her hands were knobby with arthritis.

'Seamus wasn't so bad till the wind started up; then he caught a chill. The doctor's afraid that he'll catch the pneumonia, so I have to keep him all wrapped up.'

'Great ugly porcupines,' said Seamus, with a string of dribble swinging from his lower lap, and glistening in the firelight. 'Snakes rolled into knots. Little fat bears with bristling hair.'

Elizabeth went across to the fireplace and laid her hand on his shoulder. He rolled his eyes up to look at her, but he seemed to be having difficulty in focusing.

'Those were the snowflakes, weren't they, Seamus?' she asked him.

He squinted at her intently. Then he nodded, and nodded again, as if a bright wave of enlightenment had washed into his mind. 'The snowflakes. White, white, dazzling white, the Snow

378

Queen's guards. That's what they were. Great ugly porcupines, snakes rolled into knots.'

'Little fat bears with bristling hair,' Elizabeth finished, for him.

'He's been on about that for days now,' said Mrs Patrick. 'Sometimes I wish you'd never read him that story. It's all I ever get.'

Elizabeth turned to go, but Seamus struggled an arm out of his blanket and caught at her sleeve. His eyes were wilder now, and worried.

'She's *close*,' he declared. 'She's very close! Terrible icy-cold! She breathed on the young ones as she passed, and all died of her breath save two. Salt lord mole's eye.'

Mrs Patrick said, 'I think it's best you leave him now, Lizzie. He gets awful distressed.'

'All right,' said Elizabeth. She held Seamus's hand and gave him a smile. 'Don't worry, Seamus . . . it'll all turn out for the better, I promise you.'

Seamus whispered, '*Sad the man, mind the man, day after day . . . flowers and clouds, flowers and clouds.*'

They walked back up the snowy driveway. Although it was midday, the landcape lay sunk in a brownish half-light, everything frozen, everything tightly locked. Icicles had formed in the branches of the trees, in the shape of spears and necklaces and starving knights.

'I've never seen him so bad,' said Laura, gripping her fur collar tightly around her mouth.

'He's very sensitive to changes in the weather,' Elizabeth told her. 'He can always feel electric storms coming, or a cold front sweeping down from Vermont. I think he's sensitive to spirits, too. After all, what did Mrs Patrick always say? He was kidnapped by the little people, and taught magic.'

'You don't believe that, do you? That was just something she

379

used to tell us when were younger, so we wouldn't think that he was loopy.'

'I don't know . . . I always thought that he could hear things that normal people couldn't. He used to sing songs, remember, and sometimes they had beautiful tunes that nobody had ever heard before. And he always said that he could *see* things, didn't he? Faces looking out of empty windows; old women walking down empty streets; dogs and cats where there weren't any.'

They reached the house, and to Elizabeth's delight she saw Lenny's bright red Frazer parked outside. They hurried indoors and there was Lenny, still wearing his hat and his brown tweed overcoat, poking the sitting-room fire into life.

'Lenny! It's so good to see you!' She put her arms around him and they kissed.

'Careful,' he laughed. 'Red-hot poker. I'm sure glad your front door was open, or I would've frozen solid by now.'

'Hi, Lenny,' said Laura, reaching up to kiss his cheek. 'Lizzie thought you were in Hartford.'

'You don't think I'm going to stay in Hartford when Lizzie's here, do you? Besides, I've got some great news. I met a guy in Hartford who runs a private life-and-pension fund specifically aimed at office workers. It's a great scheme, it really is. It has all kinds of benefits, health-care, loan-back, you name it.'

'Will you get to the point?' laughed Elizabeth. 'You're trying to sell me one of your policies already.'

'Oh, well. The long and the short of it is that the greatest concentration of office workers on the Eastern Seaboard is – where?'

'New York, of course!'

'So that's my news. I'm moving to New York at the end of the month. They're arranging an apartment and a new office, and everything's hunky-dory!'

Elizabeth grinned at him. 'You're really coming to New York?'

'End of the month, definite.'

'Well . . .' said Laura, archly. 'Looks like fate has brought you together again.'

'That's my opinion,' Lenny agreed. He was looking at Elizabeth more seriously now.

'How about a cup of something hot?' Elizabeth suggested.

Laura made them three mugs of hot chocolate, and then they sat by the fire. Elizabeth sat close to Lenny, holding his hand, and for the first time in a very long time she began to feel part of somebody else. She could stroke the back of his hand and his skin felt like her skin. She could touch his hair and it felt like her hair, too. She found that she couldn't stop looking at his profile, his long eyelashes and his straight nose, and the firelight-filled dimple in his chin.

They lit cigarettes and Elizabeth told Lenny what had happened to Bronco and Vita, and the way in which they had exorcized Billy.

'You took mescal?' Lenny frowned. 'Isn't that stuff dangerous?'

'Well, there *is* a risk, but not so much if you have somebody with you when you take it, somebody who knows what they're doing, like Eusebio.'

Lenny shook his head and blew out smoke at the same time. 'I don't know what to say about you doing that. If I'd been there – '

Elizabeth squeezed Lenny's hand. 'We didn't have any choice. If Billy had kept on pestering Bronco for the rest of his life, he never would have written again. He would probably have ended up killing himself. Besides, I had a selfish motive, too.'

'What do you mean?'

'Laura, tell Lenny what happened to you.'

Hesitantly, discursively, and without mentioning the worst of what Raymond had done to her, Laura told Lenny about Aunt Beverley and Chester Fell. When she had finished, Lenny said, quietly, 'I read about that in the paper, two movie producers frozen in their own pool. Me and a couple of the other insurance people were trying to decide what the life-policy liability would be for somebody dying in a freak accident like that. But you think it was – ?'

Elizabeth nodded. 'I don't think there's any question about it. Anybody who hurts us or upsets us or looks like they're going to get us into trouble – the Peggy-girl makes sure they're never going to do it again.'

'And you want to track her down, the same way that you and Bronco tracked down his brother Billy?'

'Think what our lives are going to be like, if we don't.'

Lenny stubbed out his cigarette. 'It sounds too damned dangerous to me. You don't know what you'd be getting yourselves into. And from what you've been saying, you might not be able to get back out of it, once you're in there. What did that Eusebio say, about people in a coma? I don't want to be married to somebody who never wakes up.'

Elizabeth stared at him with her mouth open. 'Did you say *married*?'

Lenny flushed so deeply that his face was almost maroon. 'I – uh, what I meant was, if I was married to you, if I was married to anybody – and they were in a coma – you know, they never woke up – no matter who it was, whether if was you or not – '

He stopped flustering and ruefully rubbed the back of his neck with his hand. 'I have to admit that I was going to ask you, right after I told you that I was moving to New York. In fact I arranged to move to New York on purpose, so that we could be together. I could have gone to Boston instead.'

Laura crowed with delight, and kicked her slippers in the

air. 'He's *proposing* to you, Lizzie! He's actually *proposing*! And I'm a witness! I love it, I love it, I love it!'

One of her slippers landed straight in the fire, and Lenny had to rescue it, smoking, with the fire-tongs. After he had slapped it against the hearth and trodden on it to put it out, the romance of the moment had passed. They were all laughing too much.

Lenny sat down, and looked at Elizabeth with a questioning smile. She reached across the couch and held his left hand between both of hers, and smiled back at him.

'Can you give me some time to think about it?'

'Of course. I'm sorry it slipped out that way. I feel like such a dope. I was going to get down on one knee, and give you this.'

He reached into his pocket and took out a black velvet ring-box. Laura was beside herself with glee. 'It's so romantic! I can't stand it!'

Elizabeth opened the box and there was a diamond-and-sapphire engagement ring, sparkling brightly in the firelight. It must have cost Lenny hundreds. She looked up at him, and saw the expression on his face, and it was so warm and hopeful that she melted. She slipped the ring on her finger and said, 'That's time enough. I've thought about it. The answer is yes.'

He blinked. 'The answer is yes?'

'Do you have wax in your ears?' demanded Laura. 'I wouldn't let my precious sister marry a man with wax in his ears.'

Lenny leaned over and kissed Elizabeth on the lips. 'I love you,' he whispered. 'And, thank you. You just made the New York vice-president of Hartford Life and Loan a very, very ecstatic vice-president indeed.'

As he kissed her, a strong cold draught blew through the house. It moaned and whistled at the front door, and stirred the heavy drapes across the sitting-room doorway. It blew into the fireplace, so that the flames cowered beneath the logs, and a fine cloud of sparks and wood-ash was blown across the hearthrug. It was so cold that Elizabeth felt the hairs rising on the back of her neck, and she shivered.

'God – what a draught!' she said. It moaned away through the library, almost like somebody invisible, sweeping through the house wearing an icy cloak. They heard the french doors in the library rattling, and the thin shriek of the draught.

'Somebody walking over our graves, if you ask me,' said Laura.

But Elizabeth sat up, and looked around, and then she stood up and walked to the sitting-room window, and stared out into the gardens. The naked trees trembled, and the wind was blowing snakes across the snow. Elizabeth went across to the next window, and stared out of there, too, looking for any movement in the half-light.

'Anything?' asked Lenny.

Elizabeth shook her head. 'Not that I can see. But that doesn't mean that she isn't there. Seamus has been acting up – that's a sure sign that Peggy's around.'

'Isn't it time you just ignored her?' asked Lenny. 'Maybe she only comes because you imagine that she's going to come. She might be just as much a figment of *your* imagination as she is of her own.'

'What happened to Chester and Raymond wasn't a figment of *my* imagination,' Laura countered. 'Neither was Bronco's brother Billy a figment of Lizzie's imagination.'

'Seriously, Lenny,' said Elizabeth, 'I don't think you should get too close to me till we've got rid of this Peggy-girl. Heaven knows what she might do to you. Look at Dan Philips – and the worst thing that he might have done to me is think some suggestive thought. He probably didn't even do that. More than likely, the Peggy-girl was jealous, that's all.'

Lenny said, 'Lizzie . . . I believe in all of this stuff. I've seen it for myself. I know it's real and I know it can be dangerous. But

384

you can't expect me to keep away from you, and you can't expect me not to protect you. Anyway – how *are* you going to get rid of her? And when? You're not thinking of taking that mescal again, are you?'

Elizabeth went over to a side-table and took out a small paper package. 'I brought four mescal buttons back from Arizona. As soon as we can see any sign of the Peggy-girl, I'm going after her.'

'You could kill yourself.'

'There's a very slight risk of asphyxiation if I take too much, but Laura will be watching over me, the same way she did in Arizona.'

'I won't let you do it.'

'You can't stop me, Lenny. And, besides, there's no other way.'

'You've agreed to marry me, Lizzie. I won't let you do it.'

'You won't be able to marry me unless you do. Look what happened when we kissed just now – we had a cold wind through here like the Snow Queen's breath. She could kill birds just by breathing on them, and men just by kissing them.'

'You really believe that hooey?' Lenny demanded.

'Yes, I do,' said Elizabeth passionately. 'I really believe it. It's true. People leave their bodies when they die and they can sometimes turn into characters out of their own imagination. *Yes*, I believe it.'

'And so do I,' said Laura.

Lenny turned his face away. 'The trouble is, so do I.'

Elizabeth said, 'We'll do it as soon as we can – maybe tomorrow. I just have to think what character I can be, so that I can deal with the Snow Queen. Gerda is the strongest character in the story, the little girl who refused to give up, but Peggy's already chosen her. There's a little robber-girl in the story, and she's quite influential. She holds a sharp knife against her reindeer's throat just for the fun of seeing it panic. But she's not as strong as Gerda.'

'Does it have to be a character from the same story?' asked Lenny. 'I mean, supposing you turned yourself into some witch or something . . . a witch who had more magic than the Snow Queen?'

'Yes!' said Laura. 'Or what about the Angel in *The Red Shoes*, do you remember, in his long white robes, and with wings that reached from his shoulders to the earth.'

Laura and Elizabeth quoted the Angel together: "Dance thou shalt," said he: "dance on, in thy red shoes, till thou art pale and cold, and thy skin shrinks and crumples up like a skeleton's!" '

But Elizabeth shook her head. 'I couldn't become the Angel of God, I just couldn't – quite apart from the fact that he's a he, and not a she. I think you're right, Lenny – I *could* be somebody from another book, but it would have to be somebody stronger than Gerda, and somebody who had the means of driving away the Snow Queen, too.'

Lenny said, 'I should come with you. I should eat the mescal too. You can't do this alone.'

'No, you can't. Peggy would never do anything to hurt *me* – but she wouldn't hesitate to hurt you. She really wouldn't, Lenny. Think of the Reverend Bracewaite; think of Miles. And if you had seen for yourself what happened to Dan – he broke into *lumps*, Lenny. He literally broke into lumps.'

'So what can I do?'

Elizabeth looked at her wristwatch. 'I want to see my mother this afternoon. I need to know if the Peggy-girl has been visiting her recently. Maybe you could drive us out to Gaylordsville.'

'Sure. Maybe we could tell her that you and me are engaged, too.'

Elizabeth kissed him. 'You're no fool, are you, Lenny

386

Miller? You know that's the main reason I want to go. It's not every day a girl gets proposed to.'

'It's not every day she accepts.'

Laura went through to the kitchen, to make sure that the range was well stoked up. It was an old-fashioned blue-nickel Wehrle, which had probably been installed before the First World War, but it burned everything – coal, softwood, even corn-cobs – and it gave out tremendous waves of heat. As she came in through the kitchen door, however, she felt intense cold, rather than heat. The stove was still alight, the fire was still burning, but it was giving out no warmth whatsoever.

'Lizzie!' she called. 'Lizzie, come here!'

She approached the range very cautiously, her heart beating so loudly that she could almost hear it. She had laid the fire early this morning, and by now the whole kitchen should have been uncomfortably hot. The range itself should have been impossible to touch, except with oven-gloves. But it was cold as a cast-iron coffin. In fact, it seemed to emanate cold. Laura stood close to it, and she could see her breath vaporizing, little clouds of panic.

Elizabeth came into the kitchen, closely followed by Lenny.

'The range,' said Laura. 'Look at it, it's burning at full blast, but it's *cold*.'

Elizabeth went up to the range and stood beside it. It was icy-cold. The warming closet at the top, the nickel-plated rail, the hotplates themselves, all icy cold.

'This isn't possible,' she said.

'Maybe it isn't,' said Laura. Her fear made her irritable. 'Maybe it isn't, but it's happening.'

'Oh, come on,' said Lenny. 'The fire's burned itself down, that's all. My grandma used to have one of these old ranges, and – ' Lenny laid his hand flat on one of the hotplates. Instantly, there was a sharp sizzling noise, and Lenny shouted out in pain. He tried to tug his hand away, but his skin was stuck to the metal, and he lifted the whole hotplate out of the oven-top. He shouted, and twisted around, and shook his wrist again and again, and at last the hotplate clanged onto the floor, and rolled away, with the skin from the palm of his hand still stuck to it, like shrivelled grey tissue-paper.

'Christ it hurts! Jesus Christ, it hurts!'

Elizabeth pulled him over to the sink, and turned on the cold tap. She held his wrist tight and the palm of his hand wide open, so that the freezing-cold water could gush all over his burn. He stood next to her, alternately letting out gasps of pain and short bursts of shocked laughter, until at last the water numbed his hand, and he began to relax.

She wrapped his hand in a dry clean tea-towel, reached up and touched his cheek. She felt so frightened for him that she didn't know what to say. You love me, you want to marry me, so you're probably going to die, by one of the most agonizing deaths ever known? Together, she and Bronco had exorcized Billy; but she wasn't at all sure that she could get rid of Peggy quite so easily. Everything had been different in Arizona; hot and strange and slightly magical, with Eusebio to guide her. She was beginning to doubt that peyote magic would work in straight-laced New England, in freezing winds, in territory where no Piman or Papago Indian had ever walked. The land that Eusebio worked may have been the land of the dead; but Litchfield was the land of a different kind of dead – trappers and Puritans, witches and Redcoats in powdered wigs and men who rode furiously by night, on all kinds of arcane and hair-raising errands.

Lenny said, 'Look . . . it's a little raw, but it's nothing.'

'Maybe it *is* nothing, But you should see a doctor. We should take you to the hospital.'

'What? It's only one layer of skin. It's sore, but it'll heal. And what will the hospital do? Give me a tube of hydrocortisone, a cheery pat on the back, and charge me $50 for the pleasure?'

'I'd better call the clinic and tell mother we won't be visiting today,' said Laura.

'No, no,' Lenny protested. 'I can wrap my hand up in some surgical gauze, and put a glove on over it. I'll be all right. It doesn't even hurt that much. Let's go see your mother. We need to, don't we? I *want* to.'

'Okay,' said Elizabeth. 'If you say so. But if we were married – '

'We're not,' said Lenny. 'And, until we are, please let me have *some* freedom.'

Elizabeth kissed him. 'I'm sorry,' she told him. 'I guess I'm just being over-protective, like Peggy.'

They stood in the chilly kitchen with the draught shrieking high-pitched through every crevice and every window frame, and roaring soft-throated in the chimney, and Elizabeth felt that her life was at a crossroads, where one sign pointed to purgatory, and another to peace. But there was another sign, too, which was blank, waiting for her to paint her own destination on it, if only she knew what that destination could possibly be.

Her mother was in bed now. She was so thin and frail that she could have been eighty-five years old. Dr Buckelmeyer said that she wasn't eating properly, that she seemed to have lost all will to live. She talked constantly of show business, and El Morocco, and the Stork Club. Her body was collapsing in a clinic bed in Gaylordsville, Connecticut, but her mind was still whirling around Manhattan, in the glittering days of Cafe Society.

Elizabeth and Laura sat on each side of the bed. Lenny stood by the door, with his hat in his hand. The view from the window was plain and bleak. Leafless bushes, leafless trees, and a long dull slope of snow. The room smelled of lavender toilet-water and minced beef.

'Mother, how are you?' asked Elizabeth.

Her mother turned her head to look at her with rheumy eyes. 'Happy,' she said.

'You've given up smoking?'

'Dr Shitmeyer won't let me.'

'Are they treating you well?'

'I think so. I don't notice them much. They come and they go. I've decided to go back, you see, and live it out all over again . . . the *good* parts, the happy parts. I'm going to Jack and Charlie's tonight and there's nothing they can do to stop me.'

'Mother . . . you remember Lenny?'

'Lenny, Lenny, Lenny . . . yes. I think I remember Lenny. The one who went to the war?'

'He's here. He has something he wants to ask you.'

Margaret Buchanan blinked furiously. Lenny approached her bedside from the back of the room, and stood close beside her, too close for Margaret's comfort, looking down at her.

'Mrs Buchanan, I've asked Lizzie to be my bride, and I'd like your approval.'

Margaret lay slowly back on her pillow. Her eyes, first moist and uncontrolled, suddenly became shifty. 'You want to marry my Elizabeth?'

'That's the idea, yes.'

'And Elizabeth wants to marry you?'

'She's agreed, ma'am, yes, and she's accepted my ring.'

'But what will Peggy say? Peggy will be furious!'

Laura took hold of her mother's hand. 'Mommy . . . you have to accept it. Peggy's long dead.'

'How can she be dead when she came to see me this morning?' Margaret shrieked at her. 'How dare you say such a thing!'

'Mommy, she drowned in the pool and she's dead.'

'You're a liar! You're such a liar! She visits me nearly every day! She came today! She's coming tomorrow! Dead? How can you say that she's dead?'

390

'Do you want me to show you her grave?' Laura shouted back at her. 'Do you want me to have her dug up, so that you can look at her body?'

'How dare you!' Margaret screamed. 'She came today – and I'll tell you what's more – she knows about this engagement – she knows – and she'll kill you all – she'll kill you – rather than see you married to *him*!'

Elizabeth stood up. She didn't know what to say. Her mother was seriously ill; and rambling; and no matter what she said to her, it wouldn't really matter. You can't inflict pain on those who live their whole lives revelling in pain, as her mother had. You can't disappoint those who expect nothing but disappointment. All they ever do is drag you into their pain, and blame you for their disappointment, and never feel better whatever you do, because they simply don't want to. The only pleasure they ever get out of their lives is in making you feel worse, and that isn't much of a pleasure for them, either.

Laura said, 'We can't leave yet.'

'Oh, yes we can,' Elizabeth retorted. 'This woman isn't my mother. This woman isn't even my friend.'

Lenny put his arm around Elizabeth's shoulders and drew her close. 'Come on, Lizzie. You're right. It's time to put the past behind us.'

As they walked out of the clinic, a man in a maroon-striped robe stepped out of a side corridor – the same man that Elizabeth had met before, with his slicked-back hair and his six-o'-clock shadow. 'You're leaving in a hurry,' he said, with a smirk on his face.

'What's that got to do with you?' Lenny asked, aggressively.

'Nothing at all,' the man replied. 'I just wanted to wish you good luck. Tomorrow we'll run faster, won't we, Lenny? Stretch out our arms further? And one fine day . . . well one fine day . . .'

'Come on, Lizzie,' Lenny urged her, and tugged her arm.

391

But Elizabeth hesitated for a moment, and said to the man, very softly, 'Are you *really* who I think you are?'

'It depends on who you think I am.'

'I think – I think you could be Jay Gatsby.'

The man said nothing at first, but smiled very broadly. Eventually, he said, 'Remember what I said to you about dead people, that's all.'

'You said, "It takes one to know one." '

The man lifted his hand in a mock-salute. 'Truest word you ever spoke.'

Twenty-Three

Elizabeth spent all evening in the library, rummaging through books. By midnight, however, she still hadn't decided who she could be to outwit Gerda and destroy the Snow Queen. If she had been a child again, perhaps she might have been able to think of some fairy story, in which there was somebody more powerful, somebody colder, somebody with arteries flowing as cold and as white and as thick as glaciers. But she had forgotten most of her fairy princesses, and most of her hobgoblins, and even her club-carrying ogres stood unremembered in the background of her mind, like knobby rows of pollarded plane trees.

The range was still cold, so they went to Endicott's for hamburgers, and sat under unflattering fluorescent lights watching the youth of the town combing its greasy quiffs and propping its feet on the table and talking loudly about 'cats' and 'chicks' and how Jackie Brenston's record 'Rocket 88' was really the most.

Outside Endicott's the north-westerly gale screamed along Oak Street, and soon the snow started too, thin at first, and whirling in the wind, but quickly thickening up, until the street was almost blinded with white.

'Time to get back,' said Lenny. 'It looks like a bad one.'

They struggled out to the car. Already the lights along Oak Street were being switched off, one by one, as shopkeepers closed up to go home. The snow pelted in their faces like the Snow Queen's warriors, and stung their cheeks. Lenny's car was already humped with it, and when they opened the doors to climb in, they dropped heaps of snow onto the seats. They drove in silence back to the house. Although it was midwinter, and blizzards weren't at all unusual, they had a bad feeling about this one. The wind was so strong that it rocked the car, and the wipers could barely cope with the furiously-falling flakes. Elizabeth felt a deep sense of relief when they finally drove down the slope towards the house, and pulled up outside the front steps.

'Come in for a drink before you go,' she asked Lenny, as they opened up the door, and stepped into the hallway.

'I should get back, really, before it gets any worse.'

Laura was dancing a mazurka on the doormat to knock the snow off her boots. 'You could always stay. We have plenty of spare beds.'

'Oh, come on,' Elizabeth coaxed him. 'We do have something to celebrate, after all.'

Lenny said, 'Okay . . . but just one, and only one. Otherwise mom will start worrying.'

'We do have a telephone, you know,' said Laura.

'So did Alexander Graham Bell,' Lenny retorted.

'Oh, sure . . . but you're handsomer.'

Elizabeth went around the sitting-room, drawing the curtains. When she reached the last window, she paused, to watch the snow. A wan light was falling across the garden, so that she could just make out fir trees, and the handrails around the swimming-pool steps. So many years had passed since she had first moved here, and since Peggy had drowned. But even after all these years, she was tied here still by what had happened, by memory and by superstition. She longed so much to be free of this house, to be free of fairy stories. The time had come to grow up, and to face the world with maturity and understanding and wit. Icicles and swords and magic spells were no longer enough. Imagination was no longer enough. This was a time for real responsibility.

Touching Lenny was real. Caring about Lenny was real. It was time that the spindly dreams were swept away. It was time that the Peggy-girl was swept away, and the Snow Queen with her.

The fire crackled in the bedroom hearth. The shadows leaped around the room like Isadora Duncan's dance troupe. Elizabeth lay in bed watching Lenny undress, half-silhouetted by the flames. He was so lean and tall. He wasn't a muscle-man, but there wasn't a spare ounce anywhere. His chest was flat and his stomach was flat and his thighs were two hard curves. His bottom was high and rounded and small. He wasn't hairy, apart from a small crucifix of soft black hair in the middle of his chest. His right shoulder-blade was marked with a crude white scar, like a teacher's tick of approval. A mortar had exploded ten feet away from him, on an island whose name he couldn't remember, or wouldn't.

He turned towards her, and she glimpsed his penis, rearing high and thick and very hard. He sat down on the edge of the bed, and touched her cheek, and she kissed his hand.

'Can you manage?' she said.

'I think so . . . these bandages don't help.'

She heard the tearing of the sachet, followed by the snapping and stretching of the rubber. Then he was climbing into bed, and lying next to her, almost on top of her, his skin chilly, his penis hard.

'Don't rush,' she whispered, kissing his ear, kissing his hair. 'Don't rush, my darling . . .'

His hand cupped and massaged her breast, and she felt her nipple harden. He kissed her, and his fingers coursed down her naked side, right down to her hip, so that she shuddered. They were clumsy and unfamiliar with each other at first, as lovers always are. But at last he lifted himself on top of her, and she guided his rubber-sheathed penis into her wet vagina, and he thrust and thrust until he shuddered at last, breathed a long, luxuriating, 'Oh,' and climbed off her.

But she held him close, and slipped off his rubber, and massaged his soft spermy penis with her fingers, because she had adored every moment of it. His lovemaking would become more assured, and she would get to know him better, and in any case she loved him, his flat ironing-board body and his scar and his big tight balls. She licked him in his ear, and licked his stubbly cheek, and his lips, too, and climbed on top of him.

'I think I died and went somewhere better than heaven,' he said.

She ran her fingers through his hair. 'I love you.' She whispered. 'I love you so much.'

She was just about to kiss him again when the wind whined and screamed in a sudden gust, and the windows rattled and a door just across the corridor slammed shut with a deafening bang.

Lenny screamed, '*Mortar!*' and twisted out from underneath her like a muscly anaconda.

'*Down!*' he yelled at her. '*Down!*'

'What?' he said. 'Lenny, what are you – '

Lenny shouted, '*Down!*' again, and smacked her head so hard that she tumbled sideways across the bed and almost fell off the other side. Her left ear was singing and she felt as if her cheek were ballooning out. She sat up, dragging the blankets around her, and stared at him in bewilderment.

'Lenny?' she said. 'Lenny, can you hear me?'

His back was turned. His head was dropped between his shoulders.

'Lenny . . .' she repeated. She shuffled her way towards him, and laid her hand on his back.

'I can't do it, can I?' he said, and he was sobbing. 'I can't get over it.'

He smeared the tears away from his eyes with the back of his hand. 'So young . . . They gave us training, but they never trained us for Guadalcanal . . . they never trained anyone to have their legs blown off or their faces on fire or the guts falling out all over the beach.'

He stared at his bare feet on the bedside mat. 'We've been talking about spirits. But the spirits of those guys are going to haunt me for ever; until I die; and I'm afraid to meet them when I do.'

Elizabeth held him close. She didn't know what to say. All she could hear was the wind rising, and the snow pattering urgently against her window.

She fell asleep shortly after she heard the hallway clock chime two. The wind was still whining, and a distant shutter was banging – *pause* – banging.

She dreamed that she was walking through a frigid palace, in a time long after she was dead. The palace was silent and dark, and there was nobody there. They had all left years ago, so that only she remained, walking hopelessly from room to room. She knew that she would never find her way out; and that even if she did, the palace was set in the middle of a vast and snowy waste, thousands of miles from anywhere warm, thousands of miles from summer gardens where children played and every flower told its own story.

She reached across the bed, feeling for Lenny's naked back. He was gone. All she could feel were cold white sheets, with snaking wrinkles in them like the snow.

'Lenny?' she said, and turned around, and sat up. 'Lenny – where are you?'

The fire had died, and the bedroom was dark. The wind was screaming now, like a demented beast. Elizabeth dragged herself across the bed and switched on the bedside lamp. No doubt about it, Lenny was gone. But his clothes hadn't gone, and neither had his wallet or his shoes. *Oh, I have left my –*

'Lenny?' called Elizabeth. Maybe she didn't have anything to worry about. Maybe he had gone to the bathroom, that was all, or hadn't been able to sleep.

He had shocked her and upset her, hitting her like that, but at least she could understand why he had done it. She had met more than one veteran who seemed to have escaped the war uninjured: Peter Vanlies from Freestone Books, Rudge Berry from the *New Yorker*. Friendly, balanced, equable men – until something inexplicably frightened them or riled them, and then they became Marines again, instantly, capable of any violence, out of control.

She climbed out of bed and walked across the bedroom naked to pick up her robe. It was then that she became aware of an unexpected coldness in the air, even colder than the wind that was blowing, even colder than the snow. She turned around, and there was the Peggy-girl, floating at the end of her bed, her face whiter than ever, her eyes even darker, her lips even bluer with frostbite.

Her dress was soiled now, soiled and greasy, and it stirred listlessly in the wintry draught. She held out her thin, blue-veined arm, with its frostbitten fingers, and said, 'Lizzie . . . you've betrayed me.'

'Betrayed you? I haven't betrayed you! Why can't you leave me alone? I don't need you, Peggy. I don't want you! Just go, and go for ever, and leave me alone!'

'Lenny hit you, Lizzie. I can't allow that.'

'Lenny hit me because Lenny has problems. I didn't like him hitting me, and I never want him to hit me again, but I know what his problems are, and I love him, and I want to help him to solve them. Can you understand that?'

'Lenny won't ever hurt you again.'

Wide-eyed, terrified. 'What do you mean? What?' Oh God, don't tell me . . .

'We haven't killed him, don't worry,' smiled the Peggy-girl.

She danced a slow aerial ballet around the bedroom, her feet barely skimming the floor. Her smugness and her dirtiness were frightening. So was her ever-encroaching frostbite. Her feet and her ankles were so black now that she looked as if she were wearing boots.

'Where is he?' asked Elizabeth, hoarsely. 'What have you done with him?'

'Don't you *know*?' teased the Peggy-girl. 'Can't you possibly guess?'

'Tell me,' said Elizabeth. 'Please.'

'I was Gerda, wasn't I? You guessed that much. But I didn't have a Kay.'

'You've taken him.'

'Yes, we've taken him. The Snow Queen took him on the sledge and carried him away, and now he's sitting in her palace, naked as naked, on the Mirror of Reason, cold as cold, trying to form the word Eternity, so that he can escape . . . which he never will.'

'You *bitch*!' screamed Elizabeth. 'You horrible little *bitch*!'

The Peggy-girl looked taken aback. 'He hit you, Lizzie. He took his hand to you, and hit you.'

'Yes, he hit me! But it's my decision what I want to do about it! Mine, do you understand me, not yours! You have no right whatsoever to interfere in my life and take Lenny away from me! You had no right whatsoever to kill the Reverend Bracewaite, or Miles Moreton, or those movie people that Laura knew. You had no right to mutilate Aunt Beverley. *You had no damned right at all, and I'm going to make you pay for this, believe me!*'

The Peggy-girl was hop-skip-jumping in front of the hearth. 'Oh, yes, Elizabeth? And how are you going to do that?'

It was four-thirty in the morning and Elizabeth and Laura were sitting in the library, close to the fire. Even so, the house was so cold that they were wearing their overcoats.

'I can't think of anybody,' said Laura, in despair. 'And God almighty . . . it's nearly dawn.'

'I have to be somebody *strong*,' Elizabeth insisted. 'If I'm going to have any chance of saving Lenny, I have to be somebody *strong*.' She felt distraught, exhausted, too frightened for Lenny to think straight.

'What about Scarlett O'Hara?' Laura suggested.

'Can you really see me as Scarlett O'Hara?'

'Maybe you don't have her temper, but you have her looks. And if you burned Atlanta, wouldn't that melt all the snow, and the Snow Queen, too?'

Elizabeth thought for a moment. 'Burning,' she said.

'Well, that's right, burning. The Snow Queen's afraid of fire, isn't she? That's why the Finland woman kept her house so hot, to keep the Snow Queen away.'

'*Burning*,' Elizabeth repeated. She stood up, and looked quickly at all the books in the library. 'Not here,' she said.

'What isn't here?'

'*Bleak House*. Can you see it anywhere?'

'It's in your old bedroom. I saw it there yesterday when I went in to borrow your robe. What do you want *Bleak House* for?'

'Esther Summerson, that's what I want it for. I always adored Esther Summerson. She was Ada's companion, don't you remember?'

'I never read *Bleak House*. There was never anything literary to read at Aunt Beverley's, unless you count *Variety*.'

'Esther Summerson was blonde and very beautiful . . . but more than that, she was strong and calm, and that's just the person I need. Gerda was strong, too, but her greatest strength was her persistence, not her depth of character.'

'And the burning? You said "burning", as if it was something important.'

'It *is* important. Esther knows Mr Krook, who keeps a rag and bottle shop by the wall of Lincoln's Inn. Mr Krook dies of spontaneous combustion. He catches alight, and burns, and there's nothing left of him.'

'I've heard of spontaneous combustion. There was an article about it in the *Saturday Evening Post*. Some old farmer was sitting in his kitchen in Nebraska or somewhere like that, and they found his body half-burned down to the waist, even though the linoleum floor that he was lying on was hardly scorched.'

'Exactly,' said Elizabeth. 'I'm going to be Esther Summerson, and I'm going to take Mr Krook to meet the Snow Queen, and see how the two of them get along together.'

Laura slowly shook her head. 'Listen to us,' she said. 'Listen to what we're saying. We must be going out of our minds.'

'If we're going out of our minds, where's Lenny? Don't tell me he walked off into the snow and left all his clothes behind.'

'All right, then,' said Laura, standing up, and wrapping her overcoat tightly around her. 'When do you want to take the peyote?'

'As soon as I can . . . now.'

'Don't you think you ought to change your clothes, like you did when you were Rosita? You ought to look a little more Dickensian.'

'I could wear great-grandma's bonnet, couldn't I? This coat will look all right, and nobody's going to see what I'm wearing underneath.'

She hurried upstairs – first to her old bedroom, where she found a tatty paperback copy of *Bleak House* on the shelf next to her showjumping books and *The Last of the Mohicans*. Then she went through to her father's room. His great-grandfather had been so grief-stricken when his great-grandmother died that he had kept all of her clothes, of which the last surviving remnants were her tiny patent-leather button-up shoes, so small that Elizabeth had no longer been able to wear them when she was eight years old, and the grey velvet bonnet which she used to wear on Sundays.

Elizabeth lifted the bonnet out of the musty, varnished hatbox. She put it on her head, and it was uncomfortably tight, but it would have to do. She went back downstairs. Laura was waiting in the hallway, holding the mescal buttons in her hand.

'You look terrific,' she said. 'But do you really want to do this?'

'Laura, this has got to be ended, once and for all.'

They went into the library. Elizabeth sat down on the leather sofa, with *Bleak House* open on her knees. She closed her eyes for a moment and said a prayer, the prayer that Gerda had recited in *The Snow Queen*. Then she looked up at Laura and said, 'I'm ready.'

'Remember what Eusebio told you . . . chew it slowly.'

She took the mescal button, and she was just about to put it into her mouth when the wind, already furious, let out a shriek that sounded almost human. It came screaming down the library chimney, so that the logs were hurled out of the hearth, blazing and cartwheeling across the room. At the same time, the french windows burst open, and the blizzard came lashing in. The heavy velvet curtains flapped and rumbled, and snow flew around them like angry white bees. It was so fierce that rows of books toppled from the shelves, and fell with their pages flapping to the floor. Papers whirled in the air, and the desk-lamp tipped sideways and smashed.

'Lizzie!' screamed Laura, in terror. The noise of the storm was deafening. The french windows flapped and banged, flapped and banged, until the glass shattered. Snow tumbled across the floor and began to pile up in the corners of the room, and on the chairs. The coldness of the wind was unbearable. Elizabeth held her hand up in front of her face to shield her eyes, but she still felt as if the skin of her cheeks were being scrubbed with a cold wire brush.

The wind and the snow extinguished most of the logs, but one was still burning underneath her father's desk. She kicked it out of the kneehole and into the open, and stamped on it. As she did so, however, she dropped her mescal button, and it disappeared somewhere in the snow.

'Laura!' she shouted. 'Keep hold of that peyote! I've just lost mine!'

But Laura shouted back, '*Look!*' and pointed frantically to the garden.

Walking towards them through the blizzard was the Peggy-girl, her white dress flapping, her face black-and-blue with frostbite. Her expression was angry and haunted, and even though her feet didn't quite touch the ground, and she left no footprints in the snow, she seemed to be flagging as she approached them, as if the snow and the icy winds were taking their toll on her.

But it wasn't the Peggy-girl that had alarmed Laura so much. Behind her, in the darkness, a tall black shape was approaching them, too. It was only visible because the snow was flying off it, and it looked like a huge ungainly woman in a cloak.

'Oh God, she's bringing it here,' said Laura.

She turned to run but Elizabeth caught her arm. 'Peggy won't hurt us, you know that. She's here to protect us.'

'You think so? Then why is she leading that thing here?'

'She won't hurt us. She can't.'

'You can believe that if you want to. I'm not going to stay to find out.'

She ran to the library door, but when she tried the handle it wouldn't turn, and it was so cold that it flayed her fingers, the way that Lenny had burned his hand on the stove.

'It's frozen solid!' she called out. 'Help me open it!'

'Leave it!' said Elizabeth. 'You won't be able to!'

'Then I'm going the other way!' Laura shouted at her. 'Come on, Lizzie! You can't just stand there and wait to be turned into ice!'

The Peggy-girl had already reached the snowbound patio, and was gliding towards them with those strange, tired footsteps, rather like an exhausted skater. Close behind her, the huge black shape of the Snow Queen grew larger and larger, and Elizabeth was sure that she could hear it, over the shrieking storm. It was making a deep, thunderous sound like a subway train passing beneath her feet, mixed with a clashing noise, like hundreds of scissorblades. Beneath its cowl she could make out a long pale horse-skull kind of shape, which must have been the Snow Queen's face, if it had a face.

She tried to turn to Laura but she couldn't. She suddenly realized that she was paralysed with fear. She couldn't move, she couldn't speak. She could hardly even breathe. Laura snatched her hand and tried to pull her toward the french windows, but she couldn't think how to make her legs work.

'Come on!' screamed Laura. 'Lizzie, for God's sake, come on!' The cold was so appalling that she couldn't say any more, and the temperature was falling like a stone down a well.

Laura pulled her one more time, and then gave up. She stumbled out of the windows, and across the patio, heading for the tennis-court. But she hadn't gone further than the patio wall when she tripped on a step that was hidden beneath the snow, and fell, and knocked her head. The knock was so loud that Elizabeth could hear it over the wind.

'Laura!' she called, and managed to walk stiffly towards her. But as she reached the french windows, the Peggy-girl came and stood in front of her, with both hands raised, palms forward, as if willing her to stop.

'Laura's hurt!' Elizabeth protested. All the same, she glanced behind the Peggy-girl at the black hunchbacked shape which loomed in the darkness. If it came any nearer, she was going to try to run, too.

'I know what you're trying to do,' said the Peggy-girl, dispassionately. 'But you must stay as you are, and lead your life as you always wanted to. You don't want your Lenny to suffer, do you?'

'Leave us alone!' Elizabeth shouted at her. 'Why can't you leave us alone?'

'You have to be protected, Lizzie. I don't want anyone to harm you.'

'I don't need protecting! I don't want protecting!'

The Peggy-girl said nothing more, but turned her back, and glided away through the teeming snow. At first Elizabeth thought that the Snow Queen was going to come closer, but as soon as the Peggy-girl had passed it by, it turned away, too, and within seconds it had vanished in the blizzard.

Elizabeth limped over to Laura and knelt beside her. Her face and hair were already covered in a thin veil of snow. Her eyes were closed and her breathing was very shallow. She looked almost as white as the Peggy-girl. 'Laura!' she called her. 'Laura, wake up!'

Laura's eyes stayed shut, her face pressed against the snow. Elizabeth took a deep breath, and managed to lift her up in her arms, and slowly carry her back into the library. She cleared the snow from the couch, and laid her down. 'Laura, wake up! Laura!'

She turned Laura's head to one side, and it was only then that she saw that her blonde curls were matted with blood and snow. 'Laura! You have to wake up! Laura!'

She went to the door and tried to open it. The lock was still frozen solid, and the handle wouldn't turn, no matter how furiously she rattled it. Desperate, she went across to the fireplace and picked up the poker. She wedged it at an angle in between the doorhandle and the door, and heaved. To her relief, the lock gave way, and she was able to drag the door open. She carried Laura into the sitting-room and laid her carefully on the sofa. Then she picked up the telephone to call for an ambulance. The receiver was dead; the storm must have brought the lines down.

Gently, she sponged Laura's head with a wet tea-towel from the kitchen. It was difficult to see how deep the wound was, underneath her hair, but Laura still seemed to be deeply unconscious and her breath kept catching. Her pulse was faint and irregular. There was nothing else Elizabeth could do; she would have to borrow Mrs Patrick's pick-up and drive to the doctor's, and bring him back to help her. The blizzard was far too fierce to risk driving to New Milford, and she didn't want to take Laura with her to the doctor's in case the pick-up broke down, which it very often did, even in good weather.

The fire had died down to ashes, but they were still glowing, and she quickly jabbed at them to liven them up, and put on more logs. Then she took off her great-grandma's bonnet, wrapped her head in a scarf, and pulled on boots and gloves.

'I'll be back as quick as I can,' she whispered to Laura, and left her a scribbled note, *Gone to doctor*, in case Laura regained consciousness before she got back.

She went out through the front door and trudged down to Green Pond Farm through the furious snow. She kept slipping and stumbling, and the wind was so fierce that she had to lean into it, to stop herself from being blown over. It took her nearly ten minutes to walk the short distance to the farm, and by the time she passed the old pigsty her nose was so cold that she couldn't feel it.

To her surprise, the farmhouse was in darkness. Not a light showing anywhere. Maybe the power was out. The Patricks must be at home, because the pick-up was still parked in the farmyard, and there were no tracks in the snow to indicate that they might have walked anywhere, or that another vehicle had come to collect them. What was even more peculiar, the front door was wide open, and snow was drifting into the hall.

'Mrs Patrick? Seamus?' she called. She peered into the darkness and listened, although it was hard to hear anything over the wailing of the wind. 'Is anybody at home?'

She stepped hesitantly into the hall, and felt her way through to the kitchen, where Mrs Patrick and Seamus spent most of their time. The door was open and she could see that the kitchen itself was illuminated only by the ghostly, reflected pallor of the snow. It was cold, too, and her breath was visible as she looked inside.

Everything in the kitchen was covered in glistening layers of ice. The plates and jugs on the hutch were buried in ice, and the shelves were dripping with icicles. The dried flowers sparkled with ice, and even the pie that Mrs Patrick had been baking was frozen solid, with spangles of frost on it.

Mrs Patrick herself was sitting at the table, and Seamus, as usual, was sitting in his blanket beside the fireplace. Elizabeth said, 'Mrs Patrick, thank God you're – ' even as she realized what had happened to them.

She approached them cautiously and tenderly, with a feeling of overwhelming grief. Mrs Patrick was frozen so hard that her eyeballs had turned opaque, and her skin was deathly white. Elizabeth gently touched her hair, and it broke in a shower of frozen white filaments. She went across to Seamus. Her footsteps crackled on the frozen floor. Seamus sat with his head on one side, a string of ice dangling from his lower lip. He looked oddly peaceful – more peaceful than Elizabeth had ever seen him before.

On a wooden chair she found Mrs Patrick's black leather purse. It was frozen solid, too, but she chiselled it open like a big black oyster, using a kitchen knife. She looked at Mrs Patrick and said, 'Forgive me, won't you. I'll be back, when this is over.' She took out the keys to Mrs Patrick's pick-up, and went outside.

It was no use, however. The pick-up whinnied and chugged, whinnied and chugged, but wouldn't start. Elizabeth sat back in the old leather seat and let out a long, smoky, breath of resignation.

There was nothing left for her to do. She would have to use the glamour, and confront that hideous black figure that Peggy's imagination had brought to life, and try to destroy it.

Fire And Ice

'She called him by his name –
the Dreams again rushed by – and behold!
it was not him at all.'

Twenty-Four

Laura was still unconscious when Elizabeth eventually made it back to the house. It was almost six o'clock now, but the storm was screaming unabated, and the sky was just as dark as it had been in the middle of the night.

She tried patting Laura's cheeks, and coaxing her back to consciousness, but Laura remained as floppy and as unresponsive as ever. Elizabeth could only hope that she was sleeping . . . nature's way of helping her to recover. She prayed to God that she hadn't suffered brain damage.

Laura's left hand was clenched, and she carefully pried it open. Empty. The mescal buttons had gone. She looked around the floor, but there was no sign of them there, either. She forced her way back into the library, and groped around in the snow, trying to find the button that she had dropped, but she couldn't feel it anywhere. There was too much debris under the snow, too many books and pens and logs and inkstands. She went out through the french windows and braved the storm for three or four minutes, trying to find the buttons on the patio, but the snow was impossibly deep, and even the bloodstain that Laura had left on the snow had been covered over.

She returned to the sitting-room. It was well past six now, maybe she could find somebody in town to help her. She stoked up the fire as high as she dared, then wrapped up again and walked up the road to the end of Oak Street.

Sherman was deserted. In places, Oak Street was three or four feet deep in snow, and a long curving drift went halfway up Endicott's front window.

Blinking against the blizzard, Elizabeth shouted, 'Hallo! Can anybody hear me?' But her voice was swallowed by the wind.

She was about to struggle back to the house when she saw a long unnaturally-shaped lump of snow on the sidewalk. Shivering, she knelt down beside it and dug at it with her hands. First of all she felt something leathery, then something soft. She scraped all the way around it, and even before she knew who it was, it was obvious what it was. A man lying frozen, face-down on the concrete. She didn't want to dig very much more, but she cleared the snow away from his face. It was Wally Grierson, one-time sheriff, his face as white as dead pork.

Elizabeth slowly stood up. She was beginning to realize now the extent of the Snow Queen's revenge on all who touched her, all who helped her, all who denied her. God, for all she knew this blizzard had covered the whole of Litchfield County, and beyond.

She stumbled back to the house. She was exhausted by the time she struggled up the steps to the front door, and she was gasping for breath. She went inside, sniffing with cold, and slammed the door behind her. There wasn't any time to lose. She hadn't wanted to do this – not this way – but now she knew that she had no choice. She brushed the snow off her coat, and put on her great-grandma's bonnet again. Then she went into the sitting-room. She held Laura's hand, and kissed her frigid cheek.

'Please be all right, Laura,' she whispered. 'Please don't leave me, not now. I need you so much.'

She sat in the big armchair on the other side of the room. She wound her scarf around her neck and tied it in a slipknot. She tied the other end to the arm of the chair.

Pray God this works. Pray God this works. Pray God I don't strangle myself, and die.

She closed her eyes. She tried to think of Esther Summerson, the way that Dickens had described her, when she and Ada first met. 'I saw in the young lady, with the fire shining upon her, such a beautiful girl! With such rich, golden hair, such soft blue eyes, and such a bright, innocent, trusting face!'

She leaned sideways in the armchair, so that the slipknot tightened around her neck. The scarf began to squeeze her larynx, and made her gag. But she kept on leaning over, further and further, until her breath was coming in short, harsh whines, and she felt as if she were throttling. Her vision darkened, and she could hear the blood rushing in her ears. She started to panic, and claw at the knot with her fingernails, but somehow she managed to tell herself to stop, to stay calm, to think of Laura, to think about Lenny.

'Esther Summerson,' she whispered. 'Esther Summerson.'

Her vision darkened and darkened, until she could see nothing at all. She heard herself breathing in high-pitched squeals of constricted air; but then even that sound seemed to fade away, and she was sure that she was walking, not sitting, and that somebody was walking beside her. She heard shouting, and jeering, and the sound of horses' hoofs and iron-rimmed carriage wheels.

'It's here,' said a woman's voice, very close to her ear.

She opened her eyes. She was standing outside, in the slush, on a foggy winter's morning. A woman in a brown Victorian cape and shawl was standing next to her. She looked around her, and saw that they had reached a narrow back street, part of a ramshackle collection of courts and lanes. The wind had dropped, but the air was extremely raw, and there was an acrid stench of coal-smoke and horses in the fog.

'It's here,' the woman repeated. 'You were asking for Krook's, wasn't you? It's here, right in front of your nose.'

Esther found herself in front of a shop, over which was written, in spindly letters KROOK, RAG AND BOTTLE WAREHOUSE, and KROOK, DEALER IN MARINE STORES. In one window a sign announced Bones Bought. In another, Kitchen Stuff Bought. In another, Old Iron Bought, and Waste Paper Bought, and Ladies' and Gentlemen's Wardrobes Bought. In all parts of the window there were quantities of dirty bottles – blacking bottles, medicine bottles, ginger-beer and soda-water bottles. There was a tottering bench heaped with shabby old books, labelled Law Books, 9d Each. Inside the shop's entrance, Esther could see heaps of old scrolls and law papers, and heaps of tags, and second-hand bags of blue and red, all hanging up like hams.

It was so gloomy inside the shop that Esther couldn't have seen very much, except for a lighted lantern carried by an old man in spectacles and a hairy cap. As soon as he saw her, he turned, and came towards the entrance, and confronted her. He was short and withered, his head sunk sideways between his shoulders as if he were slowly collapsing from within. His breath fumed in the fog. His throat, chin and eyebrows were frosted with white hairs, and his skin was so gnarled with veins and puckered skin that he looked like an old root that had been left out in the snow.

He addressed her, stepping out of the shop. 'Have you anything to sell?'

'Mr Krook? My name is Esther Summerson. I badly need your help.'

The old man stepped back, and eyed her up and down. He smelled of dust and ink and candle-grease and yesterday's luncheon, whatever that had been.

'Help, what manner of help?' He peeked under her bonnet. 'Hi, hi! Here's lovely hair! I've got three sacks of ladies' hair below, but none so beautiful or fine as this!'

'I didn't come to sell my hair. I need you to come with me. I'll pay you well.'

'I don't care for pay,' said Mr Krook. 'It's things, that's

what I want to lay hold of. I have so many parchmentses and papers in my stock. I have a liking for rust and must and cobwebs. All's fish that comes to my net. Besides . . . I can't spare the time. I have rags and robes to weigh, bones to sort.'

Esther could dimly see her reflection in the shop's grimy windows. A very pretty, fair-complexioned girl, with gentle eyes, and slightly-pouting lips. She wondered why she seemed so unfamiliar, so unlike *her*.

Mr Krook turned, and hobbled back into his shop. It was then, however, that Esther saw another room, almost an invisible room, superimposed on the rags and the junk and the law books. A sitting-room, with a fireplace, and a long-case clock. She felt a tight constricting feeling around her throat, and she realized who she was, and why she was here.

'Mr Krook!' she called. 'I have a whole house for clearance, a whole house crammed to the ceiling with books and papers and kitchen stuff and furniture! You may have it all, all of it, if you assist me now!'

The old man stopped, and came back. 'Is this true?' he wanted to know.

'All you have to do is to put on your coat and come walk with me.'

'Walk with you? Where?'

'I won't detain you for long. Mr Krook. Why, if we fall to pleasant conversation, you might even persuade me to sell you my hair.'

The old man stopped, looked hard at her, looked down into the lantern, blew the light out. Esther waited in the street while Mr Krook donned his overcoat, a worn arrangement of greasy black, with a black astrakhan collar. Then together they walked along the slushy street.

'May I know our destination?' Mr Krook inquired. Esther wished that he wouldn't draw quite so close to her, and that he didn't smell quite so rank.

'Somewhere else,' said Esther. 'You should stop at this corner, as I do, and close your eyes, and think of somewhere else . . . Lapland, where it always snows, all the year round.'

'Lapland? Why should I wish to go to Lapland?'

'You wish to have the contents of my house, don't you?'

'Mmyes,' said Mr Krook, grumpily.

'Then close your eyes and think of Lapland.'

They had reached the corner of the street. A hansom cab rattled past, followed by a horse-drawn dray, from the back of which half-a-dozen ragged children were hanging. A man in a bowler hat was standing on the opposite side of the street with a mournful expression and a placard that said, simply, Fish.

Esther stood close to the wall so that she wouldn't be jostled by passers-by, and closed her eyes. 'Are your eyes closed, Mr Krook?'

'My eyes is closed, Miss Summerson, though the Lord knows why.'

'Are you thinking of Lapland, Mr Krook?'

'I am, Miss Summerson, though the Lord knows why.'

They seemed to be standing on the noisy street-corner in Dickensian London for an age, without anything happening. Then, quite suddenly, Esther became aware of a chilly wind blowing against her face, a fresh cold wind that carried no odours of horse manure or coal smoke – a wind that smelled only of fir trees and frozen distances. She opened her eyes and she and Mr Krook were standing on an endless plain of pure unmarked snow, under a sky that was seamlessly black. It was bitingly cold, but it wasn't snowing, and the air was so pure that she could almost hear it ring. This was the imaginary world in which Peggy had been dancing when she fell through the ice into the swimming-pool. Esther had arrived here at last.

'Mr Krook!' she said. 'You may open your eyes now!'

Mr Krook opened first one eye and then the other. He

looked around him with his mouth hanging open, revealing rotten yellow stumps of his teeth.

'Where are we? What the devil happened to Lincoln's Inn? Where's my shop? You've spirited my shop away, haven't you? That's what you've done! You've stolen my bottles, and my rags, and my law papers! That's it, ain't it?'

'No, Mr Krook, I've done nothing of the kind. I've taken you to Lapland, to meet my sister. She lives here, amidst the ice and snow.'

Mr Krook closed his eyes tight shut. 'Take me back again!' he demanded. 'Take me back to Lincoln's Inn, or by all-that's holy – '

'*No*, Mr Krook,' Esther insisted, and firmly took hold of his mittened hand, and began to pull him across the snow. Reluctantly, grumbling, he opened his eyes and started to walk with her.

'Who would live in such a place? Where's the houses? Where's the people? Where's the rags and bones and bottles?'

They hadn't walked for more than a mile before Esther saw a small white shape in the distance. She knew instinctively what it was. She was more than a character in a book, as Mr Krook was. She was Elizabeth as well as Esther. She had influence over her own imagination, so that she could change where she was, and what time it was, and who she should fancy to meet.

The Peggy-girl came nearer and nearer across the vast and flawless plain of snow. The air was so clear and lens-like that she seemed to become larger by optical magnification, rather than perspective. Not far behind her, a huge black shape loomed, its cloak billowing in the Arctic wind. Esther could hear its thundering tread when it was still more than a mile away, like the thundering of a distant iron foundry.

'Hi! What's this?' said Mr Krook.

'My sister's coming,' Esther told him.

'Your sister? And what else? I shan't take another step. I detest this place. I detest this tedious walking, too.'

'Then stand still,' said Esther, in the clearest of voices.

The Peggy-girl reached them and stood in the wind, staring at them with a cold and disapproving expression on her face.

'Lizzie,' she said. 'Why did you come here? This is my place, not yours.'

'I came for Lenny. I want him back, and I won't be leaving without him.'

'Who's this?' asked the Peggy-girl, turning to Mr Krook.

Mr Krook dragged off his fur cap and gave her the deepest and most sarcastic of bows. 'They call me the Lord Chancellor, my dear, although I'm not the salaried Lord Chancellor, my noble and learned brother who sits in the Inn. They call me that because both he and I grub on in a muddle, never cleaning, nor repairing, nor sweeping, nor scouring; and because he and I can never bear to part with anything, once we've laid our hands on it.'

'Why did you bring him here?' the Peggy-girl wanted to know. Behind her, in the middle-distance, the black shape of the Snow Queen was bearing down on them like a huge transcontinental locomotive. The ice began to tremble under their feet, and the air began to twang and crack.

'I want Lenny,' Esther insisted. 'You didn't have any right to take him. More than that, I want you to leave me alone. Stop protecting me. Live here, if you want to, with your Snow Queen and your fairy stories, but leave me alone!'

'God's teeth,' breathed Mr Krook. The black shape was almost on top of them now, taller than two men, with a hideously hunched back. Mr Krook looked at Esther in alarm, his rheumy eyes bulging out of his head, and took two staggering steps backward. 'What is this thing?' he asked, his voice thick with panic. 'Does it mean us harm?'

The Peggy-girl circled around Esther, one blackened toe

pointed downward, ballet-like, so that she left a perfect circle in the snow. The air was so cold now that Esther's coat was stiff with ice, and her bonnet glittered. The black shape rumbled and thundered only a few feet away, towering over them, black against a blacker sky. Still the temperature fell, until the air itself began to crackle like cellophane, and every breath formed diamonds around their mouths and nostrils.

'You should know where Lenny is,' said the Peggy-girl, and her eyes were impenetrable. 'Where do all our loved ones go? Where did little Clothes-Peg go?'

'Let him free!' Esther shouted at her. 'Peggy, for the love of God, let him free and leave me alone!'

'Don't you want me?' asked Peggy, plaintively.

'No, I don't want you! Go away!'

'Don't you *love* me?'

'No, I don't love you! I hate you! Go away!'

The Peggy-girl stayed silent for a moment. Then her hair rose up in the air, as stiff as icicles, and she screamed and screamed until Esther thought that the ice would crack beneath their feet.

At the same time, she heard a clashing metallic snarl, and a rumble of heavy material, and the so-called Snow Queen threw back her cape and bared her head.

'Save me!' screamed Mr Krook, dropping to his knees. 'Saints and angels, save me!'

The head that emerged from the Snow Queen's cape was monstrous and bony, and white as death. It was a grotesque parody of a woman's face, long and skull-like, with blind white tentacles writhing around its neck. Its eyes were dark and unreadable, like the Peggy-girl's, but the jumbled rows of jagged teeth that encrusted its jaw were drawn back in a hideous and obvious grin of triumph. Out of the cloak reached a claw-like hand, fleshless and shrunken, and Esther thought that she could glimpse naked flesh, white with cold, and dangling and swinging with extraneous growths and tags of skin.

'Hel, the daughter of Loki,' she breathed, and even her breath hurried away in terror.

The Peggy-girl stood close to her. 'That's right. How did you know? The Snow Queen was always Hel. "Hel into darkness thou trew'st. And gav'st her nine unlighted worlds to rule. A queen and empire over all the dead." '

Mr Krook had been silent all this time, his head bowed, kneeling.

'Mr Krook!' called Esther. 'This is Hel, the gatherer of spirits.'

'I shan't look!' Mr Krook called back. 'I shan't look, not until it's gone!'

'Hel wants the spirits of criminals and sinners, and those who die without shedding blood!'

Mr Krook stood up, slowly and painfully, and stared up at the monstrous bony-headed apparition that now stood over him.

'Thing!' he screamed at it. 'You may have me not!'

There was a split second's pause. Then the Snow Queen suddenly lashed out, and her claws snagged into Mr Krook's arm and belly. She lifted him clear off the snow, kicking and struggling and screaming, her claws penetrating right through his overcoat, in one side and out of the other, and blood spraying from his coat-tails with every frantic kick. She threw back her grisly head and stretched open her jaws, and a long black tongue slithered over her gums like an anaconda. At the same time, she let her cloak drop down to the ice, and Esther cried out loud at what she saw.

The Snow Queen's skin was white and thin, almost transparent. Inside her misshapen abdomen, Esther could see the arms and legs and faces of naked men and women, scores of them, dead but frozen, like a ghastly catch of fish. Every time she moved, the bodies slid and tumbled inside her, an arm sliding, a leg falling sideways, a torso pressed against her skin.

Mr Krook, writhing on the Snow Queen's claws, saw it too, and stuck out his arms and legs, totally rigidly, and screamed. Blood sprayed out of his mouth, but he didn't stop screaming, even when the Snow Queen shook him from side to side, and his overcoat tore, and his stomach tore, and his intestines fell below his hemline, and swayed wet and bloody between his feet.

'Mr Krook!' screamed Esther. 'It's time for your moment of fame. Mr Krook! What will we always remember you for?'

Mr Krook was only a character in a book; or perhaps he was something more than that. Even characters in books have a sense of their own destiny. Whatever he was, whatever he knew, he embraced the Snow Queen as tightly as he could, he held her close, while the white bodies of her victims wallowed around inside her, their dead and desperate faces staring through her skin.

At first, Esther saw only smoke, issuing from his overcoat – thick, oily smoke. Then suddenly he screamed, and gripped the Snow Queen even more ferociously. His white hair burst into flame – the sort of guttering, greasy flames you might have expected from a tallow candle. Then his coat began to blaze. The Snow Queen uttered a terrible clashing sound and tried to pry him free from her. But Mr Krook held onto her like grim death itself. He was burning so fiercely now that his fingers were probably convulsed, and he couldn't have released her even if he wanted to.

The Snow Queen screamed, and when she did so, Mr Krook incandesced. He blazed brighter and brighter, like magnesium, so bright and blue that Esther couldn't even look at him. His body fats spat and sizzled with heat, his bones popped, his intestines roared like fat on a red-hot stovetop.

The Snow Queen began to burn, too, and everything inside

her. Her skin shrivelled, and fire took hold of her, until she was nothing but a mass of flame.

Esther lifted both arms to protect herself as the Snow Queen literally exploded in a fiery eruption of human flesh. Her horselike head dropped down into her blazing ribcage, her arms folded in. Then she exploded again and again, until the snowy plains were scattered with burning human debris, hands and arms and torsos and disembodied heads.

Esther turned to the Peggy-girl, who was standing beside her with her head bowed. Gradually, the Peggy-girl began to fade, and the snowy plain began to fade. Gradually, Esther became aware of somebody shaking her, and shaking her, and saying, 'Lizzie! Lizzie! Wake up, Lizzie!'

Almost vanished, almost completely transparent, the Peggy-girl raised her head and looked wistfully at Esther with those dark, smudged eyes. 'Oh, I have left my gloves behind,' she whispered; but her voice was so soft that it could have been the draught, blowing under the door.

Elizabeth opened her eyes. Laura was shaking her, and she was coughing and choking. Her throat was swollen and bruised, and she could hardly breathe.

'Laura!' she said, 'Laura, what's happened?'

'You almost died, for God's sake! You almost died!'

Slowly, Elizabeth sat up. Her throat hurt so much that she could barely swallow. 'I did it,' she said. 'I did it. I went there . . . I found Mr Krook. I burned her.'

'You almost strangled yourself! How could you do that? You almost strangled yourself!'

'I'm all right. Please, I'm all right. My throat hurts but I'm fine. How's your head?'

Laura promptly sat down on the sofa and burst into tears. 'It hurts,' she wept. 'It hurts, and when I woke up, I saw you strangled with your scarf, and I thought you were dead.'

They sat for a moment in silence, while Elizabeth drank a

glass of water and tried to clear her throat, and Laura wiped her eyes.

'Did you find Lenny?' asked Laura.

Elizabeth had been thinking about it, hardly daring to face it. What had the Peggy-girl said to her? '*Where do all our loved ones go? Where did little Clothes-Peg go?*'

Exhausted, bruised, she lifted herself off the sofa and walked through the kitchen to the back door. She opened it up, and saw that it was lighter outside already, and that the wind had dropped. She crossed the garden to the swimming-pool, and even before she was halfway across the lawn she could see the footprints on its frozen surface, and the darker shadow where the ice had broken.

She stood on the edge of the pool, looking through the ice. Lenny swam cold and lifeless, his skin as white as snow, staring up at her through a window through which living people may never pass.

She heard Laura calling her, 'Lizzie! Lizzie! What's wrong?' Her voice echoed flatly across the cold snowy garden.

She walked across to the snow-covered garden shed, and reached down underneath it, into the crevice where she used to hide her love letters when she was young. Her fingertips found the damp and mildewed pages of a book, and she carefully tugged it out.

The Snow Queen. It was so blotched and stained that it was almost illegible. All the same, Elizabeth ripped it in half, and tore the pages out one by one, and scattered them all across the snow.

Laura was waiting for her when she returned to the house. They put their arms around each other, and held each other in silence.

Epilogue

All this happened nearly fifty years ago. Only two or three people in Sherman, Connecticut, now remember the winter of 1951, and how many people died.

Aunt Beverley recovered from her accident with disfiguring facial scarring and became a care-assistant at a retirement home in Pasadena. She died of an overdose of aspirin and alcohol in 1958.

Margo Rossi married a Massachusetts hotelier and never worked in publishing again. Her present whereabouts are unknown.

Laura Buchanan became a TV actress, and appeared in several episodes of *The Dick Van Dyke Show*. She died of cervical cancer in 1963.

Elizabeth Buchanan resigned her editorship at Charles Keraghter and moved to Arizona, where she lived with Johnson 'Bronco' Ward until he died in 1959. He never completed another novel.

Today, Elizabeth Buchanan is still alive and living in Scottsdale, Arizona, where she edits *The Pen*, a magazine for would-be writers. Sometimes, from a distance, she thinks she glimpses a man in a white uniform, watching her. Not bothering her, but watching her.

Every time she sees him, she whispers, '*Arriba los manos, senor*,' and tries to smile to herself.